Praise for *The Pelican Bride*

"Fresh as a gulf breeze, *The Pelican Bride* is the perfect pairing of history and romance. Finely tuned characters and a setting second to none make this a remarkable, memorable story. Beth White's foray into colonial Louisiana is historical romance of the highest quality."

—**Laura Frantz**, author of *Love's Reckoning* and *Love's Awakening*

"Not your usual setting, not your usual historical romance—*The Pelican Bride* breaks new ground in the historical genre. Choosing to write a story set in the French colony that became Mobile, Alabama, draws the reader into a new and exciting period. I fell in love with Tristan Lanier just as Geneviève Gaillain did. Who can resist a kind but fearless heroine and a hero who refuses to be molded to fit what others think is right—when he knows what is right and will do it? A winning beginning to a new historical series."

—**Lyn Cote**, author of The Wilderness Brides series

"New France comes alive thanks to intricate detail."

—*Publishers Weekly*

"Returning cruelty for cruelty is just a part of the reality of relations between European [illegible] the brutal New World of 1704, [illegible] fast-paced romantic adventure. [illegible] in spite of the horror in her you[illegible] n's choice to truly believe, lead t[illegible] rter."

—*RT Book Reviews*

"White's carefully researched story, set in what would become Mobile, Alabama, is filled with duplicity, danger, political intrigue, and adventure. This unique book will appeal to a wide range of readers."

—*Booklist*

"A fascinating and little-explored historical setting peopled with strongly defined characters and no lack of romance makes an intriguing start for White's new series."

—*CBA Retailers & Resources*

"A lush and highly detailed historical setting sets an atmospheric tone for this tale of love and life in New France. The well-researched story of the Pelican girls, so named for the ship that brought them, is an unembellished look at a slice of the human experience not often told. Recommended for fans of historical fiction."

—*Library Journal*

"The characters of *The Pelican Bride* will come alive as readers get into their heads. Readers see demonstrated, in the various characters, the seven deadly sins. This book is a must-have for any historical fiction collection; few stories are written on this time period and area."

—*Congregational Libraries Today*

THE *Creole Princess*

Books by Beth White

GULF COAST CHRONICLES

The Pelican Bride

The Creole Princess

GULF COAST CHRONICLES • BOOK 2

THE *Creole Princess*

A NOVEL

BETH WHITE

a division of Baker Publishing Group
Grand Rapids, Michigan

Published by Revell
a division of Baker Publishing Group
P.O. Box 6287, Grand Rapids, MI 49516-6287
www.revellbooks.com

Printed in the United States of America

Library of Congress Cataloging-in-Publication Data
White, Beth, 1957–
The Creole Princess : a novel / Beth White.
pages cm. — (Gulf Coast chronicles ; book 2)
ISBN 978-0-8007-2198-5 (pbk.)
1. Alabama—History—Revolution, 1775–1783—Fiction. 2. Christian fiction. 3. Love stories. I. Title.
PS3623.H5723C74 2015
813′.6—dc23 2014046426

Scripture used in this book, whether quoted or paraphrased by the characters, is taken from the King James Version of the Bible.

This book is a work of fiction. Names, characters, places, and incidents are the product of the author's imagination or are used fictitiously. Any resemblance to actual events, locales, or persons, living or dead, is coincidental.

The author is represented by MacGregor Literary, Inc.

15 16 17 18 19 20 21 7 6 5 4 3 2 1

To Debo, my lifelong mentor—
Yoda of storytelling, cake baking, cymbal playing, doll dress making, and innumerable other creative pursuits.
This one is for you.

1

MOBILE, ALABAMA
AUGUST 1776

Lyse Lanier danced on bare feet along the Water Street wharf with her crab bucket bumping against her leg, face lifted to a welcome early-morning breeze off the bay. The end of a long, hot summer had brought the usual stifling humidity, warm brackish waters, and rising threat of fall storms. Still, she was glad to be outdoors, free to poke about among the shrimpers docked alongside the merchant ships, fishing boats, and ferries. She was sixteen and a woman now, no longer confined to the classroom. In fact, it might be time to put up her hair, lengthen her skirts, maybe think about practicing some of the ladylike skills other girls her age found so important.

Lifting herself to the balls of her feet, she imagined herself in a spangled gown, walking the parapet of a gilded castle, high-heeled slippers pinching her toes, corset so tight she could barely breathe. *Head high, back straight, my girl. The duke may ask you to dance tonight.*

The sunbaked odors of salt and fish and oil became the smoke of a hundred tallow candles and expensive perfumes wafting from the silken clothing of her ball guests. Landing chains creaked against boats. Ship hulls sawed against their piers. The music of the wharf was an orchestra that flowed through her as she turned, head tipped back to follow a bank of clouds shifting across the hot summer sky.

Swaying, she closed her eyes and envisioned a young man pushing through the crowd with aristocratic authority. A clean-lined French face with serious eyes and . . . and a sword like Grand-pére's—

"Hey, girl, I want a place to spend the night. Help a sailor out!"

The rough voice dissolved her daydream like waves on a sand castle, and she whirled to scan the crowded waterfront to find its source. Market day had brought merchant ships from Havana, Pensacola, Baton Rouge, New Orleans, and ports beyond. Men of all ages, color, and social strata abounded, but few women. Few ladies, anyway, for the eastern edge of the city was home to sailors, slaves, shopkeepers, and travelers. And women of easy virtue.

Her gaze lit upon a swarthy, bearded creature leering at her over a pile of canvas near the closest pier. Dressed in sailor's garb of ragged sailcloth, with oily curls straggling from beneath a dirty knit cap, he was a signally unprepossessing sight.

"Try Burelle's," she said. Pray God the quiver in her voice didn't betray her fear.

"He's not as pretty as you."

She laughed and kept walking.

Simon had warned her this morning to take their young stepmother along. But Justine was due to deliver her fourth child any day and waddled like a cow. "I can take care of myself," Lyse told Simon, reaching inside her bodice for the scabbard sewn into her shift. She'd jerked her little knife free to wave it under her brother's disapproving nose, then tucked it away again before he could grab it.

Now, she *hoped* she could take care of herself.

The odor of old sweat and fish came up fast from behind. An iron grip caught her upper arm, jerking her around to face him.

"Think you're too good for the likes o' me, little girl? I fancy a little café au lait of a mornin'."

She stared into the sailor's twitchy eyes. "Matter of fact, *little* man—" the wicked point of her knife snicked beneath his chin—"I think you got me mixed up with somebody else. I'm the town barber, specializing in the extra-close shave." Dropping the bucket, she braced to jab upward.

"Permiso, señorita," came a deep voice behind her.

She jerked out of the grip of the sailor, barely noticing that he took the opportunity to melt away among the crowd, and turned to look up into a pair of sleepy brown eyes set in a good-looking olive-skinned face.

"What do you want?" She'd been looking forward to drawing a little blood, thus proving to Simon that she could protect herself.

"Eh, *pardon*." The young man's French was just as lazy as his Spanish. "Do you not speak Spanish?"

She switched to English. "You can apologize in any language you choose—just mind your own business." One by one, she flicked the knife under the three ornate silver buttons adorning his waistcoat and smiled as they bounced onto the boardwalk.

"Lud, what a destructive little mite it is," he said in English, watching the buttons roll into a crack and disappear. "Ah, well, saves me the trouble of doing them up from now on." He gave her a lopsided grin.

"Perhaps you'd like me to cut the rest of it off you," she said, "since dressing is such a—Hey! Give me that!"

He held her knife close to his Castilian nose and examined its beautiful carved ivory handle. "Oh, I shall. In a moment." He tested the blade against the pad of his thumb, frowning when a thin pink line of blood welled. "My dear," he said faintly, watching his blood drip onto the boardwalk, "perhaps you could direct me to a doctor. I seem to have injured myself with your little skiver."

"Do *not* faint!" she gasped, looking around for help. "You're too big for me to carry! And give me my knife!"

"Very well, if you promise not to perpetrate further damage to my wardrobe." Sliding his arm around her shoulders, he slyly tucked the knife into its scabbard—how did he know where it had come from?—and sagged against her. "Would you be so good as to direct me to Master Burelle's establishment? I believe he is holding a room for me."

"Make up your mind. Do you want the doctor or the inn?"

"I want to sit down. Anywhere will do." He closed his eyes, giving her the opportunity to admire eyelashes that would have been the envy of any debutante.

Lyse, however, refused to admire anything about him. Whoever he was. "All right, you big baby. Come along." Grunting under his solid weight, she wheeled him toward Royal Street. "There's a barbershop and surgery across the street from the inn."

"Mademoiselle is too kind . . ." The young man had switched back to French, perhaps sensing it was her native language, but his deep voice maintained its languid, sibilant Spanish cadence. "I regret that we have not been properly introduced. I am Don Rafael Maria Gonzales de Rippardá, merchant of New Orleans, at your service."

"I would say, rather, that it is I at *your* service." She looked up at him and caught a mischievous dimple creasing one lean cheek. "Oh, you are such a faker!" She dipped out from under his arm. "What a fuss for such a little bit of blood."

He gave her a wounded look. "Mademoiselle, it is not so! Every drop of one's blood is infinitely precious!"

"How do you know I am *mademoiselle* and not *madame*? Hm? You are very forward, for a stranger to our city."

"Are you indeed *madame*? Your poor husband must be obliged to beat you daily. Only see the damage you have inflicted." He held open his mangled waistcoat. "One wonders why anyone would come back, after such a welcome."

"You *are* welcome—to go away and *never* come back!"

He blinked at her sadly. "Are you really not going to tell me your name?"

She regarded him tight-lipped for a moment, arguing with herself. He was too lazy to be dangerous, despite his height and the clever way he had relieved her of her knife. And he *had* frightened away the nasty sailor. Also he smelled very good, faintly of sandalwood. "I am *Mademoiselle* Lyse Lanier. Of Bay Minette," she added, surprising even herself. "I'm not usually rude, and I thank you for sending away that—that miscreant."

She was treated to the full impact of Rafael Gonzales's flashing white teeth and sparkling dark eyes as he swept off his tricorn, making its extravagant red plume quiver. He bowed deeply at the waist, twice, a ludicrous exaggeration considering her ragged and barefoot state.

"You are utterly forgiven, beautiful mademoiselle, señorita, miss—and what an enchanting name for an enchanting young lady! If all the women of Mobile are so gracious as you, I am doomed to enslavement! Perhaps I should, like Perseus viewing the Sirens, go about blindfolded in order to maintain my sanity."

She laughed and took his arm, tugging him in the direction of Burelle's. "Then you would certainly be in trouble, you ridiculous man! Odysseus is the hero you're thinking of—and he had his sailors plug their ears and tie him to the mast, for it was the Sirens' song and not their beauty that was so dangerous."

He waved a languid hand. "One of those moldy Greek fellows is so much like the other, I can never keep them straight. But I assure you, if you begin to sing to me, I shall run away in terror."

Lyse had never had a conversation like this with another human being, ever. He spoke with the musical syntax of the classical heroes in her grandfather's library. She waited for Rafael Gonzales to inquire how a tattered Creole girl came to know the difference between Perseus and Odysseus.

But he continued to saunter alongside her, whistling something that sounded like "Down among the Dead Men," until she finally said reluctantly, "I can't sing."

"That is of no moment. I can sing well enough for both of us." And, to her astonishment, he burst into a sweet tenor rendition of *"De Colores."*

The street was crowded, and people were turning to smile and stare as they passed. Lyse clutched his arm. "Stop! This is not New Orleans. People do not sing on the street."

He broke off a liquid melisma to give her one of his sleepy stares. "Do they not? How very inconvenient. Next time I shall bring my guitar."

"We do not play the guitar in the street either." She couldn't help giggling. In front of the inn she halted. It was the largest building outside the fort, a two-story with a broad front gallery graced with several large rocking chairs and a swing. "Here is the inn. Would you like to sit down before claiming your room? I can go inside and get someone to bring you a tankard of ale."

"You are very kind, mademoiselle, but if I could trouble you for one more favor, I should like you to deliver a message to Major Redmond for me."

"Major Redmond?" What business could Daisy's gruff father have with this lazy, musical young Spaniard?

"Do you know him?" Gonzales's black brows came together. "I have not stopped at the wrong fort again, have I?"

She laughed. "His daughter is my dearest friend. What would you have me tell him?"

Gonzales smiled, clearly relieved to be in the correct port. "I have brought a hundred pounds of sugar from Havana, being off-loaded even as we speak. And I would like to entertain him for dinner this evening, if he is free."

Lyse nodded. "I will tell him." She privately doubted the busy major would be interested in leaving the fort to share a meal with a young merchant who couldn't be bothered to deliver his own invitations. But she hadn't seen Daisy for several days, and she was now provided with an excuse to visit. She backed toward the street. "Are you sure you don't want me to find a servant to help you in?"

"No. I thank you." He flapped open the beautiful red brocade waistcoat, sadly lacking in buttons, to display his trim middle. He reminded her strongly of a preening cardinal. "As you see, I am quite restored. No need to worry after all." Propping one hand on his sword hilt, with the other he caught her fingers and carried them to his smiling lips. "Adieu, mademoiselle. Adios, señorita. Goodbye, milady. We shall meet again, I vow."

Lyse dipped a curtsey, recovered her hand, and hurried to the street before she could betray the odd flutter in her stomach at the touch of that warm mouth upon her skin.

Jackanapes, she thought as she hurried toward the fort. How Daisy would laugh when she told her about this absurd young Spaniard.

~

Daisy was not amused. "And why were you at the waterfront by yourself? You know Simon has forbidden it!" She set aside her embroidery and rose, her blue eyes worried. "You could have at least taken along one of your little brothers."

Lyse snapped her fingers. "*That* for Simon's pronouncements! He is neither my father nor my master." But she couldn't help smiling at her friend's idea of protection. "And what possible good would a five-year-old be if I were attacked by brigands?"

"He could run for help!"

"Pooh." Lyse reached around Daisy to pick up her needlework. She studied the tiny stitches in awe. "I don't know how you keep from going blind. Justine's is nowhere near this fine."

Daisy was not to be distracted. "You are fortunate this Spaniard came along to frighten away the sailor. I will make Papa reward him handsomely."

"He is quite handsome enough already." Lyse grinned as Daisy rolled her eyes. "Don Rafael doesn't need money. He just wants to talk to your papa, which is the least I can do in return for his . . . chivalry."

"He sounds like a proper fop. Did he really faint at the sight of his own blood?" Daisy drew her lacy shawl from the back of her chair and led the way to the front door.

Incurably honest, Lyse shook her head. "He was only looking for an excuse to put his arm around me." A laugh bubbled up. "I think you'll like him, Daisy. At least he smelled good!"

"Which is more than I can say for your brother," Daisy said with a rueful laugh. "He always smells like fish."

Lyse smiled as she went down the gallery steps. "He would say that is the smell of bread and butter. He'd better bring in a good catch today, or we're all going hungry. I sold out of everything we had by midday—which is why I went down to the docks to begin with." Shading her eyes against the glaring sun, she paused at the bottom of the steps to look up at the looming main gate of the fort. "Is your papa on duty?"

"Yes, he'll be in his office in the administration building. He told me to have supper ready by seven, as he's bringing a couple of junior officers with him." Daisy gave a ladylike snort. "He keeps hoping to take my interest away from Simon."

"A French Creole fisherman will never be good enough for you, Daisy. Especially one who is the grandson of a slave." Lyse said it without self-pity. It went without saying that many of the British military and civilian population of Mobile disapproved of the deep friendship between the two young women. The budding romance between Major Redmond's daughter and Simon Lanier had developed into quite a scandal.

"But the *other* side of your family is one of the oldest in the city.

And Simon is my best friend's brother." Daisy hooked her arm through Lyse's and marched her toward the gate. "Papa will just have to get used to the idea that I'm not going to marry a soldier, no matter how many redcoats he makes me cook for."

"At least you can cook! I sometimes wonder if part of Simon's interest isn't prompted by the prospect of escaping Justine's fish stew!"

"Now, Lyse . . ." Daisy gave her a reproachful look. "Poor Justine—"

"*Poor* Justine knew what she was getting when she married my papa." Lyse bit her lip against further criticism. Her young stepmother was a beautiful paper-skull, but she did not deserve the hardships that accompanied life with a charming drunk, two willful adult stepchildren, and three—almost four—children under the age of five.

As usual, Daisy followed her thoughts. "How much longer, do you think, before . . ."

"Before the new baby comes?" Daisy's manners might be too delicate to directly refer to the subject of childbirth, but Lyse had no such qualms. She had helped to deliver her youngest siblings, Geneviève and Denis, and had vivid memories of Luc-Antoine's squalling arrival into the world.

Daisy's cheeks pinkened. "Papa said I might send a pork pie or something else nourishing when the time comes."

"I'm sure a pork pie will cheer her right up," Lyse said with a twinkle. "It shouldn't be much longer. Lord knows she's big as a whale. She quite shakes the house when she walks from the kitchen to the back porch."

"Lyse!" Daisy burst into a fit of giggles. "That's very—unkind!"

"But true." Lyse mimicked Justine's waddling gait, one hand at her back for balance, then suddenly twirled on her toes, arms gracefully aloft. "Oh, Daisy! Your pork pie makes me want to dance! How can I ever thank you!"

Arms about each other's waists, shaking with laughter, the girls saluted the guard who opened the gate for them and passed into Fort Charlotte—formerly known, under the long French regime, as Fort Condé. The British had rebuilt the crumbling fort and renamed it for their queen eight years ago, but its timbers were already rotting again under the onslaught of hot, moist summers and continuous infestation of bugs. Lyse fully expected the stockade to topple under the next hard rain.

She would never have dreamed of entering the fort alone, but Daisy had free rein. The two of them often had occasion to run errands which took them to Major Redmond's office. As they walked toward the headquarters building, situated on the far side of the drill green, Lyse looked for familiar faces. During the past year, a few boys with whom she'd grown up had declared loyalty to the British Crown and enlisted as soldiers.

She recognized no one today, until a young officer hurried out of the gatehouse and caught up to them.

"Miss Redmond!" he said breathlessly, falling into step. "Lyse—I mean Miss Lanier! May I escort you to—wherever you're going?"

Daisy halted long enough to give him an annoyed look. "Thank you, Niall, but we're capable of finding our way across the green."

Removing his misshapen tricorn, the ensign executed an awkward bow and rose with clanking of sword and sweat dripping off his spotty brow. "I'm sure you are, but your papa told me not to let you—that is, he asked me to look out for you, if you should come this way—"

"For heaven's sake, Niall," Lyse interrupted. "Where is Major Redmond?"

Niall plopped his hat back onto his rusty curls. "He's with Colonel Durnford—but you can't go in there!" He scampered after the girls, who had looked at each other and resumed their walk. "Hey! I said—"

"I heard you," Daisy said over her shoulder. She quickly mounted the steps onto the gallery and pushed open the heavy oaken door of the admin office, Lyse and Niall right behind her. Daisy paused at the desk of her father's subaltern. "Corporal Tully, I would speak with my father."

Tully looked up from some task he'd been concentrating on. He sighed. "Miss Daisy, you know you can't come barging in here without a by-your-leave. Major'll have my head." He gave an uneasy look at the closed office door. "He's got Colonel Durnford with him."

Daisy opened her mouth to argue, but Lyse blurted, "We heard. Why?" In her experience, the arrival of the lieutenant governor of West Florida generally preceded some unpleasantness.

"That would be nothing I could discuss with little girls—even supposing I knew." Tully scratched his head, disarranging the thinning sandy hair. "They've been in there close on two hours and not a peep out of 'em." He frowned. "So best you two go home and play with your dolls."

Daisy's gentle expression frosted. "Corporal Tully, you overstep—"

The office door opened, and Daisy's father stuck his head out, along with a virulent cloud of cigar smoke. "Daisy? I thought that was your voice. Are you all right?"

"Yes, Papa. But Lyse brings you a message." Daisy took Lyse by the elbow and tugged her closer. "Tell him, Lyse."

Lyse hesitated. She and Daisy had been friends since the day they'd met as small children, but the handsome, bewhiskered major still gave her the shakes.

And the impatient dip between his thick brows didn't help. "What is it, girl? I'm in rather an important meeting."

Lyse studied the two uniformed men inside the office—a youngish one puffing on a big Havana Special cigar, and the other, a grayer version of Redmond, nursing a snifter of French cognac.

She gathered her courage. "Sir, I apologize for the interruption. But I bear a message from a young man I met this morning on the waterfront—Don Rafael Maria Gonzales de Rippardá, merchant of New Orleans." Reeling off the young Spaniard's litany of names, she quelled the urge to roll her eyes. The busy major would never take her seriously.

But Redmond opened the door wider. "Rippardá! In truth?" He grinned. "I'm surprised he didn't come with you! Where is the young scalawag?"

Lyse exchanged looks with Daisy. "He—he's settling in at Burelle's, sir. He told me to say he wants to entertain you for dinner tonight—or at your earliest convenience." Well, she added that last bit herself, for courtesy's sake.

Major Redmond didn't seem to notice. He turned to address the officer with the most gold braid on his uniform, the young one with the cigar. "Colonel Durnford, you'll want to meet this young Spaniard. Protégé of Oliver Pollock—a wealthy Irish merchant with quite a bit of influence among the Spanish military."

"It's the Spanish crown I'm most concerned about," Durnford growled. "King Carlos tells the military where to go and provides the coin to get it there." He stuffed the cigar between his teeth and spoke around it. "I've heard of Pollock. If you think this boy might connect that coin toward us and away from the rebels, it's worth the time."

Redmond nodded and turned back to Lyse. "Can you find Rippardá and convey another message?"

Lyse dipped a quick curtsey. "Of course, sir."

"Good girl. Tell him . . ." He turned the cigar in his fingers. "Thank him for his invitation, but say it would be more convenient if he would join my family in my home." He nodded at Daisy. "Daughter, you'll need to lay six more places at the table this evening. Rippardá, plus the Durnfords."

Daisy swallowed. The Durnford clan included two little girls and a boy, all under the age of six. But she curtseyed obediently. "Yes, sir." She gave her father a cozening look. "Could Lyse come too? I'll need help with preparing all that extra food."

"Yes, yes, whatever you think, my dear." He backed away, already disengaging from the conversation. "Run along, we're very busy here." He had already shut the door before Lyse and Daisy had time to curtsey again.

They looked at each other, laughing, and Daisy put a hand over her mouth. "*Only* six more for dinner!"

Lyse sobered. "I hope Justine can do without me tonight. She wasn't feeling well this morning. What if the baby comes early?"

Daisy shrugged. "You'll have another little brother or sister, and I'll manage."

"True." Lyse smiled at Corporal Tully as she and Daisy left headquarters arm in arm. "How about this—you drop a message at the inn for Don Rafael, and I'll go home and check on Justine, then come back to your house. What are you making for supper? Want me to bring some oysters?"

"Good idea. They'll fill out the gumbo. And you can make the cornbread—yours is so much better than mine."

"All right." Lyse grinned. "I can't wait for you to meet Don Rafael. His accent is so droll!"

"And yours isn't?" Daisy laughed and mimicked Lyse's Creole patois. "Come, my little cabbage, let us dance the night away under the moonlight."

"Oh, you English, always so serious. Come on, *cher*, I'll race you to the gate." Lyse dropped her friend's arm and took off running.

The French girl was the one to keep in his sights, and not only because she was good to look upon. Behind those golden eyes lurked a dangerous intellect.

As she ladled Miss Redmond's excellent gumbo, thick with

oysters and shrimp, aromatic and steaming, into his bowl, Rafa gave her his most inane Don Rafael grin. "Mademoiselle, you are kind to notice my great famishment. Will you not be seated, so that I could serve you as well?"

Her gaze flicked to their host, who was entertaining Colonel Durnford at the far end of the eight-foot table. "Thank you, monsieur, but I am not . . . hungry." The quirk at the corner of her generous pink mouth deepened.

Puzzled, he watched her glide to serve one of the Durnford children, her movements unhurried, graceful, but efficient. What had she implied by that hesitation? That she was not welcome at the Redmonds' table? But why? Clearly she and Miss Redmond were great friends. The dynamics here were very strange. But perhaps it was simple British snobbery at play.

Do not be distracted, he reminded himself. His mission was not to flirt with a girl who walked like a dancer through places no lady should go. If he hadn't happened along this morning when he did, she might have found herself dragged into an alley by that sailor.

But what a surprise—and delight—to find her here, a quasi-guest in the Redmonds' home.

Lyse. Her name was Lyse. He deliberately removed his gaze from the curve of her waist, made even more alluring by the glossy black curls that clung to her apron sash. He turned to Daisy Redmond, seated at his left, and found her watching him with a twinkle in her large blue eyes.

"*Caray!*" He thumped himself in the forehead. "I have turned my back upon my hostess, when she is so kind to take in a stranger and feed him the most excellent of creole dishes!"

The twinkle became a dimpling smile. "Lyse taught me to make it, *señor.*"

Do not look at the French girl, he told himself again, as he blew across the steaming fish stew and spooned it carefully into his mouth. She was like the spices melding upon his tongue, with her Gallic-accented English and dark gold eyes in that caramel-skinned face. Such Creole girls walked all about New Orleans, as common as flowers, so that one eventually became dulled to their exquisite beauty. But this one was different, and he wanted to know why.

He swallowed, closing his eyes in ecstasy, then smiled at Miss Redmond. "You are a student to be commended. My nose thanks you. My belly thanks you. Indeed, I am your slave forever. Only tell me your lightest wish, and I shall cross a hundred seas to grant it."

She laughed. "Lyse was right. You are droll."

He contrived to look hurt. "Droll? My English is not of the best, but I think I would rather be intrepid or gallant—or even irresistible. Droll, Miss Redmond? Really, you wound me."

Her mouth pursed even as her blue eyes danced. "I beg your forgiveness, Don Rafael. How may I make it up to you?"

Rafa placed a finger between his brows and crossed his eyes, as if the act of thinking were painful. "Hmm. Perhaps you might . . . Yes!" He beamed at her. "I will allow you to take me on a tour of the fort and the city on the morrow. Then we shall once more regard one another with mutual respect and admiration, *sí*?"

This time she laughed outright. "I'm very sorry to turn down such a wonderful offer, but Thursday is my day to teach the children of the town their letters."

"Ah, that is very much too bad." He gave the French girl a sidelong look, unable to resist teasing. "Then perhaps, if I solemnly promise to refrain from singing or playing my guitar, Señorita Lanier would agree to take your place."

Lyse was bending over the littlest Durnford child's dish, picking the shell off an oyster. Hearing her name, she looked up and gave him her crinkle-nose grin. "Your restraint is admirable, sir. But it seems I have given you the impression that I dislike music—when nothing could be further from the truth."

Miss Redmond was looking from her friend to him and back

again, clearly perplexed by the conversation's subtext. "But do you have a guitar with you? You must entertain us this evening!"

Rafa shrugged. "I was a cantor as a child, so, yes, I have been trained. But I didn't mean—" He saw Lyse's satisfaction. "I mean, of course I will sing. Allow me but to fetch my guitar from the antechamber."

Miss Redmond caught her father's attention by clinking her spoon against her goblet. "Papa! When everyone has finished eating, let us adjourn to the salon, where Don Rafael will give us a bit of a concert, shall we? Timbo—" She turned to the elderly slave who had been quietly removing empty dishes and refilling wine glasses. "Will you set up the tea cart in the large salon?"

"Yes, miss." The man inclined his grizzled head and backed out of the dining room.

As he dealt with his dinner and fielded Miss Daisy's prattling, Rafa covertly watched Lyse Lanier as she took her place at the table, opposite Daisy. He couldn't quite place her in the social strata. The French of New Orleans, he had noticed, tended to hold a rather inflated view of their importance, despite the fact that they were a conquered people in a Spanish colony. Here in British West Florida, less than two hundred miles away, he had expected the same. But Lyse gazed upon him, not with superiority, but rather as if she found him entertaining—a sort of egalitarian amusement which oddly heated his blood.

He swallowed a sigh along with the last of his dinner ale. How he wished he could shed Don Rafael's shallow persona, just long enough to prove to her that he was a man, and not a musical manikin.

Ah well, he had neither time nor mental energy for serious courting, even had she been so inclined.

Still. She was *very* good to look upon, in a wildflower sort of way. He mentally entertained himself by imagining her family. She lacked the polished femininity of Daisy Redmond, whose smooth golden hair, milky skin, and blue eyes proclaimed the aristocratic English lady; indeed, Lyse's coppery complexion, wild black curls, and exotic mouth bespoke native or African descent, belied by the beautiful gold-shot eyes, which would be an anomaly amongst the dark browns and blacks of the African, mulatto, and mestizo slave culture.

Parsing that culture was part of his assignment here. As they all adjourned to the salon, the two British officers, Major Redmond and Colonel Durnford, lagged behind the ladies. Daisy took her place behind the tea tray, settling in with a precocious matronliness that was as funny as it was charming. Her lady mother having succumbed to yellow fever shortly after the family's arrival in Mobile, Daisy had functioned since as mistress of the house.

The fact that she served the town as schoolmistress only added to her general air of *I am in charge, so do not cross me*. Rafa kept expecting her to remind him to tuck in his shirttail and not to belch in public—which he wouldn't have done in any case, as his own dear mama had drilled him endlessly on the *etiqueta* of a gentleman while he was still in short coats.

He was pleased to discover that the men and women did not separate in the parlor, as was customary in many places he had visited. Even the children gathered to play Spillikins in a quiet knot at their mother's feet, while the adults conversed over their heads.

Rafa sat listening for a moment, taking in his surroundings with the eye to detail his father had taught him long ago. The Redmonds' home was built in the French fashion, a square two-story construction elevated on stilts above the muddy ground, with a broad front porch facing Conception Street. Inside, it was two rooms across, with a breezeway between—one room for family living space, the other for dining. At the other end of the breezeway, he presumed, one would find the kitchen and another service room, with bedrooms upstairs. Judging by the softening wood and wattle of the walls, the house was about four years old, comfortable without being overly fine.

Rafa shifted in the sturdy, ugly armchair to which he had been assigned; it was short of back, high of arm, hard and uncomfortable as only a stiff-rumped Englishman could conceive. He thought wistfully of his mama's elegantly appointed parlor in New Orleans, with its rich jewel-toned rugs and curtains, plush upholstery, and tasteful artwork. She had taught him to appreciate fine architecture, good books, and the French love of cuisine, to complement his father's head for commonsense military and business practices.

Fortunately, his own quirky sense of the ridiculous rescued him during these ever more frequent trips to barbarous outposts like Mobile and beyond. That, and a certain talent for extracting—and planting—pertinent information.

"Colonel Durnford," he said, firing the opening salvo, "it is my hope that British ports along the Gulf Coast will not be closed to Spanish merchants such as myself—now that the crazy colonials in the northeast have elected to cut off the nose of their collective face. We Spaniards, of course, have no interest in making war with our best customer."

Durnford's mottled complexion darkened. "You heard about that, then?" He did not, Rafa noted, answer the question.

"'Tis news likely to spread at the rate of fleas in a kennel." He spread his hands in a gesture copied from his Gallic friends in New Orleans. "This so-called *declaration of independence*, which is as stupid as it is appalling, is like to create shock waves in all manner of unexpected places."

"It was indeed ill-advised." Durnford exchanged glances with Redmond. "What do you know about it, Don Rafael?"

Rafa smiled and brushed an invisible speck of lint from his breeches. "That your King George is the grossest villain since Caligula. He has, they say, 'obstructed the administration of justice,' making judges dependent on his will alone. That he and his minions subject colonial citizens to a 'jurisdiction foreign to their Constitution and unacknowledged by their laws.' That he has erected a multitude of new offices and sent 'swarms of officers' to harass people and to eat them out of house and home. That he levies taxes without the people's consent. That he has, in short, fundamentally altered all aspects of British government."

Rafa had kept his voice quiet, but by the time he finished, he was aware that a certain intensity colored the words. The women had abandoned the topic of fashion and turned to listen, Mademoiselle Lyse staring at him with wide golden eyes.

He would have given much for a window into her brain at that moment. Many French Americans resented British presence but were, for a variety of reasons, unable to leave their homes and businesses in order to start over elsewhere. Those who did remain were required to swear at least nominal loyalty to King George.

Before he could ascertain anything like truth, the heavy lashes fell, shielding her gaze.

Daisy Redmond sat forward, her small fists clenched. "How dare they make such absurd claims! King George is—is . . . Why, he's the king! He has a perfect right to tax anyone he chooses! And how else could he pay for the military protection provided by my papa and his soldiers?" She glared at Rafa. "How *dare* they?"

"I am only repeating the main phrases that have been passed along the information circuit."

Colonel Durnford tapped his fingers against his lips. "That is quite a mouthful of accusation. And you say they have literally declared themselves independent of their sovereign nation?"

"It would seem so." Rafa sipped from the fragile cup in his hand. "Personally, I think it's all a tempest in a teapot, so to speak."

He got the expected laugh from that. Miss Daisy sat back, and the conversation veered to less volatile topics, such as the price of sugar and the problem of freebooters who infested the shipping lanes between Havana and Pensacola.

Fortunately, as he had hoped, Rafa seemed to have laid to rest any suspicions the officers might have harbored regarding the purpose behind his visit. Both men continued to treat him with a mixture of amusement and mild disdain.

Which was perfectly acceptable. Desirable even.

Eventually Miss Daisy remembered that he was to have entertained with his voice and guitar. Agreeably he rose and fetched his instrument, a beautiful rosewood guitar designed and built by his grandpapa. He pulled it from the protection of its red velvet drawstring sack, made by his grandmama, grinning at the expected gasp of admiration from his audience. The inlaid mosaic of colored chips of turquoise and ebony encircling the sound hole made it a thing of great beauty as well as augmenting its resonance.

He rippled off a minor scale and chord progression, grimacing to find it out of tune, then bent to pluck the strings and turn the pegs to his satisfaction. Finally he tried the same cadenza and shrugged, glancing at the French girl. "It is as good as I can make it in this terrible heat. What would you like to hear?"

Lyse straightened, apparently startled to find herself the one being addressed. "The rest of '*De Colores*,'" she blurted.

"*Bueno*." He fingered a few arpeggiated chords, held her eyes, and began to sing. It was not a love song, but he made it so. Such was the gift he'd been given.

She stared back at him, her quizzical expression softening until her lips began to curve in a smile.

Then he remembered he was to charm the English young lady and not the French. *Caramba*. Sometimes the *estúpido* act became all too real.

2

Lyse awakened early, with the first calling of the birds. Leaving Daisy asleep, lying neatly on her side with hands tucked under her cheek, she slipped out of the high bed and dropped onto the cool plank floor. Dressing started with brushing and replaiting her hair, then securing her stockings above the knees with ragged ribbons and lacing on her stays. She stepped into her old blue linen petticoat, tied it over her shift, then pinned the open-front dress atop it all. She took a squirming moment to adjust the tight-fitting bodice, wishing there were money to purchase fabric for a new dress. Her body had filled out in disconcerting places over the summer, slimming down in others, until she hardly felt like the same girl who'd joined Daisy for lessons with her governess last spring.

She padded on stocking feet down the stairs, carrying her shoes and trying not to hit the creaky spots. She had promised to meet Don Rafael outside Burelle's midmorning, as Major Redmond had all but ordered her to do. She was early, hoping to beg a beignet from the inn's kitchen before her appointment.

Frankly she would be surprised if the Spaniard remembered to meet her. The song she requested of him, the so beautiful *"De Colores"* . . . eh, bah, he'd intended it for Daisy after all. After one line of liquid music, he'd turned that bovine gaze on Daisy, looking at her as if the sun and moon rose in her blue eyes.

Not that her friend noticed any man who wasn't Simon Lanier. Daisy had smiled at the Spaniard with sunny indifference that bordered on insult and asked him if he knew "Drink to Me Only with Thine Eyes."

Smiling at the memory of Don Rafael's incredulous expression, she quickly slipped on her shoes, left the Redmonds' house, and swung down the street toward the inn. The town was still sleepy on this bright midweek morning. Sailors who had spent the previous evening carousing were still abed, fishermen not yet returned from a night of shrimping, crabbing, and fishing. The shops would open around ten, when housewives and chefs sent their servants out to market.

A few young working women like herself were out and about, drawing water for the day or executing other errands. Lyse waved at people she knew, but didn't stop to talk as she might normally have done. As she reached the corner where Burelle's sat next to the livery and blacksmith, her stomach gave a loud rumble. Joony, the inn's cook, should have hot beignets coming out of the grease by now. A beignet was an absolute necessity.

"*Hola!* Señorita Lanier!"

She stopped, skirts lifted to jump over a puddle, and looked up and down the muddy street. Then movement on the inn's deep second-floor balcony drew her eye. Don Rafael, dressed in buckskin breeches and white shirtsleeves, leaned upon the wrought iron rail, waving a red handkerchief. The brilliant waistcoat was nowhere in evidence.

Lyse waved back. "Good morning, monsieur! You are risen early! I was just about to go round to the kitchen for breakfast."

"I beg you will join me in the dining room instead. I'm on my way down." Before she could say yea or nay, he disappeared through the French door behind him.

Lyse was left to jump over the mud onto the brick pathway which led to the inn's front gallery. Her family's history with the Burelles was a long and colorful one. Her great-grandmother had baked for the present owner's grandfather in the Old Fort Louis tavern before the town had moved in 1711 to its present location at the mouth of Mobile Bay. Over the years, members of the two families had intermarried until mutual cousins often sprouted in the most unexpected places.

Monsieur Burelle's married daughter Brigitte was sweeping the porch and greeted Lyse with a cheerful "Good morning" as she mounted the shallow front steps.

"*B'jour*, Brigitte!" Lyse smiled without stopping to talk. She hurried into the inn's dining room, where the houseman was popping open a fresh white tablecloth and letting it float down onto a table by the open window.

Zander gave her his usual wide grin as he smoothed wrinkles from the cloth. "M'sieur be lookin' for shrimps, come time for makin' de gumbo."

"I don't have shrimp yet, Zander," she said, pausing with a hand on the door lintel. "In fact, I haven't seen Simon since yesterday morning." She glanced at the kitchen door. "I was hoping there might be hot beignets . . ."

"My Joony got the grease a-bubblin' since dawn. And we got sugar brought in yesterday!" He kissed his black fingers.

Lyse laughed at the slave's wicked grin. "Sugar? Then I better hurry before the word gets out and they're all bought up!"

"Oh, señorita, please don't abandon me when you have just arrived!" Don Rafael Maria Gonzales de Rippardá, resplendent in a dark-green jacket with deep lace-trimmed cuffs, over fine buckskin breeches and a scarlet-and-gold waistcoat, descended the stairs. "I must be insulted!"

It appeared they would be conversing in English today—the neutral tongue.

Lyse looked at Zander. She couldn't afford to actually *pay* for beignets. Joony could usually be counted upon to give her a sack full of the droplets that splattered off the spoon into tiny, mouth-watering, grease-laden confections.

"Come, you must be my guest. I insist!"

Guest? She wavered. She had never dined in the tavern as a paying customer. If Monsieur Burelle came in and saw her here, he might shoo her out like a mosquito.

Apparently Don Rafael mistook her reluctance, for genuine hurt seeped into his expression as he executed a formal bow. "But I see that you are quite busy, so I will excuse you—and I will eat alone." With a set smile he sauntered toward Zander's table.

The thought of beignet scraps flew out of her head. "Oh, no no! Of course I will join you, it's just that I never—"

"Ma'm'selle forgot to ask me to set two places 'stead o' her usual one," Zander interrupted smoothly. "Come, ma'm'selle, while I get another plate for m'sieur." He stood behind a chair and waited for her to be seated, then pulled out another one for Don Rafael. With a friendly nod, he headed for the kitchen.

Feeling as if she'd suddenly been transported into her daydream from the pier yesterday, Lyse looked at the snowy linen napkin on top of her plate. It had been folded in the shape of a peculiar, long-necked seagull. She glanced at the porch. Brigitte was going to come in and evict her at any moment.

Don Rafael seemed unaware of her unease. He picked up the seagull in front of him and destroyed it with a careless snap, then draped it across his lap. Propping his elbows on the table, he fixed her with sleepy brown eyes.

She couldn't make herself ruin her napkin bird, so she set it aside and tried to return that unsettling regard. He was an empty-headed popinjay. A practiced flirt. Nothing to be scared of.

She cleared her throat. "What would you like to see first this morning?"

"I have already seen it," he said with a smile.

A silver-tongued popinjay, she amended. She willed herself not to blush. "Wait until you see Joony's beignets and seafood omelet. They should be in an art gallery."

Fortunately Zander returned with another plate and setting of flatware. He addressed Don Rafael with the respect due a wealthy patron of the inn. "I like to recommend the chef's specialty of the mornin', m'sieur. The omelet—"

"Belongs in an art gallery, I understand." The Spaniard winked at Lyse. "I defer to the collective wisdom. Yes, and an order of beignets and—do you have the chicory coffee? I develop the taste for strong drink since I live in New Orleans."

Zander kissed his fingers again in approval. "Oh, yes, she will grow the hair on m'sieur's chest! And for ma'm'selle?"

"Regular coffee for me." If she was going to be shooed out of the dining room, she might as well enjoy it first.

After Zander ambled away, she picked up her napkin, cupping it in her hands. One more minute and she would put it in her lap.

The Spaniard's eyes were caressing her face. "You live in the Mobile for all your life, Señorita Lanier?"

She nodded. "I am Creole—native-born Louisianan. My papa runs the ferry across the bay." When he wasn't in gaol. "Also my grandpapa and his brother own ships here and in New Orleans. Perhaps you know the Lanier Brothers Transport company?"

Don Rafael tilted his head. "I have seen the ships. This is an important business, I think."

The popinjay had beautiful manners. She couldn't tell from his expression whether he considered it strange for a descendant of such a well-known family to be walking about barefoot.

"I suppose." It always came down to Papa and his rash decisions. But then, if he hadn't made those rash decisions, she wouldn't be here. She took the napkin bird by its beak, shook it briskly, and laid it in her lap. "We can take the ferry down to Dauphine Island today, if you like. It's a pretty day to be on the water."

~

Holding her skirts clear of the mud and standing water, Daisy took the schoolhouse steps two at a time, praying nobody would see such an unladylike and undignified dash. But she had discovered from unfortunate experience that if the primer spelling list wasn't on the chalkboard before the students arrived, she would face an hour of mayhem from which the day might never recover. She had thought Lyse might wake her, but the other side of the bed was empty, and no trace remained of her friend's presence except a slight dent in the other side of the bolster.

Hurriedly she fished in her pocket for the key and let herself in. The one-room building, adjoined to the brick hospital situated on Conception Street, was constructed on a raised platform in the vain hope that frequent floodwaters wouldn't rise into the schoolroom. This morning the floors were still damp from a heavy rainstorm earlier in the week, but at least there was no standing water under her desk, which happened to be the lowest point of the room.

Straightening desks along the way, she hurried to the blackboard at the front of the room and found a small piece of chalk in her desk drawer. Her father had the desk made for her as soon as he realized she was determined to stuff education into the children who wandered the downtown streets like feral cats. Tongue between her teeth, she started writing the spelling list.

She dearly wished that she might hold classes at least five days a week, but so far she had not convinced her father to allow her more than two. He insisted that she must reserve time for supervising the upkeep of their home. Besides, many of the children she wanted to teach were needed in running the various business endeavors of their parents. She herself had had the benefit of a governess who had taught her her letters, as well as deportment and a smattering of languages and music. Dear widowed Mrs. Calder had willingly included Lyse in the lessons, and both girls grieved when she caught yellow fever and passed away last fall.

Determined to pass along the benefit of her expensive education, she tried to convince the young mothers she met socially that their children would make more capable artisans, businessmen, fishermen, *citizens*, if they knew at least the basics of arithmetic, reading, and writing. To her joy, her little class had grown to the point that they must soon look for a bigger room.

Until then, she must find ways to contain the chaos.

She had just written "decision" in her best copperplate when footsteps sounded on the steps outside. Someone was early today, she thought, glancing over her shoulder. Probably nine-year-old Emée Robicheaux, precocious and hungry for learning. Daisy could hardly keep up with her requests for more books to read. She'd had to ask Lyse to start bringing books from her grandfather's magnificent library.

But when she recognized the tall figure standing in the doorway, backlit by the morning sun, she almost dropped the chalk. "Simon!" She laid the chalk on the rail under the blackboard, dusted her hands, then the front of her dark-blue worsted dress. "What are you doing here?"

He sauntered in with his rolling gait, his usually pleasant expression replaced by something . . . odd. "I'm looking for my sister. Have you seen her?"

"Lyse?" Of course he meant Lyse, little Geneviève was only four. "Yes, she spent the night with me, but she left the house early this morning. She was going to . . ." Then it occurred to her that Simon might not know anything about Don Rafael Gonzales. She had never lied to Simon, but perhaps she shouldn't blurt that out.

"Going where?" Now Simon was scowling, one of his famous *Lyse is in trouble* scowls. He braced himself against her desk and folded his arms.

Daisy practically worshiped the ground Simon walked on, but he could be overprotective of his little sister. "I'm so glad you came into town this morning," she said, swishing closer to him with a smile. "I need fresh water from the spring for the children. Would you mind taking the bucket and—"

"Of course. After you tell me where Lyse is." He wasn't angry, at least not with her, not yet. Just implacable as only Simon could be.

Daisy had known him since she and Lyse were six and Simon was a ten-year-old miniature version of his handsome father. The day they met, shortly after her mother died, she'd been trailing behind her bewildered, grieving father in the Emporium. The Lanier children, ragged but happy, had been engrossed in racing a box turtle against a frog down a back aisle, while their beautiful mulatto mama bartered at the front of the store with Monsieur Gerard over the price of a pair of men's stockings for her husband.

Daisy had of course instantly fallen in love with Simon and followed him around for months—until he took to jumping out at her unexpectedly from behind trees and making her cry. For a while after that, she refused to acknowledge his existence. Then on the day of her thirteenth birthday, she came upon him sitting on her back steps. He was waiting for Lyse and puzzling over a pamphlet that Reverend Garrett had left in a stack for Papa to distribute among the soldiers.

"What is this—this—nonsense?" He'd thrust the paper toward her, black eyes blazing. "*Papist idolaters*? Is that what you think of me?"

"I—I—of course not." She shut the kitchen door, took the paper, and sat down beside Simon. She turned it over in her hand. "Where did you get this?"

"It was lying on the ground right here by the steps. Your family is Anglican, don't try to deny it." His voice, deepened to a velvet rumble since the last time she'd spoken directly to him, shook with something that almost sounded like hurt. It pierced her tender heart.

"Yes, but I don't believe everything in that pamphlet. In fact, most of it I don't even understand. Please, Simon, you know I'm your friend—Lyse's friend, I mean." Afraid to look at him, she gripped her hands tight in her lap.

"Well . . . I love God just like you do. And you shouldn't leave things like this around where they will hurt people you care about, especially if you don't even believe it."

She peeped at him, relieved to hear the softening of his voice, to see the calming of those stormy eyes. Lyse's aggravating older brother had turned into a man while she wasn't looking—harder along the jaw, leaner and bonier in body, tall enough to tower over her.

And she was thirteen now, a maiden who had just that morning put her hair up for the first time. As he stared back at her, something bloomed between them. She felt it in the heating of her cheeks, saw it in a subtle shift in his expression. He was no longer angry, just intrigued.

Now, three years later, standing in the schoolroom with her desk between them, she was fully aware of her power over him. If she wanted to distract him, all she had to do was walk a little closer, lay a hand on his wrist.

But he suddenly grinned and stood up. "No, you don't, my lady. You will not look at me with those blue eyes and hope I forget all about what I came to find out. What mischief is my sister up to this morning?"

She gave him the pouting smile that usually got whatever she wanted. "Simon . . ."

He stared at her, unmoving.

She looked at the clock and sighed. She wasn't going to finish the spelling list now. "It's seven-thirty, and the children will be here at eight. Come sit on the porch with me, and I'll tell you about Don Rafael Gonzales de Rippardá."

~

Rafa lounged back in his seat on the *Princesse*—an ancient but apparently seaworthy bateau captained by its scowling owner, Simon Lanier—and tried to convince himself that his only interest lay in ascertaining British strength along the Gulf of Mexico.

Unzaga would not be pleased at his delay. At least, not until he heard Rafa's report of intelligence gathered during this delightful interlude with his charming little Creole maiden. That she was one of *those* Laniers was an interesting detail indeed. That she had the alluring face of a gypsy princess was a delicious fact that his commander need not know.

She sat facing him with one hand gripping the side of the boat, the black spirals of her hair coming loose to blow like silk ribbons in the wind, eyes narrowed to topaz slits against the fierce morning sun. Every so often, she would lean and point, drawing her dress so snug across her bosom that he could hardly focus on landmarks with musical names like Bay Minette, Chacaloochee Bayou, Mullet Point, and Bay Bon Secours. And then the peevish brother Simon—who had apparently discovered the proposed tour from Daisy Redmond and then raced to the pier to chaperone—would give him a warning look, reminding Rafa that he could not afford distraction.

"Señorita Lyse," he said to divert the protective brother, "you must tell me how it is that you come to be related to the Laniers of New Orleans."

He watched Simon Lanier's expression shift from protectiveness to outright hostility. Where the girl's eyes were that innocent dark gold, his were black and stony, the eyebrows slashing above an arrogant nose. His skin was baked a darker brown, the curly black hair pulled into a no-nonsense queue. The similarity between the siblings was in the generous mouth, the design of the white teeth—which were now bared like a wolf's fangs.

"We have nothing to do with them," Simon Lanier said coldly. After a moment he looked away and applied himself to adjusting the sail.

Lyse leaned closer to Rafa, her hair blowing across his lips, her frown apologetic. "There is bad blood among my family." She glanced at her brother. "It has to do with the former Louisiana governor, O'Reilly—"

"Lyse, you will not speak that man's name." Simon spat over the side of the boat.

"But Simon, this is unreasonable! We cannot bring back Uncle Guillaume—"

"I said, don't speak of it! I let you bring this Spaniard onto my boat because we need his silver, but you will not divulge our private business to him. Pére wouldn't like it. *Comprendre?*"

Lyse stared at her brother, her delicate pointed chin trembling, tears standing in her eyes. "I understand you are a big blockhead. The world is a chessboard, and King Louis got himself mated out of the game. But we who are neither black nor white still have to live here, and discourtesy will not undo what has been done."

Simon clamped his lips together. After a moment or two he looked away and began to vigorously pole the boat away from an approaching sandbar.

Lyse met Rafa's eyes, her expression distressed. "I beg you will overlook—"

"Please, señorita, it is of no moment." He took her hand and gently kissed the scarred knuckles. "I have the habit of impertinent questions. My mama beats me for it daily." When he won a small smile, he sat back, satisfied.

Maybe he hadn't been able to coax the so-beautiful English rose into taking him about the city of Mobile. But as a substitute, the French camellia looked to be blooming under his touch. There was no end to what she might divulge before the day was done.

Don Rafael had gone back to New Orleans, leaving Lyse to help Simon tie the boat up at the pier and wait for another ferry customer.

The very fact that she had conversed with someone who bore the title *don* caused her to look at the world differently. Before today, she had felt some of her brother's resentment for the Spanish race. She hadn't known her uncle Guillaume as well as Simon had, but she understood the grief his death had caused her father and her grandfather. Defending this particular Spanish gentleman, however, painted a different color on the canvas of her feelings.

She elbowed Simon, who sat beside her on the dock with feet dangling over the side, fishing pole in hand. "Simon, why do you suppose Uncle Guillaume got involved in the revolt against the Spanish but Papa didn't?"

Simon gave her a funny look. "It was the same year Maman died, don't you remember?"

"Maybe I'm like Papa and blocked out everything except that."

She'd been about eight, old enough to understand that when people died, they went to heaven and never came back. Maman had been sick with something that made her beautiful café-au-lait skin turn ashy, the whites of her amber eyes the yellow of poached corn. For days she had burned in an agony of fever, twisting in her bed until the smell of the room became nigh unbearable. Papa, for one, couldn't stand the sight of his beloved Cerise fading like a tide going out. He'd begged Grandmére Madeleine to come attend Maman, while he'd retreated to his fishing boat and a brown jug that turned him surly as a dog with a sore tail.

On that day—that horrid, endless day of defeat and sadness—Grandmére called Lyse and Simon into Maman's room and bade them say goodbye. Grandmére had washed and tended Maman, then changed the bedclothes, so that Maman looked like the frail, translucent shell of a sleeping angel. Simon, uncharacteristically diffident, gripped Lyse's hand so tight her fingers ached and approached their mother with lagging steps. He'd brushed a kiss upon her brow, then backed away with his stringy young throat working. Abruptly he dropped Lyse's hand. Releasing a guttural sob, he ran.

Lyse looked up at her grandmother, who placed a gentle hand upon her head. "Go ahead, *cher*," Grandmére murmured. "She knows you're here, and she won't leave without your blessing."

Her heart felt as if it would melt from her chest, but Lyse found courage in her grandmother's presence. She swallowed and knelt beside the cot. "Maman," she whispered. "I love you. I'll take care of Papa and Simon."

Her mother's eyelids fluttered. "My precious girl. Strong and sweet as a rose." A faint smile curved the blistered lips. "Listen to Grandmére. Read every . . . every book in Grandpére's library."

"I will." Because she didn't know what else to say, Lyse knelt there, praying wordlessly with tears dripping off her chin.

After a time, Grandmére touched her shoulder. "Come, *cher*. It's time for your father to say goodbye."

Lyse hadn't known he was there, but as she rose and reluctantly backed toward the doorway, the strong scent of spirits overpowered the sickroom smell. She turned.

His face was awful in its grief. Pushing Lyse aside, he stumbled into the room, grabbed fistfuls of his own hair, bent double as if he were the one in death throes.

Lyse felt Grandmére pull her out of the room. In the kitchen, she flung her arms around Grandmére's waist and burrowed into her in an attempt to block out the sound of Papa's sobs.

Grandmére held her tight for a minute, then gently led her out to the gallery. "Let's sit on the steps. I have something for you."

"I don't need a present," Lyse said as she plopped down beside her grandmother on the top step. All she wanted was her mother. She crossed her arms over her knees and laid her head on them. She could still hear Papa crying through the open window.

"No, it's something my maman gave me when I needed it. Now it's time to pass it on to you."

Lyse turned her head. "Which maman?" According to family legend, Grandmére had been adopted as an infant, her real mother being Grossmére Geneviève's unmarried sister Aimée.

"The one who loved me enough to give me her Bible and teach me to revere its author."

Lyse frowned, trying to disentangle Grandmére's meaning. "Grossmére Geneviève?" she guessed.

"Yes. She came to Louisiana when it was little more than a rotten fort and an Indian village or two. People say she came just to marry my papa, but she really came because of this Bible. She believed every word of it and read it every day."

"Like you do?"

Smiling, Grandmére leaned over and picked up the Bible, which had been lying on the seat of one of the rocking chairs on the gallery. She sat there every morning as the sun came up, reading and rocking and praying under her breath. "I wanted to be just like her."

Grandmére was the happiest person Lyse knew. She slowly reached for the Bible. It was heavy, leatherbound, scarred from years of use. It pressed on her lap with the weight of wisdom. "Will you help me understand it? Grandpére says I'm smart, but—" she looked doubtfully at the Bible—"there's an awful lot of big words in there."

Grandmére nodded. "There's hard truth and stories of cruelty and evil as well, but there will also be help and encouragement when you need it. And stories of heroes who lived for God. Women who followed him even when their lives were difficult. Geneviève

Lanier was a woman like that. She had to keep her faith quiet for a time, but God protected her."

Lyse had heard the stories of the Huguenot persecution in France, how Geneviève and her sister Aimée had gotten on a boat with twenty-three other French brides-to-be, to come to New France and choose husbands from among the king's explorers. Tristan Lanier had been a man among men, one of Bienville's trusted advisors. When the settlement was moved downriver from the twenty-seven-mile bluff, he had been instrumental in choosing the present location. Still, he and Geneviève had built their home apart from the fort so that they could practice their Reformist faith without interference from the king's Catholic prescriptions.

"Why didn't God protect Maman from the fever?" she asked.

"Lyse, everyone dies, some sooner than others. We cannot know what lies behind God's mighty purposes for those who love him. What you *can* know is that he is with you always, even now. He understands your grief, he weeps with you, he will hold you through it. Look at me, little one." Grandmére took Lyse's chin. "You must keep your eyes fixed on Jesus, no matter what happens."

Remembering that scene, Lyse looked at her brother with new eyes. He hadn't been as close to Grandmére as she. No wonder he had a hard time with faith and forgiveness.

Simon put an uncharacteristically gentle hand on her shoulder. "It was a hard time for us all, *cher*. Grandpére submitted to the British here in Mobile in order to keep his property. He tried to stop Uncle Guillaume from going to New Orleans, knowing the revolt was pointless and dangerous." He shrugged. "It turns out, he was right."

Politics had never interested Lyse, except when her family was directly affected. But this young Spaniard had awakened something . . . restless within her. "So are you going to marry Daisy?"

He heaved a moody sigh. "Of course I want to. But the major doesn't particularly like me. And I can almost understand why."

One side of his mouth curled up. "My prospects aren't particularly bright."

"Why don't you ask Grandpére to teach you the shipping business? You could be a great help to him."

"I don't want to sit in an office running accounts. I want to be outdoors on my boat, working with my hands." He paused. "Besides, Daisy is young. She thinks she wants me, but she also thinks her father is going to give in and give us his blessing. I'm afraid we may have to go away if we want to be together." He scowled. "Don't you tell her I said all this, Lyse."

He hadn't talked to her in such depth since they were children. She shook her head. "I won't. You've thought about this a lot, haven't you?"

"Of course I have. I can't just marry Daisy and move her in with us over at Bay Minette."

Lyse laughed. "No. And that really isn't funny, is it?"

"No." But he smiled. "I hear things at the docks, Lyse. Changes are coming, now that the Americans are trying to throw off the Brits. They're going to be cracking down on trade, embargoes are likely, and I've got to find ways to keep us fed. As long as fishing is good, we'll be all right . . ." He shook his head.

Simon might be the most cautious one in the family, but he wasn't afraid of anything. Hearing him express these doubts was sobering. Lyse knew better than to press him about the Spaniard.

Who she'd likely never see again anyway.

The line jerked. "Simon, you've got one!"

Fishing was a much more productive enterprise than wishing one's life away.

3

March 1777

Lyse was helping Simon unload a workboat full of tobacco up from the island, when Niall McLeod's bright red head popped from behind a towering stack of crates. The whites of his blue eyes were round as eggs.

"Lyse, you've got to come now! Your pa's got himself in trouble again."

She shifted the heavy crate in her arms onto a new stack, then stood up with a hand to her back. The days of lazing about with a charming Spaniard on a boat tour down the bay, as she had seven months ago, were long gone. If it was true that an army marched on its stomach, the British troops of West Florida were going to subsist mainly on cigar fumes. She and Simon had been shuffling tobacco crates all morning, with no signs of stopping before dark. The British frigate *Hinchinbrook* had brought her valuable cargo from Carolina, sailing around East Florida via Havana, and had orders to leave port at dawn on the morrow.

Reluctant to take Niall seriously, Lyse glanced at Simon. He hadn't heard, or he'd be exploding with anger. He was arguing with a porter whose wagon had been commandeered to transport the tobacco to the fort. Their father should have been here to deal with cartage so Simon could focus on the boats, but they hadn't seen Papa all day. "Papa's always in trouble," she said with a shrug. "What's the problem now?"

Niall edged between the crates and stood before Lyse, rotating his hat between his hands. "Drunk and disorderly again. I talked the sergeant out of putting him in the guardhouse, but you've got to come get him. Now. Please, Lyse."

She looked down at her work garb—Simon's outgrown breeches and shirt topped off by an ugly, shapeless homespun coat, with homemade moccasins on her feet. Necessary for hauling freight on the dock, but unacceptable for walking about in town. "Niall, I can't come now. Don't you see we're in the middle of—"

"Either you come get him and take him home, or I'm letting him go to the guardhouse." Niall's round face was set in uncharacteristically obstinate lines.

Papa must have really done it this time.

"All right, I'll come." She glanced over her shoulder. Simon couldn't be spared, so it would have to be her. "Simon! I have to run an errand—I'll be back in an hour."

Guiltily shrugging off her brother's angry objection, she followed Niall. They dodged the longshoremen, sailors, merchants, and slaves who crowded the dock, Lyse pulling her hat lower to cover her eyes and hide her face. Her hair was braided and tied out of the way under a scarf, so maybe nobody would recognize her and tell Justine she'd been working at the wharf again.

She tugged Niall's sleeve. "What did he do this time?"

Her old friend hesitated. "There was a faro game at Coup de Chance."

Faro. Mixed with rum and politics, no doubt, and—judging from Niall's involvement—off-duty soldiers. A combination which Antoine Lanier would be unable to resist.

When she didn't answer, only sighed, Niall said, "I tried to get him to come out. I told him you and Simon had work down at the quay, that you needed him." Niall shook his head. "He just said something about 'all those mouths to feed' and called for another round."

"All those mouths" included herself right now—which was why she spent her days either working at the dock or fishing for her supper—but Lyse would not feel guilty for refusing the first offer of marriage to come her way, from a friend of her father's who already had three children. She was only sixteen, and there would be more. She sneaked a glance at Niall. He would ask her, she was sure, as soon as he got up enough nerve to brave Simon's contempt. Papa would say yes, relieved to be shed of her.

Niall looked at her again, his face flaming when he met her eyes. He wasn't handsome, but he was a good boy, and he didn't seem to mind her complicated, slightly seedy family. If she married him, she would be a British soldier's wife.

Which would be little better than marrying Bertrand Robicheaux.

Feeling her throat tighten, she snatched for joy. Nobody said life should be easy. Even Daisy, who lived about as charmed a life as anybody she knew, faced her father's reluctance to let her marry Simon. But God was good, and something would work out.

Lyse smiled and bumped Niall's shoulder with sisterly gratitude. "It will be all right. You'll see."

It seemed God had been listening to her prayers, for nobody they passed gave her and Niall more than a cursory glance as they trudged up from the quay to turn onto the street which ran past the gate to the fort. They stopped at the gatehouse, where Niall exchanged salutes with another young infantryman. "Reporting back to Sergeant Adamson."

The guard looked happy to have his solitary boredom interrupted. "Who's this?" He looked at Lyse with mild curiosity.

"M-Monsieur Lanier's . . . son," said Niall, tugging at his uniform collar. "Adamson's request."

"Oh. Yes. Take him in." The young guard looked doubtful. "You might need a wagon, though. I doubt he can walk in his condition."

Lyse's heart sank. Please, God, let him be sober. Otherwise she'd never get him home. Simon was going to be furious.

It was a prayer without much hope.

Lyse followed Niall past headquarters, hoping that she wouldn't run into Major Redmond or anybody else she knew. She couldn't help remembering the day last August when she and Daisy had delivered the message from Don Rafael. It had been a highlight in a bleak season, as British military presence tightened over the port, limiting trade with "suspicious parties," notably American ships. French vessels were also scrutinized, as gossip said Louis XVI was ready to ally his country with the Continental rebels.

She hadn't seen the insouciant young Spanish merchant since their tour down the bay on Simon's bateau. If he had returned to Mobile for trade purposes, he hadn't sought her out. Which was just as well. She had no time for lazy popinjays.

Niall halted, and she realized with a jerk of awareness that they had stopped outside a barracks whose door stood open to the fresh spring breeze. Smoke curled from the chimney, dissipating into a cloudless cerulean sky, and the smell of fish stew wafted from a kettle over the fire. Lyse's stomach growled. She hadn't eaten since a dried apple gobbled at daybreak. The time must be near noon.

"Wait here," Niall told her. He disappeared inside the barracks, and she heard him address someone within. "Lanier, it's time to go. Lyse and I are going to take you home."

There was a groan followed by an unintelligible mumble.

"Sir," Niall said loudly, "you can't stay. My sergeant—"

Niall catapulted backward through the door.

Lyse caught him, stumbled back, and nearly fell under his stout body, but she managed to break his fall, letting him roll hard onto his stomach.

He got up spitting dirt. "You crazy old bear! I'm trying to help you!"

Lyse went to the door of the barracks. "Papa! It's me! What's the matter with you? Why did you hit Niall?" After the brightness of daylight, the room was stuffy and dim, filled with shapeless forms of furniture, hanks of tobacco, ropes, and tools hanging off the walls, the smoke and smell of the stew strong enough to choke.

Something on the closest bunk shifted, growled like the bear Niall had called him. "Lyse? What you doing here?" Papa's French was slurred, rough.

"I'm taking you home. You can't stay here." *I can't either,* she thought, uncomfortably aware that she stood in a bachelor dwelling. Her reputation, shaky at best, would collapse if anyone else knew she was here, dressed in her brother's clothes.

"Can't go home." Papa flopped back onto the bunk with an arm across his eyes. "Poor Justine. She hates me."

This was absurd. When had she turned into her father's confidante? "No she doesn't. She just wants you to come home tonight. She misses you."

"The children need shoes. *You* need shoes. But I lost yesterday's shrimp money, and Michel Dussouy's given his business to the British pigs. I don't know what to do."

Lyse gritted her teeth. She loved her handsome papa, but he was the biggest trial on two continents. He hadn't even the common sense to keep his controversial political comments to himself. No wonder Justine had sent him fishing.

"The weather is getting warm enough so none of us will need shoes for long. Let's go home, Papa. We'll pray about it and figure out what to do."

"There are some things praying won't fix, little one." But he sat up, scrubbing his hands over his face. Apparently he had cat eyes, for he gave her a disapproving look. "What are you wearing?"

"I was working with Simon at the dock." *And I wasn't the one who lost all my money at cards,* she wanted to add, but she held her tongue. "A dress isn't practical."

"No daughter of mine walks about in male attire." He rose, swaying, and stumbled toward the door. He brushed Lyse aside and glared at Niall. "*You* still here?"

"Yes, sir." Niall stood his ground. "I escorted Lyse. Sergeant Adamson told me to make sure you both made it home." He gulped. "He said you're not to come back to town until you've paid your taxes."

"What is he going to do, arrest me?" Papa's expression folded into belligerence.

"Yes, sir, he will. In fact, he was going to this time, but I—I—" Niall's face suddenly flamed as he glanced at Lyse. "Come on, let's just get out of here. It doesn't matter now."

"Niall, what did you do?" Lyse clutched his arm.

"Nothing." Pulling away, Niall shoved his shoulder under Papa's armpit, taking most of the older man's weight, and started hauling him across the drill field.

"Niall?"

But Papa was laughing drunkenly. "I remember now. Boy, you've thrown your leg over a wild mustang this time." He looked over his shoulder at Lyse. "Young Niall here convinced his commanding officer not to arrest his betrothed's papa."

"*Betrothed?*" She darted around the two of them, planted her hands on Niall's chest, and shoved. "Are you as crazy as he is? I'm not marrying you!"

Three or four men came out of the other end of the barracks to stare. "Is that a girl?" asked one of them.

Niall planted his feet wide to keep Papa's unbalanced weight from pulling him down. "Lyse, be quiet. Come on, we've got to get out of here." He looked around. "I'll explain when we get to—"

"We don't need your help!" Wildly she grabbed her father's other arm and started hauling him toward the gate, Niall supporting him on the other side. She could hear the soldiers behind her laughing. Humiliation stung her eyes and the back of her throat.

They made it to the gatehouse, where the guard let them out with little more than a yawn. Lyse paused to lean against the stockade, her shoulders aching from the effort of keeping pace with her father's stumbling gait. He had fallen into a morose stupor. "We've got to have a wagon. It's too far down to the quay."

They stood there for a forlorn minute, resting as foot traffic proceeded up and down Esplanade. One or two inhabitants on horseback clopped by, followed by a well-dressed man and woman in a carriage.

Niall took off his hat and swiped his sweaty forehead against his sleeve. "I could maybe go to the livery . . ."

She gave him a scornful look. "You can't afford the livery any more than I can."

Even more doubtfully, Niall said, "You want me to go for Simon?"

Another carriage approached and came to a halt in front of them. "*Buenos días, señorita*," said a cheerful voice. "Perhaps I may be of assistance?"

Lyse squinted against the sun. She knew that voice from somewhere. She shifted, tilted the brim of her hat to block the glare. "Don Rafael? What are you doing here?"

~

Rafa could see that his little Creole saucepot was not happy to see him. And, indeed, he could hardly have run across her at a more inopportune time. Brigadier-General Bernardo de Gálvez, governor of Spanish Louisiana since New Year's Day, impatient with former governor Unzaga's good-hearted but chaotic method of handling diplomatic relations between Britain and her rebelling New England colonies, would court-martial Rafael if anything happened to the cargo waiting at the Dauphine Island port.

But an engagement with pirates encountered off the coast of Dominica had left the main course and mizzen course sails damaged, and they must be repaired before the *Diamante* could put back to sea and head for New Orleans. And, since information could be as valuable as gold in these days of pre-war, it was incumbent upon Rafa to make good use of the time.

However, as he looked down into Lyse Lanier's uptilted face, shaded by the wide-brimmed felt monstrosity she probably intended for a hat, he could not bring himself to abandon her to the dubious protection of these two ruffians—a stout young redcoat with a spotty chin and rusty hair dribbling from beneath his tricorn, the older one belligerent and, to all appearances, at least three sheets to the wind.

He saw no reason to answer her question directly. Instead, he wrapped the reins around the horn and jumped lightly to the ground. "As you can see," he said in English, since the other three had been speaking that language, "I have once more arrived to rescue the damsel in distress. I will not ask why she is dressed like a page boy in a penny opera. Instead I will introduce myself to her escorts and offer the use of my carriage, should it be required. Sirs, I am Don Rafael Maria Gonzales de Rippardá, at your service."

He bowed with a precise concoction of irony and courtesy, then stood with his beautiful new plumed hat over his heart while expressions of equal parts chagrin, anger, reluctant gratitude, and amusement chased across Lyse's expressive little kitten face.

The older man lurched away from the girl, the threat in his balled fists significantly mitigated by his unsteady stance. "You dare address my daughter in this familiar way, you Spanish court card?"

Rafa blinked, all but leveled by Señor le Papa's toxic breath. "I meant no insult, señor. I wish only to help." He turned to the girl. "Perhaps I misunderstood the difficulty?"

Under the misshapen hat, her clear caramel complexion had bloomed camellia pink. She stepped in front of her papa to look up at Rafa with humiliated golden eyes. "You didn't misunderstand, monsieur. In fact, you are purely an answer to prayer. My papa is . . . ill. We were—this is my good friend, Niall McLeod." She glanced over her shoulder at the young redcoat. "We were trying to help Papa walk down to the quay, where my brother is working. Perhaps it wouldn't be too far out of your way, to take us up in your carriage and drive us that far?"

Rafa, who considered himself a good noticer, absorbed three things all at once. First, the "good friend" McLeod seemed to be prepared to unsheathe his sword and detach Rafa from his head. Second, Papa Bear wasn't so drunk that he couldn't inflict quite a bit of damage, should he perceive real or imagined insult to his little girl. Third, said little girl seemed already to be regretting her request for aid.

All of which, due to a perverse twist of his personality—so obstinate that even his imposing *madre* had been unable to beat it out of him—made Rafa smile and take her hand, bringing it gently to his lips. He stood there studying the small grubby hand with its broken fingernails and silvery scars, which proved she was a woman who worked for every morsel of food that went into her sweet mouth. If he had not been in love before, that little hand flung Cupid's arrow straight to the center of his heart.

She gave an impatient tug of the grubby hand. "Do I take that to be a yes? Papa, allow Niall to help you up and let us go. We are blocking the street." She put her hand on Rafa's shoulder and hopped onto the bench seat of the carriage.

Rafa was left on the ground with McLeod and Señor Lanier, who had little choice but to obey. He turned to help the soldier boost Lanier up beside his daughter, and she slipped her arm securely through his to keep him steady.

"Niall, thank you for your help." She leaned across her father, holding out a hand to McLeod. "I don't know what we'd do without you."

The soldier reddened, taking her hand and squeezing it awkwardly. "Don't worry about the—you know, what I told my sergeant. It was a stupid thing to do, and I'm sorry."

"Very stupid, but you meant well." She smiled kindly as she sat back.

Lanier scowled down at the young man. "Keep your mouth shut about it, boy."

"Yes, sir." McLeod backed away, cowed.

Rafa gave the horse leave to start and glanced at the girl. He could feel the pleasant warmth of her small, curvy body all along his side, wedged as she was between himself and her father. He decided to take the scenic route to the quay.

"One must ask what it was McLeod told his sergeant," he said after a moment.

"Nothing useful." Lyse pressed her lips together, then burst into a peal of infectious laughter. "He told the sergeant that he'd just got betrothed! To me!" The laughter bubbled again.

Rafa frowned. "And that is funny because . . ."

"Oh, Don Rafael! You yourself said I look like a little boy!"

"Hmm. So I did." He couldn't tell her he'd said that to keep from scooping her up in his arms, so surprised and delighted was he to see her, not thirty minutes after his arrival in Mobile. So he just winked and began to whistle an air from *The Gulf of Sirens*.

All too soon, they arrived at the quay. Before Rafa could draw the horses to a complete stop, Lyse had dropped her father's arm and jumped to her feet.

"Papa, Simon's boat is gone!"

Rafa scanned the quay, which ran the length of the shoreline as far as the eye could see. "Where is everyone?" Activity had ground to a halt, leaving only a few dock workers engaged in lethargic tasks. There was not a British officer or soldier anywhere in sight. Gálvez would be interested in the lackadaisical state of the port.

"Most go home for lunch," Lanier said. "Some walk down the bayou for fishing, others to the taverns." He slid down from the carriage seat, listing as his feet hit the boardwalk. "I'm going to lie down in the shade." Avoiding Lyse's hand as she reached to steady him, he shambled toward a canvas awning pitched near the end of the nearest pier.

Lyse quickly scooted to the far end of the seat and turned sideways to slide down as her father had done.

"Wait!" Rafa jumped to the ground. "I'll help you." He barely made it around the carriage in time to soften her landing. The folds of the oversized coat couldn't disguise the smallness of her waist under his hands. He held her, looking down into her face, vaguely aware of her irascible papa nearby.

He closed his eyes, counted to ten, and stepped away.

Lyse flung her hands about and glared at the back of her father's head. He was already collapsed under the awning, snoring. "Now what am I going to do?"

Rafa was wondering the same thing. He must find a reputable sailmaker with all speed, but he couldn't abandon the girl.

He cleared his throat. "Señorita. Miss Lyse. I think your papa is not so very ill."

She turned to look at him, frowning.

"Perhaps if you leave him to . . . sleep it off, he will be improved enough to get himself home. Or perhaps your brother will come back to get him."

She looked away. "You don't understand. Justine—Papa's wife—is worried about him. He's been gone for three days, and—"

The ragged edge of her voice pierced his heart. "This Justine is not your mother?" She had not mentioned this name during their tour last fall.

"My stepmother. But she's not much older than me, and there are four little ones . . ." Straightening, she tucked her hands behind her back. "But this is not your concern, and you must forgive my complaining." She bestowed upon him a tight smile. "Thank you for the kind use of your conveyance. Good day to you, Don Rafael."

She expected him to drive away and leave her here to deal with her selfish, miscreant father, the surly brother, and a houseful of dependents? He shook his head in disbelief. It was not the Spanish way. It was not the Gonzales way. His mother would beat him about the head.

Still he spoke carefully, for she was very proud. "I understand your reluctance to allow a stranger into your family difficulties. But I have an idea." He paused, watching her face. She was guarded, naturally, but at least she was listening. "I am in need of some gifts to take back to my family in New Orleans, but I must also complete some business with regard to my ship—and time is of the essence. Perhaps, while your papa regathers his strength in expectation of your brother's return, you might do me the favor of executing the purchase of those gifts. In return, I could pay you a small commission."

He could all but see the wheels of her brain turning. Gradually the golden eyes brightened, and her lips curved. "You would pay me to go shopping?" The sound of her laughter was like the bells of the Church of St. Louis. "Monsieur, I think you have been too long in the sun. What kind of gifts?"

"Come with me. I will drive you back to the market and talk to you about my beautiful mama and my sister Sofía."

~

To choose a gift for Don Rafael's strict mama, as well as the much-beloved Sofía, who also shared the name of Lyse's French-Canadian great-great-grandmére, was a difficult responsibility.

In Gerard's Emporium she had found an imported satinwood tea caddy with ebony line stringing, sandalwood marquetry inlay, and polished brass hinges and hasps. Even Daisy didn't own anything so fine. It would take most of the Spanish coin given her by Don Rafael, but she knew Madame de Rippardá would adore it.

If someone gave it to Lyse, *she* would adore it.

But now she stood at the dry goods counter, reverently handling an ell of fragile Alençon lace. There were women of the city who still wore dresses trimmed with this beautiful stuff, though she personally knew very few of them. Perhaps the French and Spanish ladies in New Orleans were accustomed to dressing more extravagantly than here in this British military outpost. Since hostilities had broken out between England and the thirteen northernmost colonies, life in loyalist East and West Florida had become increasingly frugal. British merchant ships were often waylaid by American privateers and prevented from sailing into the ports of Pensacola, Mobile, and Baton Rouge. Prices had soared until only the very wealthy could afford luxuries like dress material, lace . . . and tea caddies.

Reaching into her pocket to touch the velvet bag of gold coins Don Rafael had given her—what an honor that he had trusted her with such riches!—she glanced over her shoulder at the tea caddy, displayed grandly inside a glass-fronted cabinet at the front of the store. She wished he would come back and help her decide.

She turned as the little bell at the top of the door tinkled. Her cousin Scarlet, carrying an armload of packages and a parasol, backed through the door. Closing the parasol, she held the door open as her mistress entered with the ceremony of a Parisian duchess.

Madame Dussouy, ugh. All of Lyse's pleasure in gift-buying evaporated like rain on hot brick. She would like to have snatched a whispered word with Scarlet, but she was still dressed in Simon's clothes and would inevitably draw the matron's sniping.

Madame Dussouy looked around, mouth pursed like a dried lemon. "Monsieur Gerard? Where are you? I need assistance, if you please!" She began to search the shelves as if Monsieur Gerard might have hidden himself under a rug or behind a clock.

Hoping the imperious society dame would be well occupied with ordering about the owner of the Emporium, Lyse hurried to greet Scarlet with a hug. "My cousin! What a good surprise!" She stood back, searching Scarlet's sweet face. Relieved to find no fresh bruises or scratches, she squeezed her hands. "You look well."

Scarlet glanced over Lyse's shoulder to where Madame was now fingering the same laces Lyse had just been looking at.

"I am," Scarlet whispered. "But we can't talk long. If she sees me talking to you, I'll pay for it when we get home."

"It is so wrong! We have the same grandmother—" Lyse broke off the useless words, words that always came when she thought of Scarlet being abused for nothing more than talking with her cousin.

Scarlet shook her head, a sad smile on her full lips. "What's done can't be undone." She looked around again, always on guard. "So tell me what you're doing in here. I know you don't have any money."

Lyse couldn't help the bubble of excitement that lightened her voice. "But I do! Look at this." She withdrew the little pouch of coins from her pocket, opened the drawstring, and held it so Scarlet could peer inside.

Scarlet's big brown eyes flashed up to stare at Lyse. "Is that—?"

"Yes, Spanish gold." Lyse hefted the bag so that the heavy coins jangled against one another. "Do you remember the Spanish don I told you about? The one who visited Mobile last August?"

"Yes. Is he back?" Scarlet sucked in a breath. "He gave that to you? Lyse, what have you done?"

"Yes, Lyse, what have you done?" Madame Dussouy pushed between the two girls and snatched the velvet bag.

Startled, horrified, Lyse grabbed for it and missed. "Give that back to me! It belongs to—"

"I'm sure it doesn't belong to you!" Madame poured the shining coins into her hand. A handsome woman of some forty years, as always impeccably dressed and coifed, she fixed Lyse with her steely blue eyes. "Who did you steal this from? Monsieur Gerard!" she called without taking her eyes off Lyse. "Come here and see what I found."

4

Rafa drew the carriage up in front of the Emporium where he had earlier deposited Lyse, tossed the reins to a boy standing about ready to deal with customer equipages, and leapt down onto the brick drive path. What a long and frustrating, but highly invigorating afternoon it had been, negotiating for the repair of his sails and establishing trails of information that Gálvez would undoubtedly find helpful.

In fact, it occurred to him that he might pursue a more long-term arrangement for his employment in Mobile when he next conferred with the governor. In the meantime, it looked like he would be stuck here for at least a week before the sails would be ready and he could complete the delivery of uniforms, powder, and blankets intended for transfer to American operatives waiting in New Orleans.

Doomed to endure the beautiful smiles of Señorita Lyse Lanier—assuming she had not absconded with his gold coins and left him to purchase his own gifts. Smiling at the absurdity, he swung into the Emporium.

He stood looking up at the grand beamed ceiling, soaring to nearly twelve feet above, where dusty afternoon light poured in through open transom windows, illuminating the merchandise displayed on polished wooden glass-fronted shelves and open counters. Finally it dawned on him what was so odd: the empty aisles.

But a definite disturbance roared from the back of the store. Raised voices, both male and female, the clang of a bell, scrape of steel—

Rafa, who never liked to appear in a hurry, took off at a run. He arrived at a door marked "Office" just in time to observe a lady dressed in puce, with a nose like the prow of a ship, raising her hand to strike a tall young Negress who stood protectively in front of someone else. A well-dressed white-haired gentleman with a pair of silver-framed spectacles dangling from a strap around his neck stood by, arms folded, impassively watching the proceedings.

"Pardon me," Rafa said, "but I'm looking for Señor Gerard."

The puce lady's hand connected with the Negro girl's face, but possibly with less force than intended, as she jerked around to assess Rafa with a pair of the coldest eyes he'd seen outside of a fish tank.

The man with the spectacles, looking relieved at the interruption, stepped to the door. "I am Gerard," he said. "How may I help you?"

"Well met, señor." Rafa bowed, trying to see who stood behind the dark-skinned girl, though he suspected he knew. "I am Don Rafael Maria Gonzales de Rippardá, and I have lost a young . . . relation of mine." He had noticed that the more names one rattled off to new acquaintances, the higher his rank was assumed to be. He sensed the importance of impressing these people.

Suddenly Lyse dodged from behind her friend, took the girl by the shoulders, and kissed her reddened cheek. "Scarlet, you needn't hide me. I can take care of myself." She glowered at the blonde woman. "Don Rafael, I'm so glad to see you! Please tell Monsieur Gerard I didn't steal those coins!"

The puce lady looked down her large, sharp-ended nose. "As you can see, there are no Spaniards here, sir. It seems you are mistaken."

Rafa smiled broadly, removing his hat and bowing again, as if he had just taken notice of her. "Señora," he purred, rolling the *r* with deliberate exoticism, "you must forgive my faulty manners in overlooking your gentle presence. But it is indeed Señorita Lanier I seek—and of course she is not Spanish, for our families are only very distantly related." He took in Lyse's high color and dangerously wet eyes. "My dear, has there been some misunderstanding about the coins? I should not have burdened you with my little errand if I'd known there would be trouble. I am such a bad . . . cousin!"

"There is no misunderstanding, only very much of the stupidity." Lyse shot a resentful look at the puce woman and slid her arm through that of the young black woman. "I was only showing them to Scarlet, and explaining how you asked me to buy the gifts, but Madame Dussouy refused to believe anyone would trust me with such an important task! And she slapped Scarlet for standing with me. Have you ever heard of such injustice?"

Rafa bit the inside of his cheek. He agreed with Lyse, in fact wanted to kiss her for her brave words, but interfering between a mistress and her slave was a grave social faux pas that Don Rafael would never commit. He endeavored to look bored. "Yes, yes, little *prima*, but remember we are in a hurry this afternoon. We must collect the gifts and be on our way." He turned to Gerard as if just remembering. "I believe you have my coins, señor?"

"Oh! Yes, of course!" Gerard handed over the velvet bag with its heavy jingling contents. "I'll be happy to wrap up whatever you wish to purchase. Please forgive my—" He caught the puce woman's steely gaze. "That is, before you go, may I introduce Madame Dussouy, who was sincerely trying to help. I beg you will blame only me for any confusion in the matter."

"Why, there is nothing to forgive," Rafa said, with a deep bow to the woman. "I am pleased to make your acquaintance, Madame."

She gave a regal nod of her blonde head, the purple feathers stuck in the curls bobbing absurdly. "Don Rafael, I hope you won't take it amiss if I caution you against allowing this little hoyden to traipse about dressed like a boy! Look at her, flaunting such a great amount of money to anybody and everybody. *My* slaves are trained to resist temptation, but not everyone is so diligent in discipline."

Lyse opened her mouth, clearly ready to speak, but Rafa forestalled her with a sly wink. "You are indeed a . . . paragon, madame," he said, proud of his improving English. "I will keep your advice in mind." He let his gaze flick over the slave's face, noting the distinctive almond shape of her eyes and the delicate, narrow chin. Forestalling Lyse's clear intent to introduce her friend, which would only make a bad situation worse, he clasped her hand and tucked it firmly into his elbow. "Come, *prima*, show me what you have picked out for Sofía and Mamá."

The puce woman stopped him by waving a large ostrich-feather fan in his face. "Wait! Don Rafael, before you go—"

Fighting the urge to sneeze, he raised an eyebrow. "Señora?"

The ostrich tucked itself under her arm. "I had a notion that if you aren't otherwise engaged, you might like to attend a little soirée I am holding this evening. My husband and I are patrons of the arts and have engaged a traveling string quartet that is purported to be quite good. There will be dancing, and my cook is considered the best in the city . . ."

Rafa had planned to spend the evening trolling the drinking establishments along the waterfront for news. But the opportunity to solicit information from the upper classes, especially those with French roots, could hardly be passed up.

He folded himself into another bow, lower than the first. "Señora, you are too kind. I should be most happy to give up my lonely room above the tavern in favor of your gracious offer of entertainment."

Madame simpered. "Excellent. We are located on the shell road northwest of town. Ask anyone, and you'll be able to find us."

"Until this evening, then. *Adiós*." Rafa hustled Lyse from the office, overriding her incipient protest, trailed by the profusely apologetic Gerard.

Safely outside the Emporium in his carriage—with an exorbitantly expensive tea caddy and enough lace to decorate the curtains of Versailles in a package stowed under the seat—he gave the horses leave to start.

After a strained moment, Lyse heaved a gusty sigh. "I'm very sorry for the trouble, Don Rafael."

"Three times, señorita. Three times now have I rescued you from disaster." He glanced at her, smiled at her dejected expression. "In the fairy tales this is a significant number."

"It won't happen again, I promise," she said, hunching her shoulders.

"Somehow I doubt that." When she failed to laugh, he sighed. "Who was that dreadful woman, and why was she screeching about hoydens and ragamuffins and slaves?"

"Madame Dussouy, as Monsieur Gerard said. She is married to one of the richest Frenchmen in town. You arrived just in time to keep me from landing in gaol." The dimple flickered in her cheek. "I am three times grateful, *mon cousin*."

"You are three times welcome, *mi prima*. But if I may be so bold, I have a small favor to ask in return."

"Anything, m'sieur!"

"I ask only that you accompany me to the señora's soirée. I fear that if I attend alone, I should be as a goldfish among the, um, matrimonial sharks."

Her eyes widened. "I could not! I wasn't invited. I would never be invited!"

"Come, little cousin, you aren't . . . afraid of the Harpy? Are you?"

"Of course not! Well, only a little."

"In Spain, the guest of my guest is my guest. Surely the good señora wouldn't risk offending me by turning you away. You have said you would do anything for me."

She stared at him, white teeth worrying at her lip. "I have nothing fit to wear."

"I will not insult your intelligence by disagreeing," he said with a grin. "But perhaps your friend, Miss Redmond, would consent to loan you a dress for the occasion."

"She probably would." Lyse folded her arms and sat silent for a stubborn moment. "All right. I'll ask her, and you may collect me at her house. But if Madame tosses you out on your Spanish . . . um, ear—don't say I didn't warn you!"

~

This was a terrible idea.

Don Rafael clearly had no concept of the wasp nest he had stirred into a noisy, stinging disaster, and Lyse had just as obviously lost every scrap of sense she'd ever possessed to have agreed to it.

She could feel every eye following her as the two of them progressed through Madame's gold-and-green salon, could literally hear the volume of conversation drop to scandalized whispers as hands covered mouths and mouths went to ears. She gripped her escort's forearm as if it were a rope and she drowning in a surging sea of outrage. Even the fine dark-green Aubusson carpet beneath Daisy's gilt-painted slippers seemed to drag at her like an undertow.

To be sure, the Dussouys' rheumy-eyed old butler had offered no resistance to her entrance with Don Rafael, but he would hardly have recognized tomboyish Lyse Lanier in the frilled-up doll Daisy had created that afternoon out of whole cloth. Indeed, she feared to turn her head, lest her hair come tumbling down from its tower of curls pinned to a padded contraption Daisy called a *toque*. Lyse had refused to wear powder, but the gold-and-cinnamon-colored ribbons threaded here and there were *très à la mode*.

Daisy had fretted that her only dress long enough for Lyse's tall frame was years out of date. But in the cinnamon brocaded robe à la française, with its low-cut, fitted bodice and voluminous folds of satin draping from the shoulders to drag behind her like a train, Lyse felt like a veritable princess. And Don Rafael's eyes had widened comically when she had descended the Redmonds' stairs, her wide, panniered skirt filling the breadth of the stairway. He had bowed low, then kissed her hand before tucking it into the crook of his elbow.

Now, promenading with him through the finest salon in the city of Mobile, surrounded by people no more finely dressed than herself, she understood for the first time the depth of her family's poverty.

"My Creole princess is perhaps in need of refreshment?"

At the sound of Don Rafael's voice, she blinked, startled to realize they had come to a stop in the center of the crowded candlelit room. His expression was quizzical, his dark brown eyes kind.

"Not really." She wrinkled her nose. "I'm afraid my bum has twisted sideways."

His laughter, infectious and uninhibited, rolled over her. "Señorita, if that means what I think it means, that is perhaps one difficulty I cannot help you with."

Heat bloomed in her face, but a surreptitious glance around told her that people had gone back to their own conversations. She leaned in to whisper, "It's just that I'm not used to wearing so many . . . appendages, under my dress and on top of my head! Besides the, um, bum problem, there is a ribbon tickling my neck, and I can't lift my arm to reach it. Please, Don Rafael, I would be so grateful if you would just yank it out."

"I'll be happy to oblige, if you promise to leave your wicked little knife in its sheath." Still chuckling, the Spaniard turned her so that he stood behind her, his hands cupping her shoulders. He leaned down so that his voice rumbled deep in her ear. "But if we are to be cousins, then you must call me Rafa instead of the so-stuffy Don Rafael." He moved the offending ribbon, tucking it into her curls.

She held her breath as his lips hovered close to her neck. He would not be so improper as to . . .

She jerked around to face him, in the process using her elbow to shift the padded bum under her skirt back into its correct position around her hips. "Thank you, *Rafa*," she said, dipping a saucy curtsey. "And you need never fear my knife, so long as you keep your . . . waistcoat out of reach."

He gave a great sigh and once more offered his arm. "To borrow one of your so-apt French words, *touché*, cousin Lyse. *Touché*." He tilted his head as the music changed from a stately allemande to a lively reel. "Would you care to dance, or would you prefer to tweak the Harpy's nose and see how long it takes her to recognize you?"

Lyse had almost relaxed into forgetting her terror. The knot under her rib cage suddenly tightened. "I really don't think—"

But it was too late.

"Don Rafael!" came the cultured, but carrying tones of their hostess, rapidly approaching. "I was so afraid you would forget to come!"

Rafa patted Lyse's hand, which had suddenly gripped his arm again, and murmured, "Courage, infant!" His blinding smile bloomed as he towed her with him in the direction of Madame Dussouy's ostrich-feather coiffure, which waved above the crowd. "Of course I remember to come, Madame Señora! And I bring my little *prima* with me, because I know it will make my Grandmama the Doña Magdalena de Ibanez y Rippardá so happy that our Lyse has been presented to your fine company."

Oh, this was such a ridiculous charade, and nobody was going to believe his lies, because everyone here had known her family since before she was born. Even as she dropped into an awkward curtsey, Lyse wanted to dash out of the house, skin back into her own comfortable clothes, and never show her face in town again.

But Madame Dussouy was staring at Don Rafael with her stupid mouth ajar. Her eyes darted to Lyse, then back to the Spaniard. One could clearly see her inability to reconcile this outrageous dilemma. "Ah, of course," she said at last, looking stricken by rigor mortis. "You are most welcome, and I pray you will avail yourself of refreshments. In fact, here comes Scarlet with hors d'oeuvres right now. Scarlet! Set that tray down, and bring mint juleps for Don Rippardá and . . ." She flapped a hand. "Mademoiselle Lanier."

Lyse rose jerkily and whirled to meet her cousin's—her *real* cousin's—astonished brown eyes.

"Lyse?" Scarlet squeaked, juggling the teetering tray. "What are you doing here?"

Madame rounded on her. "Girl, how dare you address the guests directly. Obey me instantly!"

Scarlet managed to land her heavy tray on a nearby table and, after one more frightened look at Lyse, hurried away toward the butler's pantry.

Lyse wanted to run after her, but she felt Rafa's long fingers gently squeeze her hand. A slight shake of his head and a sly wink kept her from flying to pieces. She forced herself to smile at her hostess with composure. "It's kind of you to accept me, Madame. As you can see, Don Rafael is . . . difficult to resist when his mind is made up."

"Yes, indeed," Madame said with a frosty smile. "Besides, I would never have it said that my charity is lacking." With Lyse firmly set in her place, she turned to Rafa with a flirtatious flip of her fan. "Don Rafael, I believe you have not met my husband." She turned to call to a tall, stooped gentleman in a powdered wig holding forth nearby in a cigar-smoking circle of men. "Monsieur Dussouy! Come here, sir! There is someone I would have you meet."

Lyse had met Michel Dussouy on a number of occasions, usually at church, and she had found him to be kind, absentminded, and yet a remarkably astute businessman. Whatever his wife's personal prejudices, his business dealings with the Lanier family had generally been conducted in fairness and without rancor.

Dussouy shook hands with Rafa, acknowledging the introduction, and when his gaze lit upon Lyse, he simply bowed courteously over her hand without even a raised eyebrow—for which she would have liked to kiss his pocked cheek.

Instead she smiled and dipped a curtsey. "Monsieur, I wanted to thank you for giving my stepmother your seat at mass on Sunday morning."

"Please do not mention it. At the rate she's going, Madame Justine will soon need a whole new pew to seat the Lanier clan!" As Lyse laughed, Dussouy turned quizzical gray eyes on Rafa. "My wife has told me all about the young Spanish don marooned in our city for ship repairs. I hope you have secured what you need, but if there is aught I can do to assist, you have but to stop by my offices just down on St. Francis. We deal in ship repairs and merchant marine supplies of all sorts."

"Kind of you, sir," Rafa said. "It looks to be nearly a week before the necessary materials can be pulled together. In the meantime, my partner, Señor Pollock, has given me leave to dispense with all cargo likely to spoil before we reach New Orleans."

Dussouy's face creased in a smile. "Are you indeed associated with Oliver Pollock? I met him once on a trip to New Orleans, back before the American rebels took to blocking trade between our cities. Capital fellow! Hair as red as a rooster's comb!"

Rafa laughed. "Indeed, sir. And a temper to match. He'll have my head if I can't make it back to port by the end of March." He paused and leaned in. "Are your ships indeed having difficulty reaching their markets? I would have thought the British military presence enough to keep pirates and privateers at bay."

Dussouy's thin lips compressed. "You didn't hear it from me, but there's a shadowy devil based out of the islands near Mobile Point, who has chased my lads into shipwreck more than once.

Some say he's American, others claim he's a Frenchman, looking for Spanish gold."

Rafa looked skeptical. "So shadowy that the lines of the ship cannot be identified? I find that hard to believe."

"She's small and fast, and according to my men, the captain's disguise bars any discovery of his identity."

For some reason, Lyse's pulse jumped. "What kind of disguise?"

Dussouy waved a hand. "Scarf over the head, face blacking, indistinguishable clothes. Clever sort."

"My brother fishes out of the islands near the Point. He's not mentioned anything like that." Lyse watched Rafa's face, wondering if he'd seen any such pirate.

He merely looked vaguely confused. "Why would the French be this far north and west? Their ports are all in the Caribbean."

"Laddie, this was a French port for sixty years. Just because a British flag flies over the fort doesn't mean the French are gone completely to ground." Dussouy spread his big hands. "Besides, as I'm sure you know, we—the French, I mean—entered treaty with the Americans some weeks ago. Lafayette himself has put on a uniform and come over to aid Washington."

"Monsieur my husband." Madame firmly took her husband's arm. "Everyone knows *we* are loyal British subjects now and have no knowledge of what the French would be up to." She gave Rafa a coy smile. "Though I wouldn't be surprised to hear that our Spanish neighbors have thrown in their lot with those bourgeois continentals. King Carlos is notoriously interested in gaining back his control of Gibraltar and Minorca."

Rafa laughed. "Madame, you are pleased to jest with your guests. Why would His Majesty give aid to a group of colonists rebelling against their monarch, when that would endanger his own God-given authority? Have you not heard about the American captain who took port in New Orleans? Captain Gibson was apparently selling rum in an attempt to cover purchase of clothing and blankets and gunpowder for their little uprising. I assure you Governor Gálvez arrested him in short order."

"And rightly so," said Dussouy, frowning at his wife. "Women, as you will discover, have only a vague understanding of politics as it applies to the daily running of a household, and none at all of its international complexities. Monarchies aside, Carlos is far too fond of his treasury to risk it in such a fly-by-night endeavor as colonial self-government."

Lyse had heard her grandfather and her papa arguing over just these subjects on many an occasion—and had been taught to vigorously participate.

Before she could object, however, Rafa smiled down at her and patted her hand. "One must agree that such topics are tedious in the extreme, when there is music to be danced to with the loveliest of partners. Señorita, would you honor me with the minuet?"

She had not noticed that the dancing had stopped, and the musicians were retuning. She cast a desperate look around. It was a test. A mild, but signally cruel test. The minuet—complex, dignified, and performed one couple at a time while everyone else watched—could establish one hopeful debutante and set another up for a future of obscurity and social ruin. What could it do, she wondered, to a girl who was neither debutante nor hopeful?

The Spaniard held her eyes with a lazy smile as she slowly dipped into a curtsey. Grandmére Madeleine had once taught her and Simon the dance, though of course they'd had little opportunity to practice. What if she forgot the steps? What if this stupid bum roll decided to shift again? What if her hair fell down from its tower?

The thought made her want to laugh. Rising from the curtsey, she went palm to palm with Don Rafael as they performed the opening honors to each other and then the audience. She would show him. She would show them all!

Dancing parallel to Rafa, she followed him in the lead-in figure. To her relief, she found the stately four-step, six-beat pattern coming without conscious thought. Curving sideways, they met at the rear of the open space, then danced forward to the middle, where Rafa wheeled her in a three-quarter turn and danced her sideways to a corner. By the time they had completed the initial crisscross figure, her knees had stopped trembling.

Though there was nothing particularly seductive about the dance—except for her partner's refusal to let his sleepy gaze drop from her face—this was far different from dancing with her older brother. By the time they came to the two-hand turn and ending, Lyse felt as if the blood beneath her skin might burst into spontaneous flames. She was aware of the calluses on the palms of his hands, the blood-red signet ring worn on his left index finger, the small moon-shaped scar at the corner of one eye. Together they honored the audience, then, turning face-to-face, she curtseyed to him as he bowed. She held the curtsey, heart thudding, breath coming in shallow gasps. Surely if she moved she would fall.

As if he had seen her terror, he reached down to grip her elbow. "Come, *prima*, don't faint on me," he murmured, boosting her to her feet.

"How could you do that?" she whispered, regaining her balance. "You know I'm no society girl."

"What? Have you no faith in my leadership?" He guided her toward a corner of the room amid a patter of polite applause.

With her back to the wall and his tall figure between her and the rest of the room, there was nowhere to look except at his snowy, elegantly tied neckcloth and the firm chin above it. "Faith? I barely know you! I must balance your kindness in dealing with my father against the silly way you serenade my friend with love songs and antagonize my brother with nosy questions. For all I know, you are the pirate Monsieur Dussouy was describing earlier."

His mouth pursed in a soundless whistle as he stared at her. For a moment the brown eyes had narrowed, darkening to a frightening near-black. She thought she saw a flash of not only intelligence but hurt.

Ashamed that her discomfort had led to thoughtless words, she placed her fingers over her lips. "I am sorry, Don Rafael," she mumbled. "There was no need to be rude."

Easy laughter dispelled the darkness in his expression. "A pirate! You have caught me out—and how clever I should be to damage my own ship so that I might steal the gold in my hold and hide it from myself!"

"No more ridiculous than paying someone else to buy gifts for you."

He bowed in genial self-mockery. "And so we have established that Don Rafael is ridiculous and silly. I refuse to be drawn into bickering over the obvious. I am much more interested in discovering what is your relationship to the pretty little slave named Scarlet—who has already caused you such grief this day."

Ah. And here it was. If she didn't tell him, someone else was bound to. Besides, he already knew that she was a fisherman's sister and daughter of a drunken ferryman. There was little reason to withhold the whole truth.

She focused her gaze once more upon the garnet pin nestled in the folds of his neckcloth. "It is a long, tedious story, I warn you."

He smiled and tucked her hand into the crook of his elbow. "Then let us find refreshment and walk about the room. I am not in any hurry."

"Very well."

The refreshment table was a six-foot buffet table placed between the French windows opening onto the front gallery of the house. An obscene amount of sugared pastries on tiered silver trays flanked a crystal punch bowl filled with some pale liquid that might have been champagne but was probably watered lemonade. Rafa filled a goblet and handed it to her.

"Thank you." She sipped, resisting the urge to make a face. Some drinks were made for decoration.

He toasted her lightly with his own goblet. "I'm fairly certain we shall both survive."

Arm in arm they began to make the round of the salon. After a quiet moment, Lyse peeked up and found Rafa observing her contemplatively.

"Come, *prima*," he said. "Out with it."

She smiled in spite of her reluctance. "You have met my papa."

"Ah, the papa. I felt certain he must be somewhere in this long tale."

"Yes, but he wasn't always so—so—*outré*."

"*Outré*? I am not familiar with this word."

"Unconventional. Outside the accepted social norm."

"And what has your unconventional papa to do with the Harpy of la Mobile?"

This time she did chuckle. "My papa and Madame Dussouy were at one time betrothed!"

5

With a tray of dirty champagne flutes balanced in her hands, Scarlet stood on the back porch, facing the freestanding kitchen. Music and conversation poured through the open French windows at the front of the house, lashing her skin like the thongs of a poisoned whip. Not for you. Not for you, girl. No dancing, and don't speak to the guests, even if the same blood runs through your veins.

How had Lyse come to be in Madame's salon dressed like a French doll? She'd nearly dropped that whole tray of sparkling drinks, so unbelievable was the sight of her cousin promenading on the Spaniard's arm. Judging by the masterful way he had managed Madame this afternoon in the Emporium—she had been all but cooing as he extricated Lyse from her talons—he must have been the one to arrange for Lyse's invitation. She'd heard it said that Spanish men came equipped from birth with a certain *hubris*, an awareness of masculinity and authority that emanated from their pores like an exotic scent.

Scarlet was the one who had borne the brunt of Madame's sharp temper afterward. Questions, all the way home from the Emporium. Why would Don Rafael entrust so much money to barefoot, dirty-skinned Lyse Lanier? Why had Scarlet thought it permissible to ignore her mistress and converse with free persons in a public place?

With nothing to be gained by arguing or explaining, Scarlet had remained silent, further angering her mistress. If she hadn't been needed to help prepare for the party, Scarlet would doubtless have spent the rest of the day, hungry and alone, in the windowless carriage house. And she wouldn't have spoken to Lyse—which had only gotten her into further trouble.

She shut her eyes against useless tears. With Madame, there was no peace. Every second she stood here invited reprimand and punishment. Oh, how she missed her mother. Her father, a field hand who had been sold when she was a young child, was barely a memory. But Maman had had a way of reminding her whose bondservant she really was. That persecution was God's purification tool. That joy was more than beautiful clothes and rich food.

But God had taken Maman away too. Last summer she had died in Scarlet's arms, gripped by a fever that came with an infected tooth, of all things. Madame had been so angry to have lost her seamstress that she almost sold Scarlet in a fit of pique. But M'sieur intervened, gently reminding his sulking wife of Scarlet's value as a breeder and her talent with a needle, that Madame would not likely be able to replace her for the money. He'd given Scarlet a compassionate, cautioning look that told her to keep quiet.

M'sieur would release her if he could afford to do so. He had once told her so. But he could not, and that was that. She was lucky that she had been mated with the Dussouys' young blacksmith, though they couldn't legally enter into a marriage contract. Cain treated her with shy, inarticulate respect bordering on terror, and she liked him well enough. Her circumstances could be much worse. The field slaves were considered livestock. At least she lived in the house, in a room off Madame's bedchamber where her clothes were stored. She followed Madame to church every Sunday morning and sat in the balcony with the other slaves, and she was allowed to spend the afternoon with Cain and his parents and two older sisters.

She almost had a family.

But Lyse *was* her family. Same blood. Free blood under God.

Pulled by some compulsion outside herself, she carefully set the tray of flutes down upon the porch, away from the door so that they wouldn't be knocked over, then crept down the porch steps and ducked under a low limb of the magnolia tree beside the house. The night was dark and still, thick with spring fog, the ground moist and cool under her bare feet. As she slipped around to the front of the house, the violins grew louder, harmonizing with the music in her head, and the rhythm tugged at her feet until she was dancing. If she were caught here, she would be whipped, but she couldn't make herself go back.

From the shadows, she watched the swirling guests through the window, and Lyse went by, still on the arm of the Spaniard. She was looking up at him, eyes sparkling like jewels, her black curls beginning to escape from their beribboned tower to dangle against the low neckline of her dress. He bent his head to listen to her, his eyes full of some smoky emotion of which Lyse seemed unaware.

Scarlet caught her breath, pierced by unwanted but inevitable envy.

Not for you, never for you.

She sank to her knees, her heart bleeding aloud. "God, my Father," she whispered. "Oh, God, my rock and my fortress, my master. Is this truly your will? I'm asking again—deliver me, set me free! I'll serve until you do, but oh, God, rescue me from this bitterness." She bent forward, wrapping her arms about her head, heaving silent sobs. There was no knowing how long she lay there before finally she sat up, spent, aching with weariness and sadness, and dried her swollen face with her apron. "Behold the handmaid of the Lord," she sighed. "Be it unto me according to thy word."

Rafa whistled through his teeth. "Your papa was engaged to the Harpy? Truly?" Now this was a turn he had not seen coming.

"Yes—when she was Mademoiselle Isabelle Hayot, and Papa was very young and ignorant. The match was arranged by their parents. You must know that my family has not always been so down on the luck." She gave him a quick sideways glance, as though daring him to contradict her. "The Laniers came from Canada to Louisiana with Iberville and Bienville, before even the Hayots. Their family is in the transport business as well."

"But—"

"Be patient, m'sieur, and I will explain. There are two branches of the Lanier family—one being descendants of Tristan Lanier, who settled his family at Mobile Point, near the mouth of the bay; the other, those of his younger brother Marc-Antoine, a soldier of the French Marine. The two lines came together when Marc-Antoine's son Charles—Chaz, as he is sometimes called—married Tristan's adopted daughter Madeleine. My grandpére Chaz founded the shipping business and had two sons, my papa being the younger. He was, perhaps, more handsome and impulsive than wise, as things turned out . . ."

Rafa waited while she gathered her thoughts, her expression far away in a distant past. A deep love of story and a natural curiosity fueled his sense that there was more to this lovely young woman than met the eye.

After a moment, she blinked and went on. "As I said, the Hayot and Lanier family businesses were about to be joined by the marriage of Isabelle to Antoine. As a wedding gift, Grandpére Chaz sent my papa to New Orleans with money to buy a ship. But as you know, the slave market is located near the waterfront." She paused, as if this non sequitur might explain everything.

He made a noncommittal sound. "Yes. I have seen it."

"Well, Antoine stopped to observe the proceedings, as he had not seen it before. As it happened, there was a beautiful young woman for sale that day, a mulatto with café-au-lait skin and lips like ripe berries."

He glanced at Lyse's lush mouth. "So he bought her instead of the ship."

"Yes." She made a face. "But my papa was not content to bring home the beautiful slave instead of a ship. He must set her free and have the priest say words over them, so that she is bone of his bone and flesh of his flesh!"

"He married a slave? Your mother was a slave?" He should have made the connection before, and not just in the honeyed pigment of her skin, the springing curl of her hair. Not that her manners were coarse, for they were not—but there was something of-the-earth, something as fresh and natural as seawater, in her expression. And he knew with sudden clarity that, when the time came, Lyse would deeply feel and understand the ideal of freedom.

She shook her head. "She was a freewoman when I was born. But she and Papa didn't have an easy time of it. Grandpére Chaz wouldn't disown his son, but he was enraged that he lost the money for the ship and refused to give him more. The Hayots, of course, were insulted beyond redemption, and there has been bad blood between the families ever since."

"Ah. And thus the shrilling of the Harpy."

She sighed. "Yes."

"But what has this to do with the girl named Scarlet?"

She stopped walking, turned to face him. "Look at me, m'sieur. Can you not see it? Our mothers were sisters."

He did as she invited, for a long moment. He saw the rarity of a soul who dared take on someone else's battles, housed in a woman unaware of her own translucent beauty. Dangerous words trembled on his tongue. To keep them from spilling, he looked away. Finally, he managed lightly, "I see that you feel guilty for something that is not your fault."

"But that's just it! How could I be so wretchedly cruel as to come here with you—dressed this way, to flaunt my freedom in front of Scarlet—" Her voice wobbled. "Whose fault is that but my own?"

"Señorita—Lyse, listen to me." He leaned close and spoke quietly, urgently. "You will not help your cousin by raising these sorts of questions in such company as this."

"Then where am I to raise them? In church?" She laughed. "The people in this room are all good Catholics who attend mass regularly. And if they don't own slaves, it's only because they can't afford them."

"I agree that there is much injustice all around, and I understand and admire your compassion and love for Scarlet. But we are all buffeted by circumstances that can either shape us into people of strength and character—or make us bitter and vindictive."

The thick, heavy lashes slowly lifted until she met his eyes. "You would have liked my grandmére Madeleine. She said something like that to me once."

"She sounds like a woman of great good sense." He smiled. "And remember, little cousin, things are not always what they seem." Praying he had not just unwrapped a carefully laid cover, he took her gloved hand and pulled her toward the center of the room, where a cotillion was beginning to form. "Now let us dance away these sober cobwebs before Cinderella must return to her stepmother's clutches."

~

Through the black lace oak trees lining Conception Street, Lyse caught glimpses of the moon, a bright white crescent in a star-spangled sky, as Rafa drew the horse up in front of the Redmonds' cottage. She should have been exhausted after such an emotionally and physically taxing day. Yet the nerves pinged along her skin, and she found herself reluctant to bid her escort good night.

She waited while he jumped out and wrapped the reins around the hitching post at the end of the carriageway, then she leaned forward so he could take her hand and help her to the ground. Instead he reached up, grasped her waist, and swung her down directly in front of him. Caught by surprise, she stood in the shadowy yard, looking up at him.

"You're sure Miss Daisy knew you were coming back here?" His voice was quiet, deep, lending an air of conspiracy to the fact that they were alone in the darkness.

"Yes." She should have stepped back, should have run for the side door of the house. But as she'd told him, she wasn't a proper society maiden. And she wasn't ready for him to leave.

But he seemed to be aware of the proprieties. "Good, then I'll walk you to the door." He tucked her hand through his elbow. "Are you glad you came?"

What a question! Her first time to attend a party in the wealthy part of the city. Her first time to dress like a young lady. Her first dance with a gentleman who wasn't a relative. Those three things might never happen again, but like Cinderella she'd be able to tell stories to her children about it all. She stopped, hugging Rafa's arm.

He looked down at her in surprise. "What's the matter?"

"Nothing, I—" She cleared her throat, suddenly embarrassed. "I just wanted to say thank you. For—for making me go, for making me feel like a princess just for one night." Before she lost her nerve, she stood on tiptoe and kissed his cheek. "No one has ever treated me this way before."

She was about to run, but he caught her hand and stepped in front of her. "Wait. I think there is a misunderstanding."

"What do you mean?" A huge magnolia tree blocked the moonlight and shadowed his face. She wasn't exactly afraid, but there was an odd timbre to his voice, something that lit more little pinpricks of excitement under her rib cage.

"You think I feel sorry for you?"

"Well, of course you do," she said stoutly. "You are a very wealthy man, a very kind man, and I—"

"I am not kind. And I don't feel sorry for you." He stepped closer, as he had when the minuet brought them palm to palm, only this time the force of his personality seemed to wrap all the way around her, softening all night sounds, absorbing and focusing all light so that she could look nowhere except his eyes. *"Eres bella, mi corazón."*

The words might have been breathed on the wind, except she felt them against her lips just before . . . oh! Nothing, nothing in the poverty of her hardscrabble young life, had prepared her for the lush, full-blown kiss of a true courtier. He kissed and kissed her, then after a moment cupped her face with one big hand, pressing the pad of his thumb beneath her lower lip, breaking the kiss only to slant his head the other way and start again. This *soldado* of *amor* held her prisoner with nothing but sweet words and honeyed mouth, and if she didn't get away from him *now*, this very minute, she was going to break every promise she had ever made to her dear departed Grandmére, and there would be no going back to the *before*.

She jerked her mouth away with a little squeal, shoving against his chest.

He instantly let her go, stood there breathing hard, as if he'd just run a long distance.

There was a long, humming silence, during which they stared at one another like combatants in a war.

"Lyse!" he finally burst out. "I'm sorry—"

"Don't." She put both hands to her cheeks. She felt feverish as with some illness. "I brought it on myself. I—I threw myself at you, like a—but I only meant friendship, though it mustn't go any further because my brother would kill you and then I would have to—"

"Lyse! Stop it!" Now he was laughing at her, reaching out one of those beautiful seductive hands for hers.

Humiliated, she took another step back. "Yes, I'll stop it. So, good night, Don Rafael." She bobbed a curtsey. "I thank you for the treat of the party, and I wish you safe travels, for I won't be seeing you again. I have to go home in the morning, and please give my kind regards to your maman and your sister—"

"I said stop it!" This time he reached her in one long stride, seized her face in both hands, and branded her with one more brief, searing kiss. He laid his forehead against hers and muttered, "The only way to shut you up."

She closed her eyes and stood in his embrace, defeated. "I don't know what you want," she whispered.

"I don't want anything, you crazy infant. I'm only astonished you haven't pulled your knife on me. Except . . . perhaps you like me a little?"

"I like you more than a little," she admitted. "I think that is the problem. But even a barefoot Creole like me knows a lady doesn't kiss a man who is not her husband upon the lips."

He sighed. "Well . . . perhaps it was a little outside the pale, but let us blame it on the moonlight and the scent of honeysuckle and begin again. *Sí?*"

She peeped up at him but saw only apparent sincerity along with gentle humor in his face. "All right."

He looked relieved. "*Bueno.* You are perfectly safe with me, I promise. We are friends again, *si*?"

"Yes. But I really have to go inside. Daisy will be worried."

"I have a few more days in Mobile before I must return to New Orleans. Will you take me fishing before I go?"

"You like to fish?" Somehow she found that surprising.

"I adore fishing almost as much as dancing, though not as much as kissing."

She laughed. "Perhaps I might teach you a thing or two."

He gave her that charming, raffish grin and kissed her hand. "You may teach me anything you wish, my princess. Now run away to your friend before I forget I am a gentleman who always keeps his promises."

She ran, but couldn't resist one more look over her shoulder as she reached the door. He had climbed into the carriage and sat looking at her in the moonlight. When he lifted a hand, she hurried inside.

She stood with her back against the kitchen door, one hand pressed to her lips. Dear Lord in heaven, what had just happened?

"Lyse? Is that you?"

The scared whisper startled Lyse away from the door. A single candle flared, illuminating Daisy's yawning face and nightgowned figure halfway down the back stairs.

"It's me," Lyse said. "I'm sorry to wake you. I was just coming up."

"What time is it?"

"I'm not sure. Midnight maybe?"

"I should have come with you." Daisy peered at her as if expecting some injury. "Are you all right?"

"Of course I'm all right." Lyse touched her hair, hoping there was no overt evidence of Rafael's embrace. "It was a lovely party."

Daisy looked doubtful for a moment, then suddenly smiled. "I'm glad. You deserve to have a good time now and then." She held out the hand that wasn't holding the candle. "Come up to my room and tell me about it."

Lyse took her hand and followed her friend up the stairs, carefully holding the skirt up so she wouldn't tread on it. "Is your papa asleep?" she whispered. Daisy's father's room was on the other side of the large house, but she didn't want to disturb him.

"I think so. He was working late, writing a letter to Colonel Durnford and Governor Chester. He's worried about what the

French will do now that they've joined the rebels. It's getting harder to get supplies into the ports."

"I know. There was talk about that at the party." She didn't mention Monsieur Dussouy's fear of the Spanish joining the war. There was no need to frighten Daisy with rumors.

They reached the landing and turned right, where the door of Daisy's bedroom stood open. They went in, and Daisy shut the door behind them. She set the candle on the bedside table and turned Lyse around to help her undress. "I'm amazed you stayed dressed up for so long," she said, unhooking the heavy capelike train while Lyse worked on unfastening the bodice front. "I remember the first time I wore this dress, I had a headache nearly the whole time!"

Lyse peeled out of the bodice and let it fall, then untied the tapes of the skirt and petticoat. With a little shimmy, she let both drop to the rug and stepped out of the pile of fabric. "I'm glad you made me practice moving around your room and walking up and down the stairs, or I never would have managed!" Laughing softly, she removed the padded bum roll from around her hips and tossed it in a corner. "Some *man* must have invented that contraption!"

"No doubt." Giggling, Daisy steered Lyse to the stool at her vanity table. "Here, sit down. I'll take your hair down while you come out of the corset." With a quick yank, she untied the bow of the corset tapes at Lyse's back waist.

"Oof!" Lyse let out a relieved breath, then sucked in another one to the bottom of her lungs. "Oh my, that feels good!" She closed her eyes and relaxed while Daisy began to pluck out hairpins and toss them onto the vanity. "I don't know how you dress this way nearly every day."

"You get used to it." Daisy fished the toque from the thick mass of Lyse's hair and dropped it into her lap. "But I don't dress up this much all the time. The children don't expect the latest fashion."

"Neither do the dock workers. And I know my brother would love you if you wore a sack and pigtails."

Daisy smiled, and both girls fell silent. It occurred to Lyse that the Harpy, as Rafa had dubbed Madame Dussouy, would be scandalized to see the commander's daughter thus serving the offspring of a former slave. If Daisy's mother had lived to train and mentor her, Daisy would undoubtedly have been less likely to straddle the social boundaries that separated her and Lyse. As it was, the girls' mutual state of motherlessness allowed them to move seamlessly in and out of each other's worlds.

Finally, attired in a borrowed nightgown, hair combed and braided for the night, Lyse climbed into the bed beside Daisy, who blew out the candle and lay back as well.

"I wish you could stay here all the time," Daisy said on a yawn. "I always wanted a sister."

"Mmm."

It was a sentiment Daisy had repeated often over the years, the first time a summer afternoon shortly after Lyse's mother died. Lyse had been sitting on the steps outside her grandfather's office, a book in her lap, tears dripping off her chin onto the page. Daisy, walking past with her governess, stopped to ask what was wrong. Unable to articulate the depth of her misery, Lyse simply shook her head.

Daisy, ignoring the fact that her governess had already turned the corner of the street, sat down beside Lyse. "I'm sorry," she whispered and sat there quietly until the frantic governess returned for her nearly an hour later.

The girls had become fast friends that day.

But Lyse's family needed her now, and that was that. She lay on her back, listening to the settling of the old Creole cottage, the chirring of tree frogs outside, Daisy's soft breathing beside her. The question she'd been dying to ask finally burst out. "Daisy, has Simon ever kissed you? On the mouth, I mean."

There was a long silence. "That's a peculiar question," Daisy said slowly. "Why do you ask?"

"I won't think badly of you if he has. I just . . . wondered how it happened. If it happened."

Daisy sighed. "Just once. I told him he mustn't do it again until . . . well, until we are betrothed." The bed bounced as she turned on her side and said anxiously, "It was almost an accident. He had come to bring fresh water to the schoolhouse, and I got there early too, so there was only him and me. I dropped my satchel and reached to pick it up at the same time he did, and—and . . ." Finally she said, "So," as if that explained everything.

Lyse lay quietly for a moment, frustrated. That didn't sound at all like the cataclysmic event that had just happened between her and Rafael. She put her hand against the fluttering under her ribs. Perhaps it was nothing to be upset about anyway, for Rafa was going back to New Orleans in just a few days, and she would likely never see him again. What was one kiss in the grand scheme of things anyway? As he had said, moonlight and honeysuckle.

"Well," she said, "thank you for telling me. I just wondered."

"Lyse." Daisy suddenly sat up. "You won't ask Simon about it, will you?"

She was going to be so full of secrets, she would pop. "Of course not. I never talk to Simon anymore, anyway. He's far too busy."

"Good." Daisy lay back down again. "Good night, then, my sister. I'm glad you had a good time."

"Good night, Daisy. I hope your papa will let you and Simon marry one day. Then we'll be sisters for real."

They hugged each other, then turned back to back. Lyse closed her eyes. But it was a long time before she fell asleep.

~

Shoving his chair back, Rafa laid his napkin across his empty plate and rose. The food and service in the dining room of Burelle's inn had been extraordinary, on a par with any establishment in New Orleans. But his own company was beginning to pall.

Come, admit it, he admonished himself. *You miss her.*

He hadn't seen Lyse for two days, not since kissing her outside the Redmonds' house. He could have found her, he supposed, except he had been so appalled at his own lack of restraint that he had made himself focus on business to crowd out thoughts of berry-ripe lips and silken skin and jewel-colored eyes.

Ay! Maddening to find himself unable to shut her out for more than ten minutes at a time. He slammed the door harder than necessary as he exited the tavern, then stood with his hands behind his back, observing the foot and carriage traffic on Dauphine Street. At least the town sailmaker had promised to have him under way no later than this afternoon. So he must use the last of his hours in Mobile to gather as much information about the port as he could. Gálvez would expect details of fortifications, armament, citizen loyalty . . . all the things which would determine the success or failure of a Spanish siege.

And attack was inevitable. Gálvez meant to pluck every port along the Gulf Coast, from Natchez and Baton Rouge to Mobile and on over to the final plum, Pensacola. The only question was when. The shipment of gold that Rafa's ship brought from Madrid was a crucial installment of aid intended for outfitting and arming American soldiers.

He was already late in delivering it. The American Captain Gibson and his crew remained in detention, a sort of luxurious house arrest under Gálvez's hospitality, awaiting Rafa's return. In one sense, the delay strengthened the appearance of Spanish neutrality. But Rafa knew that Gálvez would be relieved when the Americans departed New Orleans. British suspicions could be allayed only so long.

"I hope your stay in Mobile has been comfortable, sir," came a rich, slow voice behind him.

Rafa turned. He'd been so deep in his thoughts he hadn't heard Burelle's servant Zander open the tavern door right behind him. The man's dark skin was creased between the eyes, his hands twisting a towel into an anxious rope.

"I've been most comfortable, thank you," he assured the man. "Good food, clean sheets, prompt service. Please don't mind my . . . overzealous shutting of the door."

Zander smiled, clearly relieved not to have been a source of displeasure. "Very good, then. If there be anythin' else I can do for you, all you need do is ask."

"No, thank you. Except . . ." Rafa tipped his head. "Zander, how long have you known Miss Lyse?"

The white smile widened. "Since she's a baby runnin' the streets with that rascally brother of hers. What one of 'em don't think up, the other pulls out of mischief's own workbox."

"Ah. So you are aware of her family's circumstances."

Zander nodded. "I know most things that goes on around this town. People talks whilst they eats, and Joony's kitchen draws hungry folks."

Rafa glanced around. Perhaps he had time for one more errand before he left Mobile. "Why do you suppose Lyse's grandfather refuses to have anything to do with her? He must be quite a wealthy man."

"Not as rich as some, sir, and I don' know where you gets that other idea from. M'sieur Chaz, he love Miss Lyse to pieces."

"But—I assumed from the state of her dress that—" Rafa swallowed his astonishment. "If the old señor loves her so much, why not present her as a young lady, as she deserves?"

Zander's old eyes took on a thoughtful gleam. "I suppose you could be layin' that down at the door of M'sieur Antoine's pride, much as anythin' else. Antoine, he don't like to be under his papa's thumb."

Rafa recalled Lyse's story of her father's rift with his family.

Impetuous decisions, no matter their justification, had a way of boxing one in, as he'd found to his cost. He thought of his sails due to be delivered in a few hours, he thought of the gunpowder and gold in the hold of his ship, and he thought of Lyse's sherry-colored eyes. Impetuous or not, he made up his mind. "Where could the old Señor Lanier be found on a lazy Thursday morning?"

"Nothin' lazy about M'sieur Chaz. But most days you find him in his office just down the street." He gave him a few of the building's details.

Rafa tossed the servant a small coin. "Thank you, Zander. I'll be back for my sea bag this afternoon and settle up with Burelle then."

He stepped into the street, which had begun to come alive with distant noises from the docks, the ring of a blacksmith's hammer just down from the inn, merchants calling their wares from the market. Royal Street was already teeming with foot traffic and the occasional horse-drawn carriage. He began to look for the brick building Zander had described.

Most of the structures of Mobile, like those of New Orleans, went two or three stories straight up, with ornate railed balconies fronting each level and roofed with wooden shingles. Notwithstanding the fourteen years of British occupation, it was still a very French city, with the fleur-de-lys in every wrought-iron design and a predilection for open door-height windows and brightly painted shutters.

Halfway down the street, Rafa stopped in front of a tall, narrow three-story brick building graced with curved iron stairs ascending to its second-level main entrance. A neat sign posted beside the central door proclaimed it the headquarters of Mssrs. Charles and Thomas Lanier, Shipping. He was in the right place, but it seemed Lyse's grandfather was in business with a relative. Who was Thomas?

Checking the fall of his neckcloth and the lace at his cuffs, he mounted the stairs with his sword rattling. Surely Lyse's grandfather wouldn't refuse to see him.

He gave the ornate brass knocker affixed to the paneled door a brisk tap. After a moment, the door opened to reveal a tall, white-haired gentleman in the dark, formal attire of a previous generation.

Eyebrows aloft, the old man looked Rafa up and down. *"B'jour!"*

Rafa smiled and bowed. "Good morning, sir." The Laniers were French, but he was more comfortable speaking English. "I am Don Rafael Maria Gonzales de Rippardá, here to see Señor Lanier—Señor *Charles* Lanier, that is."

"I am Charles Lanier," the man responded in the same language. "How may I help you?"

"I am here by reference of Señor Dussouy, whom I met at a social function two days ago. I am given to understand that if a man wants anything shipped to New Orleans, the vessels and captains of Lanier are the best."

Pride traced the older man's face. He moved back, opening the door wider. "Come in."

Rafa obeyed and followed the straight back in its outmoded full-skirted coat through a richly furnished reception room, across a Chinese red carpet that matched the silken cushions on a couple of wing-back chairs in a corner. Lyse's cheerful poverty struck him all over again, and by the time they reached the open door of a fine office, Rafa was struggling to unlock clenched jaws.

"Sit, if you please," said Lanier, gesturing toward a Louis Quinze chair facing the monstrous seaman's desk which fronted the open window. A brisk March wind blew the light draperies about and ruffled a stack of papers under a lion-shaped pewter paperweight.

"Thank you, señor," Rafa said with studied mildness.

Humor quirked the old man's lips as he sat back in his chair. "You've been hanging about the waterfront for nigh on a week, and just now ask for the best shipping the city has to offer." He steepled knobby dark fingers under his chin. "Young you are, for a man of business."

Rafa stared. "How do you know how long I've been here?"

"There isn't much goes on in this city that I don't know about." A grin lifted the lined face. "I'm also aware you squired my granddaughter to a *soirée* with those provincial Dussouys the other day too. Which means you've come to find out what sort of scoundrel would allow her to run about dressed like a veritable ragpicker, when he could easily clothe her in silks."

Rafa tried not to look taken aback by this shockingly un-French bluntness. Beyond the words, there was something alien about the old man, a harshness in the shape of the nose, or perhaps it was the flat color of the eyes. Except for the outmoded European clothes, he looked a bit like the Indians Rafa had seen trading in the marketplace. With a shrug he accepted the thrown gauntlet. "The thought had crossed my mind."

Lanier barked a laugh. "It is, of course, none of your business. But because Lyse seems to like you, I will trade information for information. And in addition I will give you a piece of advice."

"What would you like to know, señor?" Rafa crossed his legs, all lazy insolence. "My poor brain is an open book."

"I would like to know what induced Isabelle Dussouy to invite Lyse into her salon."

Rafa picked up his quizzing glass and twirled it by its velvet ribbon. "Besides my charm and address, you mean?"

Lanier snorted. "Granted, Isabelle might fall for that. But her antipathy for the Laniers is legendary—and perhaps well deserved."

"You have heard the adage that forgiveness is more readily procured than permission?"

The old man's expression froze. "A sentiment which all but destroyed Lyse's father. I would not have her exposed to Isabelle's spite."

"Ah, but you see, I am careful to count costs. Señora Dussouy very much wanted the coup of Don Rafael's presence at her little party." Rafa paused, observing his companion keenly. Lanier's black eyes, nearly buried in wrinkles, gave away little, but one strong dark hand gripped the handle of a bronze letter opener with a fierceness that reminded him of Lyse wielding her little knife under the sailor's chin. "She was in little danger of insult," he added gently.

"Eh, bah," the old man growled, tossing the knife upon the desk's blotter. "You see my frustration that my granddaughter grows into a beautiful young woman—while I am denied even the right to protect her from social harm, let alone make sure she has decent clothes upon her back."

"It would seem that you brought that denial upon yourself," Rafa said.

Lanier lurched to his feet and turned his back upon Rafa to stare out the window. "I suppose she told you about the shipwreck that is my son Antoine."

"I met him. He loves her very much, as does your grandson, Simon. They both guard her like dogs with a valuable bone. As does a rooster-combed young soldier named Niall McLeod."

Lanier produced a rusty chuckle and looked over his shoulder. "You met young Niall, then? He proposed to Lyse when he was eight years old."

Rafa didn't mention the embarrassing scene involving McLeod he'd come upon near the waterfront. "She easily inspires devotion."

Perhaps he revealed more than he meant after all, for the old man wheeled, scowling. "I suppose you are already in love with her too."

Rafa lifted the quizzing glass to his eye. "Oh, señor, I am but a vagabond minstrel-cum-merchant, doing my best to cozen the businessman who, I am told, can introduce me to the highest strata of society in your fair city. Acquit me of lasting attachments to any maiden, be she ever so fair."

"I wonder what my father would have made of you," Lanier muttered obscurely, fixing him with a suspicious glare. "It would seem there is little of our family history that my granddaughter has not already spilled."

Rafa grinned. "Perhaps. But it is not her history which I have come to discuss, so much as her present whereabouts. She promised to take me fishing."

"To take you—" Lanier positively gaped, the black eyes scudding over the lace dripping from Rafa's wrists and the beautiful tailoring of his fashionable coat.

"Yes, and as I am due to depart Mobile as soon as the winds permit, it had best be now." Rafa shrugged. "Now please tell me what is this valuable piece of advice you wish to offer."

6

Lyse was standing shin-deep in the marsh, cutting strips of bear grass for Justine's baskets, when she heard a shout in the distance. She looked up, shading her eyes against the noonday sun glaring down onto the glassy surface of Bay Minette. Just above the water, scudding clouds moved along in the wake of a salty wind blowing up from the Gulf. March could be cool and wet, but this year summer looked to be coming early.

She squinted, trying to make out the shape of the boat as it approached at a moderate clip from the direction of Mobile. No sail, just someone rowing an old-fashioned pirogue—no, two someones, both figures male—and as they got closer, she saw that one was young and vigorous, dark-haired, the other somewhat stooped, silvery hair blowing in the stiff breeze.

Who could it be? Not Simon's bateau—this boat she'd never seen before. She rubbed her eyes. The younger passenger almost looked like . . .

She jerked erect, nearly dropping the basket hanging on her arm. Rafael Gonzales . . . and *Grandpère*? Her hand clenched the haft of the knife in her hand. After disappearing for two days without a word, Rafa had rowed himself all the way across the river to her home? And in company with her patrician French-Indian grandfather, who had not visited them in the twenty years since Papa built the raised cottage?

As the boat drew swiftly nearer, she looked down at herself. The skirt of her oldest dress, a shapeless striped poplin of faded grays and blues, was pulled between her legs from the back and tucked up into the sash around her waist, forming a pair of balloon pants that allowed her to work in the water without soaking the skirt. She had plaited her hair from the crown of her head into a couple of long braids, then pinned them up in thick coils on either side, and both her arms were scratched from palm to elbow from the sharp edges of the grass.

She almost took off in a splashing run to duck behind the house and pretend she wasn't home. But then she remembered that Rafa had seen her in far worse condition. He knew she worked as hard as any slave to help keep her family afloat, and he knew she had little in the way of feminine frills and furbelows to call her own. He would not think less of her to find her thus employed.

And if he did—so what? Why should she be embarrassed by the opinion of a Spanish gadfly from New Orleans?

Absently she dropped the knife onto the damp grass in the basket and waited, a hand pressed to her aching back, for the boat to float on the current up to the pier. She watched Rafa ship the oars, vault onto the pier, and catch the line Grandpére tossed him, then crouch to tie up the boat to the cleat.

He gave the older man a hand up before turning to beam at Lyse. "*Hola, prima!* See who I have brought to visit you today!"

Truly, he was incorrigible.

"Grandpére!" she called. "It is so good to see you!" She turned and waded back to firmer ground, while the two men walked the pier, leaving the boat behind. "What are you doing here? I can't believe you came all the way across the bay!" She laughed as Grandpére caught her up in a hug and swung her in a circle.

He seemed as fierce and strong as ever, the scent of his tobacco tickling her nose.

"Your young man convinced me the fishing would be better on this side." Grandpére looked over his shoulder at Rafa, who watched them, a slight smile tucking up one side of his mouth. The beautiful mouth that had made itself quite familiar with hers.

She jerked her gaze back to her grandfather. "He is no young man of mine," she said, face hot. "Anyway, I can't go fishing today—I'm working!"

Grandpére let her feet touch the ground, though he kept hold of her hands as he surveyed her questionable garb. Shaking his head with a grin, he made a visible effort not to mention her lack of propriety. "You can stop long enough to hold a conversation with your old grandpére."

Rafa wandered nearer. "I'd be careful around her, sir. She looks innocent, but she's handy with a knife, and that one's a deal bigger than the one she pulled on me half a year ago."

Grandpére's eyebrows went up, but Lyse hooked his arm and tugged him toward the cottage. "Never mind his nonsense. Come on, Justine will want to show you the new baby." She cast Rafa a quelling glance over her shoulder. "I suppose you may as well come too."

"And thus do words sharper than any dagger pierce my wretched heart," he said with a hand over the abused organ.

"How many does this make?" Grandpére asked. "I vow all Antoine has to do is look at a woman and babies sprout like weeds in a garden."

"Weeds, Grandpére?" Lyse laughed. "Rémy is number four, not counting Simon and me, of course. He's the sweetest little thing, and just beginning to sit up by himself. He babbles and grins when the other children talk to him, so he's quite an easy baby."

Grandpére halted at the top of the steps, where the gallery floor had started to rot and sag. "This is dangerous. What if one of the children should fall through? Antoine should fix it."

"He will." Lyse stepped over the bad spot, then took Grandpére's elbow to assist him. "I keep reminding him. It's been so long since you visited! Come in and let me fix you some tea." Trying not to be ashamed of her home, she turned to meet Rafa's eyes. "Be careful, Don Rafael, it is rather—"

"I am always careful, señorita," he said cheerfully. "One never knows when an alligator might decide to make his dinner out of one's shoes. Though perhaps I could redeem the situation by making shoes out of *him*."

How was one to remain angry at one so droll? And what on *earth* had he been doing for the last two days? She hadn't exactly sat home waiting for him to call, but he could have at least tried to find her. Well, before today.

She opened the front door, stuck her head in, and looked around the empty salon. "Justine? Where are you?" She could hear the children playing outside, toward the rear of the house, and domestic noises emanated from one of the two back bedrooms. "We have visitors."

"I'm changing the baby's nappies," Justine called. "I'll be right there. Who is it?"

"Come and see. It's a surprise." She looked over her shoulder to meet Grandpére's twinkling eyes and laid a finger over her lips. "Come on in," she whispered, ushering in her grandfather and Don Rafael.

Moving just inside the door, Rafael looked around the small room. It was crowded with a variety of shabby, cast-off furniture, a table covered with half-finished baskets, and fishing equipment leaning in the corners. In his tailored blue coat, open over a fine silver-and-gray floral waistcoat with eye-popping silver buttons, he looked like a peacock holding court in a chicken coop. But he still managed to seem relaxed and curious, absorbing every detail.

He walked over to the baskets and picked one up to examine the lovely, intricate design. "These are beautiful—in fact, my mother would love to own one. There would be a market for them in New Orleans, if you would care to trust me with selling them."

"Justine is the artist, not me," she said with a shrug. "I was just helping out by cutting grass for her." Then she saw her young stepmother, baby Rémy on one hip, walking down the breezeway between the two back rooms. "Here she is—why don't you ask her?"

"Ask me what?" As usual, Justine's golden hair was piled in a haphazard knot atop her head and secured with a large tortoiseshell comb, her calico day dress well fitted to her trim figure. Her gaze fell upon Grandpére, who stood near the door, his hat tucked under his arm, a faint smile softening his dark face. Her confidence visibly wobbled. "Monsieur Lanier! Antoine didn't tell me—"

"He doesn't know I'm here." Grandpére glanced at Lyse.

She heaved a sigh. The people she loved were all at such unnecessary odds. Why could they not forgive and reach out?

She supposed it was up to her to bring them together. "Justine, this is Don Rafael, who took me to the soirée at Madame Dussouy's. He wants to know about your baskets." She clapped her hands and kissed little Rémy as she took him from Justine. "Come, angel-cake, Grandpére wants to play with you!"

Trusting Rafael to put Justine at ease, she plunked the wiggly, gurgling baby into her startled grandfather's arms. "Don't worry," she told him with a laugh, "he's been fed and changed, so he should be dry for . . . a while." Satisfied that the company would sort themselves out, she scooped up the abandoned basket of grass and pattered down the breezeway. With Justine occupied, someone needed to keep an eye on the other three children.

She found them under the porch. Six-year-old Luc-Antoine, self-appointed general, had marshaled his troops in the time-honored tradition of his French Marine forebears. Clutching a bucket, he squatted on his haunches, while five-year-old Geneviève and three-year-old Denis sat on their bottoms digging in the sandy soil with a couple of bent spoons. Three short cane poles lay nearby.

Lyse crouched, hands on knees, to peer in at them. "What are you doing, *chéris*?"

Luc-Antoine looked around. "Papa said he would take me fishing if I got a bucket of worms."

"I go fishing too. See?" Denis showed Lyse his spoon, upon which squirmed a large brown earthworm.

"You can't go," Geneviève said, rolling her big brown eyes. "You're too little."

Denis's mouth crumpled. "Rémy's the baby now!"

Lyse hiked her skirt up and crab-walked under the house to hug Denis, wormy spoon and all. "Of course he is. But I think you'll all have to wait a bit, since we have company now. Where is Papa, anyway?"

Luc-Antoine gave her a Simon-like scowl. "He went to borrow Simon's boat. He *promised*."

"I know, but your grandpére has come to see you, with . . . another gentleman. Maman wants you to come wash your hands and say hello."

"Will the other gentleman take us fishing?" Geneviève asked.

"Fishing!" Denis echoed.

Lyse sighed. "Not this time."

"Now's as good a time as any. I told you I came to fish." Rafa's deep, sibilant voice came from behind Lyse.

She looked around and found him peering under the wooden underpinning of the porch. His eyes were alight with laughter.

She frowned at him. "You were supposed to be talking to Justine."

"A charming young woman, but she was obviously afraid your grandfather might drop the baby on his head, so I took pity and let her go rescue them both." He dropped into a crouch. "Hello, *niños*! This is a most peculiar place to drop one's hook! Might I suggest the fish might be more abundant at the water's edge?"

"We ain't fishing under the house," Luc-Antoine said seriously. "We're digging worms."

"Ah. And you are quite expert, I'm sure. Can I see?"

Luc-Antoine hesitated, then turned to crawl toward Rafa, the bucket clutched under one arm. Denis and Geneviève followed, leaving Lyse to bring up the rear more slowly, careful not to brain herself on the beams under the porch.

When she emerged, she found the three children clustered around Rafa, who squatted with Denis's fat grub close to his face. Geneviève was giggling, the two boys elbowing one another to get closer.

"I believe," Rafa said with the gravity of a magistrate, "that this fellow is big enough to catch an alligator at least. Or maybe a whale."

"There ain't any whales in Bay Minette," said Luc-Antoine, the literalist. "The water's too shallow."

"Did you ever see a whale?" Geneviève demanded.

Rafa gently laid the worm in Denis's palm. "As a matter of fact, I have. I once sailed to Venezuela with my father, and there was a big pod of them, spouting like giant fountains, out in the middle of the ocean."

Lyse felt her mouth going round, right along with the children's. "I would love to see that one day."

Rafa's warm brown eyes met hers, his expression soft and quizzical, oddly more intimate than the kisses they had shared.

"M'sieur." Geneviève tugged on his sleeve. "Are you gonna take us fishin' or not?"

"Genny, the gentleman's name is Don Rafael," Lyse said, hoping he hadn't noticed her blush. "Don Rafael, I would like to introduce to you my sister Geneviève and my brothers Luc-Antoine and Denis."

Rafa shook hands with the boys, then got to his feet to offer a deep, courtly bow to little Geneviève. He grinned when she jumped up and bobbed a curtsey. "I am enchanted, señorita. You are every bit as charming as your big sister." He glanced at Lyse. "Are you ladies sure you want to . . . ah, bait hooks and handle wet, scaly fish?"

Lyse took a scoffing tone to cover the fact that her heart had melted into a goopy puddle. "Papa taught me to bait my own hook when I was Denis's size. I'll show you alligators!"

Half an hour later, cane poles in hand and lines in the water, they sat on the end of the pier with the water lapping under their feet against the pilings. Rafa had removed his beautiful coat and dropped it behind him, drawing Lyse's gaze to the big shoulder muscles flexing and bunching under his fine linen shirt as he reached to keep little Denis's pole from tangling in Geneviève's.

He had come to see her after all. Gone to the trouble of locating her grandfather and somehow instigating this wonderful and wholly unexpected visit. She couldn't help trying to imagine Grandpére's conversation with Justine. It was necessary that they be allowed to make their peace, but how terrified poor, bashful Justine must be.

Rafa glanced at Lyse over the heads of the children. "You said your father was gone to borrow Simon's boat. Does your brother not live here as well?"

"No. Not since . . . last summer." Lyse rarely shared personal information outside the family, but Rafa knew of the strain between Simon and their father. "They get along better, now that Simon built himself a little houseboat over at Chacaloochee."

"Ah."

She could tell he wanted to ask more questions. But she had questions of her own. "I had thought you already back in New Orleans."

"Lyse."

She reluctantly looked at him.

He was holding Geneviève's pole steady, his expression anxious. "I couldn't go back without seeing you."

Her pulse sped a little, and she raised her chin. "Now you have met my whole family. And you have even charmed my grandfather. How did you come to meet him?"

"I went to his office. I wanted to see . . ." He hesitated, glancing down at Geneviève, who regarded him with worshipful brown eyes. He smiled. "Yours is a most interesting family."

"More than you know. Did you know that my grandmother's father is the Comte de Leméry?"

He blinked. "The old man looks at least half Indian."

"He is. His mother was of Koasati origin, though of course his father, Marc-Antoine Lanier, was Canadian. Grandmére Madeleine's father, Tristan Lanier, was Marc-Antoine's half-brother through their mother. Tristan's father, the Comte de Leméry, legitimized him just before his death, though Tristan never returned to France to take up the title. He had already built a life here—and besides, his wife was wanted for the murder of a French dragoon." She laughed at Rafa's confused expression. "Sometime I will draw you a diagram of the family tree."

"Perhaps, after all, I should address you as 'your highness.'" He grinned. "Though I have lately begun to wonder what real difference a connection to aristocracy—or lack of, for that matter—can make in these modern times. I have become acquainted with certain . . . Americans—" he cut a glance her way, as if testing her reaction—"who make a good argument in favor of the concept of every man created equal. My own father has a rather plebian ancestry and gained his rank through courageous action rather than an accident of birth."

Lyse hesitated. "And yet, *Don* Rafael, an accident of birth attaches that same rank to you."

"Yes." Rafa shrugged. "And we shall see whether I live up to it."

At that moment, Geneviève shrieked and yanked her pole out of the water. "A fishy! I got a fishy!"

Rafa leaned over to help her unhook the wriggling, flapping fish, heedless of the spotting of his immaculate shirtsleeves and breeches. "What you have here is a pet." He showed the four-inch fish to Geneviève. "Too big for bait, too little to eat."

"We can't have pets," said the literal Geneviève, her face falling. "Papa says we gots enough mouths to feed already."

Rafa laughed. "Then I recommend sending this fellow back to his mama so that he may grow big enough for your supper next time." The fish landed in the bayou with a shallow splash, and Rafa wiped his hand on the leg of his breeches. "Somebody pass me a worm."

But Lyse shook her head. "It is past time I took the children in to greet their grandpére." When all three children set up a predictable wail, she firmly began to wrap her line around her pole. "All fine things must come to an end, my little cabbages, even so useful and engrossing an occupation as baptizing the occasional worm."

Resistance would no doubt have lasted a great deal longer but for Rafa's loud, awkward, and highly comical attempt to copy Lyse's efficient movements. By the time he ended with the line wrapped round his legs and its barb hooked in the back of his shirt, the children were giggling and competing to show him the best way to dispose of one's line, and Lyse had to drop her pole and untangle him.

There might have been, she suspected, another motive behind his feigned ineptitude. He was so tall that he must bend over, resting his hands on his knees, in order for her to reach the hook caught in his collar. She stood with his silky black hair tickling her chin, his aristocratic nose buried in her neck, and his warm breath raising goosebumps along her collarbone. He was real flesh and blood under her hands. There was no moonlight or scent of honeysuckle to blur the lines of social caste, only sunshine and the excited shrieks of the children and the lap of the bayou against the pier. They were, quite simply, a boy and a girl caught in an attraction as inevitable as the tide. She knew it, even before, as she finally worked the hook free and dropped her hands away from his big shoulders, he slowly lifted his head, letting his lips brush along her jawline.

"Thank you, *prima*," he whispered, looking into her eyes with a wicked twinkle. "You have saved my fishing expedition from complete disaster."

"I wonder exactly what you have been fishing for," she replied breathlessly, trying not to laugh.

"If you don't know, then I am the saddest excuse for an angler there has ever been." With a crooked smile he straightened and looked around for the children. His eyes widened. "Uh-oh."

Lyse followed his gaze, expecting some new prank created by her siblings.

But all three had run back to the end of the pier, where they jumped up and down, waving at a boat drawing closer and closer to the pier. "Papa!" Geneviève shrieked. "Papa! Come see who's here!"

Rafa knew he should have gone with the morning tide. The ship was laden with goods, its sails repaired, his crew rounded up and put to work, the captain apprised of imminent departure.

But the elderly Señor Lanier's agreement to make the trip to visit his son's family had settled the question. He must have one more look into Lyse's gamine face to assure himself that no one could be so enchanting as he remembered. That she was only a woman, and a very young one at that. Just a drunken fisherman's daughter, though perhaps brighter and more educated even than his own sister, and possessed of laughter that would charm the stars from the sky.

Oh, yes, and a depth of spirit that drew him like the siren's song at which he'd stupidly scoffed so many months ago. A way of looking in his eyes and finding the man he wanted to be.

He blinked and saw her father vault onto the pier—miraculously sober and looking as if he might like to haul Rafa into the bay and drown him like an unwanted puppy. Unsmiling, one by one, Antoine Lanier patted his children leaping at his feet, then inexorably put them aside and strode along the pier.

Rafa thought of the responsibilities that awaited him in New Orleans, he thought of the ship and its precious cargo which must find its destination with all dispatch, and he weighed the present crisis which would determine the happiness of his heart.

He stepped forward and a little in front of Lyse. She must not suffer for his selfishness. "Señor, I bid you welcome."

Lanier's response was an inarticulate growl and a quickening of his pace.

Behind Rafa, Lyse gasped, and her hand slipped inside his elbow. "Papa, we have been watching for you! The children—"

Lanier cut her off with a slash of his hand. "Take them inside the house. Tell Justine I am home."

"But Papa—"

"Step away from my daughter, you infernal Spanish whelp," Lanier snarled at Rafa. He turned with a scouring look at the children, who stood wide-eyed at the end of the pier. "Get in the house!"

They all ran.

"Papa, I was just taking a hook out of his shirt!" Lyse's voice was high with strain.

Rafa deliberately turned his back on Lanier and looked down at Lyse. The fear and chagrin in her big eyes made him ill. He had not dishonored her, though the kisses they had shared on the night of the soirée had bordered on . . .

What? Had he treated her with less than the respect with which he would want his own sister to be treated? Though he could claim her invitation, he was no longer a little boy to be swayed by desires of the body. He was a man who should be capable of ruling his emotions. Somehow he must protect her and absorb the consequences of his actions.

He took her hand from his arm and lifted it to his lips. "Go to your grandfather. I will speak to your papa."

"Rafa, we've done nothing wrong. But you don't understand his hatred of the Spanish. He will kill you."

Rafa could hear Lanier's approach, the harsh breath of his rage. "Your grandfather told me. I will talk to him—now go! Hurry!"

With one last anguished look, she snatched her hand from Rafa's and picked up her skirt to run.

But it was too late. Lanier reached them, grabbing Lyse's wrist in one hand and Rafa's in the other. "I told you to leave him!" he shouted, shaking her arm with bruising force. "Don't you know he's got no good intentions toward a girl like you? Are you so loose in morals you'll give him leave to handle you in whatever way he likes?"

Rafa's instinct to swing at Lanier was overwhelming, but he couldn't risk hurting Lyse. She had suddenly gone still, as though she knew struggle would invite more violence. And that realization ignited in him a flare of red rage that threatened to burn every thought to cinders.

He forced himself to relax, to look beneath the insulting words of his adversary. A man's daughter was his property, and he would not let her go without payment of some kind. Then Rafa must think like a merchant. What would Don Rafael do?

Producing a bewildered smile, he stared at the big fist wrapped around his arm. "My dear sir, there is no need for this, er, energetic method of arresting my attention. I assure you, I am listening." He brightened. "But then, of course you didn't know. In your absence, your daughter and I were arranging to hire your ferry to transport me and my luggage out to my ship anchored at Dauphine Island." He squinted up into Lanier's fierce dark eyes. "But perhaps you have no need of the enterprise?"

There was an infinitesimal relaxing of the grip upon his wrist. Lanier's expression became cagey. "I might have. But Lyse cannot speak for me. She is a child."

Rafa suppressed the urge to challenge the man's absurd denigration of one to whom he clearly owed his dignity and probably his livelihood as well. "Ah, then it is good that you arrived when you did. I should hate to have taken my business elsewhere." He laughed, casting another confused look at Lanier's grasp on his arm. "You can let me go now—I vow I shall not escape."

For now, Lanier's anger seemed to have been diverted. With a snarling "*pah!*" he released both Rafa and Lyse and turned to stalk toward the cottage. "Come into the house, you Spanish dandy, so that we can strike a deal over a tankard of ale."

Rafa followed, resisting the urge to take Lyse's hand. Truly it was in the mercy of God that this man maintained any business at all. A more contentious, sodden derelict he had yet to meet.

"Papa." Lyse hurried to catch up to her father and took his elbow. "Before you go in the house, you should know we have a guest. I was trying to tell you when—"

"You mean besides him?" Lanier jerked a thumb over his shoulder.

"Yes." Lyse glanced back to give Rafa an apologetic smile. "Papa, Don Rafael has brought Grandpére to visit us."

Lanier stopped dead still to stare at Lyse. "*What*? Why?"

"He wanted to see the children, especially the new baby." Lyse's eyes filled. "Papa, he loves us very much. Please be kind to him."

Rafa couldn't tell from Lanier's stony expression whether his daughter's plea reached him. He resumed walking, but at least he didn't shake her off. At the house he opened the front door and planted himself in the doorway, leaving Lyse and Rafa on the porch behind him.

"*Mon pére,*" Lanier said with little apparent affection. "I don't know why this sudden desire to gloat over us, but now that you have satisfied your curiosity, I hope you will take yourself back to your British mansion and leave us be."

Rafa heard the hiss of Lyse's indrawn breath. "Oh, no," she whispered.

He gave her a cautioning look. "Let your grandpapa handle it."

There was a moment of tense silence, broken only by the gurgling of the baby. Then Charles Lanier's cultured French, "It is not so, my son. There is no gloating, only regret that I didn't come sooner."

Antoine Lanier moved stiffly into the room and stood, arms crossed, staring at his father, who, still holding the baby, occupied the room's only comfortable chair. With a nod, Rafa encouraged Lyse to enter as well, and he followed close behind. The two of them hovered just inside the door. Justine and the children clustered around the rough pine table, which had been cleared of the baskets.

Little Geneviève bounced to her knees on the bench. "Papa! Grandpére brought us all lemon drops! See?" She opened her mouth for his inspection.

Antoine's face softened. "Yes, I see." As if compelled, he looked at his father again. "Thank you, Father. We are all glad to see you."

"I miss you, Antoine," the old man said softly. "Especially now that your mother is gone. I would that you would bring the children home, so they could come to know their heritage."

"Their home and heritage are here," Antoine fired back. "When they are old enough, they may visit you on their own—as do Lyse and Simon." He turned to glare at Lyse. "Though I'm beginning to think I have allowed them entirely too much freedom. They both seem to be short on good sense."

"Antoine," Justine said, gently chiding. "Not in front of our guest." She rose to take little Rémy, who had begun to gnaw on his grandfather's watch fob, and smiled when the baby buried his face in her neck. "Come, little one, it is dinnertime for you. Lyse, perhaps you'd like to prepare tea for everyone? Bring the children and come with me." Without waiting for a reply, she dipped a curtsey and glided from the room.

Lyse gave Rafa a helpless look. "Would you like tea?"

Tea was the last thing on his mind, and the stepmother was clearly a beautiful widget. "Of all things, señorita," he said with a smile.

As she herded the children in a noisy exit toward the back of the house, Rafa and Antoine seated themselves at the table. He couldn't help comparing the stark simplicity of this small room to the grand salon in which the Dussouys' soirée had been held. Here there were no Aubusson carpets, no imported furniture or gilt-framed portraits to please the eye. No rich pastries on silver trays and no candelabra with scented tapers to soften the glare of the afternoon sun. No bejeweled guests providing bright conversation to accompany the lilting strains of a string ensemble.

Just three silent men in a fisherman's cottage.

Rafa waited, prepared to act the mediator.

Antoine finally cleared his throat. "Justine and her tea," he said gruffly. "I have a keg of ale on the back porch." He made to rise.

Charles stopped him with an abrupt gesture. "No, my son. I see I'm not welcome, so I'll not stay. I just wanted to hold the children in my arms once, before—well, before it's too late." He glanced at Rafa. "Giving you a chance to earn some Spanish coin was excuse enough. If you'll conclude your business, we'll take ourselves back across the bay and relieve you of our unwanted presence."

Antoine thumped a fist against the table. "You make me the churl, when it is you who cast me out!"

The old man's lips tightened. "It is you who wanted to go your own way. I merely allowed the consequences to fall where they would."

"The consequences rest on your grandchildren. They bear the burden of your selfishness."

Alarmed at the storm boiling to the surface, Rafa half rose, deliberately jarring the table against his thighs. "It seems, gentlemen, that it would be more to the purpose for the two of you to join forces in convincing your British masters of the benefit in allowing free trade for Spanish ships wishing to take port in your fair city. They do no one good by allowing freebooters to make off with merchandise that would strengthen commerce here."

"Allowing freebooters?" The old man barked a laugh. "French, American, and Spanish ships alike are being robbed by the English navy, while the Regulars turn a blind eye. And King George does his best to tax us all into penury. My family has owned property here for three-quarters of a century, and it's been all I can do to hold on to it in the face of his majesty's greed."

Antoine turned on him. "And the Spanish are no better—the dogs took New Orleans by the throat and slaughtered anyone who protested."

The rational side of Rafa's brain understood the Frenchman's bitterness against the commander who had ordered his brother's execution. Still, he was young and proud enough to resent the insult. He stood blinking until he had a grip on his temper, then said carelessly, "I defy you to claim New Orleans isn't better off with Gálvez in command of the city." He shrugged. "Besides, that is all water under a very old bridge. The question now is how to get one's cargo through the gauntlet of pirates patrolling the Gulf of Mexico."

Antoine considered him with narrowed black eyes. "My boat is armed, as is my son's. Besides, we navigate coastal channels the British are too lazy and undermanned to frequent. Your merchandise will be perfectly safe."

"That is good to know." Rafa hesitated. "I had wanted to set sail before the evening tide."

"We can leave immediately." Antoine skewered Rafa with narrowed eyes. "But try to make free with my daughter again and you will find yourself missing some essential parts."

~

He was going back to New Orleans, and she would never see him again, Lyse reminded herself as she carefully placed the chipped teapot and four mismatched cups on Justine's silver tray. Her young stepmother had brought the tray with her as part of her dowry, and it was one of the few really fine items in the cottage's shabby little kitchen. It was reserved for use with the most honored of guests, like Grandpére.

And Rafael Gonzales.

She knew she walked the razor-thin edge of Papa's temper, and if she stepped wrong, she risked his wrath not only upon herself but on Justine and the children as well. It was her place in this family to facilitate peace. To help them love one another, as Grandmére Madeleine had taught her.

Grandmére, who had been born of shame but reared in grace, had understood the blessedness of peacemakers. Lyse found daily purpose in honoring her memory.

So, if she could not have Rafa's presence in her life, she could at least send him away without the bitter aftertaste of discord. Squaring her shoulders and recovering her smile, she picked up the tray and entered the salon.

She found the three men on their feet, evidently prepared to leave the house. "Papa! Where are you going?"

Papa, all but shoving Rafa through the door ahead of him, looked over his shoulder. "The Spaniard has hired me to take him down to his ship at Dauphine Island. Tell Justine I will be back later."

"But what about the tea?" She looked down at the tray. "Grandpére, don't you want to—"

"We'll have tea another day," Grandpére said gently. "I'll come again, *cher*." He walked over and bent to kiss her cheek, then whispered in her ear, "And so, I imagine, will Don Rafael."

Her gaze flew to Rafa, who blew her an insouciant kiss over her father's stiff shoulder. Papa pushed him out of sight and growled, "Well, old man? You wanted to come. The tide will not wait."

Lyse set down the tray and flung her arms around her grandfather. "Please come back! We have missed you!" She lowered her voice. "And tell Rafael thank you for coming. And that I will pray for him."

Grandpére kissed her again and let her go. "He is a blessed man." He followed Papa out the door.

Lyse ran to the rotten porch and watched the men untie the boats—Papa in Simon's, and Rafa and Grandpére in the hired boat—and begin the short trip over to Mobile. She might never see Rafael Gonzales again, but her life was forever changed because of him. He had seen in her more than a drunken fisherman's daughter. He had stood beside her in the face of Isabelle Dussouy's arrogance and shown her the woman's essential cowardice. He had even sparked hope that Scarlet might one day be free—if she could find a way to be brave and persistent and very clever.

Those three things she was determined to be, God willing.

7

Port of New Orleans, New Spain
March 22, 1777

The *Valiente* limped into New Orleans with more than her sails in disrepair. The port side of her upper gun deck had been broadsided, and the berth deck was carrying water. Two of her three square-rigged masts had been clipped so that she listed badly.

Rafa, nursing a hole in his shoulder from which a scrap of iron had been removed by the ship's surgeon, hobbled down the gangplank with less than his usual swagger. He frankly dreaded the coming report. Gálvez was likely to hand him his head—if Pollock didn't do it first.

The gold was gone.

He could still hardly credit it. That he'd survived the pirates' attack seemed even more miraculous.

He stopped, eyes tightly clenched against the sensation of the quay shifting beneath his feet. The wounded shoulder throbbed, and his stomach heaved like seas in a northeast storm. He'd wanted nothing so much as to keep to his cabin. But reporting in must come first. By now, word of the attack would have reached Gálvez, and delay would only make it worse.

He pulled himself together, set one foot in front of the other, and crossed Decater Street toward the governmental offices of the Cabildo in the *Places d'Armes*. Behind him the docks throbbed with activity—shrimp boats, barges, and tugs clogging the piers, and longshoremen hauling barrels, crates, sacks, and every imaginable container onto the quay. Laughter, profanity, and shouts in every language of the globe competed with the shrill of whistles and rattle of carts and drays along the wharf. On coming home, Rafa would normally have stopped to absorb and revel in the stabbing color and sound and odor of his adopted city.

But today . . .

This day, every sensation focused on the loss of twenty-four thousand *pesos* for which he must give account. The noise around him only added to the headache that threatened with every step to send him to his knees.

He didn't even stop to admire the beautiful Church of St. Louis, the center of the *Places d'Armes*. Arriving at the Cabildo, he was greeted by a yawning young adjutant in sloppy uniform and gigantic powdered peruke, too busy admiring himself in a pair of shiny Italian leather boots to spare more than a cursory glance at Rafa's credentials. Making a mental note to report this lackadaisical guard, Rafa rapped upon the governor's door.

A moment later Gálvez himself appeared. His impatient scowl turned to surprise and welcome. "Gonzales! I was beginning to think you'd absconded with the king's gold. Come in and tell me—" The general's heavy black brows twitched together. "Sit down first, before you fall down. Here." He hooked the leg of a chair with his foot and pulled it over before pushing Rafa into it.

"Thank you, sir." Rafa struggled to sit upright and hold his superior's frowning gaze. "I'm . . . all right. But I'm afraid I have bad news."

Gálvez stood over Rafa, arms folded. "It would appear so. Have you seen the surgeon?"

"Yes, sir. I've a hole in my shoulder and a killer headache, but I'll recover after a bath and a day's rest." Rafa swallowed. "It's the gold. It's gone. We were ambushed by pirates just past the tip of Dauphine Island. We're lucky they didn't find the gunpowder."

Gálvez stared for a moment. "Pirates took the gold, left the gunpowder, and released the ship?" He sat heavily against the edge of his desk. "That makes no sense."

Rafa allowed himself to slump, sliding down until his head rested against the back of the chair, closing his eyes against the lurid images that had played in his head for the last twenty-four hours. "Yes, sir, I know. If I hadn't seen it, I wouldn't have believed it."

"Start at the beginning, then. Tell me all."

"We had sailed four miles out of the Dauphine Island harbor into the Mississippi Sound. The weather was good, with a brisk southwest wind, calm seas. I was on the bridge with Torre at the helm, keeping an eye out, since privateers are known to hide in the bayous. The lookout in the upper rigging shouted that a corvette approached from behind, coming up fast. Wasn't long before I could see her with the naked eye. She was sixty feet long, maybe seventy tons berthen, carrying ten guns and flying a British flag. Fast, sir—so fast I knew we wouldn't outrun her." Rafa rolled his head against the back of the chair. "She fired a wide warning shot and I knew I'd better stop or return fire."

"Were you in British waters?"

"Probably, though I could argue not."

"No sense initiating aggression," Gálvez said reluctantly. "So you dropped anchor."

"Yes, sir. I chose caution—and paid for it."

Gálvez grunted. "What happened?"

"After we hove to, their captain and three mates prepared to board, all armed to the teeth—and, here's the thing—" Rafa gritted his teeth. "They were disguised—face paint, shaved heads, crazy plaited beards. I'd swear they were British, except the captain's accent was a little off. French, maybe?"

Gálvez shrugged. "The Acadians hold long grudges. But why hide under an English flag?"

Rafa struggled to sit up. "I don't know, but as soon as I realized we'd been tricked by pirates, I signaled our cannoneers to fire. Pretty quickly the scene was smoke and noise and blood, and I went down, from a musket ball." Remembering the searing pain of the hit, he gripped his aching shoulder. "Seems they thought I was dead. I came to in a puddle of blood, saw the pirates were forcing my men to haul off the crates of gold, and knew I had to do something. So I crawled backward into a niche where I'd hidden a loaded musket and ammunition. I'd set up a series of signals for contingencies, whistles mostly." He chuckled, remembering the enemies' consternation when their captives suddenly dropped the cargo and dove back onto the *Valiente* while Rafa covered them with musket fire. "My men all deserve medals, sir. We were under way before they could stop us, limping but alive."

Gálvez was quiet for a long moment. "I will think," he finally said. "Disasters occur, and one must rework and recover."

There was no rage. No blame. Rafa knew that many commanders would have him court-martialed—or hung. And this was the heart of his loyalty. How could he repay such grace?

"I will get the gold back, sir. I will return to Mobile, I will find the pirate's lair, and I will bring him back to you."

"Yes, but first you must have your shoulder repaired. While you do this I will have Pollock commandeer the powder and supplies. Later we shall worry about the gold."

"The longer we wait, the less chance we have to recover the loss."

"Patience," Gálvez said, raising a hand to keep Rafa in his chair. He moved to sit behind his desk. "You have the letter from our friend in Pensacola?"

"Yes, of course." Abashed to have forgotten such an important item, Rafa reached into his coat pocket. "Here it is." He handed Gálvez the thick packet he'd carried safely in spite of everything. "At least this didn't fall into enemy hands."

"Yes. If anything is more valuable than a hold full of gold, this is it." Gálvez broke the packet's seal, unfolded it, and swiftly perused the closely written missive. A wolfish grin spread across the patrician features. "And taking into account the details of Fort Charlotte in Mobile that you have provided, Spain will soon control the entire Gulf Coast." He looked up at Rafa from under heavy brows. "You are dismissed, Gonzales. Clean up and report to Pollock. After you have briefed him, tell him I want to see him forthwith."

"Yes, sir." Rafa managed to get to his feet and salute. "Thank you for your trust. I won't fail you again."

When Gálvez merely waved a hand and kept reading, Rafa backed out of the room, already formulating a plan to return to Mobile. He *would* recover the gold. And if in the process he managed to capture an hour with a certain beautiful Creole, so much the better.

~

Mobile
March 1777

The Chacaloochee Bayou was alive with returning spring. Wildflowers sprang up in niches along the Indian trails through the greening woods, tempting Lyse to slow down long enough to pluck a fragrant handful. Blue, her favorite color, clustered around dark-brown centers, making her think of Rafa singing *"De Colores."* She walked along, scuffing her feet through the pine straw the wind had blown across the path, brushing the flower's delicate petals against her fingers.

She supposed he must be back in New Orleans by now. Perhaps

he'd given the tea caddy to his maman and the lace to his sister Sofía. Sofía was a very lucky girl, to have such a brother.

Of course, she thought with instant loyalty, Simon was a brother among brothers. Which was why she came to be walking through the woods, confident in her ability to persuade him to move back home.

Well, mostly confident. Simon could be quite disagreeable when he thought Lyse had been interfering overmuch between Papa and Justine.

But really, what else was she to do? Since Grandpére's visit, Papa had been drinking more and more—despite Lyse's persistence in pitching every jug of ale she found into the bayou—and bringing less and less in the way of foodstuffs home for the children to eat. Last night he had raged about like a bear with a sore paw upon the discovery that his stash beneath the gallery steps had gone missing.

Yes, she would brave Simon's impatient scolding a thousand times, if he would only come and try to talk Papa into moderation.

Lyse couldn't help thinking of happier times, when Luc-Antoine was a baby, Papa and Justine still love-drunk newlyweds, and she and Simon pretty much left to their own devices. Sometimes she wished she could go back to those innocent days of tea parties with Daisy, while Simon and his friends fished the bayous and hunted the verdant woods—before she became aware that her skin would never be fair, though she scrub her face raw, and her hair would never have the silken texture of Daisy's blonde mane.

Ever since the two of them had begun putting up their hair and lengthening their skirts, life had gotten exponentially more complicated. Her choices became limited to scrabbling for food to stave off physical hunger for herself and her little siblings, while the longings of her heart and mind found release only in the pages of the books in Grandpére's library.

There were boys in the city and its environs with whom she could probably build a tolerable family life of her own—but that would mean abandoning Justine and the little ones to God only knew what difficulties. She wasn't quite stonehearted enough to do that yet.

Stumbling a little over a limb in her path, she tossed the flowers aside and dashed an annoying film of moisture from her eyes. Rafa wasn't coming back, and dreaming would never feed anybody, as Simon had reminded her many a time. And since he was the eminently practical one of the family, he was going to have to help her find a way to get past Papa's unending ill humor.

She caught a glimpse of Simon's houseboat through the trees and started to halloo. But a flicker of light bouncing off the water stopped her on the indrawn breath. Odd. She knew every knot in every tree trunk between here and Bay Minette, and she knew when something was off or out of place. She slowed, listening. There was a rhythmic *chink*ing noise, as of someone digging in sand.

What was Simon up to?

She crept closer, moving from tree to tree, until she could make out her brother, knee-deep in a long sandy swale some fifty yards from the boat landing, wielding a shovel with efficiency and single-minded concentration. Was he digging something up—or burying something?

She hesitated just at the edge of the clearing, wondering, putting together Simon's long periods of disconnection from the family circle, Daisy's gentle frustration with his refusal to communicate with her, and rumors running about town that new sources of money had begun to siphon into local commerce. Should she make her presence known? Continue to observe?

Again she thought of her conversation with Grandmére on the day her mother died. Her grandmother's words had bequeathed to her some supernatural craving, and she'd found herself through the ensuing years a seeker after vision—searching for Jesus in the mundane, the odd, the bizarre events and people in her life. Sometimes she heard him in Daisy's infectious laughter, felt him in the childish kisses of her small siblings, saw him in the grand depths of the ocean beyond her bedroom window. Dancing with Rafael made her yearn with an inexplicable, indescribable fire. Had that been God?

Perhaps.

But where was God now, when Rafa was gone, her mother gone, her grandmother gone, her father sodden with drink, and even her friendship with Daisy curtailed by their separate responsibilities?

Let me look, Father. Let me see.

She blinked, straightened her spine, and moved from her hiding place. "Simon! What are you doing?"

He jerked upright, pulled the shovel across his body defensively. "Lyse! What are you doing here?" He glanced back at the partially covered hole in the sand. Obviously there was no way to hide it, so he didn't try. But he didn't look happy to see her. And he hadn't answered her question.

The shovel head slid to the sand. Simon waited for her, mouth clamped in a straight line.

Lyse approached, guarded, not afraid of him but wondering what she could say that would make him tell her the truth. "I needed to talk to you." The hole in the sand drew her gaze. She could see the top and side of a canvas sack. Impossible to tell what was in it, but its shape was irregular, bulky, ridged.

"Is something wrong with the baby?" Simon had been around when Justine's first three children came along, and he understood the difficulties that could arise.

Lyse shook her head. "No, Rémy's perfect. It's just . . ." She took a step closer. Simon was not a thief. "We're out of food. Papa doesn't fish anymore, he gambled away the boat, and he's drinking up any money I bring home from selling Justine's baskets. He might listen to you—"

"Wait. He lost the boat *gambling*? When he came to borrow mine, he told me his sank." Simon's face was dark with anger. "Lyse, where is my boat?"

"Papa took it over to Mobile yesterday, and we haven't seen him since. Simon, you've got to do something!"

He jammed the shovel hard into the sand. "The first thing I'm going to do is get my boat back and never loan it out again. After that—I plan to build my own life here and never look back." He must have seen the hurt and disbelief in her face, for he looked away. "I don't know what else you expect from me. Papa is a grown man who has had every chance to succeed, but he cannot seem to discipline himself to do so. I am very sorry for Justine, but she chose to marry him and must live with the consequences."

Lyse stared at her brother. How had he become this stranger?

When she didn't answer, Simon sighed. "Lyse, you know I care about you. But if you really want Papa to wake up, you and I have both got to stop shoring him up." He glanced over his shoulder at the houseboat rocking on the water. "There isn't much room here, but you're welcome to move in until you marry and establish a home of your own."

"Move here? Leave Justine and the children?" Lyse felt as if the sand were shifting under her feet. "Marry who?"

"The whole town knows Niall McLeod would take you in a heartbeat. For a smart girl, Lyse, you are an idiot."

"Niall would *take* me? What basis is that for getting married?"

"It's a very practical basis. Niall has a steady job with regular pay. He's in good standing with the Brits, and has the means to purchase land if he wants it." Simon made a comical face. "And God knows why, but he is very fond of you, in spite of the disgraceful way you've treated him."

Lyse grabbed for her spinning thoughts. "Niall is almost as much like my brother as you, and anyway, that's not the point! I cannot leave Justine by herself with four children to care for. If I could, I would go live with Grandpére. Did you know he came to see us just a couple of days ago? I thought he and Papa might reconcile, but—" she swallowed against the lump in her throat—"things have only gotten worse."

Simon's expression softened. "You should go to Grandpére. He needs you too, maybe as much as Justine. And you could live like a lady. You wouldn't have to marry Niall, if you're so dead-set against it. Maybe someone else would court you—maybe one of the British refugees pouring down here from places they've been run out of by the Americans."

Lyse stamped her foot. "I don't *want* to live like a lady, not if it means sugaring up to people taking property away from those of us who claimed and settled it generations ago! As much as I love Daisy and her papa, I'm not British, and I never will be."

"Not with that attitude, you won't." Simon scowled. "You'd best express a little gratitude to the folks in power who make the laws and keep you safe. You're not sympathetic to those American rebels, are you?"

"I don't know anything about American rebels. In fact, I don't give a *sou* about politics at all." Her shoulders sagged. Clearly Simon was invested in his own pursuits and had no intention of doing anything about her request. Her gaze fell upon the sack half-buried in the sand. "What *is* that?"

Simon looked over his shoulder. "It's—something I found."

"Something valuable? Money? Simon, what have you done?"

"Nothing illegal, Miss Nosy-Rosy." He stared at her a moment, the famous Lanier eyebrows twitched together above his handsome nose. "Do you swear you won't tell a soul?"

"I will if you stole something."

"Lysette, you know me. But you've got to promise not to tell. I'm not sure yet what I'll do with it, and it's got to stay buried until I figure it out."

Lyse wavered between curiosity and indignation. "All right," she finally said. "I'll keep your secret. If you'll help me figure out a way to make Papa stay home and work."

Simon nodded and threw down the shovel, then reached for the neck of the sack sticking up out of the sand. He hauled something obviously heavy out onto the dry sand, untied the opening, and thrust both hands inside.

Lyse heard the shivering chink of metal coins. Simon turned and rose, hands cupped under a pile of bright disks that winked in the hard morning sun.

Gold.

~

Scarlet was hanging out the wash when Lyse's little brother Luc-Antoine ran across the yard and ducked under a pair of M'sieur Michel's underdrawers before scooting into the blacksmith shop. It had been a fine spring morning, with birds calling to one another in the magnolia trees, a soft breeze to stir the sheets, sending the pungent fragrance of lye and jasmine against her face, and the knowledge that Madame wouldn't be home for midday meal. In fact, Scarlet almost enjoyed her task, because it got her out of the house and out from under the caustic tongue of Madame's housekeeper, Martine. Martine also happened to be Cain's mother and had taken it upon herself since the death of Scarlet's maman to personally direct every breath she took—and tell her when and where to let it out.

Martine claimed to be the best cook on two continents, which gave her a certain cachet within the servant hierarchy of the Dussouy mansion, but Scarlet would be switched if she'd let the woman tell her how to properly starch and iron Madame's beautiful pintuck lace petticoats. Scarlet's own maman had taught her how to launder fine fabrics, how to keep them in good repair with small invisible stitches, how to fit a woman's changing body through pregnancy, childbirth, and a certain middle-aged spread. Scarlet knew her worth, never mind what Field Marshal Martine might say.

She'd been singing a song Maman had loved—the one about Beulah Land and what a good, good time they'd have there—but broke off mid-run to duck beneath the last sheet she'd pegged and go after the boy. Luc-Antoine wasn't exactly her cousin, since his maman was the white lady Mrs. Justine. But he was Lyse's little brother, which made him next thing to family, no matter how Madame looked down her nose. He was supposed to be at school, not chasing through the Dussouys' yard or bothering Cain in the blacksmith shop.

Scarlet marched toward the tidy little tin-roof building that was Cain's domain of a weekday morning. The wash would have to wait.

The smithy smelled of metal and oil and woodsmoke, and the heat made Scarlet instantly break out in a sweat. She didn't immediately see Luc-Antoine, but through the smoke she made out Cain standing at the forge with his back to her, big and black as the iron he worked, raising a monstrous hammer like some Olympian god from the stories Lyse had read in her grandpére's library. Shivering with pleasure, Scarlet watched the hammer slam down with a mighty clang on a red-hot sheet of metal lying across the anvil. Cain was the strongest man Scarlet had ever met, yet gentle and shy as a lamb when he touched her. His leashed power and sleepy smile made her weak in the knees.

But Maman had also taught her that the secret to managing a man lay in a woman's ability to keep him mystified.

Setting her hands to her hips, she swayed her way toward the forge. "Cain! I'm going to the big house for a cat-head biscuit and syrup. Want me to bring you one?"

At the sound of her voice, he turned, pulling down the red kerchief tied across his mouth and nose. His slow smile as he watched her approach brought the familiar warmth to her body, and she had to suppress a smile of her own.

"I be hungry," he said. "How'd you know?"

She stopped a safe distance from the forge. "You always hungry. When you gonna stop growing?"

Shaking his head, he laid the hammer on a worktable and rubbed his huge hands together. "'Twixt you and my mama feedin' me, maybe never." His laugh rumbled out. "I'm gonna grow right out the roof like Jack's beanstalk. Does Madame know you in here?"

"She's gone to town."

"Then come here and kiss me. I'd rather have you than a biscuit."

"You had me yesterday, and too many treats makes little boys spoilt and lazy." She laughed at his chagrin. "Besides, it's hot as the gates of Hades in here, and I could smell you all the way to the clothesline. Or maybe that's the little mouse I just saw scamper in here. Did you see Luc-Antoine Lanier run through?"

Cain dragged his gaze from her face to look around. "No, but I been busy, last hour or so. Madame wants new carriage wheels."

There was something odd in his expression. She frowned. "This isn't the first time he's done this, is it? Where is he?"

"I said I don't know. I ain't see him today." Cain turned back toward the forge. "I got to get back to work. But I would like a biscuit, if Mama's got an extra one."

Scarlet stood tapping her foot, staring at his broad back. "Hmph. We'll see." She whirled and stomped toward the door. The big liar. What was he hiding? Outside, she skirted the corner of the shed, flattened herself against the wall, and listened. She could hear Cain pumping the bellows, the roar of the fire.

Then a small, childish voice. "Hey, Cain, reckon she'd bring me a biscuit too? I'm pretty hungry."

Aha! She hadn't been mistaken. Vindicated, she swept back inside just as Cain, a resigned expression on his gentle face, turned to greet his young visitor, who was peering out from behind Madame's wheel-less carriage parked along the side wall.

"How'd you get back there without me seeing?" Cain dropped

the bellows and wiped his sweaty face with the kerchief. "You gone get us both in trouble."

The boy grinned. "You really didn't see me? I was real quiet."

"No but *I* saw you!" In one outraged step Scarlet grabbed Luc-Antoine by the ear and hauled him out from behind the carriage. "Why you not in school, boy?"

"Ow! I was bored. And hungry." The boy looked up at her sullenly from under an untidy mop of brown curls. "Maman didn't have nothing to send with me for lunch, so I went hunting." With a jerk of his head, he snatched loose. "Cain gives me something to eat most days. Don't you, Cain?"

Cain shrugged, looking at Scarlet uneasily. "When I got extras, I do. You can bring back two biscuits, can't you, Scarlet?"

She scowled at Luc-Antoine, avoiding Cain's pleading eyes. She knew how Madame felt about the Laniers. But then she noticed the almost translucent texture of the little boy's skin, the prominence of the high cheekbones. When his stomach gave a loud rumble, she sighed. "All right. I'll be back in a minute. But you got to go back to school after you eat, you hear?"

"Yes, ma'am!" he said with a dimpled grin so much like Mr. Antoine's she slapped him affectionately upside the head.

"I ain't no ma'am." She turned on her heel and headed for the big house.

Martine, always contrary where Scarlet was concerned, seemed reluctant to part with even one of her famous cat-head biscuits. But when Scarlet told her they were for Cain, the older woman packed half a dozen in a cloth-lined basket and tucked in a jar of cane syrup and some links of pork sausage as well.

Scarlet hauled her prize back to the smithy and set it down on Cain's worktable with a thunk. "I swear your maman is the most ornery colored woman in Mobile. No you don't!" She swatted Luc-Antoine's dirty little paw as it reached for the basket. "Wash your hands first! Both of you." She gave Cain the look.

The two males, one big and black, the other small and pale, headed for a bucket of water Cain kept on hand for regulating his fire. They scrubbed their hands and faces, then reported to Scarlet for inspection. Using one of Madame's silver table knives, she spread the biscuits with the thick, fragrant brown syrup and gave one each to Cain and Luc-Antoine. "Wait!" she said, just as the boy crammed a quarter of one of the giant biscuits into his mouth. "Didn't your maman teach you to say grace?"

"Yes'm," he mumbled around his mouthful, reddening. "Sorry."

"Bow your head," she said severely, winking over his head at Cain. "Dear Lord, we thank thee for these thy bountiful gifts. Help us to live our lives in gratitude to you and charity toward one another as you have shown it to us. Amen."

The words were hardly out of her mouth before Cain had disposed of one biscuit and reached for another. "Amen," he said, eyes twinkling.

They ate together quietly for a time, with Scarlet supervising to make sure the boy didn't drip syrup onto his clothes nor lick his fingers. Cain she didn't have to worry about, as his maman had refined his manners until he could've eaten dinner with the governor in the big house. There were some things she could be grateful to Martine for.

She watched him, enjoying the roll of shoulder muscles under his thin cambric shirt as he moved his arms and the play of a shallow dimple in one cheek as he chewed. His head was perfectly shaped, the coarse hair cut close to keep lice at bay, and his ears flat and well-proportioned. He would make a fine father for her babies. She put her hand on her stomach, imagining the swell and flutter.

"I can't eat no more, I'm full."

Scarlet blinked and focused on Luc-Antoine. He had both arms wrapped about his belly. Probably not used to eating so much all at one time. Say what you would about Madame and M'sieur

Dussouy—they fed their slaves well. "You ain't gone be sick, are you?"

Luc-Antoine shook his head. "No, ma'am. That was sure good." He glanced at the basket, where one lone biscuit remained. "Could I take that home and split it with my brother and sister? The baby don't eat nothin' but Maman's—"

"'Course you can," Cain said with laughter in his voice, tossing the biscuit to the boy. "Now you get on back to school 'fore Miss Daisy comes after you again."

Scarlet grabbed his arm. "She knows he comes here? What if Madame finds out?"

"Finds out what?" The sugary-steel voice drew Scarlet's attention like a gunshot.

Her mistress stood outlined in the doorway, kid-gloved hands clasped at her waist, her head tipped to one side with the feather in her hat poking out like a hen's tail.

"Madame!" Scarlet slid down from the barrel she'd been perched on. There was nothing else she could say. Nothing was going to make Luc-Antoine disappear.

"Yes, it's me," Madame said coldly. "What do you all think you're doing? Is this a tea party?"

"Oh, Madame, I'm so sorry," Scarlet babbled. "We just stopped for lunch, I finished pegging the wash, Cain is working on your carriage, and it seemed like the Christian thing to do, feeding the little boy—"

"I was hungry," Luc-Antoine said, disastrously drawing Madame's gaze.

"You're one of the Lanier children," she informed him.

"Yes'm," he said with no visible sense of self-preservation. "I'm Luc-Antoine."

Madame inspected him top to toe. "So I see. You look like your father." This did not seem to please her. "You also look like a rag-picker. I am all for charity, in moderation, but if I allow one child to leave the school and come to me for food, I'll soon have hordes here every day." The sharp gaze suddenly returned to Scarlet. "You knew it was wrong to encourage him—didn't you?"

Scarlet stared at her mistress for a long moment. She knew what she ought to say: *Yes, ma'am. It was wrong. I'll never do it again.*

But she *would* do it again.

When the silence apparently went on too long for Madame to bear, she took an angry step inside the shop. "You are the most ungrateful little snippet I've had the misfortune to be responsible for! I feed you well, give you my clothes—even let you spend Sunday afternoons with Cain, as if you were a married couple. And you repay my generosity by sneaking off from your work and stealing my food for little vagrants like this one." The wintery blue eyes focused on Cain. "And you—I had thought better of you. Scarlet has obviously bewitched you. Clearly I can no longer trust either of you." She drew in a pained breath. "Well, I'm sorry to say, there will be consequences. I must pray for guidance on how to handle this . . . this situation."

Scarlet had expected to be slapped at the very least. Though Madame didn't whip her house slaves as many did, her anger sometimes took physical forms.

She didn't trust this display of restraint. And Luc-Antoine was involved now. "Please, Madame, let me take the boy back to school. I'll make sure Miss Daisy doesn't let him run off again."

Madame's expression was unreadable. "No, I'll take him myself. You and Cain get back to work. I'll deal with you later."

"No!" Luc-Antoine jumped to his feet. "You ain't my maman, and you can't tell me what to do. You—you leave Cain and Scarlet alone. Alls they did was give me a biscuit."

Madame gave a disbelieving crack of laughter. "You are right. I certainly am not your mama, and isn't it a good thing? But you *will* respect your elders, little man. My pony cart is in front of the house. You will bring it around here to pick me up, and if you disobey again, you will be very sorry. Is that clear?"

Luc-Antoine stared at her mutinously for a moment. Finally he looked down, muttered "Yes, ma'am," and scuffed past Madame out of the shop.

Scarlet exchanged an anxious glance with Cain, then dipped a curtsey and moved to do Madame's bidding. She wouldn't help anything with further argument. *Please, God, give me grace.*

~

When the schoolroom door abruptly opened, Daisy looked up from reading Emée Robicheaux's essay.

Emée, who shared a desk with Suzanne Boutin, the doctor's youngest daughter, sucked in a breath and whispered, "I told you he was getting in trouble, Miss Redmond."

The clearly prescient Emée referred to Luc-Antoine Lanier, who stood, clamped by the shoulder, at the side of the town's most terrifying grand-dame, Mrs. Isabelle Dussouy. And Madame did not look pleased to be here.

There was little for Daisy to say but "Good morning, Mrs. Dussouy. I see you have found Luc-Antoine."

The older woman released Simon's brother with a little shove into the room. "I have indeed. I found him eating food stolen from my larder and socializing with my slaves. I believe he belongs in school with you?"

The implication being that Daisy had been derelict in her duty. Was she supposed to have left her other students alone while she went on a fruitless search for a little boy who had made a profession out of escaping adult supervision? Even Simon was inclined to shrug his shoulders. *Well, that's Luc for you. He'll come back when he's hungry.*

Daisy drew herself up, as she had seen her father do when challenged by an impertinent enlistee, and injected a touch of frost into her tone. "I thank you for your concern, ma'am. I shall make sure he pays for his imposition and works off the meal by helping to muck your stables every morning the rest of this week." She turned her darkest schoolteacher frown on the miscreant. "Will you not, Luc-Antoine?"

His mutinous expression folded when she continued to stare with relentless calm. "Yes, ma'am." He turned to Mrs. Dussouy. "I didn't mean to steal. And please don't whip Cain or Scarlet. They was just being nice to me."

"*Were* being nice," Daisy corrected him.

"Were." Luc-Antoine sighed. "Couldn't I just feed the horses? Or exercise 'em? I'm a good rider."

Mrs. Dussouy looked outraged. "I wouldn't let a little—"

"No." Daisy reached to take his dirty little face in her hand, turning it up so that he met her eyes. "And you will go to Mrs. Dussouy's early so you may be on time for school. You have missed several assignments, and you must work hard to catch up. Emée and Suzanne have quite passed you up today."

The challenge of competing for honors with a couple of *girls* had the expected effect. Luc-Antoine plunked into his seat without another word.

Which left Daisy facing Mrs. Dussouy. She had never felt so young and unsure of herself. She straightened her spine. "You may depend on me to follow through with the boy's punishment, ma'am. I don't think he will try this particular stunt again. Thank you for returning him to me."

"Well." Madame sniffed. "One can hardly expect refined behavior from one of his mongrel pedigree, I suppose. But the damage to my slaves' discipline is a serious matter. Once they get the idea they can converse on an equal basis with their betters . . ."

Daisy bit her lip, thinking of the deeply spiritual talk she'd had just this morning over breakfast with the family's houseman, Timbo. Was she "better" than him? She was his mistress, in the sense that her father owned Timbo's papers, supplied the food, clothing, and shelter that kept him alive, and demanded his unquestioning obedience. But she depended daily on the wisdom gained from his gentle, slow-spoken answers to her often anxious questions. Timbo was in many ways the grandfather she'd never had.

She also thought guiltily of the book hidden under her bed, a book which had irrevocably altered her thinking on subjects like freedom and equality. Her father, like Mrs. Dussouy, would be scandalized to know she'd so much as cracked the cover of such subversive literature.

"You must do as you see fit, of course," she said calmly. "As I must do with my students. Again, I'm sorry Luc-Antoine disturbed you. Please forgive me if I return to our lesson." She dipped a quick curtsey and turned to walk to the chalkboard.

"Well!" Mrs. Dussouy huffed, but after a moment Daisy heard the door open, then shut with a bang.

The children tittered. She ignored them and continued with her spelling list. Simon would laugh when she told him about the morning's kerfuffle. Even the "mongrel pedigree" remark would strike him as funny, as his forbears had been ruling over a large chunk of New France when the Dussouys were still trapping furs in Acadia.

Not that that mattered. She loved Simon for his humor and good sense and strength of character. And a certain expression when he looked at her that could make her weak in the knees.

"Miss Redmond, I think you misspelled 'attention,'" said Emée behind her.

"Oh, dear, I certainly did." Red faced, Daisy corrected her mistake and scolded herself not to daydream. She was getting as bad as Lyse.

8

New Orleans
May 1777

Rafa, dressed in one of his more sober evening suits of black velvet decorated with black satin frogs along the cuffs and tail vents, handed his tricorn to the Pollocks' butler with a smile. He took a moment to check his appearance in the fine Valencia mirror, which he himself had brought back from Havana in March, then climbed the stairs to the great salon which fronted Chartres Street.

As he waited in line to greet his host, Rafa reflected that everyone who was anyone must be here tonight. Governor Gálvez held court beside his chosen lady, the beautiful widow María Feliciana de St. Maxent d'Estrehan, near one of the magnificent French windows. The windows stood open to the mild spring breeze, spilling the light of a thousand candles onto the street below. As usual forgoing the finery due his exalted position, Gálvez had favored a uniform even more severe in lines than Rafa's own, a restraint that served as a deliberate contrast to his lady's extravagant Gallic beauty.

With his heart firmly in the possession of a certain other Creole lady, Rafa found himself inspecting the exquisite Doña d'Estrehan with the detached admiration one might accord an expensive painting: wondering how much it cost and how long it had taken to compose. Her dark curls had been piled over some towering contraption and threaded with ribbons and silk flowers, with a few long ringlets allowed to cleverly trail along the low neckline of her golden voile gown. Amber and ruby jewels twinkled from her small, dainty ears and about her throat, and the large, tip-tilted dark eyes had been subtly enhanced by a faint rouging of her high cheekbones.

Small wonder that Gálvez scarcely took his eyes from the lady's face.

"The governor is clearly smitten, is he not?"

Rafa turned to find Pollock's wife, Margaret, smiling as she stood on tiptoe to kiss his cheek. He grinned. "Without doubt. It is but a matter of time before she becomes Doña Gálvez. Wagers say before Christmas."

"Oh, well before that," Pollock said, firmly shaking Rafa's hand. "And one hopes that she will give him an answer soon, so that his attention may be focused on the business at hand."

"I've noticed no lack of discipline." Rafa rubbed his shoulder, just now becoming free of the ache from the scrap-iron wound.

Pollock leaned in, touching the side of his large nose. "Gálvez may bark, but he's pleased with the intelligence you brought. In fact, the king has authorized us to send more blankets and gunpowder up the river."

Before replying, Rafa looked around. Mrs. Margaret had turned to the next guests in line, an indigo merchant and his well-dressed wife. There were spies everywhere, and he had to believe that if he had been so easily able to infiltrate Pensacola, the likelihood of the British returning the favor was great. Gálvez had sternly warned them all not to speak out of turn.

With a tilt of his head, he invited Pollock to follow him to a quiet corner where they could converse with their backs to the wall, in no danger of being overheard. Rafa folded his arms and said softly, "Gálvez may have forgiven the loss of the gold, but I'm going to get it back."

"The governor is both fair and practical. He will never penalize a man for what is outside his control—and pirates are parasites who unfortunately ride the tails of any coastal political conflict. We're lucky that's the first major cargo we've lost to this point. And to have escaped with no loss of life—" Pollock shrugged—"that is truly a blessing. How do you plan to recover it?"

"I've thought about it. As I reported, the people of Mobile and Pensacola are not eating well. Their stores of flour are all but depleted, and summertime fevers will soon be setting in." Rafa met Pollock's sharp gaze. "What if, as a gesture of goodwill, I take them some of the quinine that just came from Peru and a hundred fifty or so of those barrels of Brazilian wheat? I could also take a fully armed crew, poke around the docks, pretend to carouse a bit." He grinned at Pollock. "You know. Take it from there."

"In other words, everything that young Don Rafael is so good at." Pollock rolled his eyes. "I think it's a brilliant idea, and if I were a younger man, I'd go with you. I'll outfit you, because I think it's worth trying to get that cache of gold back in our hands. The Americans need every scrap of help we can send their way." He paused, said in uncharacteristically diffident tones, "What did you think of the Adam Smith treatise?"

Rafa straightened. "I read it. Compelling stuff, and you add that to Thomas Paine's work . . . well, I'm not ready to renounce my Spanish citizenship, but I want to see this American experiment work out." He looked away. "I know people who don't now have the freedom to make their own choices, and they deserve better."

"People?" Pollock, always discerning, had an uncanny knack for prying information out of Rafa. "People in general, or people in particular?"

He didn't answer for a moment. The dancers' rhythmic patterns in the center of the room made him think of Lyse and the way she had anxiously followed the touch of his hands, the direction of his gaze, as he guided her in the minuet. Her guilt that she could enjoy a party when her cousin Scarlet could not—and her valiant efforts to keep her poverty-stricken family afloat. "Rather more specific than not," he said with an oblique smile.

Pollock laughed. "I understand the need to be careful, given the present company. Speaking of which, look who has just arrived. I must go speak to your mama—and perhaps, in your father's absence, you might come with me to fend off the young puppies who'll be sitting up to beg for your little sister's favor."

Rafa turned just in time to witness the grand entrance of the two most powerful women in his life—Mama, still beautiful, even with her black hair beginning to gray in delicate wings above her ears, and Sofía a younger copy, looking like some exotic little bird in a dress decorated with the lavender lace Lyse had selected for her. They were quickly obscured by the onrush of uniformed men seeking to fill Sofía's dance card.

"*Ay,*" he muttered, gave Pollock a rueful glance, and took off toward the crowd.

He pushed through to Sofía's side just as a young adjutant, notable for a prominent Adam's apple and a nose the approximate size and shape of a mast in full sail, claimed her hand for the next country dance.

After retrieving her dance card and dismissing the poor adjutant with a careless wave, Sofía seized Rafael in an enthusiastic hug. "Rafa! You must see how beautifully your Mobile lace has made up! Am I not adorable?" She stood back to pirouette for his benefit. "You must go back and find more, only perhaps you might look for that delicious shade of celery that I saw in *Fashionable Miscellany*."

Trying not to wince at the clench of pain in his shoulder—or her unfortunate use of the word *delicious* in the same sentence with *celery*—he took her hand, tucked it into his elbow, and whisked her away from her disappointed cadre of admirers. He guided her toward the refreshment table. "You are of course adorable, little sister, and naturally I exist to provide your modiste with dress materials. I hesitate to remind you, however, that further travels must wait until I have enough merchandise to fill another ship."

Sofía pouted, then giggled and leaned in to whisper, "Oh, I have missed you! Where have you been keeping yourself the last few weeks? Mama said Mr. Pollock undoubtedly had business matters for you to attend, but I can hardly believe you wouldn't at least come by and take me driving of an afternoon. And Rafa, you haven't been to mass at all! Padre Juan wouldn't tell me if you'd been to confession, he says it is none of my concern, but truly it *is* my concern for your spiritual—"

"Take a breath, Sofi," Rafa said, laughing. "I promise I have not put myself beyond redemption. In fact—" He stopped himself abruptly. How to explain the overwhelming urge he'd had, ever since returning to New Orleans, to pray about everything? His family would think him mad. And anyone who knew Don Rafael, merchant and man about town, would certainly not credit him with any serious engagement of the spirit. He let out another laughing breath as he picked up a glass of lemonade and handed it to Sofía. "In fact, I have tied up some loose ends which leave me free to join you and the parents for services tomorrow evening."

"Really? Oh, Rafa, that is excellent! Mama will be so happy, and maybe Papa will stop growling about your selfish absences."

Rafa suddenly regretted that lemonade seemed to be the strongest libation available at the party. He bit his tongue, then after a moment blurted, "If I were wearing a uniform as Papa wished, he would not see me even every three to six months as I manage now. I'd be serving in Peru or Dominica or some other godforsaken outpost, unable to do more than write the occasional letter."

"I have hurt your feelings," Sofía said, tears in her big brown eyes. "I don't understand why you and Papa cannot forgive one another and cease this interminable sniping through me. I'm *glad* you're not military! I don't want you in danger of being shot at or—or run through with a bayonet or—Because it's bad enough that Cristián and Danilo—" With a strangled sob, she crammed her gloved fist against her mouth and turned away.

Rafa cursed himself for upsetting her, particularly in a public setting such as this. His older brother Cristián had been absent from the family fold for nearly two years, and Danilo, younger than Rafa by a scant ten months, had shipped off to the southern colonies just after Christmas. He bolstered his determination that neither Sofía nor their mother should know how close to his heart the pirate's iron had come.

He sighed and put his good arm round her shaking shoulders. "Come, Sofi, I'll make up to Father, I promise. And we'll light ten candles each for Cristián and Nilo tomorrow. I know God will keep them safe."

Sofía wiped her eyes with her gloved fingers and gave a blubbering laugh. "*Why* do I never have a handkerchief when I start to cry? It is so aggravating!"

"That is why you have a dandy for a brother," he said and handed over his large, lace-edged handkerchief. "Mop up, and I'll let you go dance with your Roman-nosed adjutant. I'm sure he won't notice how pink yours is."

She blew her nose, then handed back his handkerchief with a watery smile. "Please don't ever change, Rafael. I love you just like you are, dandified or not."

It was a small comfort, but he took it. He escorted his sister back to her swain and went to work, circulating the room in search of spies and information. The governor had asked for a meeting in the morning, and if he expected approval for a return to Mobile, he had best be prepared to justify it.

Mobile
October 1777

Lyse pulled her shawl around her shoulders as she followed Daisy down the schoolhouse steps into the street. A sudden snap of fall had tugged brittle brown leaves off the water oaks, sending them swirling along with the breeze. In August the school had been moved to more spacious quarters on Conception Street to accommodate the children of Loyalist refugees fleeing the northern colonies, and Daisy had begged Lyse to help by teaching the youngest children.

When her father unexpectedly encouraged her to move in with the Redmonds, Lyse timidly broached the subject to Daisy and found herself smothered in a hug and all but deafened by her friend's shrieks of joy.

With little further ado, Lyse settled into a contented routine for the first time in her life.

The only thing marring her peace came whistling round the corner of St. Peter Street with his tricorn pushed to the back of his red head and his musket propped on his shoulder. At the sight of Niall's delighted grin—as if he didn't know she and Daisy started the walk home at three o'clock every afternoon—Lyse turned to dive back into the schoolroom.

But Daisy was already tugging her along, smiling and waving. "Niall! How nice to see you! Are you off duty this afternoon?"

"Yes, until this time tomorrow. May I walk you ladies home?" Niall turned hopeful blue eyes on Lyse.

She didn't have the heart to crush him. Besides, Daisy was squeezing her arm so hard there were sure to be bruises later. "Of course, if you're not too tired."

Niall fell into step, suppressing a yawn. "I'm tip-top, not tired at all. Sentry duty is so boring, I don't know why the major bothers.

We're perfectly safe down here on the gulf. They say the Americans are getting ready to come down the river and attack, but everybody knows their navy ain't worth spitting at. Now the Spanish, that would be another thing—" Niall suddenly clamped his lips together, looking sideways at Daisy. "I'm sorry, don't mean to criticize your father. He's got to follow orders, after all."

Lyse exchanged glances with Daisy. They'd been discussing this very topic off and on over the past few days. Major Redmond had lately been by turns silent and terse in communication, his high, handsome brow etched with new lines. Lyse strove for a casual tone. "Niall, why would the Spanish come here? They're a neutral party in the war—aren't they?"

Niall shrugged. "They claim to be. But they stopped one of our ships that tried to enter New Orleans harbor, wouldn't let her in, while at the same time that tricky Gálvez is harboring American smugglers who've been pillaging up and down the Mississippi for half a year or more."

"How do you know that?" For reasons she couldn't explain to herself, much less Daisy, Lyse found herself fascinated with anything having to do with the Spanish of New Orleans.

Niall didn't seem to hear the tension in her voice. "Another family of refugees from Natchez came in late last night. That's the third group this month. The major assigned me to find them temporary places to board, and a whinier lot I've yet to meet." He put on an exaggerated nasal drawl and minced along with a hand at his waist. "'It is so *hot* in this mosquito-infested bog, ensign, I don't know how you people stand it. If King George knew what we put up with out of loyalty to the Crown, I swear he'd knight us all, instead of allowing the rebels to run us out of our own homes!'"

Lyse and Daisy both laughed. "How much longer do you think the war will drag on?" Lyse asked, sobering.

Niall shook his head. "No idea. Could be a month, but more likely a year, since the French came in to complicate things. Depends on—" breaking off, he looked over his shoulder—"depends on how the next campaign goes. I hear we might invade New Orleans, if the Spaniards double-cross us."

Lyse felt her face drain of blood. "Invade? But surely there's no reason—"

"Now, there's no cause to be frightened," Niall said, clearly aware that he had stepped wrong. "Like I said, Colonel Durnford is suspicious of Spanish motives, but he can't prove anything, and besides, I'm just speculating—and you know how low on the chain of command I am!"

There was a long, uncomfortable silence as the three of them passed the Emporium, which loomed starkly empty, devoid of paying customers. They reached the Redmonds' cottage and paused on its brick walkway.

"Would you like to come in for lemonade, Niall?" Daisy asked politely.

"I would, but—" He shuffled his big feet. "Please forget I said anything, girls. I could get into real trouble if your pa hears I've been talking out of turn."

Daisy touched his arm. "You didn't say anything I haven't heard people all over town gossiping about. You and Lyse sit here on the porch swing and enjoy the breeze. I'll get us something to drink and be right back." Before Lyse could object, Daisy pattered up the steps to the house.

Lyse was left alone with Niall, her hand lightly tucked through his elbow. She suddenly felt his solid weight, his anxious attraction to her. Stepping away, she turned to walk up the steps, but he awkwardly grabbed her shoulder.

"Wait, Lyse, I—before Daisy comes back, I wanted to—to ask you—" He gulped. "There's a dance at Burrelle's tomorrow night. I want to—could I escort you?" His ears were bright red, and his eyes shone with hope. He was such a kind boy, gentle and hardworking and familiar as a pair of house shoes.

Justine and her father liked him. The children liked him. Even Simon liked him.

How could she say no?

"Lyse! Lyse! I ran all the way to the school to look for you!"

She whirled. Luc-Antoine was running down the opposite side of the street toward her, dodging a cart and mule in front of the Emporium, jumping over a mud puddle, arms and legs pumping and hair flying.

Her little brother had, against all odds, managed to please her high-and-mightiness Isabelle Dussouy enough that she had offered him an apprenticeship with Cain in her forge. He had been given a pallet in the servants' quarters, three meals a day, and the privilege of attending school three days a week. In return, he was bound for ten years to spend every other waking moment running errands and fetching things for the young blacksmith as he learned the work, a job which the boy was thrilled to do.

He did not look happy at the moment. As he drew closer, Lyse could see smears of tears on his flushed cheeks.

She grabbed him as he flung himself at her, burying his dirty face in her second-best fichu. "Luc, what is it?" Meeting Niall's puzzled eyes, she stroked her brother's sweaty head. When he didn't answer, she caught his face in her hands, lifting it to look for some injury. "What's wrong?"

"It's Scarlet!" Luc-Antoine let out an angry sob. "Madame Dussouy sold her! A Mississippi trader come took her off this morning!"

~

The candles in Burelle's windows glowed like fireflies in the distance as Lyse walked beside Niall the few short blocks from the Redmonds' house. She couldn't help remembering the night she'd attended the Dussouys' soirée with Rafael in the spring. She'd felt like a princess that night in Daisy's beautiful gown, with her hair dressed high and the sparkling slippers upon her feet.

Daisy had offered to loan it to her again, but Burelle's wasn't a place where one need pretend to high fashion. Instead she wore the newer of her two gowns, a soft blue striped merino with embroidered cherries scattered over the skirt and a red military-style jacket frogged at the bosom with black satin. Her ruffled cap added the maturity appropriate for a schoolteacher.

Niall had apparently bathed and shaved, taming his red curls with some kind of pomade that made Lyse sneeze every time she took an incautious breath. He had traded his red uniform coat for a sober brown tailcoat and buckskin pantaloons that clung to his stocky, heavily muscled frame, worn with clocked stockings and shoes ornamented with large paste buckles.

Once the formality of bidding adieu to Daisy's father was over with, Niall seemed to have lost his voice completely, except for an occasional nervous harrumph that put her in mind of Grandpére's favorite mule, Charlie.

Finally she could stand it no longer. "Niall, I won't be very good company tonight, I'm afraid. If you want to go on to the party without me, I wouldn't blame you."

He hesitated. "I'm not sure you need to be alone. I know you're angry and upset about Scarlet, but—"

"I'm not upset, Niall. I'm outraged. How abominably cruel can one person be—to separate a husband and wife? It's just one more way of getting back at my father for jilting her all those years ago."

"Well, I wouldn't do it, but it's not outside the law and not even unheard of. Lyse, as much as you loved Scarlet, she isn't a free citizen. Madame Dussouy owned her and had the right to sell her if she wasn't satisfied with her."

Lyse pressed her lips together to suppress the scream that wanted to escape. Niall's words were true, but they scraped a wound so raw that she thought it might never heal. The thought of her gentle cousin hauled off by a strange man, terrified and lonely, maybe physically abused, was almost more than she could bear. If she'd known where the trader went, she would have gone after him. She should have found a way to set Scarlet free a long time ago. Then this would never have happened.

"Cain is beside himself with grief," she said when she could speak calmly. "Madame had to chain him to keep him from running off to try to find her. She beat him, Niall. After stealing his wife away, she whipped him like an animal."

Her voice clogged in spite of herself, and Niall reached for her hand. "I know," he said, "but they weren't really married. He'll get over it and mate with another girl. You'll see."

Lyse stopped, snatching her hand away. "Do you really think that? That because his skin is dark and there's a piece of paper making him a slave, that he doesn't have feelings?" When Niall just looked at her, shaking his head mutely, she blurted, "People say Scarlet and I look like sisters! Our mothers were twins! What if something happens to me, Niall? Are you going to get over it and mate with someone else?"

The words were crude, unladylike, and torn from a place in her that she rarely let anyone see. But if Niall truly wanted to wed her, as she knew he did, he'd better know what he was getting. She was no princess, nor even a lady. She was the daughter of a freed slave and a drunken fisherman.

His mouth fell open, and his eyes filled with something between shock and sorrow before he turned his face away. "How can you say that? You know I . . . love you, Lyse. I always have. There won't ever be anyone else." When she didn't answer, he summoned the courage to look at her again. "I know I'm not as fancy as that Spanish fellow, but I could take care of you, and the major says he'll help me find a little house we can live in until I'm posted elsewhere."

The "Spanish fellow" figured in this situation not at all, but her stomach flipped all the same. Even Niall had seen her infatuation. How humiliating. Pride sharpened her tone. "I'm taking care of myself just fine, thank you very much." She counted to ten, hanging her head. "Niall, you are such a good man, and you deserve a girl who will love you wholeheartedly. Me, I'm too impatient, too independent, too—too—everything! I'd make you miserable inside of a week."

Niall stepped close and tried again to take her hands. "Don't say no, Lyse. I'm willing to wait for you. I wasn't going to speak so soon, but you—you kind of forced it." He laughed softly. "Which is one thing I love about you. You won't let things lie untouched. You have to turn everything over, examine it, talk about it, *fix* it if you can."

He was utterly sincere, utterly dear, and stubborn as that old mule. She backed away, shaking her head. "No promises, Niall."

"I'll wait. Come on, I hear the music." He proffered his arm, and there was nothing to do but take it.

As she and Niall entered the inn's small, crowded ballroom, Lyse pasted on a smile and chattered and danced as if she hadn't a care in the world. Inside, she felt like a boiling inferno of rage and frustration, and with no apparent outlet, she knew it wouldn't take much to provoke a messy explosion. Would God have her marry a man who refused to push back—who simply flattened in a soft cushion of acceptance, no matter what she said or did? There was no doubt that Niall could be a good provider. But was that enough for marriage?

On the other hand, what if she waited for something more, and that something never came? The thought of living the rest of her life as a spinster schoolteacher was both terrifying and suffocating. She loved the children and found great reward in opening their minds to the peoples and worlds found in the pages of a book. But sooner or later, please God, Daisy was going to find a way to marry Simon, and Lyse would be left to run the school alone. Could she be satisfied to love and teach their children, never knowing the joy of bearing and rearing her own?

With an effort she blinked away her eddying thoughts and focused on the scene around her. Brigitte had outdone herself in turning the tavern hall into a gay harvest celebration. The tables and chairs from the small restaurant had been pushed against the walls to make room for dancing, and the rough plank floor swept clean. Bright orange pumpkins, flanked by purple and golden gourds, decorated hay bales in cozy corners for those who wanted a bit of private conversation. The company, dressed in Sunday best, whirled in time to the music of a couple of fiddlers playing on a small dais at the back of the room.

Lyse touched palms with Niall and jigged down the country dance line. There was no reason she should be sad. She had a paying job, a clean and safe place to live, congenial company. If she'd been hungry, there was plenty of good food on the bar right behind her. She hadn't, in fact, had anything to eat since yesterday noon, but even the thought of food made her light-headed. Niall kept giving her worried looks, and she tried once more to smile. Perhaps she should give it up and insist that he take her home.

The dance turned, and across the room near the front door, she saw Rafael Gonzales, Daisy Redmond clinging to his arm.

9

She had grown up in his absence.

Rafa hardly knew what to think. He had expected the sparkling, exotic little girl who had turned him on his head, with her French-accented English and kissable lips and quick, incisive humor. He stood stupidly staring at this quiet, pale-faced version of his Lyse until someone pinched his arm hard.

He closed his mouth and looked down at Daisy Redmond, who said under her breath, "Come, Don Rafael, let us proceed, or everyone will think I have hauled in some particularly unwieldy statue of Don Quixote instead."

He laughed, patted her hand, and managed to unstick his feet from the tavern floor. "Do you want to dance?" he said as they made their way through the crowded room. "Or should we wait for the next one?" Do not look at Lyse, he told himself.

But why not? that stubborn oaf Rafa wanted to know. She was the most exquisite thing in the room, like a priceless painting dimmed by bad lighting. Why was her beautiful hair covered by that awful cap? And why was she dressed like his grandmother?

And why in God's name was she dancing with the young British rooster—Niall? Was that his name?

"I think we'd better dance after all, sir. You are attracting attention." Daisy tugged him toward the end of the country dance, pushed him none too gently in line with the other men, and picked up her skirts to skip past him.

Mechanically he performed the steps. Not knowing where Lyse would be when he arrived in Mobile, he'd decided to first complete his business by delivering the wheat to Major Redmond. The major had invited him home for a drink, where, fortuitously, Daisy had told him about the dance—and that Lyse had been invited.

Now he was here, Lyse was here, and everything felt wrong, as if he'd sailed into the wrong port, as he'd joked about with her so very long ago. But really not so long ago as that; it had only been just over a year since he'd confiscated her deadly little knife and metaphorically taken it into his heart.

She danced past him, eyes downcast. No, there—a flash of topaz eyes, just before she escaped to round the end of the line and disappear. He was mad to follow her, but the music surged to an end. Daisy curtseyed in front of him, and he was obliged to bow.

"Thank you, my lady." He took Daisy's hand upon his arm. "I suppose there must be refreshments somewhere. Are you thirsty?"

She pulled a lacy fan from her pocket and plied it to her flushed face. "I am indeed. But take me to Lyse first, if you please."

He bit the inside of his cheek. "Must we?"

"If you don't wish to stand glowering at her across the room, I do indeed suggest it."

"I am not glowering."

"Scowling, then. You look like you ate an unripe persimmon."

He gave up and allowed her to steer his reluctant feet toward a corner of the room where Niall's fiery head could be seen beyond the powdered wigs of two or three substantial gentlemen and their ladies.

No scowling. No glowering. His tongue felt like a side of bacon.

What was *wrong* with him tonight? He never had trouble thinking of what to say to a woman.

He and Daisy rounded the last powdered gentleman and there she was. The demure dress was buttoned up to her chin, the hideous cap covering nearly all those glorious black curls. He wanted to yank it off, thrust his fingers into the curls, and kiss her smiling lips.

Instead he gave her what he feared was a supercilious smirk. "Miss Lanier! Well met. And Mr. . . . Mr. . . . Oh dear, I'm afraid I don't remember your name, sir."

"McLeod." The rooster made an awkward leg. "How d'ye do, Lord Rafael? Are you in town, then?"

"I believe I must be," Rafa said. "Unless you perceive me to be somewhere else, in which case I must hurry up and arrive . . . er, here." He grinned. "I've important business with the major, you see."

"Major Redmond is in that corner with the Guillorys and Sergeant Anderson." McLeod glanced over his shoulder. "But I wouldn't bother him if I were you. He's been in a bit of a snit lately, begging your pardon, Daisy."

"Oh, we've already conversed today," Rafa said. "I just delivered a hundred barrels of wheat to Pensacola, and brought another fifty to leave here in Mobile."

He was watching Lyse, and his words brought her eyes to his face. She clung to McLeod's elbow as if she were about to fall down. What exactly was going on here? Had she promised herself to the rooster while Rafa was in New Orleans?

McLeod seemed aware of his regard, for he patted Lyse's hand in a revoltingly familiar way. "How nice. Lyse and I were just about to step outside for some air."

But Lyse pulled her hand away and stepped back. "I'm not—I mean, no, let us not go yet, Niall." She blushed. "Don Rafael, you are very kind, to go to so much trouble to bring us foodstuffs. We haven't been able to get wheat because of blockaders along the

Alabama River, and—oh, it will be so good to have real bread again!"

"It is my pleasure to bring you pleasure," Rafa purred, pleased to see the darkening of McLeod's freckled young face. "Would you like to accompany Miss Redmond and me to address the major? I need to speak with him again regarding arrangements for transfer of the wheat."

"I imagine you have to return to New Orleans right away," McLeod said hopefully.

"Oh, no, I shall be here for quite a while—a week or more at least." Rafa extended his free arm to Lyse. "Coming, Miss Lanier?"

She glanced at McLeod's stubborn expression and lifted her chin. "Yes. I am."

And just that easily, Rafa walked away with the two most beautiful women in the room, one on either arm, leaving Niall McLeod to fume and plot whatever revenge he wished. Rafa simply did not care. The warmth of Lyse's hand tucked close to his body filled him with a euphoria that no amount of self-scolding could dispel. He wanted to hear her voice.

"Miss Redmond tells me that you have been helping to teach the little children their letters—and that you have come to live in town with her and the major. I confess, I'm curious as to what brought about such a change."

Lyse's shrug was matter-of-fact. "Sooner or later one grows up and wishes to be less of a burden upon the family purse strings. In fact, I have been able to contribute somewhat to my siblings' welfare." There was quiet pride in her voice, and Rafa could only applaud her loyalty and unselfishness.

Still, he sensed there was something she hadn't told him—something perhaps Daisy didn't even know. He longed to get Lyse alone so they could speak more freely.

Patience, Rafa, he told himself. Secrets often unlocked themselves if one waited long enough.

"Lyse is too modest," Daisy said warmly. "I don't know how I should have managed this fall without her to take the primary levels. The school has nearly doubled in size since the spring."

"Indeed?" Rafa would have inquired further, but Major Redmond looked around at that moment.

Redmond smiled at his daughter. "Well met, my dear!" He turned to the companion on his left, a stocky gentleman in stiff evening clothes and a powdered wig. "Guillory, see who Daisy and Lyse have brought to the party! Our good friend Don Rafael, always a welcome visitor to Mobile."

The wigged gentleman smiled. "Indeed. Our Joony will make good use of the wheat as soon as it can be milled."

Rafa thought wryly that if one's notoriety depended on delivery services, then he was destined for immortality. He bowed. "I am only too happy to provide Miss Joony with material for her beignet genius—which played no small role in my determination to remain for several days."

Guillory laughed. "Your room is already prepared, sir, and I assure you, you may stay as long as you wish."

Rafa scanned the crowded tavern. "You've attracted quite a large company this evening."

Major Redmond nodded. "Loyalist emigrants from the northern colonies have flooded into West Florida in droves. One wonders if they will stay here after His Majesty's troops have quelled the rebels."

Rafa could detect no lack of confidence in the major's voice. Clearly he believed British victory was only a matter of time. Rafa stifled a yawn. "No understanding why a man would voluntarily return to all that ice and snow when the scenery is so pretty here in the south." He winked at Daisy.

"Don Rafael, you are laying it on too thick." Daisy tossed her curls and took her father's arm. "Perhaps you should try your blandishments on some of those northern girls. We southerners are awake to your nonsense—aren't we, Lyse?"

Apparently caught off guard at being addressed, Lyse took a sharp breath and allowed her gaze to flick upward to Rafa's. Her teeth caught that sweet lower lip.

He stared at her, helpless to come up with further witticisms.

"Awake," she finally said, looking away. "Yes, of course."

Daisy rolled her eyes. "I hear the Tully brothers tuning up for another jig. Why don't the two of you join the set that's forming, while Papa and I find some refreshments. I declare, I'm parched."

Rafa nodded, relieved to have the decision made for him. "I'd be honored, Miss Lanier."

Lyse hesitated, then once more slipped her hand through the crook of his arm. As they crossed the room, her gaze remained downcast, her body stiff. "I don't feel like dancing," she muttered.

"Then come outside onto the gallery, where we may converse. I knew something was wrong." Sorry for her discomfort but giddy with relief that he wouldn't have to remain separated by the movements of the dance, Rafa steered her toward the front door and then outside into the thick darkness. A lamp threw a smoky splash of light beside the door, but a wooden swing waited in the shadows at the far end of the gallery. He headed there without hesitation. Allowing her to sit first, he settled beside her, close enough to hear the rustle of her skirts and breathe in the faint fragrance of her hair.

After a few moments of silence underlaid by the muted strains of the dance, she sighed. "Your English has improved since I saw you last."

"As has yours." He laughed. "Your accent has become so very . . . British."

"Time spent with Daisy," she said, and he could hear the smile in her voice. "And the children. They're constantly correcting me."

"And—Ensign McLeod?"

She hesitated. "He doesn't correct me."

"Wouldn't have the nerve, I'm sure. You seem very close." There was no jealousy in his voice, he was quite confident. Probably. "I mean, I believe you have been friends for a long time, have you not?"

"We have." Her voice was barely above a whisper. He wished he could see her face, somehow interpret her emotions. "Rafa, he asked me to marry him."

He found that he could hardly breathe around the pain. Somehow he managed, "Did he? And what was your answer?"

"I haven't—I didn't say no, but—you have been gone for a very long time. I didn't know if you were coming back—"

He took her face in both hands and crushed her mouth with his. After a long moment, when he felt something warm splash against his thumb, he broke the kiss. "You knew I would return," he said hoarsely. "I told you I would."

"Men lie. You meant it at the time, I told myself, but one cannot live on promises."

"I am not like your father."

"Neither is Niall. He is very good to me."

"But you do not love him." She would have said so if she did.

"Of course I love him. Wait, Rafa!" With a shaky laugh, she put a hand against his lips. "No more kisses—please!"

He kissed her palm, then held it against his cheek. "Why not?"

"Because I can't think, and I need to think!"

"Thinking is unnecessary in some instances. What does your heart tell you?"

"Oh, Rafa! My heart is so unwise. I cannot trust it, especially when you appear without warning, on a day when I am crushed by grief and worry—"

"What? What has happened? Has someone hurt you? I will kill him!"

"No—no, it is not like that. Of course you mustn't kill anyone! It is very bad, but there is nothing one can do. It is my cousin, Scarlet. She has been sold to a slave trader, and I don't know where she is or—or if I'll ever see her again."

Rafa's eyes had adjusted to the darkness enough that he could see tears flowing freely down her cheeks and dripping off her chin. "That woman is a she-devil."

"Yes, she is." Lyse uttered a shaky laugh. "But cursing her will do no good. If only I knew where the man took Scarlet, I would—but Madame Dussouy refuses to tell. She locked Cain up and slapped my little brother when he tried to let him out." Drawing back from Rafa, she swiped at her eyes. "It's a very bad situation."

"Yes. It is. I shall fix it, somehow. Depend on it."

"You are very much like Simon, you know. He doesn't know the meaning of the word *impossible*." She said it the French way, spitting the word as if it were something nasty.

Perhaps it was. "I find that most things can be remedied with a little ingenuity and persistence." He grinned at her and touched her nose. "You will find that we Spaniards are a very persistent race. Now come, let us return to the party before I forget my good intentions and persist in kissing you senseless."

~

Daisy watched Lyse come back into the hall with Don Rafael and knew a pang of envy—not because she wanted the Spanish gentleman's attention, but because Lyse's cap was askew, her lips were berry-red, and a significant beard burn marred one cheek. What would she not give to be held in Simon's arms and feel his kisses as her friends had clearly enjoyed one another! But Simon had lately become so circumspect, so—so careful of her reputation, of her father's good opinion, that he refused even to be alone with her.

Every time the door opened, she turned, hoping to see him swing through, bearing the fresh scent of salt air and his unique bold energy. But he had told her he would not come, had no time for frivolities like dancing. No, he was working on some errand of which he would only vaguely speak, except to say that it would enable him to someday apply to her father for her hand in marriage.

Someday! While time marched on, and beautiful days they could have spent together passed. She wasn't so ridiculous as to claim loneliness, for she had her father to care for and Lyse's friendship, and of course her students filled her days with intellectual challenge and laughter. But she longed to share with Simon the sweet oneness she had observed in her parents' marriage.

"Miss Redmond—*perdón*, Miss Redmond!"

She blinked and focused on Don Rafael's smiling face. "Oh dear! Were you speaking to me?"

"Well, I was, but if you are busy, I will take myself off and speak to someone else."

She laughed, unable to tell if he was serious or seriously stupid. With him, it was hard to tell. "I was woolgathering, I'm afraid." She looked around and saw that they were relatively alone, tucked away in the corner she had gravitated to when she realized Simon really wasn't coming. "Where is Lyse?"

"Serving weak lemonade to thirsty soldiers and fishermen." He tipped his head toward the refreshments arrayed on the bar, where Lyse officiated with evident pleasure. "Apparently that is all we are to partake of, on this night of free entertainment. Our tenderhearted Miss Lanier was concerned that you might be feeling abandoned and sent me to fetch you—or better yet, to ask you to dance." He bowed with extravagant grace. "Would you care to dance, Miss Redmond?"

He really was the veriest dandy, and she should be grateful for his attention, but all she wanted was to go home and take off her shoes and corset, have a cup of tea, and go to bed. She sighed and stood up. "I suppose so."

Rafael winced. "And I am thus most firmly put in my place."

"Ah, Don Rafael, I didn't mean—"

"Of course you did." He shook his head. "But never mind, I am commanded by the queen of my heart to make you dance, so dance we shall."

Laughing, she allowed him to tuck her hand through his arm and lead her into the set forming. The men bowed, the women curtseyed, partners crossed and hooked arms, and the dance began.

Don Rafael, the musician, demonstrated a keen sense of rhythm and a remarkable ability to keep less-experienced dancers from embarrassing collisions. However, there was nothing he could do about Daisy's wandering attention. When Simon's tall figure entered the ballroom, she stopped stock-still, heart beating like a kettledrum. *He has come for me.*

The other dancers stepped around her with curious looks, then, following her gaze to the doorway, moved on with indulgent smiles.

She had never in her life expected to see him dressed thus—like a prince out of some fairy tale. She had heard stories of the American General Washington's sartorial splendor: the coats imported from France, with buttons ornate but never ostentatious, boots made of fine Italian leather, and a variety of waistcoats in beautiful jewel-toned silk brocades. Yet tonight her Simon would surely have put Yankee Doodle George firmly in the shade.

Watching him, she stood shaking like a leaf in a winter wind. The Song of Songs flitted through her mind—*This is my beloved, and this is my friend.*

He went away from her, threading the crowd along the wall, until he reached the corner where her father stood in conversation with Sergeant Anderson, the Guillorys, and Niall McLeod. She watched her father look around in surprise when Simon touched him on the shoulder, saw his gaze flick up and down, taking in the beautiful evening clothes and hair neatly tied back with a dark blue ribbon.

Was Simon going to ask to court her? Now? In this room full of people?

Suddenly aware of the dancers circling awkwardly around her, she skipped to find her place in the set, blushing when Don Rafael teasingly chided her for leaving him partnerless. There wasn't time to reply, as the motion of the dance pulled her away again. She was peripherally aware of Simon and her father excusing themselves from their companions. They wound back through the crowd to the door and disappeared into the night.

The next twenty minutes were exquisite torture. Daisy laughed at Don Rafael's nonsense, tried to cheer up poor Niall, whose obvious jealousy threatened to spoil the party for everyone, and somehow kept one eye on the door. What would Papa say? When she was a little girl, he had treated Simon—when he happened to tag along with Lyse—to the good-natured pity one would accord a half-starved young alley cat. Then, when a more specific affection blossomed between Daisy and Simon, everything changed. Simon became the interloper—the thief come to steal a beloved possession—and he was tolerated with gritted teeth.

Only Lyse seemed to understand her anxiety. Her eyes were soft with concern, and once she gripped Daisy's hand and whispered, "Don't worry, it will be all right."

Daisy couldn't help glancing at the door, which remained firmly closed. "Maybe," she whispered back.

How many sleepless nights had she prayed for this time to come? How many times had she begged God to soften her father's heart, only to watch the distance grow between the two men she loved?

She didn't realize she had drifted toward the door until it opened and Simon came in alone. His eyes sought hers. His sun-bronzed skin had an ashy undertone, as if blood-leeched to deter some dreadful disease, and his mouth was set in a tight line.

Dread nearly suffocated her as she waited for him to reach her. He bowed over her hand, the heat of his lips burning through her lace mitt, his long fingers clasped loosely around her wrist. She stared at the back of his head, where the black curls were tied at the nape of his neck.

And then he rose, unsmiling. "Your papa says I may speak to you."

"Y-yes. All right." She swallowed against a dry throat. "Where . . . ?"

"There." Simon nodded toward a doorway that led to one of the small anterooms where guests could enjoy a private game of cards or otherwise entertain in small groups. He dropped her hand and walked off without looking to make sure she followed.

But she did. She would go with him anywhere, God help her.

Miraculously, the room was empty, lit by a candle someone had left burning on a spindly Louis XIV desk between the curtained windows. A velvet sofa and a couple of wing chairs sat upon a beautiful gold-and-scarlet rug in the center of the room. Daisy stopped just inside the door, waiting to see what Simon would do. His demeanor was so odd, his movements jerky and forced.

It wasn't as if they'd never found ways to be alone together. But this occasion, sanctioned by her father, conducted in this bloodless manner in a shadowy room with a noisy crowd just beyond a thin wall, set her adrift in an ocean of anxiety.

"Shut the door and come sit down." Simon dropped into one of the wing chairs, leaving her to choose the sofa or the other chair.

The sofa was closer to him. As she sat, the hem of her skirt fell across one of his boots, and she stared at it, afraid to look at him. He was going to hurt her in some way, and she didn't want to see it in his eyes.

"I can't ask you to marry me." He threw the words like stones into the silence.

She absorbed them. Do not cry. Do not.

He took a harsh breath. "But I will, when I come back. If I come back. Your papa said I might."

And then she looked up into his face. His deep-set eyes, so dark as to be nearly black, bored into hers with a banked passion that flooded her with such relief that she came close to fainting.

Then she realized what he'd said. "When you come back? Where are you going?"

"I can't tell you. And you mustn't wait for me. I'm leaving in the morning at daybreak."

"I m-mustn't wait for you? W-what do you mean?"

He looked away. "If I'm not back in a year, you are to find someone else to make you happy, because—because that would only be right."

She jumped to her feet. "Simon! What have you done?"

"I've found a way to gain your father's blessing. A way to make a fortune for us—so you can live like the English lady you are."

"No! I don't want that! Why did you not ask me what *I* want? All I need is you!" She had said it aloud, and if that made her a pathetic beggar, so be it.

His head bowed, and he clasped his hands across the nape of his neck.

"Look at me, Simon Lanier! I know you love me, and I know my father loves me, but in this case you are both a hundred miles away from wisdom." When he didn't move, she flung herself to her knees in front of him and put her arms about him. "Please, beloved, don't go away from me. I'll talk to Papa and make him see I'm determined to—to belong to you. If he won't agree, then we'll just find another place where we can live together in peace. I'd rather—"

"No!" He sat up, taking her hands and holding them still, his eyes blazing. "Don't you see, that is exactly what I cannot do? My father destroyed his relationship with his family forever by marrying beneath him, and I won't let you do that with me. You can't possibly know the misery that kind of poverty brings. It's—please, Daisy, I couldn't bear it."

Stubborn pride limned every angle of his face. She would not easily get around it. "All right, but there's got to be another way. What about your grandfather? Lyse says he has reestablished the connection with your father. He's still a wealthy man and would undoubtedly sponsor you in business. Or—has he already?" She frowned. From where she knelt before him, the polished bronze buttons of his waistcoat were in her direct line of vision. “Simon, where did you get these clothes?”

“I paid for them—I worked for them. Just like everything else I own. Nobody—*nobody*, do you hear me?—is going to give me anything I didn’t earn. Not my grandfather, not your father, not even you.”

“But that isn’t how love works! It isn’t earned, it’s given freely, expecting nothing but love in return.”

“And if you love me, you’ll understand why I have to make my own way. Daisy, this is who I am, it’s how God made me—like the color of my hair and the shape of my hands.” He let go of her to spread his big hands, palms up, fingertips brushing the ruffle on her fichu. “There’s something I have to do, to prove to myself that I deserve you. It’s—it’s already in motion anyway, and there’s no going back.”

She stared at him for a long, hopeless moment, sensing him retreating from her by the heartbeat. Finally, she bent to press a kiss in each of his callused palms. “All right then. But know this. If you’re not back in a year, I will come looking for you.”

10

Watching the anteroom door, Rafa conferred rather at random with the violinists regarding the next choice of music. As he stood pretending to listen to one of the fiddlers rhapsodize over a new tune called "Love in a Village," he watched the colors of the company shift like a series of glass windows in a cathedral.

Earlier, while dancing with Daisy, he had seen a tall young man whom he didn't recognize from the back approach Major Redmond. The dark blue coat fit smoothly over broad shoulders, rich lace fell from the piped cuffs, and the buff-colored breeches were carefully tailored. Curly, unpowdered dark hair was clubbed in a neat queue. There couldn't be many men in this backwater little town who dressed with such fashionable flair—so who was he?

When the younger man abruptly bowed to the major and turned on his heel, Rafa had nearly swallowed his tongue. *Simon Lanier?* When had he turned into this—this dandy? No wonder poor Daisy was so taken aback.

And what subject had so completely occupied Simon and the major that the two of them quit the room for nearly half an hour? When they returned and Simon closeted himself in the anteroom with Daisy for a most improper length of time, Rafa's curiosity sprouted like mushrooms after a rain. Something odd was afoot.

Suddenly the anteroom door opened, and Simon emerged alone. He pushed through the crowd and stalked outside again with nary a word to a soul.

Rafa turned to the violinist, waving a hand. "Yes, yes, señor, of course, but I must leave you now and return to the ladies, else they will think I've more interest in music than in dance—which is true, but not the impression one likes to leave with one's hostess. Yes?" He dodged a bow, then leapt from the dais and followed Lanier to the door.

There was time to speak to neither Daisy nor Lyse, but he took a quick look over his shoulder on his way out the door. Judging by the uniforms crowding the far corner of the room, Lyse was being inundated with offers of dance partners. Regretfully forfeiting the satisfaction of swooping her out from under the noses of all those redcoat rubes, Rafa slipped outside onto the gallery. The mission had to come first.

Lanier had disappeared into the darkness. Rafa hesitated, listening, anxiously searching the quiet innyard. There was no knowing whether Lanier had arrived on foot or on horseback, but supposing Major Redmond had given him some assignment, he would likely need some means of transport.

Before he could take action, a quiet voice rumbled from the shadows beside the tavern door. "You need some'n', sir?"

Zander, Burelle's houseman.

Rafa hesitated, decided not to waste time. "I meant to speak to Señor Lanier regarding transport of supplies out to my ship, but I see he has slipped away. I don't suppose he mentioned where he's off to?"

Zander's dark form materialized as he moved into the light beside the door. "No, sir. But he left on foot, headed toward the water. You might catch him, if you hurry."

"Ah. Thank you, Zander." Flipping a coin in the slave's direction, Rafa vaulted over the porch rail to the ground.

As he rounded the corner of Royal and Dauphine streets, he could see a few lights flickering along the wharf, where the piers jutted into the water. Fishermen, oystermen, and shrimpers were cleaning nets and dumping the remains of their catches into wagons. He walked the short block to Water Street, aware of every movement and sound. Lanier could have stopped in any doorway, and he knew he could pass by his quarry without knowing it.

He hesitated. Maybe he should forget the whole thing and return to the party. One more dance with Lyse—

Then out of the darkness came a growled half-curse, followed by an indistinguishable answer in a deep, Creole-accented voice. That second voice—Lyse's brother Simon. He'd met Lanier only once, and that nearly a year ago, but a musical ear for voices was perhaps his greatest gift. He continued toward the water, angling south toward the second pier.

The voices grew louder, amplified by the water but distorted by distance. Now Rafa distinguished two dark figures moving around on a midsized vessel. One man was bullish, with big shoulders hunched under a large head, the other tall and lithe, the build of a healthy young man in the prime of life.

Rafa slowed and slouched into a boneless, drunken meander perfected while watching the court cards of Madrid when he was at university. He began to whistle the first thing that came into his head, the air from "Love in a Village."

The argument onboard the boat halted.

"Who's there?" demanded Lanier.

The Bull sneered, "Just some redcoat wandering the wrong way back to the fort. Pay him no mind."

"Shut up," Lanier said. "Wait until he's gone by."

"Whatever you say."

Rafa staggered past a stack of empty kegs and lurched into them.

They fell with a rattle and boom of empty wood, rolling under Rafa's feet. With an exclamation he fell heavily and lay supine. After a moment he began to snore.

He could hear the men on the boat laughing.

"See, nothing to worry about," the Bull snickered.

The two men continued to shift some cargo across a gangplank. From his vantage point among the tumbled kegs, Rafa counted some twenty crates they moved from the pier to the hold of the boat, apparently heavy ones, judging by the grunts and swearing. Consumed with curiosity, he listened, trying to determine what exactly was being transported, and where.

When the last crate had been hauled over and disposed of, the two stood panting on the pier. Lanier gave the Bull a jingling handful of coins and said, "There's more if you can keep this quiet. I'll be back in a few months, depending on how long it takes me to disperse this." He paused, his tone darkening. "Not a word to anybody, hear me?"

"This is more than I've made in months, Chazet," the Bull growled. "No need to threaten me."

It was all Rafa could do to keep from sitting straight up. He had heard that name before—in reference to the pirate in the Gulf who had absconded with the king's gold.

Several pieces fell into place.

But a multitude of questions rose to take their place. How much did Lyse know of her brother's clandestine activities? Where had Simon been keeping the gold to this point? Where was he moving it now? And why? What did Major Redmond have to do with it, if anything?

Of course Rafa wanted it back. He *must* have it back, because the American cause depended on its delivery to purchase arms, uniforms, food, and other necessities. But perhaps there was a way to obtain it without bloodshed, maybe even deliver it to General Washington without further expense to the Spanish crown.

Think, Rafa.

He must get a message to Gálvez in New Orleans, because he was going to need help. Perhaps one of his brothers could meet him—but again, *where?*

Acting on instinct alone, he sat up with a snort and loud groan. He was still rubbing his eyes when he felt cold, hard metal press against his temple.

"Make a move and I will blow your head off, Spaniard."

He opened one eye and squinted up at Lanier—Chazet the pirate, Rafa reminded himself. Lyse's brother. The Bull stood right behind him, a second musket aimed at Rafa's midsection. "*Hola*, my dear señor," he said, grimacing at Lanier. "Someone, as you see, left a very untidy pile of barrels right in my path. Sorry if I disturbed you." He extended a hand. "Perhaps you wouldn't mind—"

"I wouldn't mind pitching you into the river," Lanier said grimly. "What are you doing here, and why are you following me?"

Rafa sighed. "I would be happy to tell you, but I confess the gun in my face is upsetting my already queasy stomach."

Lanier glanced at his companion, who shrugged, and both men stepped back. As he pushed to his feet, however, Rafa noticed that neither gun wavered.

He took the bull by the horns, so to speak, and shoved aside Lanier's musket, an expensive flintlock of Italian origin. Interesting. "I'm not following you," he said with less-than-absolute candor. "I came down here on a notion that I might find someone willing to help me move supplies out to my ship." He paused. "I believe you are in the family transport business?"

Lanier's frown deepened. "I saw you at Burelle's, dancing with Daisy—Miss Redmond. There was nothing stronger to drink there than the worst lemonade in West Florida. Cut line, Gonzales. You *were* following me, and you are neither drunk nor stupid. So tell me what game you are playing."

Rafa blinked. That emotion he saw in the Frenchman's eyes was mainly jealousy, mixed with the obvious distrust and puzzlement. Lanier was in love with the major's daughter. Which explained a lot. "I certainly did dance with the lovely Miss Redmond, and the lemonade is undoubtedly the source of my dyspepsia. Also, I rejoice that you perceive me to be an intellect, though my Latin tutor might disagree with you." He scratched his head. "Where was I? Oh, yes—I was looking for a man named Chazet, but if I attached myself to the wrong shadow, I sincerely apologize."

Lanier flinched. "Chazet is no longer here. What do you want of him?"

"He has something that belongs to me, and I should like to have it back."

Rafa had kept his voice deliberately cool and light, but the words hung between them, a palpable threat.

Lanier said coldly, "You shouldn't expect him to have retained whatever you lost."

"That is a great deal too bad." Rafa shrugged. "You must tell him—should you chance to see him when he returns—that no matter what style of brigand the English have been tolerating in the Gulf, our new governor Gálvez is determined to stop the smugglers using New Orleans as a clearinghouse for their wares."

"Is it so?" Lanier's lips twitched. "And what does he propose to do about it? Theoretically speaking, that is."

Rafa was pleased to note that the musket was now pointing at the ground, and Lanier's attitude seemed almost amused. Bull had taken to looking back and forth between the two of them, an expression of dumb confusion coloring his blunt features.

"Why—" Rafa spread his hands—"he has authorized and armed his Spanish majesty's navy with the means to halt, board, and search any vessel which approaches the waters of the city. If her captain does not possess proper documentation for all laden goods, Gálvez reserves the right to seize the ship and confiscate her cargo."

Lanier's amusement vanished. "That's grounds for war!"

"Oh, no, it is all quite within the most recent trade agreement between Madrid and London." With a subtle flick of his wrist that he was sure would have delighted Lyse, Rafa produced a knife from his sleeve and let its oiled blade gleam in the moonlight. "But, my dear señor, I beg you not to commence waving about that terrifying gun again, because I have a proposition that I think you will like, if you take but a moment to ponder its wisdom."

"A proposition?" Lanier sneered. "By all means, let's hear it."

"Why, simply this. I propose that you and I become . . . partners, shall we say, and enter the port of New Orleans together. If you come in under my aegis, there is likely to be little fuss about such details as documentation and cargo manifests."

"Now I know you are insane! What do you expect to gain from this—this—partnership?" Lanier spat the word as if it burnt his mouth. "And what makes you think I plan to sail to New Orleans?"

Rafa wanted to laugh. Sometimes, oh, his job was so much fun. "Well, as to that, you are clearly upset by Governor Gálvez's previously unsuspected backbone. And as to what I hope to gain . . . let us just say that I would like a share in whatever is in your hold."

Lyse lay awake late into the night, listening to Daisy's muffled sobs, wondering what her pestilential brother had said to provoke such despair—and touching her lips, where the imprint of Rafa's mouth still lingered like the taste of blackberries after rain.

What a wanton to have allowed such privilege without mention of one word of marriage. And after all, what did she know about him, beyond surface chatter at the social functions they had attended? That he had a mother and a beloved sister. He liked to fish and pretended not to be good at it. He was a merchant who spoke at least three languages. He had a delightful, whimsical sense of humor and sang like an angel. His clothes were beautiful and he could make a living as a dance instructor.

In short, she knew little—except that, with him, nothing was as it seemed. Like one of those beautiful jewel-toned lizards that in the summertime sunned themselves in the Redmonds' garden, Rafa would take on the color of the closest background. And then disappear without the least notice.

She would be wise to cast her lot with Niall, who could be depended upon to say what he meant and mean what he said.

Father, have mercy on me, she thought. *I am undone.*

She rolled out of bed and slid to her knees beside the bed. She'd always prayed in times of crisis. And her life had been one crisis after another. Surely there were calluses on her knees. And now Rafa had blown like a hurricane across her little island of peace here with the Redmonds, stirring up longings that could never be met. For all she knew, he had gone back to New Orleans without a word of goodbye. After he'd uttered those weak words "depend upon it" and left her, she'd seen him work his way to the musicians' dais. Then, while her back was turned, he had simply vanished.

Prayer would not come. She knelt with her forehead pressed to the counterpane, eyes squeezed shut, knees aching. Daisy was quiet now. Perhaps she had fallen asleep. Or maybe she lay awake as well, trying to form words of self-comfort.

Lyse pushed to her feet, found her slippers and robe, and padded down the hall to Daisy's room. She opened the door. "Daisy," she whispered. "Are you asleep?"

"No." The answer was hoarse, teary. "I just—can't sleep."

Lyse slipped inside the room. "Me either. Can I come in?"

"Of course." Bedclothes rustled as Daisy sat up. "What's the matter?"

Lyse felt her way to the bed and climbed onto it. "I heard you crying," she said, pulling her knees up under her chin. She could see the outline of Daisy's white bedcap and nightgown, a small ghost hunched in the canopied bed. "What did Simon do this time?"

"Nothing."

Lyse waited, but when Daisy failed to elaborate, she scooted closer. "I saw him leave with the major and come back for you. I've never seen Simon dressed like that before. Daisy? Did you refuse him?" Her voice rose with incredulity. "You've loved Simon your whole life!"

Daisy's breath began to hitch. "Of course I didn't refuse him! He wouldn't—he didn't—he said he had to do something for my father first, but he made me promise not to tell!"

"But that's crazy! Daisy, he loves you, you know he does. Whatever is holding him back is . . . surely not forever. You know how proud he is. He won't take anything, even from Grandpére. I'm sure he's still working to earn your father's favor. That's it, isn't it? Your father wouldn't let him speak to you!" It made sense. Major Redmond would of course want to make sure Daisy was well provided for.

But what about that cache of gold hidden near Simon's houseboat? Had he used that to buy the fine clothes he'd worn tonight? Had he offered it to the major as a bride gift?

Daisy shook her head. "No," she said in a forlorn voice. "Simon wouldn't even ask Papa for my hand. Or, at least . . . I don't think he did. He just said Papa gave him some sort of assignment that he had to complete . . . but I'm not to wait for him . . . past a year—" Daisy's voice splintered into a wail as she bent over and grasped the counterpane in both hands. "Oh, Lyse! What am I to do?"

Lyse cupped her hands over the back of Daisy's head and held her as she wept. "But Daisy . . . what do you mean, not to wait? Did he imply that he might not come back?"

Daisy groaned. "I don't know. I can't bear to think about it!"

Lyse couldn't bear it either. Now both Simon and Rafael were gone, leaving Daisy and her abandoned. She fought her own tears. Daisy would need her friendship more than ever. Indeed, they must bear one another up as Scripture commanded.

Because there was nothing else to do, she bowed her head over Daisy's shaking body and began to whisper a prayer for comfort.

But if God was listening, his silence was deafening.

When Lyse fell silent, Daisy turned her face. "There's . . . something else that makes this worse. I couldn't tell Simon, I certainly can't tell my father, but Lyse, you're like my sister. I trust you with my life. Will you promise to keep my secret?"

"Yes, of course."

Daisy sat up. "Light the candle. Then look under the bed."

Lyse realized her hands were trembling as she fumbled for the flint and lit the bedside candle. She had no notion what could be so troubling for the virtuous Daisy. At first she'd had the horrifying thought that her friend might be with child. Once she had the candle casting its flickering pool of light, she slid to the rag rug beside the bed and crouched to peer underneath.

Books? Slowly she reached for a stack of three leatherbound volumes that had been shoved far back, toward the middle of the bed. When they were in her hands, she scanned the covers, setting them aside one by one. John Locke's *Two Treatises of Government*, Adam Smith's *An Inquiry into the Nature and Causes of the Wealth of Nations*, Thomas Paine's *Common Sense*.

She looked up to find Daisy peering over the bed, watching her with reddened, tear-drenched blue eyes.

She sat back on her heels, pushing the books away hard. "Daisy? What does this mean?"

Daisy swallowed. "It means I'm a traitor."

11

Natchez
Late January 1778

During the last four months, the world had folded in upon itself. The days passed in a colorless wash of hopelessness until Scarlet found herself wishing for one of Madame's backhanded slaps just to break the monotony. Today was Sunday, but her new master did not believe in educating or baptizing slaves. So this morning, like every morning, she got up when the overseer rousted everybody out of the quarters with a snap of his whip against the side of the building. Rubbing her belly, grateful to be past the morning nausea that had made her first months in Natchez miserable, she followed the other slaves out to the privy. That chore accomplished, they all trooped over to the overseer's back porch, where they were served a minimal breakfast of bacon fat and cold cornbread.

Shivering in the wind that blew in from the bluffs, she huddled next to the steps, ignoring the old woman's persistent attempts to draw her into conversation. They called her Blackberry, and she spoke decent English, but at the least provocation she would launch into long, involved, and improbable stories of the African village she had been taken from as a child—which, judging by the depth and number of wrinkles upon her wizened face and her utter lack of teeth, must have been some fifty or sixty years ago.

Blackberry knew about the baby, of course, had guessed even before Scarlet's belly began to swell. It was hard to ignore the old woman's little kindnesses, but she was determined not to develop a fondness for anyone. Separation from Cain had been more painful than any whiplash, more prolonged and gnawing than the deepest physical hunger.

Even a glancing thought of her baby's father brought weak tears to her eyes, and she angrily dashed them away, snarling at Blackberry as if she had caused them—which, in a way, she had.

Instead of hitting back, Blackberry narrowed her little raisin-colored eyes and pulled Scarlet's resisting body close. "Little girl, little girl," the old one crooned. "You think you abandoned? You think the Master don't care? Well, you wrong, 'cause he got you right here in my arms."

"The master don't even know me," Scarlet spat.

Blackberry's raspy chuckle rumbled under Scarlet's ear. "The Master that made you and your little one does."

"Oh. You mean God," Scarlet said flatly. "Well, he's got a funny way of showing affection. I served him my whole life and I'm no more free today than I ever been. And now I got a baby to bring into this disaster. And look at you! Reckon you gonna die a slave?"

"I be God's bondslave, true enough, child. But that makes me free to love, can't nobody take that away. You a servant to hatred, and that's the bitterest slavery of all."

"See, this is why I don't talk to you, 'cause you always turn my words inside out."

Blackberry stroked Scarlet's lice-infested head. "Somebody need to turn you inside out. All that poison gon' make you sick and die."

Scarlet turned her face into the bony ridge of the older woman's shoulder. "Sometimes I think that'd be a good thing."

"Now, now. You don't want to cut off this little one's chances before he ever gets started. What if you got the future king of America riding in your womb?"

Scarlet felt a laugh bubble from her throat, but it quickly turned to a wrenching sob. "Old woman, you just crazy."

"That what they said about Jesus too."

"Yeah, and look what happened to him."

"He's seated at the right hand of the Father."

Scarlet sat quiet for a minute. Clearly arguing was getting her nowhere. Besides, it was nice to be held in somebody's arms. *Cain* . . . She sat up. "Overseer's walking back this way. We better get up."

"You didn't eat nothing, honey. You need to feed that babe."

"I don't feel like it. You eat my biscuit."

Blackberry just looked at her until Scarlet took a bite of the biscuit.

"You just like my maman used to be."

Blackberry nodded. "That's what mamas for. You'll see."

Yes, she would see, whether she wanted to or not. This baby was coming, right in the heat of the summer, probably drop in the middle of a cotton field.

Future king of America. Smiling, she got to her feet and helped Blackberry to her feet. Nothing had changed, but maybe she should quit being so standoffish. Having somebody to talk to had somehow made the misery go away. Maybe God was looking out for her after all.

~

SPRING HILL
EARLY MARCH 1778

"How much further, Lyse? I'm so excited!"

Smiling, Lyse looked down at Genny dancing along beside her like a small fairy maid. "Almost there, *cher*." Luc-Antoine and

Denis had jumped the creek and run on ahead through the woods, and she could hear them shouting as the dogs barked in greeting.

Mardi Gras season of 1778 had come to Mobile. The first signs of azalea bushes flirted their lacy pink skirts along the old shell road which ran westward from the juncture of the three rivers that dumped into the bay. Through the trees Lyse could just see the red-tiled roof of Grandpére's ancient two-story cottage.

It was a momentous occasion. Papa had finally relented and allowed her to bring the children to Grandpére's annual Mardi Gras party. She and Simon used to come when Grandmére was still alive, but when she died soon after Uncle Guillaume was executed, the relationship between Papa and Grandpére had deteriorated beyond repair. It was too bad there wasn't money for new clothes and shoes, but she had helped the children paint masks of papier-mâché they'd made at school, added a few shells and feathers picked up from the beach, and twisted up Genny's hair and her own in fantastical braids, with knots of ribbon for a festive touch. Justine and baby Rémy would be along later with Papa.

At least, Lyse hoped they would come. One never knew with Papa.

Genny tugged on her hand. "Will there be a king's cake? I hope I find the baby."

Grandmére used to make the braided cinnamon sweetbread in the French tradition, twisted into a crown-shaped oval and glazed with sugar. A gilded fava bean tucked in from the bottom represented the baby Jesus, for whom the Wise Men had searched so diligently. Good luck was said to follow the child who found the trinket in his or her slice of cake. With Grandmére gone now, there might not be a king's cake.

She shook her head. "I don't know, Genny. Maybe we can make one."

Genny twirled her mask on its bamboo stick. "That would be fun. I've missed you, Lysette."

And Lyse had missed her family to a painful degree. Since the night Rafa had come and gone so abruptly, and Simon had inexplicably deserted Daisy, life had taken on a whitewashed dullness that even her responsibilities at the grammar school failed to color.

She swept her little sister into a bear hug. "Did you miss getting squished like a jellyfish?"

"Yes! But don't mess up my hair!" Genny giggled, squirming. When Lyse let her go, laughing, Genny ran ahead, ribbon-festooned pigtails bouncing. "Don't worry, I won't get lost!"

Lyse followed at a pace more suitable for a young lady, stepping carefully over rain puddles left from yesterday's storm. There was still a nip in the air, a brisk wind whipping through the trees, and she was glad she'd chosen her good woolen dress and the matching shawl Daisy had helped her knit.

The thought of her friend brought on a fresh wave of worry. The two of them had become even closer since the night she'd discovered Daisy's secret. Lyse had at first struggled to understand how the gentle, biddable daughter of a British officer had come to sympathize with the American rebels. She remembered the night she and Daisy had first entertained Rafael for dinner, and Daisy's indignation when he'd told them the colonies had dared to declare their independence from the Crown.

Long conversations, often late into the night, revealed that Daisy's convictions were neither easily arrived at nor lightly held. She had first encountered the Locke treatise, oddly enough, while arguing with Simon about the intellectual capacity of women. After daring her to read Locke's work, which someone had given him, Simon was stunned to discover that not only could she comprehend it, but she could discuss it with him in concise and cogent terms.

And ultimately she had been persuaded that all men were endowed by the Creator with certain inalienable rights. Locke's arguments concerning liberty and moral philosophy had pierced her, based as they were upon truths in Scripture.

Once the door was opened, there was no shutting it again.

Daisy had listened as the men who visited her father debated—or, rather, sneered at—colonials foolish enough to propose government without a monarch. James Madison, Thomas Jefferson, Benjamin Franklin, and the like, madmen all. On a later trip, Colonel Durnford had left behind a copy of the Thomas Paine papers, scornfully bidding Daisy consign them to the ash heap where they belonged. Instead, she had hidden them in her room, devoured the treacherous, compelling words, absorbed their implications.

With no inbred loyalty to any king, particularly his British majesty George III, Lyse too found herself hungry to learn. Because Daisy was a gifted teacher, had always been Lyse's mentor, they eagerly discussed the exciting possibilities of living in freedom, with no person of any more value than another, regardless of birth or income.

One day Lyse hesitantly asked what Simon thought about Daisy's political conversion.

"I haven't admitted to him that I support the colonists' cause. He would be horrified at the thought of me flouting my father's authority. He understands the consequences of treason." Compassion filled Daisy's gentle features. "Your uncle Guillaume . . ."

That reminder was enough to give Lyse pause.

And all these months later, nothing much had changed. When Daisy questioned her father as to Simon's whereabouts, the major impatiently said he had no idea and advised her not to concern herself with what she couldn't change.

The major himself was, in fact, busier than ever. After news of the British defeat at Saratoga reached the West Florida command in Pensacola, Major Redmond received orders to initiate refurbishment of Fort Charlotte. With fewer than three hundred regular soldiers, plus a handful of Loyalist refugees, to do the work, he had neither time nor inclination to worry about his daughter's disappointed romance or her political leanings.

When by the first of March no word had come from Rafael or Simon, both girls had descended into a state of drifting numbly from one day to the next. With school suspended for the Mardi Gras holiday, Lyse had invited Daisy to the party, but she had elected to stay at home and take care of some spring cleaning. So Lyse made the trip over to Bay Minette to collect the children by herself—and here they were.

She stepped out of the shelter of the trees into her grandfather's flower-decked yard, where Genny and the two boys were romping with Grandpére's hounds, Castor and Pollux. She paused for a moment to enjoy the picture.

The cottage itself, which Grandpére and his brother Thomas had come into possession of when their father moved to Biloxi with the Sieur de Bienville in 1720, was like a grand old lady dressed for a tea party. Rising gracefully in the midst of a copse of live oak, magnolia, and dogwood beside a spring-fed creek, it had been constructed of local timber, its chinks filled in with the ubiquitous wattle-and-daub mud cement, and roofed with pine shakes. But possessing a flair for architecture, Grandpére had borrowed the Spanish preference for adobe and tile, adding to the original structure until it was now hardly recognizable as his father's Creole cottage. Eventually, wealthy British landowners had built summer homes around the property, giving the surrounding area the cachet of exclusivity. Here in this little clearing, though, was the Lanier family heritage. Safety and home.

With a sigh of contentment, Lyse crossed the yard to the porch, where her grandfather sat on a bench shucking oysters. She bent and kissed his cheek, then sat down on the steps. "Grandpére, what can I do to help you? Justine is bringing rice and bread pudding."

Grandpére tipped his head to the big iron cauldron suspended over a fire pit out in the middle of the yard. "Everything's good, *cher*. Let's just throw these last few oysters in the gumbo and wait for company to come." He winked at her. "Might not be as tasty as your Grandmére's was, but nobody'll go away hungry."

"I'm so glad we could come." She sighed and propped her chin in her hands, elbows on knees. "Something tells me it might be the last time for a while."

"You're mighty young to be showing signs of the second sight. What makes you say that?"

"Well . . . Simon's gone, nobody knows when or if he'll be back. Madame Dussouy almost refused to let Luc-Antoine off for the day. And me—if I marry Niall, there's no telling where we'll be next year. He could get sent anywhere."

Grandpére gave her his patented inscrutable look. "Is he still courting? I notice you didn't bring him with you."

"He—he's on duty later tonight. And he doesn't celebrate Mardi Gras like we do. He thinks it's heathen."

"Hmph." Grandpére clearly had thoughts about Niall's thoughts, which he chose not to express. "Nobody wants a party-spoiler around anyway. Do you love the boy, *cher*?"

Lyse looked away. Not an easy question to answer. "I've always liked Niall, Grandpére. He'd make a good husband."

"For someone else maybe. Not for you."

"Grandpére!" Lyse rarely heard her grandfather, the master of oblique references, speak so bluntly about anything. She stared at him. "Why do you say that?"

"If you loved him enough to marry him, you'd have accepted him a long time ago. You're dragging your feet, and I think you know why."

Lyse felt her face flame. "I am not! Dragging my feet, I mean. I'm just . . . taking my time because—because, well, because Daisy needs me at the school."

"If you say so." Grandpére shucked another oyster and popped it into his mouth whole.

There was a long moment of silence, until Lyse finally blurted, "Why do *you* think I'm dragging my feet, as you put it?"

But she knew the answer, and she ought to be ashamed that she couldn't get a dandified Spanish trader out of her dreams and daydreams. Even now she could close her eyes and feel his hands, warm and callused, cupped against her cheeks. The familiar sensation of a bird taking flight fluttered beneath her rib cage.

At Grandpére's soft chuckle, she bent double, hands over her face. "Oh! I wish he would just go away!"

"Niall? So do I."

"That's not what I mean, Grandpére, and you know it," she mumbled.

"And it would not be fair to wed Niall if your heart is given to someone else."

She looked up at her grandfather, aggrieved. "But the *someone else* hasn't spoken for me, and I'll likely never even see him again! I can't wait for him forever! Besides, my father married for love and made *everybody* miserable, even you!"

Setting aside his bowl and knife, Grandpére leaned down and took her hands. "Listen to me," he said gently. "I was a fool, and I was wrong about that. Your mother and father had a difficult time, but they were happy together. Can you imagine Antoine married to Isabelle Dussouy? Pah! What a stupidity *that* would have been!"

"But Grandpére—"

"I say *listen*. I was wrong, and I have been trying for fifteen years to crawl out of the ditch I created between my son and myself. What I want for you is the joy I had with your grandmother. We were cousins and friends, yes, but we had a union of mind and spirit that the Bible calls holy. And that, my child, is worth waiting forever for."

Lyse found herself without an answer. When she was still a little girl, her grandmother had told her something very similar. To hear it, unsolicited, from Grandpére seemed more than a coincidence.

She scooted close and laid her head upon his knee. "But what if he doesn't want me?"

"How could he not, precious girl?" The strong, gnarled hand caressed her hair. "Wait and see what God will do."

There was an odd note in his voice. "Grandpére," she said, looking up, "clearly you know something I don't. What happened that day Rafa came with you to Bay Minette?"

He hesitated. "Let me just say that young Don Rafael is a herald of changes coming to the world that my brother and I could never have foreseen when we were small boys in the Mobile Indian village. My mother married a Frenchman, and they divided Louisiana between the British and the Spanish—so who can predict the victors of this present tussle?" He tipped her chin. "There may come a time when you and the children will have to flee the city. Your Rafael will come for you, and you must go with him."

Fear crawled along her spine. "Grandpére! What do you mean?"

"The less you know, the safer you will be." His lips pressed together in a stubborn line, then he released her chin with a little push. "Our guests will be here within the hour. I've put out goods for the king's cake in the kitchen, along with your grandmére's receipt. Maybe you feel brave enough to put it together for me?"

"Yes, of course, but—"

"No more questions. Tomorrow brings the time for fasting and regret. Today we revel in God's goodness." He smiled. "And we need a cake!"

~

Fort Charlotte, Mobile

Daisy smiled up at the new adjutant on duty in the guardhouse at the wooden gates of the fort. "Would you please tell my father I'm here and have someone escort me to him? I've brought him something to eat." She showed him the covered basket on her arm as proof of her intentions.

Gone were the days when she and Lyse could sashay in without prior permission. She had not seen her father for more than half an hour at a time in the past week. Colonel Durnford had come over from Pensacola to stay, this time without his family, and the two men had been closeted in Papa's office at the fort for hours on end.

Indeed Daisy could hardly reconcile herself as the naive young girl who—less than two years ago—had been horrified at the thought of Englishmen shooting at Englishmen in rebellion against the king. She loved her father and certainly wished him no harm. But she was the daughter of a soldier. War had already come, and men of strong principles fought on both sides. The hard, cold truth was that George III had sent armed regulars to fire upon his own people, hardworking men who stood in protest of the fruit of their labor being wrested from them at the point of a bayonet.

Part of her indignation came from awareness that Papa, and men like him—including Simon—thought her too weak and too silly to understand the ramifications of the conflict. She was neither, and if that made her a rebel, then so be it.

Still, her father had to eat, and she was, if nothing else, a dutiful daughter.

She shifted the heavy basket to the other arm, impatiently looking around for anything interesting to pass the time while Ensign Whoever-He-Might-Be returned for her. There seemed to be significant improvements in the condition of the shoddy little fort since the last time she had occasion to enter. Some of the rotten wood of the fences had been replaced with new planking, and the crumbling mud wattle which stuck the bricks together had been newly cemented in critical places. Even the stone that formed the bastions had been newly shored up with a mixture of clay and dirt.

Frowning, she walked toward the east bastion, where a new cannon sat upon a wooden platform atop the earthworks. A couple of soldiers in ragged uniforms were cleaning and reloading the huge weapon. Eighty-pounder? What on earth? She knew that in January Papa had been ordered to begin refurbishing the fort, when news of the British loss at Saratoga reached the West Florida command in Pensacola. Had things gotten to such a point that, even in the relatively unimportant little port of Mobile, there was danger of an attack?

Now that she thought about it, she had noticed Indians from the surrounding villages pouring into the city, camping under their tents at the outskirts like animals seeking shelter from an approaching storm. She had thought they were coming in search of food, as they sometimes did when the harshness of winter struck. But this winter had been unusually mild, and yet there seemed to be thrice the normal numbers of savage children peeking into the schoolhouse windows and giggling at the sight of the white-skinned boys and girls stuck indoors in the middle of the day.

With a pang she thought of Simon, somewhere, possibly in danger from enemy guns. *Please, God, keep him safe and bring him home to me.*

"Miss Redmond? What are you doing?"

The deep voice behind her made her jump. She turned to find Papa's administrative assistant, Corporal Tully, mustache bristling, watching her with his arms folded across his chest.

"Oh! You startled me!" She smiled to cover an odd feeling of guilt that heated her cheeks. "Can my papa see me now?"

Tully stared at her for another moment, then nodded. "Yes. Come with me." He wheeled and stalked toward officers' quarters.

Odder and odder. She clutched the basket to her stomach, skipping to keep pace with his long military stride. Tully looked suddenly older, his usually ramrod-straight back bent like a pine tree in a strong wind. His reddish brows came together above his nose in a permanent scowl.

"Corporal Tully, are you all right? You seem . . . worried."

He gave her a sidelong look, a ghost of his dry smile appearing. "I work for your papa. Don't I always look worried?"

She smiled. "I suppose so, now that you mention it. But everyone seems more sober than usual, and isn't that—wasn't that a new cannon?"

Now he definitely looked unhappy. "You've always been an observant little thing. More than your da gives you credit for."

And he hadn't exactly answered her question. "Why are so many Indians coming into the city? I've noticed them in the market, more every time I go. Is there some news about the war?"

Tully chewed the end of his mustache. "Now, miss, you know I don't talk out of turn. You'll have to ask your da."

"Well, all right, I will. I'm sure it's nothing."

Tully grunted.

A moment later they reached officers' quarters, where the corporal rapped upon the door with his knuckles, then opened it without waiting for an answer. "Here she is, sir." He nodded at Daisy, then disappeared.

Daisy found her father standing behind a table, poring over a map with Colonel Durnford. Both men had looked up at her entrance, expressions stern.

Papa glanced at the basket. "You could have left that with Tully," he said on a note of admonishment. Then he saw her expression. "What's the matter?"

She didn't like speaking this way in front of another officer, but there was no help for it. She set the food on Papa's desk and busied herself with emptying it and arranging the contents in a tempting display. "I've been worried about you, Papa. You're eating little and hardly sleeping." Her hands stilled, clutched around a cloth-wrapped cheese. "Is—is there anything you can tell me about the progress of the war?" She looked up and caught the colonel's eye. "Forgive me, Colonel Durnford. I know I shouldn't—"

But the colonel stopped her with a raised hand. "Never mind, my dear. You're right to be concerned. I had to leave my own family in considerable distress." Exchanging glances with Papa, he sighed. "The news is official anyway, and word will quickly spread. France has declared war and allied herself with the thirteen rebel colonies. This makes our ports here and at Pensacola critical—which is why your papa and I are working hard to keep you and the other ladies and children safe."

She caught her breath. "Papa—!"

"Now, now, don't worry overmuch," Papa said. "As you can see, the situation is well under control. Our men are preparing for all eventualities. However, the time has come for you and me to make the move into officers' quarters here in the fort. I need you to begin packing your belongings—only the most necessary items, of course—and be ready by tomorrow morning. I will send around a cart."

Daisy stared at him openmouthed. "Papa, I cannot—What about Lyse?"

Papa looked uncomfortable. "There isn't room for her here," he said gruffly. "I know she has been as a sister to you, but none of her family have taken the oath of loyalty to the king. They must be treated with extreme caution, and I warn you above all not to confide in her further." His voice hardened. "I'm afraid that from now on the connection must be completely severed."

"But the school—"

"You may continue to teach any of the children who reside inside the walls of the fort."

Daisy felt as if her limbs might no longer hold her up. She dropped the cheese and leaned heavily against the desk.

No more friendship with Lyse? How could she bear it on top of losing Simon?

And where was Lyse to go now? She could hardly stay in the Redmonds' house alone. She could go back to her father's crowded little place on Bay Minette, but that would mean giving up teaching the town children. Lyse would be crushed.

And perhaps most critical of all, how was Daisy to deal with her growing restlessness in the face of her duty to her father? Holding her tongue about her libertarian convictions might become an impossible task. If that happened, would her father reject her? Expel her from the fort? Arrest her?

Dear God, what was she to do?

12

New Orleans
Mid-March 1778

In the five months since Rafa had returned to New Orleans with Simon Lanier, the city had become even more a hive of intrigue. He meandered along the muddy brick streets of the Vieux Carré, whistling a ditty he'd heard an Acadian flutist playing on a corner just that morning. Perhaps he would sit down and dash off some words to the tune, after he completed this evening's errand for Pollock. A love song, forsooth. Lyse would like a song in her honor.

That is, if the piratical elder brother could be persuaded not to part Rafa's head from his body in the interim.

The short voyage from Mobile to New Orleans had been completed with a minimum of fuss, considering Lanier's volatile nature. Rafa had used the time to get to know the fisherman-pirate and found him, naturally, not so easy to charm as Lyse. Simon was intelligent, fiercely independent, suspicious of everyone except his closest vanguard. That he had agreed to the temporary alliance with Rafa spoke to his desperation regarding that shipment of gold.

Rafa's gold.

But repining was a waste of energy. Half a shipment was better than none. And if Lanier could be turned for the cause, all the better.

But first, this meeting with the American agent, Captain James Willing. The Natchez storeowner had defected to the American cause early in the war and acted as a node in the secret supply chain to Pittsburgh and Philadelphia. When British officers in Natchez discovered his perfidy and booted him out of the city, he'd returned to his native Pennsylvania and joined the rebels with the rank of captain. Subsequently, because of his familiarity with the southern end of the Mississippi, Willing was given leave to raid British settlements southward along the river, forcing their Loyalist citizens to take oaths of neutrality or be taken prisoner.

Rafa had yet to become acquainted with Willing, but Pollock seemed to consider him an asset to the cause. Word had circulated that the British command in Pensacola were outraged that Gálvez had not only consented to harbor Willing in New Orleans, but allowed him to auction off the property of British citizens in front of their very eyes. Pollock, ever practical, had worked out a deal to maintain half the profits as a way of recouping some of what was owed him by the Continental Congress—funds which, he more and more strongly suspected, would never be repaid.

With a mental shrug, Rafa swung round the corner of the Rue Baronne. The noise from the Saturday morning market reached ear-splitting levels, a mélange of the squawking, bleating, and lowing of animals, human shouts and laughter, and the general blaring dissonance of commerce. The accompanying smells he supposed he'd never get used to, but they were all part of life in New Orleans. The general atmosphere here was always lively, but customers trying to complete their Saturday purchases before sales were halted for the holy day jammed in front of the stalls like packs of jackals around a carcass.

He pushed and shoved his way through increasingly dense

crowds until he reached the slave auction. It was a distasteful and depressing location that he generally avoided, but Willing had insisted upon meeting here so that he could oversee the dispensation of the last of the contraband taken in his river raids. Rafa took up a spot on the gallery of a drinking establishment across from the Exchange which was slightly elevated above its neighbors, and leaned upon the rail to search for Willing in the crowd.

No one around him paid him the least attention. He'd dressed for anonymity in a plain brown coat and waistcoat, with buff-colored breeches tucked into the tops of his oldest boots. His tricorn shaded the upper part of his face, and he kept his mouth turned down in not entirely feigned disgust. The stench of body odor and animal waste was more noisome than usual.

Resisting the urge to hold his nose, he turned his reluctant gaze to the auction block, where an auctioneer in an oversized coat stood arguing with an obviously British gentleman distinguished by his enormous height and missing left arm. Though he couldn't hear the words, Rafa could imagine the man's distress that his belongings were about to come under the hammer.

"Good to see these Royalists finding out what it feels like to have one's belongings stripped away without notice, ain't it?"

Rafa turned to find a small-statured man, maybe a few years older than himself, leaning upon the gallery rail and watching the auction scene with all apparent satisfaction. Rafa hazarded a guess. "Willing?"

"At your service." Willing reached into his pocket for a cigar, offered it to Rafa first, then, when Rafa refused, stuck it into his own narrow mouth. "I take it you've heard of me," he said as he lit the cigar.

"Pollock said I was to meet you here." The Irishman had actually said little about the American captain, a sure sign of his distaste. Now he saw why. "He says you have a requisition for the supplies needed."

"Yes. The transfer needs to be completed quickly. I've important things to take care of in the city today and need to be on my way north tomorrow."

Willing's arrogance was absurd, considering the debt the Americans owed to Spain already, but Pollock wouldn't thank him for being rude to the agent.

"Of course. Where shall I . . ." He stopped as a line of slaves emerged from the holding pen, herded by a handler toward the platform where they would be auctioned off. As they filed up onto a set of shallow stairs, Rafa strained to see the third woman in the line. Her face was now obscured by the gathering crowd, but he could have sworn she looked familiar.

"What's the matter?" Willing stood on his toes, trying to see what had caught Rafa's attention.

Rafa shook his head. His longing for Lyse had him seeing her image in every beautiful octoroon who passed. "Nothing. It was just—" The crowd had shifted again, giving him a clear view of the young woman's face. "Willing, I'll be back. Don't go away." Rafa vaulted the gallery rail and ran toward the Exchange.

He shoved his way past three vegetable stalls and a hatmaker's booth and came out in front of the Exchange, an enormous four-foot-high platform constructed of patched timbers. By now the crowd had become even more dense as word got around that the slave auction was about to begin. Rafa shouldered through a surprising number of women mixed with the men, heading directly toward the holding pen, until he finally stumbled into the rope holding back the crowd. He proceeded to jump it.

Someone grabbed his arm. "Here now, you can't go that way!"

Angrily he snatched away from the guard. Scarlet had turned at the commotion—all the slaves had—and her mouth was open in shock. She had recognized him.

"Scarlet!" He struggled to get to her. "How did you get here?"

"Didn't you hear me? You can't go past this rope. Time to examine the merchandise is over. If you wanted to see her, you shoulda come early this morning."

Snarling in frustration, Rafa turned to the man, a burly Englishman with a two-day beard mostly covering a dark, pock-marked face. "I don't need to see her. I know this woman. She's—she's a relative, of sorts. This is a mistake!"

The guard gave him an evil smile. "Know her, do you? I just bet you do. But I got her papers, and she's for sale—so if you want her, get in line and bid for her just like everybody else. Now move!" With a shove he sent Rafa reeling back against the rope.

Rafa scrambled to keep from falling on his rear, as infuriated as he had ever been in his life—mainly with himself. How could he be so stupid as to lurch into action without a plan? Now he had drawn attention to himself—a disaster in itself—and probably ruined any chance he'd had of getting Scarlet released.

Think, think, think. What was he to do?

Slowly he straightened, drawing on every drill he'd ever endured in military school, every evening spent attending his mother's endless receptions for dignitaries. He allowed his face to freeze over. "My dear fellow," he said coldly, "you seem to have misunderstood my intent. I shan't *bid* for this woman, because she belongs to the governor, and she has gotten into this lot by mistake."

"The governor?" The Englishman roared with laughter, but when Rafa continued to stare at him stone-faced, his amusement faded into uncertain bluster. "The governor, you say? I suppose you can prove that?"

"As it happens, I can." Rafa pointed across the esplanade to the tavern, where James Willing still stood, scratching his head. "You know that gentleman, I hope?"

"That's—that's Mr. Willing, the fellow what brung in all this to be sold."

"Yes. And Mr. Willing sent me to make sure this woman is

pulled from the lot and sent to General Gálvez as his wife's personal servant."

"I can't do that! The auction has already started!"

Rafa resisted the urge to look over his shoulder at the platform, where the auctioneer was rattling off bids for the first slave in line, a tall, well-built young Negro male. He would undoubtedly fetch somewhere near twelve hundred pounds, and the bidding would be lively.

He flicked a glance at Scarlet, just to make sure it was her. Because if he had made a mistake, this was going to be one fine mess.

The girl's thick, curly hair was a wild mess, her skin was dull from malnutrition, and there was a distinct bulge at her abdomen under the neat but ugly dress they had put on her. But it was Scarlet all right. The distinctive tip-tilted brows, the pointed chin and lush mouth—so much like her cousin that he wanted to howl with fury that she had been mistreated so.

He thought of Lyse's mother and Scarlet's mother, probably standing side by side, right here, all those years ago, one to be ransomed by a lover and one to be enslaved by a vindictive shrew for life.

He couldn't rescue all these people right now, but God help him to take this one to safety.

Giving Scarlet a warning look, Rafa spread his hands and played his trump card. "Mr. Willing will be unhappy if his desire to please the governor is frustrated in this—though I do see your dilemma. Perhaps the decision will become a bit more palatable if I . . . make it worth your trouble." He reached inside his coat for the purse he carried for just such emergencies and opened its drawstring. The sweet rattle of golden coins sounded as he dropped a few, well beyond the usual price of a young female slave, into the handler's palm. "There will be twice this, if you'll meet me at the Pelican this evening." He nodded at the tavern where Willing still waited. "I'll put in a good word for you with my captain. He says he plans to make another raid up the river soon."

All three of those statements were individually true, even if the sum of them was not.

The handler jingled the coins in cupped hands. He glanced at Scarlet, who stood stoic, eyes on the ground, hands clasped in front of that rounded stomach. He dared another look at Willing, then seemed to make up his mind. With a muffled curse, he stuffed the coins into his waistcoat pocket, pulled a knife from his belt, and swiftly bent to cut the rope around Scarlet's ankles.

Rising, he pushed her, stumbling, toward Rafa. "Take her and hurry, before I change my mind. Tell Mr. Willing he owes me a favor."

"I think it's the other way round." But Rafa took Scarlet by the arm and led her away as quickly as possible through the milling crowd. There was very little time. James Willing was waiting for him to return, and Rafa was going to need some explanation for this display of lunacy. When one was forced to lie, one had best stick as closely as possible to the truth.

When he and Scarlet were at a safe distance from the Exchange, but still well away from the tavern, he slowed, sliding his hand to her wrist. "Scarlet, tell me how you came here."

When her eyes met his, he was surprised to see tears forming. "I prayed for someone to come," she said. "I didn't know it would be you."

He shrugged. "Why not me?"

"It's for Lyse, isn't it? You love her."

"I—Never mind that. Did Willing really bring you here?"

"The little man on the big boat? I don't know his name. But he rolled into Natchez like a cannonball. Took all us slaves and anything else valuable to sell here, burned everything else in sight. Made the white masters prisoners so their families would promise loyalty to the—the other British—" She looked at him, eyes suddenly ablaze with hatred. "They're free. Why do they fight each other?"

Rafa started moving again. "It's complicated. At any rate, Willing will not be particularly happy to find out that I have bought you with his name." He glanced at her. "So, stay quiet and follow my lead in the conversation to come. Understood?"

~

MOBILE
APRIL 27, 1778

Business had lately picked up at Burelle's, which meant that Lyse spent a lot of time in the kitchen with Joony, learning her magical culinary arts. In companionable fashion the two of them prepared to help Zander serve the evening meal to the tavern's guests. The kitchen smelled of seafood and spices and the mouthwatering odor of rich roux bubbling in the gumbo in the cast-iron kettle over the fire. The rattle of crockery and chink of silver plate provided a rhythmic accompaniment to which Lyse's thoughts hummed.

Life had been quiet for the last month or so since Daisy moved into the fort with her father—too quiet, like the hours before an April storm, clouds looming, full and ready to explode with noise and wind and flood. It had been hard to let her friend go, and Daisy had probably been the more grief-stricken of the two, but there was no help for it. A newly immigrated British family had moved into the Redmonds' house, and Lyse suddenly found herself without a place to live. She might have moved to her father's or grandfather's house, but she wouldn't abandon the children of the primary school. With Daisy gone, Lyse was the only teacher they had.

When Major Redmond suggested she apply to the Burelles for lodging, she'd reluctantly agreed. Her tiny salary from the school gave her little enough to live on. But Brigitte seemed thrilled to have another woman to help Joony with chores in the kitchen, and they'd agreed that Lyse could work off her board and lodging in the evenings and on weekends. Grateful, she'd settled into a little attic room above the tavern, where she kept her few dresses in a tiny cupboard that left barely enough room to squeeze into the bed at night.

When she did lie down to rest, her body was so tired and her brain so overloaded that she often lay awake into the wee hours, thinking, praying, wondering, wishing. Brigitte Guillory, Burelle's daughter, was a jabber-jaws, and could be good company, but as a married woman, her first responsibility was to her husband. Lyse missed Daisy's steady companionship, her ready laughter, her ability to balance Lyse's own more mercurial temperament. On their last day together as they packed for the move, they had found a few moments for Daisy to put in Lyse's hands the stack of books from under her bed.

"Keep these for me," Daisy had said, her blue eyes full of distress. "If my father found them . . ."

"I will," Lyse said quickly. "And I'll read them all. I want to understand—"

"You *will* understand, I know you will. But you mustn't do anything . . . rash, do you hear me? Lyse, these are dangerous times, so please—be careful of what you say and who you talk to."

Kissing her friend's pale cheek, Lyse had promised.

But the more she read and understood the guiding tenets of the American rebels' principles, the more excited she became about the possibilities of living in complete liberty to choose one's way in life, without interference from a powerful ruling class. As a practicing Christian, she believed the Bible's assumption that all men and women—slave and free, male and female, all nationalities and cultures—were equal in value under God. It was a new concept, however, to imagine that intrinsic value functioning in political and everyday practice.

As one who had grown up in the rather amorphous class of not-black, not-white, not-Indian but a strange hybrid of all three,

Lyse had always struggled not to feel inferior to people like the Dussouys—and yet, she had instinctively recoiled at the subservience of the slaves around her. Her cousin Scarlet, Joony, Zander, and the Redmonds' man Timbo—all were her friends. How could their value as human beings be less than her own, or less than Isabelle Dussouy's, for that matter?

She wondered and prayed about those things. Perhaps, she feared, she would never understand nor be able to live out the convictions that hounded her thoughts.

And circling those weighty anxieties, like a bird seeking its nest in spring, that Mardi Gras conversation with Grandpére tormented her with longings she could barely express, even to God in prayer.

Your Rafael will come for you, and you must go with him.

The words were absurd, fantastical, like the heartbeat of a fairy tale.

Until Rafa's sudden, brief appearance in her life, no one had ever come to her rescue. She had always and only fended for herself. She had her little knife, she had her own thoughts and memories and intellect, she had her faith and prayers. Those things had always been enough. But would they always be? If Grandpére was right, terrible times were coming upon them all. To whom would she turn when that happened?

And yet . . . and yet . . .

"What's that big ol' sigh for, child?" Joony ladled gumbo into one of the bowls between them on the table. "You about to blow me off my feet."

Lyse smiled. Joony, short and stout as a cast-iron kettle, wasn't likely to budge if a hurricane came through the kitchen. "It's one of those I-don't-know-what-to-do sighs. Do *you* think I should marry Niall? Everybody else does—well, except Grandpére."

"What difference does it make what anybody else thinks? You'd be the one gettin' in bed with the rooster."

"Joony!"

"Well, you asked."

Lyse laughed, her anxiety suddenly dissipated. "I guess that would make me the broody hen."

"Guess so." Joony's dark face was sly. "So if you ain't hankerin' to lay some eggs, you better get out the chicken yard."

Lyse dropped a spoon with a clatter. "You think I'm being unfair to Niall—not giving him an answer?"

"I think you're playing him like a cheap violin."

"Wait, is he a violin or a rooster?"

"Don't matter. You drivin' this wagon, so you better think about where you going."

"What do you mean?"

"Listen, a lot of what happens in life, you don't get a choice. When you got a decision puts you on one road or another, the least you do is think about the consequences in light of what you know. Has this boy ever physically hurt you?"

"No!"

"Hurt your feelings?"

"No."

"Made you angry?"

"No. That sounds like he might be the perfect husband."

Joony snorted. "I'd say just backwards of that."

"Why?"

"Well, of course you don't want a man beats you. But if you got a man never disagrees with you, one of you ain't necessary."

And perhaps there was the very thing that made Lyse balk at saying "yes" to Niall, the thing she couldn't put her finger on. She didn't *need* him, except as a convenient way to prove her loyalty to the British crown. Niall had tried to convince her that the authorities would never question the wife of a British officer. Her conscience, or maybe her pride, had argued that that would be a terrible reason to get married.

She thought of her great-grandmother Geneviève, who had married a man she'd met only a handful of times, a marriage of convenience in a time when the choices were far fewer than she herself possessed. She thought of her mother, who had had no choice at all: marry Antoine Lanier or remain in slavery. And she thought of Scarlet, who had been torn from a beloved husband.

It seemed a powerful privilege and luxury to have the right to turn her back on a man who was "good enough"—but not the one she loved.

And yet . . . and yet . . .

There was no guarantee that Rafael would return to Mobile, no matter what he'd promised.

"Come on, child, we got to get this food served before those men tear the tavern down."

Joony's voice broke into Lyse's rambling thoughts, making her suddenly aware of raised voices from the dining room. "What on earth?" She picked up the tray, heavy with soup bowls, and hurried to the kitchen door.

But Zander moved in front of her just as she stepped inside the dining room. "Hold on, Miss Lyse. There's some language in here you ought not hear."

"What?" She could hardly hear him over the shouting. "What's going on?" She stood on tiptoe to peer over his shoulder.

"Miss Lyse—go back in the kitchen," Zander shouted. "Here, give me the tray." He tried to take it from her, but she resisted.

"Who is that man?"

Zander turned to follow her gaze to the short, red-faced little man who stood on a chair in the center of the room. "That's an American," he said as if introducing a minion of the devil himself. "His name is James Willing, and he's trying to read the Declaration of Independence to our folks."

Dressed in her nightgown, Lyse sat on her little attic bed, straining by the light of a tallow candle to see the broadside printed in four columns on a piece of cheap paper. She ran her finger across the smeary headline at the top of the page:

> In Congress, July 4, 1776, a Declaration by the Representatives of the United States of America, In General Congress Assembled.

Because of these words, James Willing was in gaol.

Zander's attempts to keep Lyse out of the dining room had fallen on deaf ears. Even Joony wanted to hear what the crazy little white man had to say. So the two women had quickly served the tavern's paying guests, then stood just inside the kitchen door, straining to hear the lively debate raging inside the public room. By the time someone pried himself away from the spectacle long enough to inform Major Redmond that "one of them demmed Continentals" had had the gall to show his face in West Florida, an undisclosed number of copies of Mr. Willing's illicit document had been distributed all over town.

And Lyse herself had managed to tuck one into her pocket.

She continued reading, murmuring aloud the words Rafael had quoted on that long-ago day when she had first met him.

Words to create a riot in a little town tavern and get a man locked up. Words to make neighbors and friends take aim and kill each other. Words of war.

What did they mean for a girl like her?

She wondered if Daisy had heard of this latest brouhaha. Would she care that James Willing was in gaol, and would she try to do anything about it?

A little flutter of panic settled under her ribs. *Please, dear God, don't let Daisy do anything imprudent. Keep her safe.*

Blowing out the candle, she folded the broadside and slipped it inside her pillowcase. She heard it crackle as she lay down on her side and tucked her hand under her cheek. Perhaps she'd better try to see Daisy tomorrow.

Daisy marched toward her father's office, too angry to care what anybody thought. She didn't give a farthing about James Willing—whoever that was—and Antoine Lanier undoubtedly deserved whatever happened to him, but Papa had locked up Lyse's beloved grandfather.

The world had gone completely crazy. Two men who had been friends for years, suddenly turned into enemies by the stubborn greed of a monarch oceans away. Warm with shame and impatience, she hammered upon the door of the administration building, then stood fanning her face. Oh, certainly her father was doing his duty as he saw it. But—Charles Lanier? A criminal?

She reached up to knock again and nearly fell into the room when the door was suddenly yanked open from the inside.

Niall McLeod gaped at her. "Daisy! What's the matter?"

"Let me in. I have to talk to my father."

Niall didn't move. "You can't. He's very busy."

"I don't care. This is important."

"Is Lyse all right?"

"I haven't even seen Lyse in over a week." Daisy paused, frowning. "Why would you ask that? Have you seen her recently? Has she been sick?"

"No—at least, I don't think so. It's just—she hasn't been following her usual routine, and I can't—I can't find her to talk to her. I think she's avoiding me, so I wondered . . ." Niall's ruddy complexion reddened even more. "Never mind. If this doesn't have anything to do with Lyse, what do you need? I'll relay any message to your father."

Daisy considered barreling past Niall. But she wanted to have a rational conversation with her father, and unnecessarily angering him would be counterproductive. Besides, she needed more information. Reining in her temper, she linked her shaking fingers at her waist. "Niall, is it true that Lyse's grandfather is in the guardhouse with that American man, James Willing?"

Niall looked wildly over his shoulder, as if looking for rescue. "I think so," he mumbled.

"Why?" The question came out perhaps more abruptly than she'd intended.

Niall flinched. "Well, I don't exactly know . . ."

"Of course you know—I'm sure you saw it happen."

"We can't talk about this here. Your father—"

"My father can talk to me, if you won't. I'll just raise my voice a little—"

"No!" Niall all but pushed her out of the way in his haste to step onto the porch with her and close the door behind him. "Come here, we'll sit on the steps and I'll tell you exactly what happened, just please—don't interrupt the major right now, or I'll end up in the guardhouse myself."

"We certainly wouldn't want that to happen." But she settled beside him on the steps, tucking her skirts around her legs. There was an uncomfortable silence. "Mr. Chaz is in the gaol . . . ," she prompted.

"Yes. He is." Niall ran a finger around the inside of his collar. "That Willing fellow was holding forth in Burelle's last night—"

"Burelle's! Was Lyse there?"

"I think so. There was such a commotion, I'm not sure exactly who was there."

Daisy gritted her teeth. "All right. Keep going."

"Anyway, Willing was handing out copies of that cockeyed declaration of independence, and then he stood up on a chair and started reading it out loud. There were a few Frenchies egging him on, but a couple of Loyalist citizens staying in the inn took offense, so pretty soon a row boiled up. Guillory sent Zander running here for help. I was on duty, me and a couple other fellows, so we took off. By the time we got there, Willing was in a fistfight with one of the Loyalists, and Antoine Lanier had the other one in a headlock. We broke it up and brought Willing and Lanier here to stay overnight."

"But Mr. Chaz—"

"I'm getting to that." Niall sighed. "Early this morning, Mr. Chaz showed up at the gates, asking to see the major. The major let him in, but shortly Mr. Chaz came out, calm as you please, and told me to put him in the guardhouse with Mr. Antoine."

"What?"

"I know—that's what I said, but then the major stuck his head out the door and told me to go ahead and lock up Mr. Chaz. He slammed the door so hard I thought the building might fall down." Niall shook his head, reluctant admiration settling in his expression. "Craziest thing I ever saw. But Mr. Chaz said when things get to where a man can't express an honest opinion or have a serious debate in a public place without being beat up or locked up, then it's time for a change. He said his son had finally stood for something worthwhile and he was going to stand with him—even if it had to be in gaol."

Daisy stared at Niall with her mouth ajar for a moment—then started to laugh. "Mr. Chaz arrested *himself*?" She propped her elbows on her knees, doubled over and laughed until she cried. "Oh, my Lord, wait until I tell Lyse about this!"

13

Mobile
May 1778

With dragging steps Rafa climbed the stairs onto the front porch of the tavern. The trip from New Orleans to Mobile had taken roughly twenty-four hours. Despite the rocking of the ship, which generally sent him to sleep like a baby, he'd been unable to shut his brain down. He'd found himself reviewing Gálvez's orders and the plans he and Pollock had made for eliciting information from the British and disseminating supplies to the Americans. He'd also wasted time in useless conjecture about what James Willing had been up to since he'd absconded from New Orleans—in spite of Gálvez's explicit request to stay put. Willing was the worst sort of ally, unpredictable and dangerous as a loose cannon.

Still, he couldn't wait to tell Lyse that Scarlet was in New Orleans, safe in his mother's care. And that she was expecting a baby. In truth he didn't know if that was a good thing or a bad thing.

He paused to glance at the swing hanging at the end of the porch, and a smile crossed his lips. He had kissed her there and promised to find Scarlet—an insane claim, no doubt, but in the providence of God he had done so against all odds. Would she be glad to see him?

His step faltered. Or would she be so disgusted that he'd left without saying goodbye that she would refuse to see him? Worse yet, what if she'd promised herself to the red-haired Ensign McLeod? What if she was already wed?

Dread clamped the pit of his stomach. He had always been a resilient sort, able to recover from the disappointments of life in full assurance that he was loved by parents and siblings and God Almighty—and what else could be more important? But this young lady, his Creole princess, had wedged herself into his life in quick bursts of time, until she filled his thoughts and prayers with a yearning he couldn't dispel.

Shaking off anxiety, which, as his mother often reminded him, would add nary a hair to his head, he opened the heavy front door of the tavern. He must not waste his time borrowing trouble.

The dining room, where he had breakfasted with Lyse on that bright morning after he first met her, was oddly empty. Despite the early-summer warmth which had made him remove his coat this morning, a stale coldness sat upon the tables and chairs lined up with the precision of a military review. The windows stood open, but foot traffic on the street outside was light, and no breeze disturbed the sheer curtains.

"Señor Guillory? Madame? Is anyone here?" Halfway expecting Zander to pop up from behind the registry desk, he crossed the room and peered over it.

No one there.

Puzzled, he turned and leaned back with his elbows on the desk. He was tired and hungry and wanted something to drink. Where was everybody? Perhaps he should give up and walk down to Lafleur's down the street. Or he could wander down to the Emporium—

"M'sieur Rafael? What you be doin' here all by yo'self? Why you ain't ring the bell?"

Rafa wheeled to find the ageless Joony standing in the kitchen doorway, dusting flour off her hands with a clean rag. Her red kerchief was wrapped round her head like the turban of a sultana, and a matching apron covered her neat gray dress.

When he failed to answer in a timely fashion, she frowned. "You get a touch of the sun this morning? Lose your hearing?"

Rafa laughed and went to kiss her hand. "My hearing is perfectly fine. It's my wits have gone begging. In fact, I was just wishing some magical genie would produce a pile of beignets and some chicory coffee."

"Ain't no genies hereabouts, you young rapscallion, just me and Zander and—" She sucked in a sudden breath. "But I can find you a beignet if you'll give me a minute to look. Here." She marched over to the closest table, yanked out a chair, and flicked her rag at the seat to clear it of some invisible dust. "Sit yourself down, sir. I'll be right back."

She was gone before Rafa could reply. Amused, he lowered himself into the chair and tipped his head back against the wall. He closed his eyes. Someone had found him. Beignets were coming.

Sometime later he jerked awake to a touch on his shoulder. He blinked up into a pair of sparkling golden eyes. "Lyse!" Leaping to his feet, he kissed her cheek and almost kissed her lips. But some warning in her expression stopped him. Instead he caught her hands in his and smiled down at her. "I am so happy to see you! Joony didn't tell me you were here."

She glanced over her shoulder at the kitchen. "She's doing your beignets, wouldn't let me help. She says I overcook them." She laughed. "She's the one who taught me, and I'm actually quite good at it."

There was something . . . odd about this conversation, something he couldn't quite put his finger on. "What is the matter, *mi corazón*?"

She stepped back, pulling her hands away. "Don't call me that."

"But you are my heart. Which is why . . . *eh*, the words fail me when it most matters. All is not well with you—but I have the most excellent news, and you have almost made me forget to tell you!"

Her expression remained wary. "What is it?"

"I do not understand why you mistrust me so." More puzzled than alarmed, he took another quick look around the room. Was someone out of sight watching and listening? "Come with me." He took her hand and pulled her toward the door.

"But the beignets—"

"Later." He marched her out onto the porch, then all but pushed her onto the swing. "I have found your cousin," he said baldly, flinging himself down beside her. "Now tell me what daring exploit I must next accomplish in order to win my lady's hand and heart."

"Scarlet? You found her?" The joy in her face was blinding. "*Where?* Is she well? You didn't leave her, did you?" She took him by the arm and shook him. "Rafa, *where*?"

"Such vehemence." He tried not to grin. "I left her with my mother, God help her, and in quite blooming health. Mama will undoubtedly make her fat as a whale by the time the baby comes—"

"Baby? What baby?"

Rafa winced. His darling had quite a strong grip for such a little thing. "Please, you are creasing my shirt." When she released him, he straightened his waistcoat and smoothed his wrinkled sleeves. "Yes, there is the little one coming, sometime in the summer, if my mama is to be believed."

"A baby . . ." Lyse blinked misty eyes and smiled at Rafa so beatifically that he barely contained the urge to kiss her. "That is good, I think. But tell me how you found her."

Rafa had anticipated this question and determined to shield her from the harshest facts of her cousin's mistreatment. On the other hand, tenderhearted though she might be, Lyse wasn't the sheltered innocent his sister Sofía was. "She had been picked up as contraband," he said carefully, "in a raid of a British plantation near Natchez. I bought her at auction in New Orleans. She was tired and sad, but otherwise not too badly off."

"Then she's still . . ." Lyse opened her hands, unable to voice the word *slave*.

"Yes, to free a slave is a complicated matter, I'm afraid. Not to mention expensive." When she just stared at him, he hurried to explain. "But she is safe! While she is with my mother, no one will mistreat or abuse her. When I have time, I will deal with the legalities of setting her free."

Lyse looked away. "You must think I'm ungrateful. I'm not—it's just that I've been so worried about her, and now there's my grandfather, in prison with that dreadful James Willing—"

"What? I knew there was something wrong! Explain, please."

"It is the stupidest thing! My father must always stir up trouble. That man, that Patriot, as he calls himself, was reading and distributing their declaration of independence here in the tavern, about two weeks ago. When people naturally got upset, what must my father do but take his side! Major Redmond had no choice but to lock them up. So—so the next day, my grandfather tried to convince the major to release them, and when the major refused, Grandpére insisted on putting himself in with them!"

The hair stood up on the back of Rafa's neck. James Willing had done the Patriot cause no favor with his raids of the British plantations along the Mississippi River. The British had tightened patrols of the Mississippi River, and people who might otherwise have been persuaded to remain neutral were now so antagonized by Willing's perfidy that King George had gained some powerful Loyalists. And now it appeared Willing had stuck his neck in Redmond's noose. Brave, yes. But also, as Lyse said, very stupid.

And now it appeared at least two members of Lyse's family had openly aligned themselves with the rebels. This put Lyse in a precarious position indeed.

He pursed his lips. "And . . . has Miss Redmond intervened on your behalf? Surely she spoke up for you."

"I haven't seen Daisy for nearly two weeks. Her father made her move into the fort with him. As you can see, feelings are . . . strained here. People are taking sides, and it's hard to know who to trust."

He had known this was coming. He was under orders to keep his activities on behalf of the Patriot cause secret, at least until there was an official declaration of war from Madrid. But he had not counted on losing his heart so completely and irrevocably.

He sighed. "Yes, I know. Lyse, I have to ask—have you taken an oath of loyalty to the British crown?"

Unnamed emotions flitted across her face. "My grandfather said I could trust you." The whispered words dragged from her, as if leaving her soul-naked to whatever he might do or say in response. "I hope he's right."

Much later, Rafa would look upon that moment as his coming of age. The adventure of skulking about, pretending to be an idiot and a dandy in a game of cozening the British out of information, had been a form of grand entertainment. Suddenly the responsibility of the lives in his hands weighed upon him so that, if he'd been a bit older and perhaps less hubristic, he might have run very fast, very far away.

He did not touch Lyse, for her decision must be rational, untainted by persuasion. "Your grandfather is correct," he said carefully, "but I have to know why you are living here at the tavern, and not inside the fort with your friends. Surely the good Ensign McLeod has petitioned for your protection?"

Lyse bit her lip. "He did. But unless I marry him, he has no say in what becomes of me. I'm still my father's property—"

"Are you going to marry McLeod, Lyse?" He had to know, *now*, before he committed some irredeemable folly.

"No!" She pressed the heels of her hands into her eyes. "I told him I don't love him that way—only as a brother—but he won't listen to me."

His relief was so great, his body all but slid off the swing. But he must be careful still.

"So you are lumped with the rebels because of your father and grandfather?"

"Yes, but . . ." She dropped her hands to her lap and faced him.

The full impact of her beautiful eyes, somehow courageous and frightened all at once, filled him with pride and respect. This woman was his love. *His*. Though he couldn't claim her yet.

"I have come to understand the principles they stand for," she said slowly. "And as much as I detest this Mr. Willing's methods of pursuing his convictions, the declaration of independence he brought and read to us is a remarkable and sacred document. If I thought it would do any good, I'd go to prison with my father and my grandfather. But with my brother Simon gone—God knows where—somebody has to help take care of my stepmother and my little brothers and sister. So I stay here in the inn with the Guillorys, cooking and waiting tables, and I teach the children—and keep quiet about my hopes and dreams of a free nation." She shrugged. "Perhaps I'm a coward. So now you know, and I don't know why I told you, except something—maybe God—convinces me you might help me and my family."

"You are *not* a coward," he said fiercely, "and you are right to trust no one. As a representative of a neutral party, all I can say to you is that I will do everything in my power to bring you safely through this contretemps between the British and American factions. Your father is perhaps in the safest place, but I will see if there is anything I can do to negotiate for your grandfather's release."

"You found Scarlet when I thought she was gone forever, and I sincerely thank you." She looked away. "If there was something I could do in return—"

"There is. Keep this conversation between us only. When the

time is right, I will come for you. In the meantime, watch and listen, be the brave girl you are." He lifted both her hands to his mouth and kissed one, then the other. "Now let us go inside and partake of Joony's so-excellent beignets and chicory. I find I am more hungry than ever." He gave her a smile intended to make her blush, and grinned at his success.

Lyse sat on the schoolroom floor with the children circled around her, one arm around little Genny, who shivered in delicious terror as Suzanne Boutin read aloud a story she had written to entertain the younger children. It was an outlandish tale—something about a red-haired princess, a Turkish ogre, and a fairy with tiny swords for fingernails—but Lyse couldn't have said who wanted what, nor why.

Her mind was far more occupied in wondering how Rafa had fared in effecting her grandfather's release from prison. He had fulfilled his promise of rescuing Scarlet—at least, he claimed to have done so. *When the time is right, I will come for you.* The words, oddly echoing Grandpére's mysterious stricture on Mardi Gras, promised so little and so much. What did he mean? There had been no mention of marriage.

On the other hand, when he asked her if she had given the oath of loyalty to England, she hadn't answered in so many words. And why would he ask her such a question? What if he was a spy?

He had adjured her to trust no one. If she were wise, that would even include Rafa himself.

"Miss Lanier! I said do you want me to leave the story on your desk?"

Lyse blinked and focused on Suzanne's perplexed face. "Oh! Yes, indeed! I will read it for grammar and spelling and return it to you tomorrow." She smiled at Suzanne warmly. "What a beautiful story. I know you worked very hard to make it descriptive and clear."

Suzanne shrugged. "I was trying to make it scary, not beautiful. But thank you—I suppose."

"In any case, your creativity is commendable." Lyse scrambled to her feet and extended a hand to Genny. "Come, children, back to your desks. It's time to start our mathematics lesson. Who can recite the 'times four' multiplication table?"

There was a general groan as the children moved back to their double desks. She had just gotten them settled when a knock sounded upon the door.

"Miss Lanier! Lyse! Open up!" It was a familiar male voice.

She hurried to open the door. "Niall!" With an effort she restrained her surprise and irritation. "Ensign McLeod, we are busy with lessons. What can I do for you?"

"Send them home for lunch early. I need you to come with me."

She stiffened. "Why?"

"Major Redmond asked for you."

"What if I say no?"

"Lyse, don't make me—"

"What? Are you going to arrest me too?"

He looked aggrieved. "The children are listening."

"So they are." She stood there a long moment, just to make him squirm. "All right. Children, put your things away for lunch. We'll recess for an hour—"

"It might be longer than that," Niall interrupted. "Miss Lanier will ring the bell when it's time for you to come back."

She stared at him in outrage, but there was little she could do. "Let me get my shawl. Wait for me outside." She shut the door in his face, then supervised the children as they put away books, dropped pencils, and slammed desk lids. Finally she opened the door so they could file out ahead of her. After locking the door, she turned, gathering her shawl and her dignity. "What is this about, Niall? Is my grandfather all right?"

"He's fine, but I'm not supposed to say anything else." He

offered his elbow, which she ignored, then followed her down the schoolhouse steps like a puppy. "I don't know why you're angry with me. I didn't do anything."

"That is true." She scalded him with a look over her shoulder. "You don't do anything but follow orders." *And the same could be said of me,* she thought with a pang of conscience. "I'm not angry with you, Niall, I'm just worried. Doesn't it bother you when honest citizens are arrested for speaking their minds in a public place?"

"James Willing is an officer in the rebel army. Your father—I'm sorry, Lyse, but he's a drunkard and rabble-rouser, just like your uncle Guillaume was."

She could hardly believe her ears. "Uncle Guillaume was executed by the Spanish, a long time ago, under very different circumstances. Do you think my papa should be hung as a traitor?"

"Of course not, but—but—now, I told you I can't speak to you about this, and you made me—" Niall grabbed her elbow, forcing her to stop. When she stared at him in resentful silence, he blundered on. "Lyse, I'm going to say one more thing, and then we're going on to the fort. My feelings for you have nothing to do with my duty to the king's guard. I love you, but if you won't let me protect you, then you'll have to take the consequences."

Lyse thought her head might explode. "Is that right? Well, let me tell you something, you pompous r-rooster! It is not your place to give me ultimatums or blackmail me with your stupid threats! You can't tell me what to believe, you can't make me turn my back on my father—drunkard or not—and you can't make me marry you!" She wheeled and charged for the gates of the fort.

"Wait, Lyse, that's not what I meant!"

By now she was holding back angry tears, banging with the heel of her fist on the gates. "Let me in!" she shouted at the sentry in the gatehouse. "Major Redmond wants to see me!"

"Lyse, stop it!" Niall took her by the shoulders.

She wrenched away from him. "Leave me alone!" The gate swung open, and she rushed inside, nearly colliding with a Negro laundress carrying a loaded basket. Dodging the woman, Lyse headed straight for the admin offices. She could hear Niall stomping along behind her.

At the last minute, he ran around her to reach the major's office first. Barely stopping to knock, he flung the door open. "Miss Lanier here on the major's orders," he panted.

Corporal Tully produced his patented lugubrious scowl. "It's about time. Bring her in."

~

The situation wasn't funny anymore. Daisy stormed across the drill ground in the center of the fort, as upset as she'd ever been in her life. How could Papa so mistreat Lyse's father and grandfather? She had just seen for herself that they had been held in the guardhouse for over two weeks, most of that time on short rations. Poor old Mr. Chaz was weak from hunger, and Mr. Antoine had apparently also been beaten, probably for information. His once-handsome face was now gaunt, livid bruises marring the sharply defined cheekbones. Raw cuts oozed at the corners of his mouth.

For a week or so she hadn't known. But eventually the soldiers began to talk about the prisoners in her hearing. When she asked questions, Papa at first answered with the vagueness of one putting off an annoying child. Then he'd resorted to ordering her to stay away from the guardhouse, had even threatened to lock her in her room if she disobeyed.

Well, today she had disobeyed.

She had found the Lanier men together in a narrow barred cell, at the low-lying end of the building that had flooded in last week's three-day spate of torrential rain. They had apparently been sleeping on the bare, wet floor. James Willing, the American who had started the whole episode, was confined as well, but as an officer, he was comparatively well fed and housed in the officers' quarters, comfortable in a room with a bed, a chair, and a writing desk.

"The Laniers are traitors," the guard on duty said, as though that justified such barbaric injustice, "worse than enemy soldiers in uniform."

She slapped the man's smug, astonished face and demanded that he move Mr. Chaz to a dry cell and give him something to eat. When he refused—unless her father gave the order—she had wheeled and headed for her father's office. Papa *would* give the order! She would make him, somehow.

Her whole body trembled as she rapped upon the door. "Corporal Tully! It's me, Daisy. I must speak with my father immediately. It's—it's important!"

Tully opened the door a crack but did not move aside. "Not now, miss. He told me not to disturb him for any reason."

Daisy stepped back, took a deep breath, and raised her voice to a shout. "Papa! I have to talk to you! Please tell Corporal Tully to—"

Tully opened the door, grabbed her elbow, and hauled her inside the room. "Miss Daisy, have you lost your mind?" he hissed, shoving her none too gently into the only available chair. "Tell me what's wrong—and I'll see if I can help you."

She bounced to her feet. "Unless you can countermand my father's order to mistreat the prisoners, I would speak with *him*."

"You know I can't—"

"That's what I thought." She raised her voice again. "Papa! I want to talk to—"

"What is the meaning of this commotion?" Her father jerked open his office door and stood glaring at her. "Have you taken leave of your senses, girl?"

"No, but *you* apparently have. I wish to know why you have treated two of your oldest friends like murderers!" *Please, God,* she thought, *don't let my voice quaver.* "Mr. Chaz is—is sick and hungry—"

"Daisy, go to your quarters immediately or, I assure you, you will regret it. Corporal, escort my daughter to her room and make sure she stays. That is an order." He started to shut the door in her face.

She slipped her arm through the opening to take hold of his sleeve. "Papa! What has happened to you? I cannot believe you would do this to me!"

"Daisy? Did you say my grandfather is ill?"

That was Lyse's voice, in Papa's office. Panic shook Daisy. Her father's face was stony, though a spasm of something like anguish passed through his eyes.

"Papa, please let me in. I'm not a child, and you can't protect me from the truth. I know there's something terrible going on."

He pressed his lips together, glanced at Corporal Tully behind her, and reluctantly nodded, moving aside so that she could enter the office.

Lyse was sitting in one of the chairs Papa kept for visitors, twisting her hands in her apron, her eyes large and shining with tears. She lunged to her feet and reached for Daisy, hugging her fiercely.

Daisy returned the embrace, rocked with emotions she couldn't have named. "Lyse, oh, Lyse. I've missed you so!"

"And I you." The words sounded choked.

Daisy pulled back to search her friend's face. "Are you well?"

"I'm frightened for my grandfather. You've seen him?"

"Yes, I—"

"Daisy, that's enough." Papa's voice was a douse of cold water. "Sit down, both of you—and stop being such maudlin little ninnies."

Daisy flinched. She released Lyse but squeezed her hands before taking the other chair as Lyse returned to her seat. "Papa, Lyse has reason to be worried—"

"I said that's enough!" Papa smacked his hand hard upon the desk. "This is a military installation, and I am its commander, at least until Colonel Durnford arrives. I insist that everything you hear within these walls be treated with the utmost discretion. I am responsible for ensuring the safety and integrity of the fort and the inhabitants of the city, as I always have been. But now that we are at war, every word uttered, every visitor admitted, takes on extraordinary tactical significance." He glared at them, as though waiting for an answer.

Lyse said nothing, but Daisy could feel her anxiety. She nodded warily.

"Good," Papa said, as if they had both agreed with him. "As I was just explaining to Lyse, before you burst in here like a hoyden, her father committed an act of grave misconduct by supporting Captain Willing's seditious attempt to seduce the citizenry of His Majesty's colony of West Florida. However, Antoine did me somewhat of a favor by coming out into the open. For some time now, we have been searching for an agent who has been passing information from Pensacola, through here and on to New Orleans, where intelligence has proceeded to the American high command at Fort Pitt."

Lyse gasped. "You think my father is a *spy*?"

Daisy's father leaned in. "I am aware of the contempt in which your whole family—with, perhaps, the exception of Simon—holds the British nation. Antoine himself hardly seemed a threat, as he is drunk a good portion of the time. But lately it occurred to me that very drunkenness might be a clever act, put on to get my enlisted men to talk. Then, when he couldn't resist backing up Captain Willing's effrontery . . ." Papa looked away, perhaps abashed by the incredulity in Lyse's expression.

Daisy herself could hardly contain her disgust and disbelief. "Yes, Papa?"

Papa harrumphed. "Well, I took the opportunity to question him." His mouth hardened as he returned his gaze to Lyse. "And your grandfather as well, once he insisted on aligning himself with his wretched son. Neither has admitted anything as of yet. I'm willing to believe, Lyse, that you had no notion of your father's duplicity, since I was taken in myself. But despite my affection for you, I cannot take my responsibilities lightly. I insist that you denounce your father and take the oath of loyalty to the king—or I'm afraid I must deport you."

14

With his guitar across his lap, Rafa sat in a rickety chair propped against the tavern wall, entertaining the early customers with an impromptu concert of noisy and frankly bawdy drinking songs. Once Lyse had gone to the schoolhouse for the day, he had composed a message to Major Redmond, requesting an audience at his earliest convenience, and sent it by a young off-duty soldier lounging at the bar. While waiting for the response, he had whiled away the time in conversation with those who entered the tavern for a drink, sifting through gossip about weather, trade, and the progress of the war, hoping for tidbits of information that might help Governor Gálvez assess the likelihood of a British attack on New Orleans, which was rumored for execution sometime during the spring of 1779.

"Another! One more!" came a chorus of shouts as he strummed the last jangling chord of "Juice of Barley."

He shook his head, grinning, and let the chair drop to the floor. "I swear, friends, after such a long song about drinking, my throat is parched! Barkeep, another round of the real juice of barley, if you please!"

"Barley won't grow here, man, only corn!"

The men roared with laughter. One slapped Rafa on the back, and offered to buy his drink.

Before he could accept, the door opened, and the young soldier Rafa had sent to the major entered the tavern. He stood near the door, twisting his hat.

Rafa rose, leaned the guitar against the wall, and casually worked his way through the crowd. He took the boy's shoulder in a friendly grip and said quietly, "Something's wrong. What is it?"

The boy looked relieved to see him. "Don Rafael, come with me—Corporal Tully sent me to get you."

"Tully?" Rafa couldn't think who that might be.

"He's Major Redmond's adjutant. I gave him your message for the major."

"Ah, yes, the excellent violinist. I met him last fall."

"Yes, sir. He looked relieved to hear from you. Said to come get you as quick as possible, because Miss Daisy and Miss Lyse are in trouble. But he said don't make a big to-do if you can help it."

Not make a to-do? When Daisy and Lyse were in trouble?

All sorts of possibilities chased through Rafa's brain as he hurried beside the young enlisted man. What had they done? Had he waited too long to pursue the prisoner's release? He should have gone straight to Major Redmond, as soon as he arrived in Mobile.

Calm yourself, Rafa, he thought. Panic strangled the brain and froze the instincts, as he knew all too well.

The short walk to the fort seemed to take an hour, though it was probably no more than a couple of minutes. The messenger saluted the guard, who opened the gate to admit both men.

"This way," his young friend said, leading the way directly across the drilling ground.

Headquarters was the largest of the interior buildings, built a foot or so off the ground on pilings and marked by a new door. The shutters at the windows had been thrown open, and curtains fluttered in the mild spring breeze. Peripherally Rafa noted several other improvements to the fort since he'd first visited in the fall of 1776. Gálvez would want to know that the English were investing in refurbishing the southern garrisons.

The door opened before they reached the shallow porch, revealing a tall, burly officer with balding pate and bristling mustache. Tully had evidently been watching for their return.

The young soldier saluted, then scurried away before he could be drafted for further uncomfortable errands.

Rafa bowed. "Corporal Tully, well met."

Tully nodded. "Don Rafael." He stepped out onto the porch, shutting the door, then said quietly, "I remember you being something of a diplomat, which is what we are in sore need of at the moment." He paused, tugged at his mustache. "I also remember you being a friend to our Miss Daisy and her friend Miss Lyse."

Rafa studied the man for a moment and found earnest kindness housed in the stiff-rumped British military man. "I am deeply admiring of both young ladies," he admitted, "which makes me anxious to discover what has transpired since I breakfasted with Miss Lanier this morning."

"The major does not always include me in his dealings, but things have gotten a bit, er, loud this morning. I understand that there has been pressure from the governor to clamp down on possible seditious activity—tighten security and all that. So when Captain Willing took it in his head to come over here, bust in with that declaration of independence the rebels are so het up over—" Tully shook his head. "All hell broke loose, if you'll pardon the expression."

Rafa merely raised his brows. Nothing he didn't already know.

Tully continued, "And yesterday one of the little Guillory girls showed her mama a paper she found under Lyse's pillow and asked her to read it."

Rafa felt sick. "What was the child doing in Lyse's room?"

"What little ones do. Poking around in places they shouldn't be. Then Mistress Guillory went looking and found some books pushed up under the bed, books no proper British lady ought to be reading. So Guillory brought it all to the major this morning, and he hauled Lyse in here for questioning. Major Redmond thinks he's being generous by giving her a chance to repeat the oath of loyalty. But in the meantime, Miss Daisy found out about the shape the two prisoners is in—"

"Prisoners?" Rafa knew he'd better be careful how much he let on he knew.

"The Lanier men, Antoine and old Mr. Chaz."

"I see. I take it Miss Daisy objected."

"Loudly." Tully pulled on his mustache again. "Then when she realized her papa was about to deport her best friend for treason, she—well, let's just say she wasn't happy."

Rafa could imagine. He could also imagine how well Major Redmond would have received his daughter's disrespect.

His original mission had just gone from difficult to all but impossible.

It was a good thing God had gifted him with a good set of brains and a hefty dose of self-confidence.

~

Lyse thought her heart might thunder right out of her chest. "Oath of loyalty?" The words tasted like chalk in her mouth. As a ward of Major Redmond, she had never been required to make such a profession. Until two weeks ago, if she had been asked to do so, she probably would have shrugged and said the words without thinking.

But something about that sheet of paper under her pillow had changed the way she looked at the world around her. Ultimately, it changed every relationship in her life.

Before she could voice her thoughts, Daisy lunged to her feet. She moved in front of Lyse, as though guarding her from attack.

"Papa, how can you ask such an absurd thing? Lyse has nothing to do with her father's political nonsense—how could she? She hasn't lived at home since last summer!"

Major Redmond came from behind his desk. "Daughter, this kind of 'nonsense,' as you call it, begins at an early age. Lyse has grown up in a French household. You know the story of her uncle Guillaume's rabble-rousing when the Spanish took New Orleans. The whole family is steeped in sedition." He fixed Lyse with his light-gray eyes, and she was surprised to see veiled sorrow there. "Tell Daisy what you have hidden under your bed, Lyse."

Daisy gasped, whirled around, and stared horrified at Lyse.

Lyse's heart hammered in her ears.

Silence hummed.

Then the faint sound of a birdlike whistle came from outside the office door. *"Love in a Village"?*

The latch rattled and the door opened. Rafa stuck his head in. "Major Redmond! Well met, señor! I have the message that you are ready to see me. Oh, hello, young ladies! Miss Lanier, you are hiding from me, I think—I have been searching the town high and low for you—only just look at you, wasting this beautiful face on old men like—" His eyes widened as he took in the major's stern expression. "*Caray*, I have stepped in it indeed, have I not?" He laughed.

"Don Rafael, this is an inopportune time for a visit." Major Redmond's voice was strained but civil. "I beg you to step outside and wait until I finish with my daughters."

"Oh, but what I have to say will take but a moment." Rafa's affable smile remained undimmed. He came inside, shut the door with a flourish, and seated himself upon the corner of the major's spotless desk, whereupon he set one well-shaped leg to swinging. "It is to do with that ridiculous American captain, James Willing, who I believe has escaped Spanish custody and run, who knows why, over here to make a pest of himself in West Florida. Governor Gálvez, knowing that I was coming this way on business, has bid me apprehend Captain Willing and bring him back to New Orleans. And today I find out from the good Corporal Tully that you have been so kind as to apprehend him for us!"

"Willing is in custody, that is true," Major Redmond said without smiling. "But he is a prisoner of the king, and I would not release him without—"

"—without a very good reason, I am sure." Rafa looped his hands around his knee. "And this I am happy to provide. You see, Governor Gálvez bids me inform you that Captain Willing took into parole two British planters on his so-naughty raid down the Mississippi River last month. Perhaps you know of a certain Alexander McIntosh and Anthony Hutchins of Natchez? They are at present free to walk about New Orleans, but unable to return home. And they have been forced to watch their belongings fall under the auctioneer's hammer." Rafa shook his head. "A most humiliating circumstance indeed."

"And I suppose," the major said slowly, "your governor proposes something of a trade? Why does he want Willing back? As you said, he is quite a nuisance."

"Oh, indeed." Rafa chuckled. "The governor is determined to seek redress for the embarrassment caused by the captain, and he cannot do that if the miscreant remains at large, so to speak. And frankly your charming planters would do everyone more good at home, taking care of their, um, plantations, rather than wandering about the city complaining of the heat and mosquitoes."

"I confess, I see no reason not to honor this request, Don Rafael—if you will give me your word as a gentleman that Hutchins and McIntosh will be safely returned to Natchez."

"It is my pleasure to do so, Major."

"What about their personal belongings? I presume there were slaves and other valuable items confiscated in the raid."

"I'm sorry to say that those transactions cannot be undone,"

Rafa said cheerfully. "But remember that you are getting two planters for the, er, price of one insurgent. Quite a bargain!"

Lyse stifled a giggle, in spite of her anxiety. She couldn't wait to hear what Rafa's fertile brain came up with next.

"Which reminds me," he said, suddenly leaning around the major to wink at Lyse. "I believe you have uncovered another foolish little rebel who must be dealt with."

"Foolish and dangerous," Major Redmond said. "There is an information leak to the Americans, and I am going to make sure Mobile isn't its source or funnel."

Rafa sighed. "I understand your dilemma, Major, but surely one young girl who spends her days teaching children to read and write and multiply can hardly be considered a national threat, eh?"

"She can if she is a particularly bright young lady who is connected to the Lanier and Lafleur families, not to mention those of the children she teaches. I've discovered that even while Lyse lived in my own house, she was absorbing the seditious writings of rebels like John Locke, Thomas Paine, Adam—"

"Papa, stop! You don't understand!"

Lyse had all but forgotten Daisy's presence, once Rafa entered the room. She caught Daisy's hand, forcing her to look at her. "Be quiet, Daisy. It's all right. I did read those books."

"No! They were—"

"Major Redmond, a word, if you please." Rafa slid off the desk, a lithe movement that put him between Daisy and her father, and which effectively halted whatever Daisy had been about to say. He leaned in toward Major Redmond's ear and murmured, "I realize that this may not be the *most* appropriate moment for what I'm about to say, but as it has bearing upon this rather uncomfortable discussion, I feel that I must suspend etiquette and ask Miss Daisy to forgive the interruption." He slanted Daisy a sleepy look which somehow caused her to close her lips and meekly retire to a corner of the room. "Thank you," he said with a graceful bow.

Major Redmond, looking perplexed, waved an impatient hand. "Yes, yes, get on with it, Don Rafael."

"Oh, well, this is very embarrassing, but part of my business here in Mobile was of a more personal nature. As I mentioned before, I had been searching for Miss Lanier—or more particularly, I was looking for her papa, because, well—in short, I wanted to ask him for his daughter's hand in marriage. You can imagine my chagrin when I discovered he had been detained for treason, of all things!"

No. Oh, no no no no. He had not just declared his intentions—*now*, at the worst of all possible times.

Lyse brought both shaking hands to her mouth. She wasn't sure if what she felt rising in her throat was a wail or hysterical laughter.

And then he looked at her. By now she knew him well enough to see beyond the slightly raffish facade to the kindness and intellect he hid from the world. And buried in his eyes, under the sheepishness, she saw a glimmer of warning, a deadly seriousness.

In an instant it was gone, so that she wondered if she had imagined it.

Rafa sighed. "I see that I have taken Miss Lanier—my dear, precious, beautiful Lyse!—all by surprise. But it is ever so when a man is in love with a woman of such humility that she can hardly believe she has created such deep and unfathomable feelings. Major, you must remember that at our very first meeting in your home, I could hardly keep my eyes from your daughter's friend. And I have created excuses to return to your fair city time and again, all for the privilege of laying eyes upon her . . . dancing with her . . . even touching her hand, if I may be so bold." He laid one elegant hand upon his breast as if unable to contain his feelings.

Lyse supposed she must be grateful that he had refrained from mentioning the unbridled kisses. Where on earth was he going with this absurd declaration?

Clearly Major Redmond wondered the same thing. He glanced

at Lyse as though seeing her for the first time. "Er, yes, of course," he said, "but what does that have to do with—"

"But it has everything to do with . . . everything!" Rafa reached for Lyse's hand, and she gave it to him as one in a trance. Or a Shakespearean comedy. Or possibly both. She allowed him to lift her to her feet and draw her to him. "When Lyse becomes my wife, should I be so fortunate, then she will be neither French nor British nor American—but Spanish. What is good enough for my admired Governor Gálvez, who has recently married his Creole lady María Feliciana de St. Maxent d'Estrehan, is surely good enough for me!"

Major Redmond scratched his head. "Lyse, do you want to marry this young peacock?"

She looked down at Rafa's fingers laced through hers. His hand was big and strong, and the blood-red signet ring on his index finger pressed hard into hers. She imagined giving herself to him as his wife, bound by law and the church to follow and obey him in everything—as he said, to forsake even her heritage and take on his.

Her choice was to remain single, to face whatever consequences came from the paper she had hidden under her pillow. But if she did that, Daisy would confess in order to protect her, and her grandfather would remain in prison as well . . .

Looking up, she tried to read Rafa's brown eyes, to discover whether there was any sincerity in his offer. He was such a theatrical clown, and yet, he could also be motivated by sheer gallantry. His expression softened, as if he understood her dilemma. She saw his lips move: *Say yes.*

The untamed side of her nature bloomed.

"Yes," she whispered.

Rafa smiled.

Cheeks warm, Lyse looked at Major Redmond. "But I want to take my grandfather with me."

He shook his head. "You are in no position to make demands."

"That would be one more dissident out of your hair, so to speak," Rafa said quickly.

Major Redmond heaved a sigh. "Yes, it would. And I have far more important things to do than continue this pointless argument. Very well, then, Don Rafael—take your American captain, your bride-to-be, and her grandfather, and get out of my city. Do not take this amiss, but I will be glad to see the back of the lot of you." He moved to open the door. "Good day, sir."

~

Daisy looked at her father, stunned. He continued to hold the door open, as though waiting for her to rise and follow Lyse and Rafael from the office. But she couldn't move, could barely breathe.

Lyse had just agreed to marry the Spaniard. She would be leaving Mobile, moving to New Orleans, never to return. Oh, maybe she would come back for the occasional visit, but things would never be the same between them.

She had been aware of Rafa's regard for Lyse. Maybe she herself had been swept up in the romanticism of their odd, teasing courtship—but never had she imagined that Lyse would actually leave the city, leave her family, leave her lifelong friends.

And Daisy would be left alone. Simon was gone. Her father—this stranger who had shut her up in the fort, as truly a prisoner as Antoine Lanier or James Willing—her father had just as surely shut her out of his heart. Or perhaps she had done that to herself the moment she opened Thomas Paine's book and made herself vulnerable to its beautiful, dangerous teaching.

She wanted to wail like a child. She wanted to run after Lyse and beg her to stay. She wanted to prostrate herself on the floor and pray for God to intervene.

But she must sit here, stoic, and pretend to obey her father, because to refuse to do so would be to admit to insanity. What was her alternative? Admit to treason, when Lyse had sacrificed herself to keep Daisy from doing so? And when Rafa clearly wanted her to hold her peace?

Why, God, why?

There wasn't even time to talk to Lyse, to get a farewell hug.

Alone.

"Thank you, Papa, for your generosity." She said it because it was expected. Her lips felt numb, so she bit the lower one, to make herself feel *something*.

"You're a good daughter, Daisy," Papa said. He walked over to her, took her limp hand, and raised her to her feet. "But I'm very busy. Find some of the other women, go back to your students . . ." He circled a hand in a vague manner. "Find something useful to do." The implication being, *Get out of my office so I can get back to work.*

She left the office like a sleepwalker, heard the door shut behind her.

Corporal Tully, seated behind his desk, cleaning his gun, looked up at her. His pale eyes were concerned, far more personally engaged than her father's had been. "Everything all right, Miss Daisy?"

"Yes, I'm just . . ." Her thoughts drifted. She blinked. "Do you know where Lyse and Rafa—Don Rafael went? I wanted to say goodbye."

Tully shook his head. "Walked toward the guardhouse with McLeod. I sent him to turn loose old man Lanier and the American, like your da said to do."

"So you heard—"

"I heard." Tully grimaced. "Not one of the major's finer moments. But Miss Lyse will be fine with the Spaniard," he hastened to add. "The boy's not as stupid as he likes to make out."

Daisy smiled faintly. "No, he's not. Well. Thank you for bringing him. I might have—well, I'm not sure what I was about to do. Probably something *really* stupid." She suddenly looked at Tully hard, saw the kindness in his face. Maybe she wasn't so alone as she'd thought. "Thank you for watching out for me and Lyse, Corporal. I want to do the right thing, but sometimes I . . ."

"Miss Daisy, you're going to be fine too." His scalp was pink with discomfort. "But if there's ever anything you need, all you got to do is send for me. You hear?"

She smiled and saluted. "Yes, *sir*. I hear."

~

The guardhouse smelled like moldy cheese. Lyse could hardly bear to breathe, and to think her father and Grandpére had been in this place for two weeks—

Her indignation boiled to the surface again, and only Rafa's steadying presence, a calming hand on her elbow, a word to be careful as she mounted the doorstep, kept her from an unseemly explosion.

Niall held the door as she entered the building, but she refused to look at him. He knew. He'd *known* Grandpére and Papa had been held here on short rations, without decent beds or baths or any other humane treatment. And he had done nothing. At least Daisy had tried, as soon as she discovered the situation, to do something about it.

The last two days had been dry and sunny, so most of the rainwater had drained through the cracks in the floor. But the boards were still soft, slightly squishy, and damp enough that the soles of her slippers were wet by the time she and Rafa walked through the darkness of the high end of the building to the cells where the two prisoners were kept. Only small glints of light slipped through the chinks between the shakes of the roof. Some small noise of dismay must have escaped her, for Rafa's hand slipped to her wrist.

"Steady," he murmured. "We'll have him out of here before you know it."

She glanced at him, nodded, but then she saw her grandfather.

He sat on a crate close to the bars of the cell, straight as an arrow, holding his hat in his hands. His head was bowed as if in prayer.

"Grandpére! I'm here! You're coming with me and Rafa." She fell to her knees. "Are you well? We'll get you something to eat soon."

At last he looked up, blinking as though waking from a long sleep. He looked as if he'd aged ten years. "Lyse? What are you doing here?"

"Didn't you hear me? I came to get you out!" Even as she reached through the bars for his hand, she looked over her shoulder. "Niall! Come open this door at once! Hurry!"

"I'm coming."

But before Niall could get the key in the lock, Grandpére was on his feet. "No! Antoine first. I can't leave without—"

"Grandpére!" Lyse felt like sobbing. "I'm sorry, but Major Redmond won't release Papa—at least not now. We'll get him later, but right now, you must—"

"I said I'm not leaving without my son. Not this time."

Lyse stared up at her grandfather's lined face, stubborn as a mule, but beautiful in its self-sacrifice. "Oh, Grandpére . . ."

Rafa stepped close and helped Lyse to her feet. "Listen, sir, the situation is a bit, um, odd here, as you know. Lyse has gotten herself in a bit of difficulty with the major—I'm sure Ensign McLeod here would be glad to explain—but to give you the short version, I'm allowed to take the two of you out of the city, and no one else." He paused, then added delicately, "I don't think it would be wise to question Major Redmond's generosity."

Grandpére's heavy brows lowered, and he fixed a penetrating glare on Niall.

Niall stood shifting from one foot to the other, until he finally said grudgingly, "He's right, sir. You'd better come, or it won't look good for Lyse." He slanted a shamed look at Lyse. "I'll watch out for your pa, Lyse. Make sure he eats, and get him a cot to sleep on."

"Pére." That was Papa's voice, coming from the shadows of the next cell. "Listen to them. Get Justine and the children, take them to your house."

In two steps, Lyse found him. He did look gaunt and ill, but he was also sober—which in one sense made him well for the first time in a long time. "Papa!" She reached through the bars to grab his sleeves and pull him toward her. "I wanted to take you too, but—"

"I know, I'm a traitor," he said roughly. "When *they* are the ones killing their citizens unjustly. I don't expect them to release me." He touched her face and whispered, "I heard them say you'd been brought in for questioning—but stay safe, precious daughter. Pray for me and take your grandfather to safety." He paused. "*Promise me.*"

Lyse choked back a sob. "All right, Papa. I promise. We'll come back for you," she whispered.

15

New Orleans
May 12, 1778

"Sofía! Where are you, child?" Doña Gonzales's voice floated down the curving iron staircase and found Scarlet kneeling at the feet of the diminutive Sofía, who stood upon a wooden step constructed just for Scarlet's use in the sewing room.

"Down here, Mama! Scarlet is pinning the hem of my new dress. You must come see! The drape through the hips is just so—ah, Scarlet, I'm sorry, I'll be still, I promise. It's just that you do such beautiful work, and I shall be very sorry when you have to go back to my brother."

Pins in her mouth, Scarlet glanced up and smiled at her bright-eyed and excitable young mistress. She, too, would be sorry to leave Miss Sofía—though nothing could be worse than service to Isabelle Dussouy or picking cotton.

After purchasing her from the slave market, Don Rafael had taken her first to the governor's wife, Madame Gálvez. Madame had exclaimed over Scarlet's pitiful physical condition, then gave her a long bath in lye soap, fed her, and made her rest for two whole days—for the sake of the babe, said Madame. Scarlet meekly complied, too exhausted and grateful for her redemption to even care what might befall her next. But when Madame called her into her private parlor the next day and bade her sit in the only other chair in the room, a finely upholstered blue voile, her confusion twisted in on itself.

"Madame, I'm happy to stand," Scarlet said, laying her hands protectively across the bulge of her stomach.

"Yes, I'm sure you would be," said Madame with a smile, "but I've no desire to crane my neck whilst we talk, so sit down, if you please."

Flustered, Scarlet sat. "Yes, Madame."

"Now, Scarlet, Rafael says you are a seamstress."

"Yes, Madame."

"And your baby will be coming . . . maybe in July?"

Scarlet nodded, wary now. "I think so." Was having a baby a bad thing?

Madame's eyes softened. She was very beautiful. It was said that her Spanish husband was crazy for her. Perhaps as much as Don Rafael was for Lyse. "I'm sorry you had to leave your baby's father," Madame said gently. "We'll try to find him, but in the meantime, there will be plenty of work for you here. How would you like to go to Rafael's mama until the baby comes?"

Scarlet picked through the words, trying to make sense of them. What difference did it make what she would like or not like? If this were Madame Dussouy, there would be some trap hidden in the question. Scarlet did not know Rafael's mama and didn't particularly want to go elsewhere, but neither did she want to offend this kind Creole lady. She shrugged helplessly. "Whatever you say, Madame."

So Madame Gálvez had given Scarlet one of her old dresses and materials to let it out in the waist, and then examined her stitches with a critical eye. Pronouncing it "exquisite work" with an approving smile, Madame had one of the houseboys walk her down the street to the Gonzales mansion. He left her in the kitchen in the care of a cook who reminded her very much of Cain's mother.

By the time Doña Gonzales sent for her, she had been fed most of a loaf of crusty French bread, along with a chunk of sausage, and she was so full she could barely stay awake long enough to waddle to the second-best salon.

Dear God, she thought, blinking at the two well-dressed ladies—one middle-aged, with Don Rafael's exquisite bone structure, the other young and possessed of her brother's mischievous brown eyes—*what sort of heaven have I landed in?*

It had taken Scarlet over a month to learn to answer direct questions without flinching or looking for hidden meanings. Eventually she realized that her talent with a needle was valued and appreciated. She was fed well and allowed to rest, and as her body grew bulkier with the baby, she was even assigned a small slave girl of her own to fetch and carry for her.

Little Dina, who had apparently never known an unkind word, chattered like a mockingbird from the moment she arose in the morning to the minute she fell asleep at Scarlet's feet at night. Scarlet found her maternal feelings wrenched at the thought of her charge having been removed from her mother's care at such a young age, until she discovered that the child actually belonged to the poker-faced cook. She resolved to be as kind a mistress as Madame Gálvez.

Now, one by one she removed the pins from her mouth and secured the dress's hem as Miss Sofía slowly turned atop the little platform. Finally she sat back on her heels and looked up at Sofía. "Check it in the mirror, miss," she said. "Does it look straight to you?"

Sofía turned and preened, smoothing her slender, well-manicured hands over her hips. The dress draped, as she had said, with perfection. "I love it," she said, beaming at Scarlet's reflection in the mirror. "I can't wait for Lieutenant Torres to see me in it."

"Lieutenant Torres had better look out for parson's mousetrap," Scarlet said without thinking.

Sofía burst out laughing. "Scarlet! You made a joke!"

Scarlet gasped and covered her mouth. "I'm sorry, miss!"

But Sofía leapt down from the stool, crouched and took Scarlet's hands. "Don't be sorry! It's wonderful to have someone to laugh with. Mama is always so very—" she looked over her shoulder and whispered, "*strict*!"

"I heard that!" came Madame Gonzales's voice from the hallway just before she appeared, hands on hips. "Someone has to be strict around here, or the place would fall to pieces." But her eyes twinkled. "Sofía, change out of that dress and run out to the garden for some flowers, so Scarlet can hem it in peace."

Madame stood tapping her foot until her daughter complied, then shut the sewing room door behind her and turned to Scarlet. "How are you feeling today?"

Scarlet had risen, a hand braced to support her back. Still shy around the matron of the house, she looked at the dress in her hands. "I feel fine, Doña Gonzales. Everyone is kind to me here."

"Good." The older woman nodded. "It is good to stay busy, but do not put too much strain on your back. Where is Dina? She is supposed to stay close by in case you need anything."

"She—I sent her outside to play so I could give your daughter some privacy." Scarlet bit her lip. "I'm sorry if—"

"No, for heaven's sake, girl, use your common sense. That is fine. I'm only concerned for you."

Scarlet risked a look at her mistress. "Madame . . . I wanted to ask . . ." When Doña Gonzales waited, brows lifted, Scarlet blurted, "Why are you so kind to me? I'm a slave in your house. Surely you don't treat all your servants this way."

Doña Gonzales looked faintly embarrassed. "Of course I don't abuse my servants. But you are something of a special case."

Scarlet took a step back. "What do you mean?"

"Madame Gálvez bade me care for you and make sure your babe arrives safely. What Madame Gálvez asks me to do—I do."

Scarlet stared at the other woman, but could divine nothing beyond the bare meaning of the words. Madame Gálvez had interceded for her. Because of *her* name and position, Scarlet was given favor, almost as a daughter of the house. Perhaps Don Rafael had something to do with that, perhaps not. It was a puzzle she could not unlock without more information.

"All—all right. Thank you, madame," she said and lifted Sofía's dress. "I'll finish the hem now, if you don't need anything else."

"You do that," Doña Gonzales said with a smile. "Sofía has the trap to set."

~

Aboard the *Valiente*
May 12, 1778

Lyse had once dreamed of flying off a cliff. She had spent two days in her grandpére's library, reading a book of travel in the mountains of Europe. There were no drawings, but the author's descriptions had taken her to the south of France, where her great-grandmother's people had lived before the Huguenot persecution drove them to the New World. She could imagine the snowy peaks, green valleys, sharp precipices, in such vivid detail that dizziness almost overtook her when she rose to go home. That night, as she slept, she found herself atop the highest of heights, looking down at a herd of wild horses grazing below. She wanted to ride one. And all she had to do was step off, fly down.

Arms wide, she did.

And awoke screaming so that Justine shook her until her teeth rattled.

It was an experience she hadn't wanted to repeat. But standing at the prow of the Spanish merchant ship *Valiente* with Rafa, sailing away from Mobile, she felt something of the same sensation.

"Are you cold? We can go into my cabin." Rafa's hands, big and warm, cupped her shoulders.

She looked up at him and shook her head. "I'm a little . . . I don't know how to say it." She wouldn't say *afraid*.

He seemed to understand, for a smile lightened his eyes. "There is nothing my Creole lady cannot conquer. The little village of New Orleans will be *that* to you!" He snapped his fingers.

"Even I know New Orleans is not a little village." But she laughed at his nonsense. "There will be singing and guitar playing on every street corner, and I shall be the veriest bumpkin." She turned to put her back to the water, and his hands came to brace against the rail on either side of her. Her hair blew wild in the ocean breeze, and she grabbed a handful of it. "Rafa, you have been the most gallant of rescuers, and I am grateful, but you don't have to—No one will ever know if you don't want—"

"If you say something like that even one more time, Miss Lanier, I may be forced to hold you down and tickle you until you scream for mercy. I never make offers I don't mean to keep." An uncertain tone crept into his deep voice. "Though I'm beginning to think it is you who has second thoughts."

She looked away from the hurt in his eyes. "I just wish—I wish you hadn't been forced to offer for me."

He was quiet for a moment. "Maybe one day I may find a way to convince you that I am serious. Until then . . ." He sighed. "Well, until then, we take one step at a time. And the first step is taking you home to meet my family."

At that, she smiled. "Which, I confess, has me terrified. I don't know how many times I've heard you say that your mama beats you daily."

"Ah, but then I am a particularly incorrigible case, as you well know." He grinned. "My mama will love you. And Sofía is already your best friend."

"But she doesn't even know me!"

"But I have told her all about you."

"What did you say?"

"I said, 'There is a girl in Mobile who threatens me with a knife if I don't give her exactly what she wants. And she kisses like an angel.' And Sofía said, 'Then she is exactly the girl you should marry.' And I quite agree."

Lyse gave a gasp of laughter. "You did not say that!" Shaking her head, she put a tentative hand upon his chest, and he covered it with his. "Rafa, you must know how grateful I am that your intervention kept me and my grandpére from harm. But we don't know each other well enough to make such a lifetime commitment. You have a whole other . . . life in New Orleans that I know nothing about. We have completely skipped over courtship, which is for learning such important things as religious faith. Education. Family history."

"You are right, and there will be time for all that. Lyse, I won't ask you to marry me right away. There are things I *cannot* tell you, because they are not my secrets. But I hope you will trust me to put your safety and well-being above all my obligations."

His eyes were deep and soft, so tender that her heart twisted. Trust him? She was on a Spanish ship with him, traveling away from her home and family and everything familiar, toward she knew not what. It was a little like trusting God, whom her grandmother had taught her was great and fearful and secretive but tender as a hen with her chicks.

Maybe trusting Rafa was a way of trusting God, after all.

New Orleans
May 13, 1778

The governor was at home this afternoon, which worked well for Rafa's plan to surprise Lyse. He wanted to take her to meet his mama and Sofía later, but seeing Scarlet would perhaps relieve some of the tension between them. He loved Lyse's independence, understood her self-protection, but couldn't reconcile the two without betraying his assigned mission. He hoped that once Gálvez met Lyse, she would be cleared for at least some level of information.

He held her elbow as they mounted the stairs up to the first-floor entry. They were both weary, a bit short-tempered, and hungry, as the journey from Mobile had been beset by contrary winds, stormy seas, and general bad luck. Half his crew had been struck by a bout of food poison, which he himself had avoided only because he'd been too busy writing reports to eat for the last twenty-four hours.

Lyse's lack of appetite came, he suspected, from sheer anxiety. She'd asked once about a bath before meeting anyone, and he'd had to explain that there was no time. After that, she'd kept her lips buttoned tightly, responding to his attempts at cheering her with monosyllabic replies and veiled expression.

Not good.

He had to admit, there was a small lump of dread in the pit of his own stomach. His mama would not be happy that Lyse had traveled for two days with no chaperone. He'd been able to give her a berth in a little cabin of her own aboard the *Valiente*, but Mama would not consider that proper at all.

He gave the door knocker a rap and, as they waited, studied Lyse's pinched mouth. She looked beautiful as always to him, but she kept tugging at the long, thick plait of wavy hair hanging over her shoulder, and brushing at the stains she'd been unable to remove from her skirt. Women were built for mystery and delight, but no man could navigate the labyrinths of propriety.

The Gálvezes' houseman answered the door before Rafa had time to talk himself into leaving. "Don Rafael! The governor was just about to send a man to find you. We heard the *Valiente* arrived this morning."

Rafa swallowed against a dry throat. "Yes, I stopped at the Cabildo first. They told me he's here. Does he have time to see me?"

"'Course, sir." The man's eyes flicked to Lyse. "Should I announce the young lady as well?"

"Ah. No. That is, I'll announce her myself."

"Very well, sir. This way." The houseman turned to lead the way past the grand front salons, where guests of state were received, then up the curving staircase to the family rooms.

Rafa followed with Lyse on his arm, mentally rehearsing what he was going to say. By the time he stood before Gálvez and the new Doña Gálvez, he felt as though a cyclone had torn through his brain, stripping away every logical and coherent thought.

Before he could do more than bow, Doña Gálvez said, "Really, Rafael, another one?"

His mouth opened and shut. Finally he said stupidly, "Señora?"

But Doña Gálvez was inspecting Lyse with interest and a good deal of amusement. "This one is a deal prettier than the other, and at least she isn't with child."

"Feliciana," the governor said mildly, "the boy has only just arrived, and clearly is not up to your teasing." He rose, took Lyse's hand, and lifted it to his lips. "Welcome, señorita. You are Miss Lanier, I presume."

Lyse managed a confused smile. "Yes, sir. I am Lyse Lanier." She curtseyed and looked at Doña Gálvez. "Madame, I apologize for appearing without proper courtesies. I have been rather . . . rushed."

"I can well imagine." The señora gave Rafa a disapproving frown. "Could you not give the poor girl a chance to sit down for a cup of tea at least, before you dragged her in to be interviewed by strangers?"

Rafa felt his ship go upside down once more. "Señora, my orders—" He looked to Gálvez for rescue. "I assumed I should report at once."

"Yes, yes, of course," Gálvez said. "We'll get to that. Here, the two of you sit on the settee there, and Eduardo will bring tea—wait, Eduardo, chicory for Don Rafael and me as well. Yes? Thank you. Now—" he turned to Rafa—"my wife's jesting aside, you will please explain what has transpired during this last jaunt into West Florida, particularly the unexpected appearance of your lovely companion."

Rafa had told the governor a bit about the Lanier family, but this invitation to speak his mind in Lyse's presence gave him pause. As he and Lyse sat down, he mentally picked through several ways to start the story. "Well, sir, as you know, Captain Willing created a bit of difficulty for us, by haring off to Mobile without leave. By the time I got there, he had already started a riot in the town's largest tavern—an establishment in which I have sojourned on many occasions."

Gálvez sighed. "I see. Go on."

Rafa looked at Lyse. "And . . . Miss Lanier's father and grandfather, apparently being sympathizers, got embroiled. Major Redmond arrested them both, and then brought Miss Lanier in for questioning. Perhaps, Lyse, you should give your side of the story." He wanted to hear her tell Gálvez that she was a rebel. Then, he would be free to—

He could hardly think past that.

But just then the ever efficient Eduardo returned with the tea cart, and the conversation shifted to mundane topics such as the weather, the quality of the seafood available in the Gulf, and the constant threat of flooding near the fort at Bayou St. John. By the time the butler bowed himself out of the room, Rafa had relaxed somewhat.

"And now, Miss Lanier," Gálvez said, "if you are suitably refreshed, I would hear your version of recent events."

Rafa's every hair stood on end. The reprieve was over.

Pulling her bottom lip between her teeth, Lyse met his eyes.

The governor continued, "But please know that anything you say will stay in this room. Spain remains a neutral party in England's conflict with her citizens, and I have pledged no harm to those who respect King Carlos's interests inside our own borders. You may speak freely, without fear of reprisal."

"Thank you, sir," Lyse said softly. She paused, gently swirling the tea in her cup. "For a long time, the conflict didn't seem to apply to me. I've only ever known British sovereignty, though my family remains French in language and culture. Perhaps you know that my father's older brother was involved in the Rebellion of '68. Then I met Rafa—Don Rafael—and I began to see that perhaps my view of the world had been very small. My grandfather is a great reader, and he encouraged me to take advantage of his library." She looked at Rafa, eyes suddenly fiery. "So it wasn't so great a leap, when my friend Daisy gave me books written by the instigators of the current revolution, to sympathize with their desire for freedom and independence."

"*Daisy* gave you those books?" If she had slapped him, Rafa couldn't have been more surprised.

"Yes. And that's the reason I agreed to—that I couldn't—"

Suddenly he saw it. She had been about to refuse his precipitate offer of marriage until she realized that Daisy would implicate herself to save Lyse. A red wave of chagrin climbed from his chest to his ears and over his scalp.

She had been trying to tell him that she didn't return his regard. In fact, she had never admitted any affection for him beyond friendship.

"So you are a rebel sympathizer?"

The governor's calm voice brought Rafa back from the verge of rushing from the room like the fool he was. He forced himself to lean back in his chair, cross one knee over the other, as if he got his heart smashed into a thousand pieces every day.

Lyse raised her chin and said steadily, "Yes, sir. I am."

~

Mobile
May 24, 1778

Daisy waited patiently, the empty basket propped against her hip, as Tully unlocked the gate with a clanking of keys. She had been given special permission to leave the fort, as long as the adjutant accompanied her during his off-duty hours.

Papa had not backed down from his pledge to keep Antoine Lanier imprisoned until he recanted his public support for the American rebels. Daisy had argued in vain that no one cared what a confirmed drunk thought. And her pleading that the little Lanier children needed their father had gone no further. Antoine in gaol was no harder on his family than Antoine lying under a table three sheets to the wind, and probably a lot less embarrassing.

In fact, as she and Tully slipped through the open gate and saw Justine Lanier, baby Rémy propped on her hip, waiting for her in the narrow shade provided by the stockade, Daisy had to admit Antoine's incarceration might just be the salvation of his family. Justine's blonde hair gleamed with health, her dress was neat and pretty, and the baby was fatter and cleaner than Daisy had ever seen him.

Justine's face lit as Daisy approached, and Rémy clapped his little hands. Justine set the squirming toddler down so that he could stagger toward Daisy.

Daisy crouched, setting the basket aside, and caught him just before he tripped. "Give me kisses, sweet boy," she cooed, burying her nose in his sweaty little neck.

He giggled and grabbed fistfuls of her hair, mashing his face into her cheek. "Day-day!"

Daisy looked up in surprise. "Goodness, is he talking already?"

Justine flushed with pleasure. "I've been teaching him your name. The other children wanted to come, but I couldn't manage them all by myself. Grandpére took them fishing," she added, at Daisy's inquiring look.

"I'm so happy you brought Rémy," Daisy said, rising with the baby in her arms. "Corporal Tully, isn't he handsome?"

Tully cleared his throat in noncommittal fashion. "Ma'am." He retreated a yard or so away, to give the women some privacy.

Smiling, Daisy scanned Justine's face. "You look wonderful. How is Mr. Chaz? Recovered, I hope, from his not-so-felicitous stay with us."

"Yes, he's well." Justine bent to pick up the lumpy satchel she'd brought. "Sorry this is a bit smelly. He insisted on sending a cheese and some sausage. The blackberries are ripe, so I made a tart too."

"All right. Just put it in my basket. I'm going to the market to buy some oranges and a few other things to put in too. Corporal Tully won't tell."

"Is Antoine well? No one believes this, but I miss him." Justine looked down, her cheeks flushed.

Daisy, to her chagrin, felt tears sting the backs of her eyes. No one understood why she still missed Simon, either—least of all herself. Did that make her as pathetic as Justine? At least she hadn't made babies with the man who deserted her. On the other hand, Antoine had finally stood up for something more important than a bottle of rum. She had no idea what Simon had run off for.

She pulled herself together by rubbing noses with the baby. "Yes, he's in remarkably good spirits. Tully and Niall McLeod keep the other men from abusing him, and now that he's sober . . ." She shrugged. "He's a Lanier. As you know, he can be quite charming."

"Yes, I know." Justine sighed. "Have you heard from Simon?"

Daisy stilled. "No."

"Daisy, he'll come back. Simon is the most stubborn man in West Florida, and he loved you. Loves you, I mean."

"He told me to wait a year." She felt her eyes drown as she held onto Rémy so tightly that he squealed. "I don't even know what that means, Justine."

Justine put her arms around both Daisy and Rémy. "It means he's coming back."

Daisy let herself melt into the other woman's motherly embrace. Oh, how she missed Lyse. How she missed the closeness she'd had with her father. "Thank you, Justine," she whispered. "I'll take good care of Antoine."

"I know you will." Justine sniffed.

"Are you crying too?" Daisy grinned through her tears. "Corporal Tully is going to refuse ever to come with me anywhere again."

"I can't help it. I think I'm pregnant again."

"Oh, Justine!" Daisy laughed. "I'm not telling Antoine that. You'll have to tell him yourself."

"Daisy, what's going to happen?" Justine stepped back, wiping her eyes, and took the baby. "Is your father ever going to come to his senses and let my husband go? What possible difference can it make for one Frenchman to be kept locked up?"

Daisy shook her head as she picked up the basket. "I don't know." She looked to make sure Tully wasn't paying attention, but lowered her voice anyway. "I'm worried that the war may be coming our way. There are letters flying back and forth between Mobile and Pensacola, more and more frequently. I hear that the French are making raids into the Gulf and the Spanish don't do anything about it. I know Papa is anxious."

Justine hugged Rémy. "Can you—will you let me know if there's anything I can do? Maybe your father will let me come in to see Antoine sometime?"

"I doubt it. But I'll try." It was the best she could do. "Let's go to the market, so I can buy those oranges. Maybe Rémy would like one too." She turned and called to Tully, "Corporal, would you carry this basket while Justine and I visit the market?"

With a resigned sigh, Tully complied. "Just what I wanted to do on my afternoon off."

16

New Orleans
May 25, 1778

Lyse wiped her pen and capped the inkwell, then reread what she had written in her journal. How boring. Grimacing, she shoved the book away and went to the window to twitch aside the curtain and stare down at the street traffic.

In two weeks she had gone from waiting tables and serving ale in an English public tavern, living as a servant in a tiny attic bedroom, to being the honored guest of the governor of Spanish Louisiana. She had enjoyed her stay with the Gálvezes, but she was becoming restless with the necessity of staying indoors. She had willingly told the governor everything she could think of that might be pertinent to Spanish success in taking Mobile from the British—apparently the war was about to take a twist shocking only to those who had been isolated on some deserted island—but for some reason no one would divulge to her, the governor and his lady had deemed it necessary for her to remain indefinitely incognito.

It was a luxurious imprisonment, to be sure. On that first afternoon, after the governor excused himself and Rafa to adjourn to his office for further conference, Madame Gálvez had one of the servants show Lyse to a guest room, where she bathed and borrowed one of her hostess's silk dressing gowns. After a long nap, Lyse woke to find a servant waiting to help her into a beautiful rose-colored dimity dress and show her down to the dining room. Rafa had apparently gone home to reunite with his family, leaving Lyse to enjoy a sumptuous but awkward dinner with the Gálvezes.

She hadn't seen him since. Madame Gálvez explained vaguely that Rafa was completing an assignment for Mr. Pollock, and that he would return . . . soon.

Whatever that meant.

Lyse found the hardest part of this sojourn—besides missing home and constantly wondering what Rafa was doing—to be the inactivity. She had been so used to intellectual and physical toil in the school and the tavern, from sunup to sundown, that now she was able to sleep at night only in short, restless bursts plagued with nightmares. Consequently, she withstood the daily routine of eating, reading, and picking at needlework with heavy eyes and frayed temper. The only relief in the monotony came from sporadic conversations with the lady of the house.

Feliciana Gálvez was a charming conversationalist, who told lively stories of growing up in the great port city of New Orleans, cherished daughter of a large, wealthy French merchant family. Her first marriage had been brief and childless, her second an almost unheard of love match. She lavishly praised her handsome, brilliant husband, whose tact and diplomacy in difficult situations had early earned him the respect and gratitude of much older Spanish authorities, including the king himself. However, she was also careful to divulge nothing of any political importance.

Lyse thought the governor was not the only one in the family with diplomatic gifts.

She was just about to fling herself into the comfortable chair in the corner of her room, when a scratching at the door caused her to drop the curtain and quickly cross the room. At last—someone to talk to!

When she got the door open, she stood, mouth ajar, staring at Scarlet. A smiling, neatly dressed, heavily pregnant Scarlet.

Uttering a little scream of joy, Lyse flung herself at her cousin.

"I hear you are in need of a maid," Scarlet said, after Lyse had kissed both her cheeks and reluctantly released her.

"I don't need a maid—I need a friend." Lyse wiped her streaming eyes. "How did you get here, and *look* at you! Rafa said you were having a baby, but—oh, my, look at you."

Scarlet laughed. "I can hardly see anything else, I'm so big! I have been with your Rafa's family. They brought me. Doña Evangelina and Miss Sofía are in the family parlor. They sent me up first so we could say hello without . . . well, you know." She shrugged.

"You are with Rafa's family? And they didn't tell me? There is something very strange going on here, Scarlet. Where is he? I haven't seen him since the day we arrived, nearly . . . eleven days ago, I think?"

Scarlet's big dark eyes softened. "I know you must have questions, some of them I can answer, some I can't. But they told me to bring you down right away, because Miss Sofía is standing on her head to become acquainted with the girl who has her brother all but living in the frontier outpost of Mobile, West Florida!"

Lyse glanced over her shoulder at the mirror. "All right, let me just—"

"You look fine, just come on." Smiling, Scarlet grabbed Lyse's hand and pulled her down the long, carpeted hallway toward the stairs.

"You seem to be familiar with this house," Lyse observed, bemused.

"Yes, I stayed here for a few days after Rafael bought me at the slave market. The Gálvezes are very kind, aren't they?"

"Indeed." At the foot of the stairs she tugged Scarlet's hand to stop her. "My cousin, I am sorry you have had so much to endure. That wicked Isabelle Dussouy will answer for her sins."

"Yes, but it is not mine to repay evil for evil. God will judge her, so I don't have to."

They stared at each other for a long moment. Lyse didn't know that she would have been so forgiving in Scarlet's circumstances. But her cousin seemed to have gained a serenity that could come from no other source. Perhaps she, Lyse, could learn from it.

Scarlet smiled and continued toward the open French doors of the family parlor. "Here she is!" She all but pushed Lyse into the room.

Lyse quickly found Madame Gálvez, seated upon a settee with a beautiful young girl who looked like Rafa in a lavender dress. A third woman, older than Madame Gálvez by some fifteen years, rose from a high-backed chair and approached her with measured, queenly steps.

"How do you do, my dear? I am Doña Evangelina Gonzales, and we have been waiting impatiently for the governor to give us permission to visit." The woman took Lyse's hands, kissed her cheek, and stepped back to examine her face as if learning a work of art in a gallery.

"Madame." Curtseying, Lyse felt a blush rise to the crown of her head. Rafa's mama, the so-critical Doña Gonzales, was herself a lovely woman, exquisitely dressed in a jonquil-colored gown that must have been created in Paris. She herself must look a complete bumpkin.

Doña Evangelina seemed to approve, however, for she released Lyse with a smile and gestured to the girl beside Madame Gálvez. "And this is my daughter, Sofía. Mind your manners, Sofi!"

But the admonishment came too late. Sofía had already bounced to her feet and flung herself at Lyse, grabbing her in a warm hug. "Oh, I am so happy to finally meet you! Rafael said *pretty*, he didn't say beautiful as a Goya painting!" Sofía let her go with an enthusiastic buss on the cheek, then whirled with a giggle. "And you have chosen this lace on my favorite gown, so I had to wear it and show you! See?"

Lyse, duly admiring the dress, murmured approval. The lace was every bit as lovely as she had envisioned. She looked at Madame Gálvez, silently begging for rescue.

Madame Gálvez smoothly rose. "Miss Lanier, you must forgive me if my desire to surprise you has perhaps been a bit overwhelming. I know you must have many questions, which my husband has given me leave to answer. Certain . . . protocols had to be in place first."

Lyse glanced at Scarlet, who remained standing near the door. "Of course, Madame. I understand." But she understood nothing. She wanted to ask about Rafa. Surely someone would explain what had happened to him, sooner or later.

"Good." Madame Gálvez nodded. "Now we shall sit down to tea—" she nodded at Eduardo, hovering near the door—"and get properly acquainted."

Lyse took the only remaining chair in the room as the other ladies reseated themselves. Her experience with such intimate social situations had been limited, but she knew enough to let the elder ladies take the lead.

Even the mercurial Sofía was now demurely settled upon the settee, hands clasped in her lap. Her dark eyes met Lyse's, dancing.

After some inconsequential chatter while Eduardo came and went, taking Scarlet with him and shutting the parlor door behind him, Madame Gálvez turned to Sofía's mother. "Doña Evangelina, it may now be clear to you why I sent Scarlet to you. She is not Rafael's lover, but a beloved relative of Miss Lanier. My husband has just completed the documentation releasing her from slavery—"

Lyse couldn't restrain a little squeak of joy as she jumped to her feet. "Oh, madame! I do not know how to thank you!"

Madame Gálvez sent her an indulgent smile that yet had an edge of seriousness. "We are coming to that, my dear."

"Oh. Yes, madame." Lyse dropped back to her chair. "But it is so wonderful." She couldn't help smiling.

Doña Evangelina seemed less sanguine. "Then whose baby is she carrying?"

"Lyse will perhaps be able to answer that," Madame Gálvez said.

"My cousin was married—well, perhaps not legally, but she considered herself married—to the blacksmith of Madame Dussouy, a society matron in Mobile. Madame Dussouy has a long-held hatred for my family, and often expressed that enmity in petty and cruel ways. Selling Scarlet apart from her husband was one such act. I don't believe she knew about the baby, or she might have done something even more horrid."

Doña Evangelina blinked. "I see." She looked at Madame Gálvez. "Please, continue, my lady."

Madame Gálvez nodded. "My husband had every intention of reuniting Scarlet with Miss Lanier, but he wanted first to ascertain that Rafael's assessment was based on fact, and not biased by personal affection."

"His . . . assessment?" Lyse stared at her hostess. Clearly there was some subtext going on beneath this very cryptic explanation.

"Yes. Even Rafael's parents have not been privy to the fact that he has been serving his country in a much more dangerous capacity than would appear. Don Joaquín, his father, has of course served honorably on the staff of both former Governor-General Alejandro O'Reilly and my husband as well, and his brothers serve in the Spanish navy. But Rafael, in taking a post as merchant in company with Oliver Pollock, has doubled as liaison between the American Continental Congress and the court at Madrid. His Majesty—and my husband, by proxy—has greatly relied upon information Rafael has procured in his travels aboard Pollock's ships, in and out of British ports along the Gulf Coast."

Lyse sat stunned. Rafa was a *spy*. She should have seen it. The extravagant inanity and dandified manners, which she knew to be a cover for a deep intellect. His genius for appearing at critical junctures. The way he had whisked her out of Mobile in the very nick of time, and his ability to locate and rescue Scarlet. He undoubtedly knew where Simon was too.

Her body shook with reaction. Everything he'd ever said, every romantic and tender action toward her, had been accomplished for purposes so clandestine she might never be able to untangle what was real and what was sham.

Mi corazón, he had called her. My heart.

No, she was his dupe.

Bracing herself, she linked her fingers tightly and lifted her gaze to Madame Gálvez. "I assume there is something you require of me in return for my cousin's freedom. I'll do whatever you ask."

The other woman seemed to understand some of her mixed emotions. Her smile was wry. "Don't be too quick to agree, my dear. There is one more thing you should know. Your family has already been of great service to us in a capacity so secret that even Rafael did not know until recently. Your brother Simon—"

"Simon! But he hates the Spanish!" Lyse blurted.

"He had reason to, but your brother is a practical young man. He and your grandfather still have strong ties to your family here in New Orleans."

Lyse thought back to the conversation she'd had with Simon after Rafa had toured the bay with them. Certainly Simon had acted as if he hated Rafa that day, but when Lyse questioned him about the rebellion, there had been something vaguely unsettling about his answer. Evidently her brother was nearly as good an actor as Rafael.

"So . . . Simon is an American sympathizer as well?" She could still hardly credit it.

"Yes. He is with Rafa now. I am not allowed to say where."

This was entirely too much for one day. One minute she was in her room, expiring from boredom, the next she was in this salon with her world spinning out of control.

"Does my grandfather know?"

"I imagine so. They were very close."

She opened her eyes and faced Madame Gálvez. "What is it you want me to do?"

~

Fort Pitt
September 2, 1778

At the juncture of the Monongahela and Allegheny rivers, where they flowed together to become the Ohio, old Fort Pitt sat like a lean, hungry cat waiting for prey. Rafa was no mouse, but he felt just as vulnerable as he waited for entrance at the gate of the fort's southern redoubt. Shivering, he turned up the collar of his coat. In New Orleans, the heat would still be suffocating, but as he and his companions had traveled north, skimming on the Spanish side of the Mississippi River past the British forts at Baton Rouge, Natchez, and St. Louis, then making their way slowly on up the Ohio, temperatures had grown more temperate. There was a definite snap of fall in the air, here in the Ohio Valley.

He wondered what Simon Lanier, whom he'd left at the barque with the crew to guard the cargo, thought about this alien riverscape. Of necessity the two of them had gotten to know one another during the last three months of travel upriver. Where Rafa tended to be impulsive and flexible, he found Lyse's brother to be brusque, quick-thinking under pressure, but infinitely patient and methodical in laying out plans. Rafa thought they made an effective team for their particular assignment: delivering 22,640 *pesos fuertes*, as well as a long list of supplies, to American Captain George Rogers Clark for use in his campaign to take control of the Kaskaskian territory.

On several occasions, Rafa had accompanied Pollock on trading expeditions along the upper Mississippi. His familiarity with the twists and turns of the river, not to mention his diplomatic skills, were invaluable, but Lanier was the true sailor. Until these strengths were sorted out, the two of them had frequently butted heads. Eventually, however, they settled into an uneasy truce.

The gate abruptly opened, interrupting Rafa's musings on the stark differences between the two eldest Lanier siblings. He bowed to the rough-hewn individual staring him down from behind a Kentucky longrifle. "Don Rafael Gonzales de Rippardá, reporting to Captain George Rogers Clark. Here is my letter of introduction from Governor Gálvez of New Orleans."

Some three hours later, he was escorting Captain Clark and a small detachment of Virginia militiamen down the incline from the fort to the river. He had found Clark to be young, affable, and thankfully bright, cognizant as he was of the great boon granted the American cause in Spanish intervention. Apparently there had been a series of attacks by small contingents of British-armed Indians during the summer, rendering the militiamen grateful for all reinforcements.

Rafa was glad to provide support, but he would be just as glad to make his way back to New Orleans before winter. Leaving Lyse without a chance to say goodbye had been excruciating. His mission with her brother had dangerous elements, as British settlers along the banks of the river were known to be increasingly trigger-happy. They flew the neutral Spanish flag, but some plantation owners had learned to shoot first and ask questions later.

For that reason, just within sight of the barque anchored a safe distance offshore, Rafa shouted a warning. "Ship ho! Rippardá coming aboard with Captain Clark!"

Lanier appeared on deck and gave orders for someone to lower a rope ladder over the side. Rafa and Clark pushed the longboat he'd left on shore out into the water, jumped in, and rowed out to the barque. As they climbed over the barque's rail, landing on their feet, Lanier reached to shake hands with the American.

"Captain Clark, I'm Simon Lanier." He glanced at Rafa. "I'm Don Rafael's . . . business partner."

Clark nodded. "And we're grateful for this timely delivery of funds. The British are moving on us from Canada, trying to secure territory here in the west, and we've got to stop them before they have our militia surrounded and river travel cut off." He paused, sent Rafa an awkward glance. "I need to make doubly sure, however, that this money is intended for my use and not supposed to be sent on to Philadelphia."

"Governor Gálvez understands the importance of your strategy, believe me," Lanier said. "And as Rippardá undoubtedly told you, an equal sum has been sent by the eastern route, for the New England front."

"Very well. Then let us begin off-loading immediately. I brought enough men to get it done quickly, and still keep us covered in the event of attack."

With Lanier supervising activity aboard the barque and Rafa assisting Clark and his men ashore, the chests of coin were moved to the fort by late afternoon. Mission accomplished, Rafa returned to the significantly lightened ship, climbed the rope ladder for the last time, and pulled it up, along with the longboat, to be secured to its sailing position.

Feeling just a bit deflated, he leaned against the rail, arms braced, watching the fort shrink as they sailed down the Ohio River on a strong south current, sails popping in a brisk wind.

Lanier joined him, shielding his eyes against the sun glinting off the water at the western horizon. "Am I the only one who thinks this whole escapade was just a bit too easy?" he said.

Rafa grimaced. "I hope you're wrong. That is a pile of money we just left. I have to pray they'll make good use of it. I agree with Gálvez. Once you decide to back a cause, you'd better be prepared to go in all the way."

"Would you carry a rifle and aim it against your countrymen, if you were an American?"

"I'm glad I didn't have to make that decision. As it is, I side with the Americans and serve my king at the same time. They win, we win."

Lanier's smile was wry. "No sacrifice for you."

He thought of Lyse's agony over leaving Daisy and her family, and her face when she'd said yes to his silent urging. He lifted his shoulders. Perhaps the sacrifice was yet to come. "How could you leave Daisy, knowing you might never see her again?"

"Gonzales, when you love someone, you want the best for them. How could I bring her with me, knowing she'd grieve for her father? Besides, here we are thousands of miles away for months at a time. I wouldn't leave her in New Orleans not knowing a soul. If I'd known you were going to get Lyse out—"

"Do you know why I had to bring Lyse? You never asked."

"I know she's in love with you—Lord knows why."

Rafa grinned. "I hope she is. But that's not why I had to get her out of Mobile. She was hiding some contraband books under her bed—books Daisy gave her when the major forced her to move into the fort."

Lanier frowned. "Books? You mean pro-rebellion books? That's treason!"

"So you didn't know?"

"She wouldn't have told me she had any such leanings, because I made sure everyone in town knew I was Loyalist so her father would favor my suit for her hand."

Rafa began to laugh. "If that isn't a fine mess. She'd have come with you in a heartbeat, if you'd just asked."

"And my sister knew this?" Lanier sounded incredulous.

"She's a very bright girl, your sister," Rafa said dryly. "And she took the fall for those books, so I had to get her out of there the best way I could."

"Like I said, no great sacrifice."

Rafa sighed. "Except, I have no way of knowing if she agreed because she has any particular affection for me—or if she was just accepting the lesser of two bad choices."

There was a long silence. The two of them stared downriver, while the sails cracked and snapped overhead, and the Ohio sluiced below.

Finally, Lanier said softly, "Whoever would have thought little Daisy would be a rebel?"

Mobile
October 6, 1778

A year had come and gone.

Daisy walked out onto the wharf and stood with her hat in one hand and ruffled cap in the other, letting the gulf breeze tear the pins from her hair so that it blew in wild ribbons about her head. She watched a river hawk wheel, then dive and come up with a fish wriggling in its talons. She wished she could fly off behind it as it soared across the river to some undisclosed nesting site.

Instead, she must return to the fort within the hour, or Corporal Tully would come after her. Or worse, he'd send Niall to find and escort her, and then she'd never have a minute to herself the rest of the day. He would give her a chiding look for her immodesty—no respectable woman went about with her head uncovered—and ask her if she would like to walk to the market or drive along the shell road or some other boring and pointless activity. And she would have to invent some excuse to say no, when everyone knew the brick walls of the fort had become her prison.

As Lyse had always said, Niall was a good man, but he always went for safe options. Now that Lyse had proven her disloyalty, leaving the city for good with the Spaniard, Niall seemed to have transferred his doglike devotion to Daisy. Likely he felt sorry for her. He knew—as the whole city of Mobile likely knew—that Daisy had held a candle for Simon Lanier since she was a child. He knew Simon was gone, and he wanted to curry favor with her father. All good reasons for a young ensign to come courting the commander's daughter.

And if she were a devoted, obedient daughter, she would respond, well, surely not with eagerness—but at least with gratitude. Niall was kind and hardworking, young and strong. He would make a good father—

Suddenly she drew in her arm and flung her hat, sending it wheeling like a straw seagull over the water. It landed upside down and quickly sank.

"I won't." She said it out loud, then shouted it. "I won't!" She balled up the cap and tossed it into the river too. It floated, full of air for a few moments, then slowly went under.

She stamped her foot. She was not an obedient daughter. She loved her father, and he had a duty to obey his orders, but she loved Simon even more. And he had asked her to wait.

So she would wait. But not passively, like a dove in a cage. It was said that sea hawks mated for life, and that was what she would be—a hawk, free to fly in search of God's will for her. She believed that she was created with the individual, unalienable right to freedom, to the pursuit of happiness, as the declaration of independence stated. There was no guarantee that she would ever see Simon again, let alone find a way to marry him. But neither did she have to settle for second best.

She was going to find a way to go to him, demand to know once and for all if he wanted her, and if not—well, then God would show her what to do next.

But first, she was going to take a walk. Without her head covering.

~

New Orleans
October 8, 1778

War was coming. Lyse and Scarlet's new life in New Orleans had been tranquil enough over the summer, as Lyse moved in with the

Gonzales family and helped prepare for the arrival of Scarlet's baby. They all celebrated Scarlet's emancipation on July 4, then the baby made his appearance just over a week later—a little boy, christened Bernardo in honor of the governor.

During the months of August and September, Lyse spent most days in the governor's mansion, learning the specifics of what she would be required to do during the coming fall social season, and also sharing every detail she could remember about the town of Mobile and Fort Charlotte. She understood the seriousness of the responsibility she had undertaken, as a provider of information that could affect the outcome of the American struggle for independence. She was at once thrilled and terrified.

She developed the habit of rising every morning at dawn, to spend the first hour of the day on her knees, praying beside the comfortable guest room bed she had been allotted next to Sofía's room. She prayed for Rafa's and Simon's safety. She prayed for Daisy's comfort and protection, as well as her father's. And she asked God to watch over her grandfather and Justine and the children. A bit diffidently she asked for wisdom for herself. Then she would open Grandmére's Bible and read a little, finding help and encouragement in the words, as Grandmére had promised.

After her devotional time, she met Sofía and her mother for breakfast. Most days, the terrifying Colonel Gonzales would have already left to meet with his staff, leaving the women free to chatter about clothes and the new baby—who everyone agreed was miraculously good about not squalling during the night more than once or maybe twice—and Rafa's multitudinous escapades as a little boy. Lyse came to quite adore these stories, told with amused affection by his mother and alternating fits of indignation and laughter by his sister.

The two Gonzales women seemed to take it for granted that Lyse would become one of the family. At first she had shyly denied the betrothal, but at their stares of patent disbelief, she not so reluctantly allowed them to assume a sincere commitment between herself and Rafael.

He would arrive soon enough, she hoped, and set them straight as to the expedient nature of getting herself betrothed to avoid hanging for treason.

On this particular muggy and overcast mid-October morning, Lyse was sitting by the fountain in the Gonzaleses' courtyard garden with Sofía. Sofía had been practicing her French, sending Lyse into fits of giggles because of her utter inability to swallow her *r*'s, insisting instead on rolling them all.

"I think we will have to admit defeat," Sofía sighed, after her final butchering of the word *respondez*. "I shall never have a chance to visit Paris anyway. Papa says it is a city fit only for vagrants and artists—which seem to be, in his view, one and the same." She tilted her head. "Have you ever had your portrait painted, Lyse?"

"Me?" Lyse laughed. "Sofía, you forget, my papa is a fisherman. Who would want to paint my portrait?"

"Rafael will, one day. He loves music and art."

Lyse stared. "I knew he could sing and play the guitar. Does he draw as well?"

"Oh yes. At least, he used to. Until Papa threw his paints away. Papa said it was a waste of time and money, and he should join the marines like Cristián and Danilo."

Lyse didn't know what to say. Her own father was often thoughtless and impulsive, but he would never do something so cruel as to discard one of his children's creations.

Fortunately, at that moment the Gonzales houseman stepped through the gate and approached, holding a tray upon which a letter lay. The man bowed, proffering the tray. "Miss Sofía, I thought you might like to see this right away. It's a letter from the governor's lady."

"Really? Oh, how delightful! Thank you, Manuel." Sofía eagerly broke the letter's seal and began to read it. After a moment, she looked up, eyes wide. "Madame Gálvez has invited us to a ball in a week's time. Lyse! This is terrible!"

Lyse laughed. "Why is being invited to a ball at the governor's mansion a terrible thing?"

"Why because! Because there is not enough time to have a new dress made! What are we going to do?"

Lyse rolled her eyes. "How very inconsiderate of her ladyship to fail to allow sufficient time for you to add another garment to a wardrobe that would already outfit half the population of Louisiana."

"Lyse! This is serious! Stop joking!"

"All right. But perhaps I have a solution. Scarlet is quite handy with a needle, you know. Have her take apart two or three of your older dresses and remake them into a new one."

Sofía's eyes narrowed. "That could possibly work. In fact, I like it! We should have her get started right away. You can play with that adorable little Bernardo while Scarlet works on my dress." She jumped to her feet and grabbed Lyse's hand. "Come on, there is no time to waste!"

Laughing, Lyse allowed herself to be towed into the house, where Sofía proceeded to shout for Scarlet.

Two years ago, never in her wildest dreams would she have pictured herself living in a house where one would be invited as a matter of course to a ball at the home of the governor of an entire colony. Of course, she used to fantasize about dancing with a duke, until she met Rafael Gonzales.

There was no going back to that naive little girl.

Sometimes she wondered if that was a good thing or a bad thing.

17

New Orleans
October 15, 1778

As she and Sofía descended the stairs to the Gálvez ballroom behind Doña Gonzales and the colonel, Lyse couldn't help comparing this harvest ball to the one she had attended this time last year at Burelle's. For one thing, the robe à la français Madame Gálvez had sent for her to wear seemed to have a lot less fabric at strategic points than had her former teaching garb.

She had worried a little when she put the dress on this afternoon, but Sofía had refused to let her look in the mirror until her hair was dressed and jewelry added. "Trust me, Lyse," Sofía said with a giggle, "you are going to turn heads tonight."

But then there had been a rush to get in the carriage, and there was no time to preen in front of a mirror. She would have to trust Madame's exquisite taste. What she had seen of the dress was stunning. Its skirt and petticoat were of a clear green satin, ruched in bands along every edge, with large leaf-shaped appliqués in green satin sewn along the open skirt front—a clever and striking design, to be sure. The bodice, of the same fabric, was edged with delicate blonde lace and ribbon, pleated to mimic the design of the skirt.

She felt elegant and fashionable, almost worthy to attend such a grand affair as a governor's ball.

Then, suddenly, she caught a glimpse of her reflection in the huge mirror placed opposite the staircase. Horrified, she grasped Sofía's wrist, and almost turned to run back the way she had come.

She would indeed be turning heads. The square-necked bodice, emphasized by the ruched lace, might be the height of Parisian fashion, but it was cut lower than any garment she'd ever worn.

"What's the matter?" Sofía, already two steps below, looked up at her in concern.

Lyse craned her neck to check the necklines of other women already in the ballroom. Most were even less modest than she and Sofía. "I'm . . . feeling a draft." She put her gloved hand over her bosom.

Sofía frowned, then suddenly giggled. "You'll get used to it."

"No. I won't. I shouldn't. Why didn't you tell me?"

"Because you're a prude. And the governor wants you to charm the gentlemen."

"But Madame didn't say . . ." She bit her lip. Madame *had* said for her to dance often, laugh a lot, and listen all the time. Governor Galvez wanted as much information as he could get about what people thought, and especially what they knew about British, Indian, and American aggressive activities. Was dressing like a Parisian courtesan part of listening?

She knew her cheeks were on fire. But perhaps that would be assumed to be a result of the excessive warmth in the room from all the lamps and candles. With mirrors everywhere, the whole ballroom seemed to be one big blaze of light and heat and glitter.

Sofía's eyes softened. "Come, nobody will think you . . . what is your so-useful French word . . . *outré*? Relax and have a good time. You have earned a little fun, *si?*"

Since she could hardly walk home alone, Lyse had no choice. She released Sofía and followed her down the remaining steps into the ballroom. The Gálvezes stood ready to receive each of the guests as they entered, and Lyse was gratified to be warmly hugged by Madame and kissed on the cheek by the governor. Wouldn't Grandpére be impressed at the company she was keeping now? She must be careful not to let pride turn her head.

Once they were out of the receiving line, the Gonzaleses were swept into conversation with friends, Lyse along with them. For the first half hour or so, she found herself buzzing like a bumblebee from one conversational cluster to another. She found that several military gentlemen whom she had met here at the Gálvezes' home remembered her, and she was relieved that they had the good manners to keep their eyes focused on her face and not skimming below her neck. These conversations led to names being scrawled on her dance card, as young men eagerly followed the lead of their elders.

Before long, she found herself enjoying the status of a "belle." As the word implied, she felt beautiful, desirable, and warmly welcomed into New Orleans society. Friendship with the charming and gregarious Sofía Gonzales didn't hurt anything, either.

She completely lost track of the time, until shortly before midnight, she allowed a young American merchant to dance her through the open French doors and out onto the balcony which looked down on the lamplit courtyard fountain. The young man had told her his name—Mr. Thornton, or some such British name, she thought, trying to remember—but her attention splintered when over his shoulder she saw a familiar dark head.

Rafa was smiling, carrying on a conversation with someone she couldn't see, but his gaze kept flicking the room.

"Miss Lanier! I asked if you wanted refreshment—I'd be pleased to fetch it for you."

"What?" She looked at her companion and found him regarding her with disappointment and chagrin. Apparently she had been edging back toward the doorway. "Oh—no, thank you—I'll get it myself."

She ducked back inside the ballroom, then stopped. Was she going to run to him the moment he stepped into the room, when he hadn't taken the trouble to look for her first?

How long had he been in New Orleans? Surely he would have gone to his family first—or, more likely, his first stop would have been at the Cabildo to debrief with Gálvez.

But Gálvez was here, so of course he'd come here first, and why would he seek out Lyse, when he had much more important matters to—

Their eyes met across the room. His smile broadened, crinkling his eyes and melting her knees. She stood very still as he came to her, adroitly sidestepping every person in his path. Her heart beat high in her throat, and she knew she was undone.

When he reached her, he took her hand and lifted it to his lips. Through the lace of her glove, she felt his warm mouth linger for a moment longer than was truly necessary. Because she wanted to fling her arms around his neck, she snatched her hand away and put it childishly behind her back.

He grinned at her. "Hello, Miss Lanier. I like your dress."

"There is a knife in the usual place."

"I do not think one would fit in that little space."

Her mouth dropped open. She should have slapped him, but instead she laughed. "I missed you."

"Yes, you did. Come here, I have a surprise for you." He took her hand and drew her in and out among the guests, until they were on the other side of the ballroom, where an open door led to a large anteroom with a billiards table in its center.

In the doorway, she jerked her hand out of his grasp. There were no women in the room, only Governor Gálvez and another gentleman, whose back was to her as he bent over a ball on the table, cue in hand.

The governor looked up at her entrance. "Ah. Miss Lanier, I see he found you. Come in."

She looked at Rafa for explanation.

He smiled, gave her a little push into the room.

The man with his back to her shoved the ball hard across the table toward the wicket at the other end, then straightened and turned in one fluid motion.

"Simon!" she shrieked and ran for him.

~

Rafa watched Lyse reunite with her brother, grateful that there was nothing more than a bullet hole in Simon's tricorn to indicate the little run-in they'd had with a British patrol boat as they sailed past Manchac. Since they'd taken time to bathe and change clothes before barging in on the party, Lyse need never know about that.

He wished he could bring her whole family out of Mobile, but there would be time for that later. For the present, he had his work cut out for him, coordinating the various streams of information entering New Orleans and helping Gálvez interpret it for policy purposes.

The governor rounded the table, cue in hand. "Those two were a great find, Rafael," he said quietly. "They're both smart and observant . . . and discreet."

"Yes, sir. The family history of rebellion under O'Reilly might have been a negative, except that it left them with no love for the British either."

"But you did say that the daughter of the commander—Major Redmond is his name, no?—is Lyse's lifelong friend?"

"She is. But Daisy's a rebel sympathizer herself. The odd thing is, sir . . . she's in love with Simon and doesn't know he's Patriot. If she'd known that, she might not have been willing to stay. I expect Simon will want to go after her, as soon as you'll allow it."

The governor shook his head. "If she's truly Patriot as well, she's a valuable asset inside the fort. We need to leave her there as long as possible."

Rafa glanced at Simon, who was laughing with his sister over some shared inside joke. "Then you'd better convince him she's safe where she is, or he'll be going in to get her."

Gálvez tapped his lower lip with a finger. "Perhaps you could take the commander another gift of some sort . . . a case of fine cigars, or wine . . . as a pretext for slipping her a letter from her friend. Ask her to write back to Lyse, but give her a code to pass us a few updated statistics. Her observations about staffing, munitions, provisioning—any of that would be helpful to us as we prepare."

"That sounds like you're expecting us to enter the war soon."

"Soon . . . maybe. Havana is careful not to give me too many specifics. But between you and me, I expect to hear the confirmation within a year—two at the most."

Rafa nodded. Gálvez wasn't really speaking out of turn, for speculation in the city was rife in just those terms. "The most interesting thing we learned as we came back from Fort Pitt was that the British had instigated a series of Indian uprisings against our forts along the Ohio and Mississippi this summer—with plans to hit New Orleans in the fall. But it seems the whole scheme fell apart. Our man Villebreuve, stationed with the Choctaw, says they—and the Chickasaw and Cherokee as well—are a bit more afraid of the Americans than the British can pay to overcome."

"Yes, that sort of activity is what tells me the British won't give away their colonies so easily. I know his majesty would like us to negotiate peace if we can—but England doesn't want peace."

Rafa leaned against the table, thinking over the implications. War was coming, and it would not be an easy overnight victory. Floridablanca, the Spanish minister of state, had carefully held back commitment to the Americans until Spain was financially and militarily ready. If Gálvez was correct—and he usually was—the time had almost come. Still, the theater of war was widespread over massive territory, and England would not easily concede.

He knew that Gálvez's planned strategy was straightforward

and simple: march north and take the British forts at Baton Rouge, Manchac, and Natchez to secure the river. Then he would sail to Mobile and capture Fort Charlotte before moving on to siege Pensacola. Surrounding the British on the western and southern fronts would bolster the efforts of French regulars, the Continental Army, and American militia along the eastern seaboard, in the Ohio Valley, and in New England.

Maintaining the integrity of every asset in place, both in Mobile and Pensacola, as well as here in New Orleans, was critical to the success of that strategy. But he also knew that Simon Lanier had a lot to lose by leaving Daisy Redmond in Mobile.

With his arm across his sister's shoulders, Lanier turned. Muscles jumped along his jawline. He had apparently heard some of Rafa's conversation with Gálvez. "Governor, you promised that if I could get that shipment of gold delivered to Fort Pitt, you'd help me find a way to go back into Mobile and bring Miss Redmond out."

Gálvez spread his hands. "I did. But I can't afford to precipitate an unnecessary crisis until we are officially at war. If you can give me another six months to lull them into complacency, I'll send you in to get her before we attack."

Lanier was clearly unhappy.

"Governor, if I may," Rafa said, hoping to defuse any reactionary eruption from his hotheaded colleague, "I like your suggestion that I take Miss Redmond a missive from Miss Lanier. Simon and Lyse both know Miss Redmond well enough to craft a message that will be useful and reassuring to her, but still covert enough to escape detection should it fall into the wrong hands."

Gálvez nodded. "All right. The three of you meet tomorrow morning for that purpose. Rafael, when you're satisfied with your letter, bring it to me. Meanwhile, Pollock and I will see what we can do about this new request for supplies you brought from Governor Henry. There are enough Americans here in New Orleans, posing as merchants, that the city is secure for now. But I'm hoping

Havana will see fit to send reinforcements before long." He rubbed his forehead as if it ached. "That's all for now. Go mingle and listen—and for heaven's sake, act like you're having a good time."

Lyse laughed and hugged her brother. "I am, now that Simon is here."

Rafa wished she'd said that about him. Patience was not his greatest strength—but perhaps he was learning it, a little, the hard way.

~

Daylight slipped through the curtains the morning after the Gálvez ball, and Rafa awoke, aware that something about the house was different. He rose and dressed, then slipped down the stairs to prowl for sustenance in the ample larder off the ground-floor kitchen.

The Gonzales family had moved from Havana to New Orleans in the summer of 1769, when Rafa was thirteen years of age. He'd enjoyed a rather idyllic coming-of-age, tutored at home with his brothers and learning the alleys and bayous of the city, until he was sixteen, when his father the colonel decided to ship him off to the Spanish Royal Academy of Naval Engineers. Upon his graduation in 1776, he'd come home to be a sore disappointment to El Papá. When Rafa applied to Governor Unzaga for employment as an officer, the general had, at least in Papá's opinion, lost his mind and instead introduced Rafa to the Irish merchant Oliver Pollock.

What Colonel Gonzales could not know was that Rafa did indeed go on the governor's payroll, on a detachment of such a delicate nature that no one outside the governor's closest staff would be privy to his comings and goings. His very first assignment had been a rather daring foray up the Mississippi River with a shipment of gunpowder that eventually made its way to General Washington, who was then quartered in Pennsylvania. Shortly after Rafa returned to New Orleans, Unzaga was replaced as governor by the even more cunning and resourceful Gálvez, who saw no reason to interrupt the creative partnership of Pollock and Rippardá.

Rafa had truly enjoyed the clandestine, rollicking nature of his role in Spanish espionage, but he found himself increasingly looking forward to those times when he could sleep in his own bed, wake up to his mama's *bollos* and *café con leche*, and irritate his sister Sofía. As he padded down the stairs, yawning, the tie-strings of his shirt hanging open at his chest, he wondered if Sofi was awake. She might like to go for a ride before breakfast, if she hadn't got lazy from staying up late at balls and soirées every other night during the social season.

Grinning, he turned to run back up the stairs—and then stopped halfway up as he remembered what was different today. Lyse was upstairs, asleep in the room next to Sofi.

His brain began an unplanned perambulation through the process of Lyse preparing for bed, dropping the naughty green dress Madame Gálvez had provided, brushing her hair . . . and then he realized where this particular journey would lead him.

You are an imbecile, he told himself sternly and set about distracting himself by listing, one with every step up the stairs, expressions of the Goldbach conjecture, until his brain was well and truly full of much more than red lips, golden skin, and topaz eyes.

He scratched at Sofía's door. "Sofi! Wake up and fix me breakfast! I'm hungry!" When a rising moan came from inside the room, he laughed. "Come on, I'll take you riding afterward. Hurry—get dressed!"

"Go away!"

"Sofi . . ."

"Take Lyse—she actually likes to get up early."

Rafa glanced at the closed door next to Sofía's room, desperately shutting down his active imagination. He should probably wake her up anyway. They would need to get started on the coded letter to Daisy.

"Rafa? What are you doing?"

He nearly jumped out of his skin. Lyse was at the bottom of the stairs, looking up at him. She wore a simple, very modest yellow dress, and her hair was pinned up askew, as if she'd done it herself without a mirror. How had he missed her approach?

Snatching at his sangfroid, he began to descend the stairs. "Good morning, little cousin! I see you are not so lazy as my sister, and I congratulate you. Would you like to join me for breakfast and then a ride about the square?"

She shook her head, further dislodging the pile of curly hair. "We don't eat breakfast here so much. But I have been thinking about how to get a message to Daisy and made some notes. Would you like to see?"

Of course he would like to see. He walked down the stairs feeling exactly like that stupid fellow Odysseus she had once corrected him about, the one who had himself tied to his ship so he could listen to a woman's beautiful voice. *She* was telling *him* how things were done in his own home? No breakfast? His world was well and truly upside down.

"Yes, but first I'm hungry." He took her elbow and towed her toward the kitchen. "Is Simon down here with you?"

"He has already gone . . . somewhere." She waved a hand vaguely. "He said you would likely sleep 'til noon, and he would be back then."

Affronted, Rafa stopped and frowned down at her. "I do not ever sleep 'til noon. And now the governor will say we are late with the letter, and I have other responsibilities to take care of today that must be postponed."

"But I've been trying to tell you, the letter is almost ready. I just need you to read my notes, and I shall copy it in my best hand, then you can take it to her."

"How can it be ready when I have not even . . . Oh, never mind. I suppose you have not even had Manuel bring coffee."

She gave him a perplexed look, then shook her head and pushed him toward a kitchen stool. "Sit there and I will bring you coffee. Steamed milk too, yes?"

He watched her flit about the kitchen, competently handling the coffee bean grinder, the heavy kettle over the fire, and the milk jug. By the time he had a steaming mug of chicory in hand and a buttered sweet roll on the table, he reached the conclusion that Lyse made quite a useful addition to the family. He should definitely convince her to stay.

She climbed up on another stool with a second mug and blinked at him over its rim. "Better now?"

"You are much more cheerful in the morning than your brother." And prettier. A hank of ebony curls drooped distractingly beside her ear.

Blushing, she tucked it back. "Daisy and I developed a way of writing to each other, after Simon found my diary and read it aloud one day. Every fourth word is the coded message. We wrote that way for years, just because it was fun."

"That's pretty simplistic. What if her father reads it before giving it to her?"

"We are two little girls to him. I doubt he will bother reading it, because he would never imagine us bright enough to pass along anything important. But even if he does, we've gotten quite good at using words to imply something other than their literal meaning. The number seven, for example, can mean 'week,' the number twenty-four is 'day,' and so on."

Rafa sat up, suddenly wide awake. "That is ingenious. So in this first letter, you set up a series of useful words she can use to pass us information, which will make the code harder to break if someone gets suspicious later."

"I'd already thought of that!" She grinned at him, drawing a paper from her pocket and handing it to him. "Here is my list of what I thought might be helpful, with their code equivalents, but you might have others to add."

He studied the list, more and more impressed with her intuition. There were a few things he'd add, but not many. "I'm glad you're on our side," he said slowly.

~

Mobile
Late October 1778

Everyone thought her papa a lion who ruled Mobile and Fort Charlotte with bared fangs and deafening roar. Daisy could have told anyone who bothered to ask that, with proper handling, one smiling young lady with a backbone of iron could bend the lion to her will.

It had taken little more than a week of persistent moping, picking at dinner, and staring out of windows to convince Papa to allow her an hour at the market without making poor, beleaguered Corporal Tully accompany her. With that concession granted, Daisy's jaunts outside the fort got longer and more distant, until twice she had gone all the way to Spring Hill to visit Justine and Charles Lanier.

Coming back from the second of these trips, carrying a bundle that Justine asked her to take to Luc-Antoine, she turned down the road to the Dussouy mansion. She hadn't had occasion to visit the French socialite for quite some time. After the onset of hostilities between France and England, the Dussouys had tried to continue entertaining, but British Loyalists were reluctant to associate with anyone of suspect ancestry, and with the blockades restricting trade, former French citizens like the Dussouys had little money to spend on frivolities. Besides, Madame Dussouy's open persecution of Lyse and her family gave Daisy no incentive to be friendly.

But Justine had been stuck in the house with sick children for weeks and had grown anxious about her eldest. Luc-Antoine used to visit his mama and grandfather on his Sunday afternoons off, but these visits had abruptly ceased in early October. Daisy agreed to drop by to check on him and notify Justine if Luc-Antoine was ill.

She followed the sandy shell lane under the shade of a series of grand magnolia trees alternating with dogwood and oaks, the white gravel crunching pleasantly under her shoes. There was a nip of fall in the breeze, and several yards away through the trees, she could hear the slight rush of one of the spring-fed creeks that ran into Dog River. Before long she could see the outbuildings, and then the house itself, mildewed and slightly seedy in its old age. Madame's family, the Hayots, had owned this bit of property for almost as long as the Laniers had theirs, the two families squabbling over the years with varying degrees of amicability over water rights, childish pranks, and wandering livestock. The rupture in relations created by Antoine jilting Isabelle in so public and disgraceful a manner had only slightly healed when she married the aristocratic but penurious Michel Dussouy. She'd brought him to the ancestral home, where they lived in a second bedroom until the old Comte d'Hayot passed to his eternal reward, leaving Isabelle and her brilliant young husband in charge of a shipping business second in profitability only to the Laniers'.

Daisy could only shake her head over the French love affair with dynasty. Families like Isabelle's, whose ancestors had come to the settlement under the command of d'Iberville and his brother Bienville, walked about with their noses firmly stuck in the air, whether they had money, land, or neither. They still called themselves Creole, in that haughty Gallic way that made one feel like the veriest barbarian.

Well, Lyse's family being the exception. Old Mr. Chaz was just as proud of his Indian lineage as being the son of Marc-Antoine Lanier, who as a teenager sailed from Canada with Lord Bienville, and he was quick to welcome anyone into his home, be he Briton, Cherokee, or the lowest of slaves.

So lost in her thoughts was she that Daisy came upon the open-air blacksmith shop without warning, the sound of its roaring fire and the ringing of the hammer on the anvil breaking upon her like the noise of a storm. Cautiously she approached. Cain, stripped to the waist, his back muscles dripping with sweat, labored at some large implement—possibly a plowshare, she thought—swinging the huge hammer high over his shoulder, then slamming it down with nigh superhuman force and an ear-bursting clang.

She didn't see Luc-Antoine at first, but a movement from what she'd taken to be a pile of cloths drew her attention, and she realized it was Lyse's little brother, sitting on a stump with an iron bucket at his feet, ready to douse any stray sparks that might burn down the building. She walked over to him and put her hand on his shoulder.

Looking up at her, he flinched, but then smiled when he realized she wasn't his mistress. He dropped the bucket handle and jumped to his feet to fling his sooty arms around her waist. "Daisy! I mean, Miss Redmond!"

Letting the bundle from Justine fall to the ground, she grabbed Luc-Antoine close. He smelled like a goat, and he was ruining her dress, but she held on for a full minute. Something suspiciously like tears dripped down his dirty face, but when he pulled back, he swiped his shirtsleeve over his face to smear them away.

"What are you doing here?" he asked. "Hey, Cain, look who's here!"

"I've been to see your mama," Daisy said, indicating the bundle on the ground, "and she sent a new shirt for you. She thought you might be growing out of your last one."

"He's growing out of everything, eating Madame Isabelle out of house and home," said Cain, who had turned around with a grin, letting the hammer fall to his side. "My mama can't keep him fed." He looked around and frowned. "Luc, let Miss Daisy have your seat, and I'll go to the kitchen to get something for us all to drink."

"Cain, you don't have to—" But he was already gone. Daisy watched Luc-Antoine swipe a rag across the stump, then she gingerly sat upon it. "Thank you," she said politely, smiling at him. "Your mama wants to know why you haven't been to see her lately. She misses you."

Luc-Antoine twisted the rag between his hands. "I've been busy."

"On your afternoon off?"

"Yes'm." He chewed his lip, looked away, then blurted, "I've been going to see my papa."

"At the fort? How did you get in?" She would have known if anyone had been admitted from the outside.

"You won't tell nobody, will you?"

"Anybody." She shook her head. "I won't tell *anybody*."

He looked frightened, but a little proud of himself as well. "There's a place near the south wall, where the brick's falling apart. It's real easy to climb, and it's hid by a bunch of vines and little sumac trees. The sentries know there's snakes back there, so they don't patrol it, hardly ever. All you gotta do is watch for them to go to sleep. There's another place on the river side too, that's even worse."

She tried not to look dumbfounded. Did her father know about those two places in the fort's wall that were in such disrepair that a little boy could breech them? "My—my goodness, Luc-Antoine, how very . . . enterprising of you. But you know, that's not wise. I won't tell on you, but what if one of the sentries sees you? You could be in serious trouble and, worse—they could take it out on your papa."

"I didn't think of that. I'll be more careful from now on."

She noticed he didn't promise not to go in again. "I keep an eye on him, you know. You really don't have to worry."

He shook his head. "My maman worries about him drinking. Did you tell her he ain't drunk no liquor since he's been in there?"

Daisy smiled, giving up on correcting his grammar. "Yes. I guess there's a silver lining for every storm cloud."

"Sure. Just like me getting caught out here eating biscuits with Cain and Scarlet. Got me a job and everything."

"You need to be in school. Your grammar is atrocious."

"Blacksmiths don't need grammar. They need to be strong and smart. And creative."

"If you learned your mathematics, you could be an even better blacksmith."

That seemed to shake Luc-Antoine's confidence a little. "Maybe. But I'll learn that, once I know everything Cain can teach me."

Daisy sighed. "All right. Now tell me all the places you know of where the wall of the fort is weak." She grinned at him. "I might need to climb out one day."

18

New Orleans
February 1779

Christmas came and went in the Gonzales household, in a flurry of gift-giving, dancing, and singing of carols. The weather was mostly rainy and mild, with intermittent blasts of wind cold enough to freeze puddles and make walking to the market a hazardous adventure.

Lyse would have enjoyed the festivities, had she not been uncomfortably aware that everyone in the family seemed to expect a betrothal announcement at any moment. She and Rafa had settled into an uneasy friendship. Sometimes she caught an odd expression in his eyes, but whenever she probed, he would make some joke, effectively quashing intimacy. Avoiding the subject of betrothals, they worked on the letter to Daisy; he delivered it safely and brought back a message, the details of which seemed to please the governor so much that they took time to put together another.

Most days, Rafa immersed himself in business activities that took him to Oliver Pollock's office or the waterfront—activities which involved much haggling, consumption of ale, and inspecting of goods. Rafa was good at both layers of his job, the overt and the clandestine, and he clearly enjoyed the mental and physical exertion. Often he arrived home in the wee hours of the night, long after the rest of the family had gone to bed, then awakened with the roosters crowing in the market and departed to begin the cycle again.

One evening toward the middle of February, Lyse, Sofía, and the elder Gonzaleses had been invited to a Mardi Gras ball at the Chartres Street home of Rafa's colleague, Oliver Pollock. The carriage stopped, its door opened, and she stepped down to find Rafa waiting to escort her up the stairs to the grand front entrance. She took his arm, gave him a searching look, and said quietly, "You look tired. Or ill. What's wrong?"

He gave her an amused glance. "Did anyone not teach you that pointing out bloodshot eyes and gray complexion is not the most tactful way to start a conversation, Miss Lanier?"

She smiled. "True, but I never have time to talk to you anymore. If I want to know something, I must ask when I get the chance."

He glanced around at the crowd of guests ahead of and behind them in the receiving line. "I'm sorry if you're feeling neglected."

"I'm not neglected," she said irritably, "but there are things we need to talk about. There are expectations—not mine, of course, but your sister keeps asking me—" She stopped, wishing she hadn't started this conversation. It was humiliating. She began to have a glimmer of what Isabelle Dussouy had been through with her father—except in that case, there had been a beautiful woman named Cerise who had created the distraction. To her knowledge, Rafa had no liaisons on the side.

But what, really, did she know about what he did all day and night? There was an intelligent, brave, warm *man* inside him . . . somewhere. But she had seen no sign of him for so long, she was beginning to wonder if he was a figment of her imagination.

"She asks you . . . ?" Rafa's tone was gentle.

"Never mind. It's not important." She gave him the brilliant, coquettish smile she'd learned from Sofía. "We are here to have a good time and learn all the juicy gossip we can. When we get inside, you must introduce me to someone you want me to pump for information."

They had paused just inside the Pollocks' grand foyer, waiting for their turn to speak to the host and hostess. Rafa looked down at her for a moment, his jaw shifting, his eyes unreadable.

"Don't ever say that you are not important to me," he finally said under his breath. "I know it's been . . . difficult. My sister must be hectoring the daylights out of you, wanting to know when we will announce our betrothal, but she is just going to have to be patient. The French fleet under the comte d'Estaing is even now gathering in the West Indies. There are events coming that will change the shape of the world as we know it. Events that keep me from—from speaking what I want to. But I have to say—" He suddenly grinned, the old Rafa clearly in evidence. "I'm glad you care. There's nothing sadder than being away for a period of time and coming back to find that nobody noticed."

New Orleans
June 1779

Rafa made two more trips to Mobile, one in March and another in April. Both times he came back with word that Daisy was holding her own—had, in fact, won some degree of freedom from her father. She was teaching again, free to visit Lyse's family in Spring Hill—the Bay Minette property had been abandoned, since Antoine remained incarcerated in the guardhouse of Fort Charlotte—and she reported that Luc-Antoine, now eight years old, was growing beyond all recognition.

More importantly, at least in Gálvez's view, was her documentation that the British were refitting defenses and building infantry in Pensacola, as well as the Mississippi River forts at Manchac and Natchez. Forces in Mobile, however, had been allowed to lapse into a baffling state of disrepair. Daisy had heard her father express his fear that the Americans would attack downriver from the Ohio Valley. She also confirmed information from other sources that British strategy involved a preemptive pincer invasion south from Detroit and up the Mississippi from Pensacola and Jamaica, encircling the rebellious North American colonies.

Armed with this information, Gálvez had been preparing for Spain's entry into the war—and he was convinced it was coming soon. In April, Minister of State Floridablanca had issued an ultimatum to Great Britain that she acknowledge the independence of the United States of America and cede Gibraltar and Minorca back to Spain or be willing to suffer the consequences of Spain's alliance with France. In May, Britain rejected the ultimatum.

In early June, knowing it was likely only a matter of weeks before Madrid declared war, Gálvez called his staff together—including Rafa, to his utter surprise. He arrived at the Cabildo well before the appointed time and found his father already in Gálvez's office, in conversation with Major General Girón, chief of staff.

Rafa's father bowed to him, stiffly. "Good morning, my son. I do not have time for you now, as I am about to meet with the governor. Perhaps later—"

"Father, Governor Gálvez wanted to see me too."

"What? I do not understand. This is a meeting of officers."

Girón clapped Rafa on the shoulder. "The time has come to bring you out of the shadows. Tell your father what you have been up to for the last three years."

Fortunately, since Rafa had no idea where to begin, Gálvez arrived, along with two other officers, and the meeting convened.

Gálvez stood behind his desk, tall, commanding, and remarkably young for one with so much responsibility. "Gentlemen, I expect within a very short time to receive official confirmation of

Spain's declaration of war against England. I intend to be ready to launch our attack when that happens. Troops have already landed in Havana, and they will arrive here shortly. We must be prepared to feed them. Girón and I have decided to send young Rippardá to Béxar, Texas, with authorization to drive two thousand longhorns here."

Rafa had been given some odd assignments over the past three years. This one was a little outside his milieu—he understood ships much better than livestock—but he knew better than to argue with Gálvez. "Yes, sir."

Apparently his father had no such qualms. "Gálvez, I love my son, but you're giving this responsibility to a civilian?"

Amusement lit Gálvez's eyes. "It's time you learned, Colonel Gonzales, that your son is much more than a civilian. He has been serving his country without a word of credit or thanks since he returned from the academy, and I am now promoting him to lieutenant as an official member of my staff."

"Sir? I don't understand." Poor Papa looked bewildered—as indeed Rafa felt. "Are you saying that Rafael has been performing some undercover assignment, gadding about at the behest of that Irish salesman, Pollock?"

"I'm saying that a great deal of what we know about British strategy and movement is a direct result of your son's character, courage, and ingenuity. His performance has been a credit to his upbringing and training. You are to be congratulated."

Rafa met his father's eyes and found there a most peculiar expression. It almost looked like pride. Slowly the colonel stood. His hand rose to form a salute.

Rafa bolted to his feet and returned the salute, then faced Gálvez. "Sir, when do you want me to leave?"

"Be packed and headed out by daybreak tomorrow. Time is of the essence." Gálvez handed him a sealed missive. "Here is your requisition for the commander at Béxar. If he asks about payment, tell him that Navarre in Havana will work that out with him later. Oh, and report to the supply officer for a uniform."

Rafa nodded, saluted Gálvez, and quit the office, thoughts boiling. Tomorrow. He had less than a day to prepare for the journey—and another two-month separation from Lyse.

Pollock wasn't going to like this new assignment either. The Irishman had grown accustomed to depending on Rafa to handle day-to-day errands related to the business when he was in New Orleans, as well as captaining periodic lucrative jaunts into ports along the Gulf of Mexico.

With Rafa's responsibilities shifting from espionage to overt military operations, he no longer owed direct obedience to the American agent. But, as a friend, he did owe him an explanation. With that in mind, he directed his steps to Chartres Street. He hoped Pollock would still be at home, so that he could begin his new assignment with a clear conscience. Then he must go home to pack.

Surely Lyse would understand his new duties—as a lieutenant! He must begin to think of himself as an officer in the Spanish army.

He wondered how she would like being a military wife. The thought was amusing. She was such a funny mixture of fearless intellect, whimsy, and tenderness. In fact, he couldn't wait to tell her about the look on his father's face when the old man discovered the truth, and share a laugh.

His pace quickened. He would miss her, but two months would go by quickly.

~

Lyse stood in the center of her beautiful bedroom. She could have walked around and touched the accoutrements of a wealth and prestige that separated her from her family more effectively than did the hundred or so miles of coastline between New Orleans and Mobile. Sometimes the excitement and glamour of her life, the sense that she was part of something grand and world-changing, dulled the ache of longing to kiss Rémy's damp cheek or smooth Genny's hair. But six beautiful dresses in a mahogany wardrobe couldn't erase the contents of the letter on the desk under the window.

She had to do something about it. She *would* do something. But what?

She walked toward the desk and stared at the letter as if it were one of the water moccasins that used to crawl under the porch of the Bay Minette cottage. Poison. Evil. Rafa had once called Isabelle Dussouy a she-devil, and the epithet wasn't far from the truth.

Lyse had known the danger of leaving Luc-Antoine under the woman's control, but there had been no alternative at the time. Now . . . now she might be far away, but she had powerful allies, and she had a powerful God who had already done great things for her. Slowly she reached for Daisy's letter, understanding how Moses must have felt when commanded to pick up the serpent by the tail.

She closed her eyes for one more desperate prayer, then walked downstairs to the family sitting room, where Sofía and Doña Evangelina had been finishing tea while she went to her room to read her letter in privacy. She had to find Rafa, because she was going to need the governor's help, and he would be the quickest way in to see the busy official. Her days of daily interaction with the governor's staff had dwindled to a bi-weekly briefing with Madame Gálvez. But because she didn't presume upon the acquaintance, she knew he would see her if she asked.

At the landing of the stairs, she stopped, heart thudding. Rafa was here. She'd know his voice among a thousand men. It came from the sitting room, so she hurried to the doorway and stopped there, suddenly uncertain, seeing him in conversation with his mother and sister. He never came home in the middle of the day. Something must be wrong.

As if he sensed her presence, he turned, his expression lighting and that beautiful crease in his cheek appearing. He didn't look worried at all.

She walked toward him, drawn like iron filings to a magnet. "Rafa? What are you doing here?"

He took her hands and kissed one, then the other, drawing her apart from Sofía and Doña Evangelina. "I came to say goodbye," he said cheerfully. "The governor is sending me off to Texas." He laughed. "It seems I am to be a temporary *vaquero*, of all things. Just what I went to the naval academy for."

"You're leaving?" she said stupidly. "For Texas? How long will you be gone?" It didn't matter how long. By the time he got back, it would be too late. Luc-Antoine could be dead. Maybe the governor would see her, but he was so busy . . .

Rafa must have seen her distress, for his smile disappeared. "What is it?"

She showed him the letter. Her hand was shaking so badly the paper rattled. "I got this today, from Daisy. All that information she gave us about the walls of the fort . . . She discovered it when Luc-Antoine started climbing in to see Papa. Madame Dussouy caught him leaving one night and whipped him, then went to Major Redmond to tell him what was going on. Now she won't even let Luc-Antoine go to Grandpére's house on Sundays, and Major Redmond moved Papa to a solitary cell and put him back on short rations. He also tightened up Daisy's restriction to the fort again. She had to sneak this letter out through Corporal Tully—" Feeling as if she were drowning, she gulped for air. "There probably won't be more letters after this."

Rafa's hands squeezed hers tightly, his eyes grim. "Don't worry. We'll do something."

"Don't worry? Rafa, you don't understand how much she hates us. She'll kill Luc-Antoine, by the slowest, most devious method she can think of! How could I have let him go to her to begin with—"

"It's not your fault," Rafa interrupted. "Lyse! Listen to me—I'll see Gálvez again before I leave, convince him to send Simon back to get Luc-Antoine."

"What about Daisy?" Lyse felt tears flood her eyes, hot and out of control. "Oh, her papa will be so angry! What if he finds out she has been writing to me?"

Rafa released her fingers to catch her face in his hands. "Simon will bring her out too, if that's necessary. You've got to trust us." He kissed her trembling lips, gently and briefly. "Now I really have to go finish packing, if I'm going to have time to speak to Gálvez about this." He kissed her again, once on each wet cheek. "You're salty," he murmured, letting her taste for herself. "I love you, *mi corazón*."

When she opened her eyes again, he was gone, leaving her alone with the other two women.

"Why does the woman—this Madame Dussouy—why does she hate you so much?" asked Sofía.

Mobile
June 6, 1779

Daisy could hardly breathe. She sat in the rocking chair in her quarters, listening to the rain beat on the roof and knitting a perfectly useless sock, which no one in his right mind would wear—except possibly Niall, and she couldn't have said he was in his right mind, anyway. If she didn't get outside soon, her own wits might go begging, like the Pelican girl Ysabeau Bonnet who, legend claimed, used to wander about the settlement of Mobile dressed only in her undergarments.

She had given the letter to Lyse into Corporal Tully's care over a week ago, and she had no idea if it had arrived or if it lay at the bottom of the Gulf of Mexico. Tully said he'd sent it on a

Dutch mail packet headed for New Orleans, but there were no guarantees of delivery.

There were no guarantees of anything, she knew that. By some standards, of course, her life was comfortable. She had plenty to eat—should she ever develop an appetite again—and the room in which she was imprisoned was quite comfortable, if one discounted that incessant rattle of rain.

But she had gotten desperately tired of her own company since Papa had curtailed her movements and company. Only Tully and Niall were allowed to speak to her, and then only when they brought meals. Neither would give her any information about Antoine, Luc-Antoine, old Mr. Chaz, or Justine and the children—not even about her students, whom she'd had to once more give up teaching. Certainly nothing about what was going on in the outside world concerning the war.

The commander's daughter was a prisoner in effect, if not officially.

She didn't know why, unless they'd discovered her writing to Lyse in code. And how they would have known that was a mystery. Tully claimed not to know why she was contained to quarters, though he wouldn't meet her eyes. Niall simply ignored her questions as if she hadn't spoken. She'd gotten so hungry for information she'd begun exploring ways to get out of the officers' barracks. Yesterday she'd started to climb out the window, but seeing a cadet lounging beneath, smoking a cheap cigar and paring his fingernails, she'd quickly pulled her head back inside, heart pounding. Perhaps she wasn't as brave as she had thought.

Now she sat here as twilight fell, thinking about Luc-Antoine and Cain, and all the possible methods Isabelle Dussouy was capable of inventing to make them miserable. And she thought about Antoine, chained in a hastily constructed outhouse near the fort's foundry, subject to suffocation from its smoke and fumes, as well as rising water from the torrents of rain they'd had in the last week. She couldn't fathom what created the heartless stone that seemed to have come to rest where her father's humanity used to reside. Duty was one thing, but every sense cried out at this relentless pursuit of retribution.

She sat praying and knitting until there was no longer enough light to see her work, and she was too tired to get up and light a candle. She must have fallen asleep with her head against the back of the rocker, for something, a thumping noise at the window, woke her with a jerk. There was another noise, this time a muffled groan, and she threw down her yarn and needles and jumped to her feet. The room was dark as Hades, but her pupils had adjusted after her nap, so she could see shadows where her bed sat against the wall and the white curtains she'd put up last summer.

"Who's there?" She felt frozen, her feet blocks of ice incapable of moving. There was no answer, just the rain, now slackened to a soft patter. Her breath came in quick pants, and she could feel every pulse of blood in her throat.

Then she realized it was someone else's breathing she heard. A moving shadow in the window.

"Daisy? Don't scream. It's me."

She almost screamed anyway, keeping control of her throat with superhuman effort. Finally she choked out, "Simon?"

"Yes." He had her in his arms, held fast against wet clothing, his heart thudding heavily under her ear.

She wanted to climb inside him. She clung to him, crying, incapable of understanding why he was here, what happened to the guard outside her window, what he was saying.

It was "I love you" that finally reached her. She tipped up her face, let him kiss her, fell into an ocean of joy that all but drowned her.

When she came to, she was sitting in his lap in the rocker. Her mouth felt bruised, but she didn't care, and the rain from his shirt had seeped into her dress, but she didn't care about that either, and he was holding her face, breathing hard, as if he'd run a long way.

"Daisy, stop," he said for the third time.

"What?" She felt drunk, though she'd never been drunk before.

"We have to go. I hit the guard pretty hard, but he's going to eventually wake up, and we . . . oh, Daisy. I mean, we really have to go."

"All right. Let me just . . . do I have time to leave a note for my father?"

"No! For heaven's sake, no! I found that place on the wall Luc-Antoine told you about. It's still not guarded, can you believe it—so we're going out that way, but you know they'll come after us, so we have to make as much time tonight as we can."

"All right," she said again. Papa would just have to wonder where she'd gone. It would serve him right for the way he'd treated her.

Simon laughed softly and pulled her arms from around his neck, kissed her quickly, and pushed her off his lap. "You're a handful, young lady. No wonder your papa kept you locked up."

"Only for you," she said with a giggle that felt very odd. She hadn't laughed in a long time.

19

New Orleans, Fort San Juan del Bayou
August 14, 1779

Little Nardo, strapped to Scarlet's front with wide strips of soft cloth, babbled a long string of nonsense as his mother squatted to lift the full, heavy laundry basket onto her head, then rose with it balanced just so. Nardo, a year old in July, could stagger successfully across a room on his own two fat legs, but carrying him was the only way to get anywhere fast. She followed Daisy and Lyse, similarly laden with baskets, down the footpath from the old fort to the Bayou San Juan, which meandered between Lake Pontchartrain and the Mississippi River.

Scarlet had been thinking all morning of the stories the old slave Blackberry had told as the two of them worked side by side, picking cotton on the plantation in Natchez. Those stories, of village women singing as they washed their clothes in African rivers, their children tied to their chests, had kept Scarlet from going mad from grief. Of course, that was before the wild American who called himself Willing had snatched up Scarlet and twenty or so other healthy slaves and took them to the market in New Orleans. Poor Blackberry had been left to undoubtedly die of starvation, with nobody there to mash or chew her food soft enough for her toothless gums.

Remembering Blackberry always made Scarlet sad, until she remembered to sing the old woman's favorite songs. Songs about going to the Promised Land, about eating manna in the wilderness, about seeing dry bones come to life. At first she'd thought them crazy, nonsensical songs, until Lyse explained the Bible stories behind the words. Then they made perfect sense.

Stories, always stories. Life, too, was a story, Scarlet could have told anybody that. Her own life had a beginning, a middle, and an end to come. There was glory to look forward to, but first you had to endure the fire, like the three Hebrew boys who dared to defy Nebuchadnezzar. Scarlet had survived a couple of fires of her own and come out golden. She couldn't imagine heaven being any better than this.

Just look at her, she thought, crouching to set the basket down at the edge of the water. She had a place to sleep with two good friends in a tidy little house the soldiers had built for them in the shadow of the fort. They had work to do and plenty to eat. Her little boy was healthy and happy and brought her unspeakable joy. Just looking in his bright eyes or patting his bottom when he slept made her think of Cain, and she was grateful all over again to have known love like that. Best of all, she was free. No matter what happened, no one could take that away.

"The bayou's higher than ever today." Daisy splashed into the water with a few shirts slung over her shoulder. Her skirt, like those of the other women, was hitched between her legs and tucked into the front waistband. "Much more rain and the whole fort will wash away."

"True dat," Scarlet said, tipping her head back and using her hand to shield her eyes against the glaring sun. Patchy, angry clouds, pink-tinged, hovered to the south. A storm was coming, like it or not.

Daisy shook her head. "Simon says another transport ship came in yesterday morning. That makes six. Where will they put more men on this little patch of ground? There are camps along the lake as far as you can see already."

"Plenty work for us," Scarlet said contentedly. She didn't mind it, though she knew it was hard on Daisy, who had never done anything more strenuous than lift a textbook before Simon brought her here.

In fact, Daisy had been in a state of such shock that it was a whole week before she could talk about her escape from Mobile. Some things she still wouldn't talk about—like what happened to Mr. Antoine. Lyse had questioned Simon, but he'd just said, "It's bad, Lyse" and refused to say more. He did say they tried to get Luc-Antoine and Cain out, but they'd already escaped, and there wasn't time to look for them. But every time Simon came around—which wasn't often, because of his duties in the governor's service—Daisy came a little farther toward normalcy. Simon would eventually marry her, and she would be fine.

As she soaped, scrubbed, rinsed, and wrung uniforms, Scarlet watched Lyse. She had been so quiet since they came here to live and work. Too quiet. Of the three of them, this new chapter of their lives had been hardest on her. After all, she had been treated like a daughter in the Gonzales household. But once it was discovered her mother was a slave, just like Scarlet's, that indeed they were first cousins—and it seemed she had lied to cover it up—there had been no mercy. She had been termed a colored gold digger, and with Rafael gone, there was no one to plead her case.

All the pretty dresses were taken away, her few belongings tied up in a scarf and handed to her. With her own eyes Scarlet had seen the coldness and confusion mask Sofía's face—and it was not a pretty sight.

Lyse had taken it in silent hurt, because there was nothing she could say to reverse the truth. Besides, she didn't want to live in a house where she wasn't wanted. By the time Simon came back with Daisy, Lyse and Scarlet had gone to Rafa's friend Oliver Pollock for help. He was a busy man, but he had helped them find this house and this position—though notably not offering to take them into his own home.

None of their circumstances were fair. But Scarlet had given up on fair a long time ago.

Still, the three of them were fighters. If they were meant to be laundresses, they would be the best laundresses in New Orleans, they would strengthen and pray for one another, and they would play their small part in birthing a free, independent nation. Even Lyse, as grimly as she held onto hope, prayed aloud daily for Rafael and Simon's safety, for the success of the Continental army, for the leaders of the Congress to make wise and good decisions.

Nardo suddenly grabbed both her ears and planted a sloppy, drooling kiss on her chin. As Scarlet laughed and hugged him, she met Lyse's smiling gaze. God had a way of bringing encouragement into the darkest of days, and she would hold onto that.

~

New Orleans, Gonzales mansion
August 15, 1779

"What do you mean—she's gone?" Rafa regarded his mother with horror, trying not to put too much meaning in the way she avoided his eyes, the way her hands pleated her skirt into a mass of wrinkles.

He had found her in her sitting room, sorting dried flowers laid out on a table: lavender to the right, progressing to pinks, then blues, and deep indigo on the left. She was arranging flowers, and Lyse was somewhere out in the city, while a strengthening hurricane lashed the coast with a fury of wind and waves. Even now, he could feel the house rocking on its pilings against the onslaught of the storm.

"I offered to let her stay," Mama said, "her and Scarlet and the baby—but she would have none of it. I told her you would sort it all out when you returned, but she insisted on leaving. I suppose we weren't good enough for her after all."

"Mama, Lyse wouldn't leave without a good reason. What did she *say*?"

"Why, she said hardly anything at all. After we had been so good to her, Sofía even treating her as a sister." One more pleat went into the dress.

Rafa stood tapping his fingers against his thigh for a moment. Every moment he wasted, Lyse could be in greater danger. He didn't know what had happened while he was gone, but clearly his mother wasn't going to help. "Where is Sofi?"

Mama circled a hand. "In her room, I suppose. You know how Sofía feels about thunderstorms."

Yes, he knew. As a child, Sofi had been caught in a storm in an open carriage that had been hit by lightning, killing the horse right in its traces. She would be somewhere in a corner, too petrified to speak.

"All right, Mama. I'm going to the Cabildo to report in. Maybe Simon will know where Lyse is." He turned, then hesitated. "Listen, if this gets worse, if you start seeing water in the house, you and Sofi should get all the servants and go up to the attic to wait it out. Already the water is over the road."

She nodded apathetically, and he left, frustrated. He stood for a minute on the porch, trying to judge the state of the turbulent sky. All hurricanes had their own personalities. Seven years ago, the family had lost most of its roof when a cyclone thrust a large pine tree through it. Two years later, all the upstairs windows had blown out as if with cannon fire. This one seemed to be a deadly combination of wind and rain, with long, intermittent squalls followed by brief eerie silences. He knew not to assume a pattern, however.

Taking a deep breath, he stepped off the porch into the swirling water.

Two hours later, he was back, this time with his father in a boat. He still hadn't found Lyse—a fact which he tried not to find terrifying—but he hadn't been able to withstand his father's plea to help move Mama and Sofía to the fort, which was on higher ground. He prayed that Simon had been able to get to Lyse, as well as Daisy and Scarlet, before navigating in the storm became impossible.

By now, the entire city was in danger of blowing away before the fury of the storm. Gálvez's expensive fleet from Havana had been scattered in the Gulf, hundreds of the troops drowned or battered by flying wood and stone. The confiscated British warship *Rebecca*—Oliver Pollock's pride and joy, which he'd had fitted out as a transport ship—was now a mass of broken timber piled, ironically enough, atop the rubble of Pollock's mansion on Chartres Street.

They found Mama and Sofi leaning out an attic window screaming. Coaxing them down to the boat was about as frustrating a task as he had ever taken on. Even when they were all safely settled, Rafa and his father battling the oars through the roiling water in the streets, he couldn't relax for fear one or the other of the women would capsize the boat.

By the time they made it to the fort, Rafa's muscles ached with tension, and he knew his father must be exhausted as well. But no sooner had they handed the women off to a subaltern keeping watch for refugees at the southeast bastion, than Rafa was hailed by Major-General Girón from another large boat.

"Rippardá!" Girón shouted. "All officers needed back at the Cabildo—Governor's orders!"

Rafa responded with a wave, then turned to his father. "Ready, Papa?"

His father's smile was more of a grimace, but Rafa took it for acquiescence.

As he shipped the oars again, he glanced up at the water sluicing down the walls of the fort into the bayou below. He could only hope that Lyse, Daisy, and Scarlet had made it here safely. They were all in for a long night.

New Orleans, Fort San Juan

Every fiber of her being wanted to run. Lyse clenched her hands on the doorpost to keep her feet from carrying her back into the other room.

They were here, Doña Evangelina and Sofía, where she could not get away, not until the floodwaters surrounding the fort subsided. She didn't know how they had gotten here, but she supposed someone's boat must have brought them—the same way hundreds of refugees had been pouring into the safety of the fort like ants escaping a collapsed hill and running to another.

"Lyse, you don't have to speak to them," Daisy whispered. She knew what had happened, how as soon as Rafa left to find Simon and send him on his way to rescue Daisy, then departed for his Texas cattle assignment, the Gonzales women had launched question after question at Lyse, until she had been forced to tell the whole story of her parents' marriage and exile.

They had treated it as some shameful thing, to be the daughter of a slave—freed though she might have been. Recoiling as if the darkness of her skin were some infectious disease. Discussing the shock of it as if she couldn't hear them.

But she *could* hear, and it hurt. It hurt because she'd thought they loved her for her own sake, and not just because Rafa had brought her to them. It seemed even Rafa's affection wasn't enough to cover her Africanness, that quarter-blend of alien blood.

And it still hurt, though she'd pretended to Scarlet that it didn't. Scarlet had endured much worse, so what right did Lyse have to whine about the turned-up noses of a couple of Castilian society belles?

She released the breath she'd been holding, relaxed her hold on the door frame. "Daisy, they've lost everything. They don't even have a place to sleep. Jesus was kind to those who crucified him. Can I do less?"

The first step was the hardest, the next a little easier. She kept walking until Nardo, who had been napping on Scarlet's shoulder in a corner of the room, started to cry, and Sofía turned around to look for the sound.

Sofía gasped. "Mama, it's Scarlet! And there's Lyse."

Lyse stopped a few feet away from her and smiled. "Yes, we've been here long enough to get settled, so we've got a pot of stew over the fire. Are you hungry?"

Sofía shook her head, but her gaze went back to Scarlet and the baby. "My goodness, he's gotten so big! Can I hold him?"

Doña Evangelina looked like she might spontaneously burst into flames, but Sofía ignored her and went to her knees in front of Scarlet. Sofi clapped her hands, then held them out to Nardo.

He stuck his thumb in his mouth and leaned over in that boneless way he had when he was just waking up.

Sofía caught him and snuggled him close, closing her eyes.

Scarlet, wide-eyed, said, "Watch out, he may pee on you."

Everyone in the room laughed, and the unbearable tension broke.

"I'm not a bit hungry," Sofía said shyly, swaying with the baby. "You eat first, Scarlet."

Later that night, as the room grew darker and the storm continued to rage outside the walls of the fort, Lyse sat on the floor with her back against the wall, listening to Scarlet tell stories by the light of a single candle. She supposed she shouldn't have been surprised that Doña Evangelina had ended up in charge of ladling soup. Somewhere in her dim past, she must have been a young officer's wife, used to making do with military rations. In any case, as she and Sofi pitched in to help make others welcome and comfortable, there was no mention of birth or social rank.

Lyse felt the wall of pride she'd built slowly crumble. She could only hope that she wouldn't be pierced again. She didn't think she could bear it.

~

She *was* here. His father had told him so, but he had wanted to see for himself.

Rafa stood in the storeroom doorway, a weak splash of dawn light showing Lyse asleep in a corner like the princess in a fairy tale, curled on her side with her hand under her cheek, head pillowed on a sack of coffee beans. He wanted to lie down beside her and sleep for a week, but he had promised his father that he would only briefly check on the women before reporting to the Cabildo once more for duty.

Outside the rain still fell in slow, fat, noisy drops, adding to the gush and rush of the swollen bayou below the fort, but at least the howling wind had died down during the night. The danger of trees and boats and dead animals being plucked up and whirled against shaking buildings was past. He should be able to safely attend to provisions for the cattle he had left in the care of the *vaqueros* who had accompanied him from Béxar—and whatever else his father saw fit to assign him.

But he hesitated another precious few moments, studying the curve of Lyse's chin, the soft droop of her lips, the fan of her lashes against her cheekbones. In a hundred years he would never tire of the sight.

"She has worked herself into exhaustion, poor dear, as has your little sister. They both have surprised me."

Rafa turned to find his mother leaning against the wall behind him, her posture weary but alert. Suddenly her face scrunched in a cracking yawn, and they both laughed.

"You surprise me too, Mama." He propped his shoulder against the door frame. "It is good to see you and Sofi serving others—as Lyse and Daisy and Scarlet have apparently been doing for weeks."

She stiffened at the note of censure in his voice. "No one can accuse me of being lazy."

He regarded her silently, respect and affection for his mother warring against the injustice Lyse had suffered. Carefully he said, "I wish you to explain to me how Lyse comes to be living here instead of in our home—and I don't believe she left on her own, so don't try that one on me."

Mama's soft lips pressed together in a thin line. "How dare you speak to me thus?"

"Mama, I am no longer five years old." He sighed and scrubbed his hand against a day's growth of whiskers. "I will give you the benefit of the doubt, if you'll only *explain*—"

"There is nothing to explain. Sofía and I overheard you talking to Lyse about the letter that got her so upset, just before you left for Texas. We naturally inquired as to the nature of her distress." She shrugged. "She explained about this Madame Dussouy and the history of her conflict with Lyse's father. When I expressed a certain amount of sympathy for the poor woman—"

"*Sympathy*? For Isabelle Dussouy?" Straightening, Rafa gaped at his mother. "Have you taken leave of your senses?"

Mama stared up at him coldly. "To be rejected in favor of a Negro slave is no small insult."

"Compared to what? Being cast onto the street because one is the daughter of that slave? Mama, think! What if you had been born into like circumstances? Would you have accepted your lot with the grace and humor that Lyse has? With all her struggles and disadvantages, would you have become half the lady she has?" Feeling his eyes glaze with emotion, he closed them. "Forgive me if I doubt it."

There was a long space of shocked silence. "You are going to marry her, aren't you?"

"If she'll have me." He opened his eyes, turned his back on his mother, and looked hungrily down at Lyse. "Which is doubtful, now that you have succeeded in alienating her."

"But, Rafael . . . you could have any one of the lovely Spanish girls among Sofía's acquaintance."

"I don't want any Spanish girl. I want this Creole girl who is brave and loyal and resourceful and a hundred other beautiful things I don't have time to enumerate." He looked wearily over his shoulder at his mama. "You'll have to take my word for it that I will not change my mind—and if you value my love, you will accept Lyse and take her as your beloved daughter. Do you understand me, Mama?"

She nodded, stricken of face. "I didn't know—"

"Well, now you do." He turned, gave her a brief peck on the cheek, and swung away, reenergized, down the passage to the outside door. That had been a difficult conversation, but now that it was behind him, he could concentrate on his other responsibilities. When given a choice between wrangling ornery cattle and obstinate women, he would choose the cows every time.

~

New Orleans, the Cabildo
Late August 1779

The Cabildo was an anthill of activity, with Spanish officers slamming in and out of Gálvez's office; Oliver Pollock—bankrupt after the storm, having decided to go along on the Mississippi River campaign—following the governor around, recording every order he made and some he didn't; and a number of American soldiers as well, trying to help but generally getting in the way.

Rafa considered it a miracle, a direct intervention of God Almighty, that Gálvez had regrouped and resupplied his fleet in less than two weeks. Gálvez was hoping to surprise the British with a quick strike after the brutal storm, and the Spanish fleet under Girón's command would sail with the evening tide, first to Manchac to take Fort Bute, then, once it was secure, heading north to Baton Rouge. Gálvez himself would advance on foot with a battalion of soldiers made up of Spanish infantry, French Creoles, Americans, free Negroes, Indians, and a mixture of all. It was a cultural gumbo of an army, built on Gálvez's charisma and leadership, fired by motivations ranging from national pride to greed to starry-eyed idealism.

Rafa would have given anything to be part of it.

But the governor had seen fit to leave him and Simon Lanier in New Orleans. Simon was to supervise the continued refitting of every available vessel that came into the port, while Rafa saw to restocking arms and ammunition in the warehouses of the Cabildo. He was also to make sure the cattle brought from Texas—which had miraculously survived the storm—stayed fed and healthy, and that other foodstuffs for the army continued to stream in from outlying farms and plantations.

As if all that didn't keep him busy twenty hours a day, seven days a week, with barely time to stuff in the occasional meal, Rafa's final responsibility involved uniform repair and replacement, including boots, undergarments, and other accessories. As Gálvez and his army marched out of the city and the fleet set sail, Rafa finally threw up his hands and turned to the displaced women who were waiting in the fort for the water to recede from their homes so they could begin cleanup.

To his surprise, he found in his mother a deep well of common sense and physical strength. That she agreed to help—truth be told, she more or less shoved him out of the way and took over—was a welcome source of amusement as well as incredulity. Doña Evangelina marshaled her troop of laundresses and seamstresses with the deftness and ingenuity of El Cid, taking over a warehouse and reorganizing it so that Rafa could lay his hands on whatever item might be required with a minimum of time and effort.

Lyse, Daisy, and Scarlet served as subordinate officers to the Little General, as he took to calling his mama, each taking on an area of responsibility and making it her own private battlefront.

Rafa couldn't have been more grateful, but there was little time to confer with his female staff. Instead he left them to their tasks and tended to his own.

One evening in mid-September, he sat down, hungry and exhausted, in the governor's empty office to read a letter from Gálvez. It informed him that both Manchac and Baton Rouge had been secured in the name of His Majesty Carlos III, and they would be moving on to Natchez soon. That was good, he thought as he laid his head down on the desk. He would rest, just for a minute.

Some time later, he awoke to an aroma that had his stomach rumbling like a kettledrum in a military band. Bacon. He would sell his soul for a rasher of bacon right now.

Sitting up, rubbing his eyes, he realized he didn't have to do anything so drastic. Someone had put a plate of fried eggs, barley toast, and—yes, bacon, here on the desk. As he ate, he almost cried with pleasure. He was mopping up the last of the egg yolk with half a slice of bread when the office door opened.

Lyse put her head round the edge of the door, her eyes bright as stars. "The Little General wants to know if her favorite subaltern has finished his dinner so she can wash the plate."

He groaned, rubbing his stomach. "Yes, but you'll have to come get it. I'm so full I can't walk."

She came in, swaying, hands behind her back. "That's too bad, because there might be another surprise . . ."

Instantly he was on his feet. "You haven't kissed me in months."

"Three months and ten days, but nobody is counting," she said, laughing, "but that's not it."

"Oh." He yawned. "Then I'm not interested."

"Rafa, I am reformed. I don't kiss men to whom I'm not betrothed."

"That's ridiculous. Of course we're betrothed."

Her pretty mouth tightened. "We are not."

Suddenly he was no longer amused. "I don't know why you say that. You agreed. Daisy is my witness."

"That was no betrothal. It was a trick to keep me out of prison. Your mother doesn't think I'm good enough for you, and you didn't—you didn't disagree with her—"

To his horror, her face screwed up, she threw a piece of cake at him, and she bolted from the room, slamming the door behind her.

What had just happened? He absently brushed cake crumbs from his shirt. Was he betrothed, or was he not?

Also, she forgot the plate. Now he would have to take it to his mother himself. And she was likely to do more than throw cake at him.

~

New Orleans
October 20, 1779

Lyse and Daisy had been sent to market by Doña Evangelina, and they were both grateful to get out of the close confines of the fort and the hard work of the warehouse. But even two months after the hurricane, the French Quarter streets were still muddy, old houses were patched together with new timber, and the rank odor of mildew turned a pleasant outing into a chore to be gotten over as quickly as possible. Lyse turned the corner which led to the slave market, intending to hurry Daisy along, until she caught sight of an ebony-skinned woman being led, hands chained, to the dais for sale.

"Daisy! Does that woman look familiar to you?"

Daisy paused to look, her forehead creased. "I'm not sure. Maybe."

"She looks like that woman who used to cook for Madame Dussouy. I saw her that time Rafa took me to the soirée. Remember?"

Daisy looked amused. "I remember when you went, because you quizzed me about kissing Simon that night, and I couldn't go to sleep for hours! But I'm not sure I've ever seen Madame's cook."

"Oh. Well, even so, she looks like Cain around the mouth. Doesn't she?"

"Tell you the truth, I don't remember much about Cain. All I know is he's Scarlet's mate and Nardo's father. Don't look at me like that—I guess they're married in God's eyes."

"Of course they are. But the point is, I'm going over there to talk to her. Maybe she knows what happened to Cain after you left Mobile."

"Wait—Lyse! You can't just walk up to a slave on the auction block and start asking questions! Lyse!"

Lyse barely heard her. She pushed through the crush of people around the dais.

"This woman is healthy and still young enough to give you many good years of service," the auctioneer yelled over the mumbling of the crowd. "I have it on good authority she was the best cook in the environs of Mobile, save maybe the woman at Burelle's Tavern. She's been cared for well, has all her teeth, and never been sick a day. Now who'll start my bid at two hundred pounds?"

Lyse stood on her toes to see between a woman with a large straw hat and another with a parasol. Someone had already bid two hundred, and someone else raised it to three. She'd better hurry. But what was her name? Scarlet had talked about her life at Madame Dussouy's, how all the slaves had been belittled and treated roughly except Cain's mother, the cook, who got uppity because of her superior value in the kitchen.

She couldn't just call out, "Hey! Are you Cain's maman?" Her name was . . . Martha, maybe? No, but something like that.

"Martine," she said aloud. That was it. "Martine!" she shouted during a break in the bidding. "Martine, look here!"

The woman turned her queenly head, the dull dark eyes suddenly narrowing, looking for Lyse's voice.

"Martine! It's Lyse Lanier! Right here!"

Martine's mouth fell open. "Miss Lyse?" Lyse saw her mouth the words.

"Yes! It's me!" Lyse pushed her way to the edge of the dais, ignoring the scowls of the auctioneer. "Do you know what happened to Cain and—and my little brother Luc-Antoine?"

"Miss, don't you see we're in the middle of a business transaction here?" The auctioneer crouched, snarling at Lyse. "You'd better get your dark face out of here before you wind up for sale too!"

Frightened, Lyse stood her ground. "I'm not a slave, and I just want to ask this woman about her son. I used to know them in Mobile."

"I don't know. You look like a slave to me."

Daisy stepped through the crowd and took Lyse's arm. "I assure you my friend is a free woman," she said firmly. "We are part of the governor's staff, and Madame Gálvez will vouch for us."

"Oh is that right?" the man sneered.

"That is right," came a cultured French-accented voice behind Lyse. "These young ladies have been in my home many times."

"Madame!" blustered the auctioneer. "I'm sorry—I did not see you with them!"

Madame Gálvez nodded with regal condescension.

Lyse had never been so glad to see anyone in her life.

"I'll be happy to pay whatever you think this woman is worth," Madame said. "I have need of a new cook."

The man's eyes squinted. "She is very expensive, Madame. The bidding has already gone up to five hundred twenty."

"That's a lie!" exclaimed Lyse.

"Never mind." Madame smiled. "I shall pay six hundred and call it a bargain. Yes?"

The man's mouth opened and closed. "Yes, Madame! That will do very well."

Madame completed the transaction and extended her hand in its elegant glove. "You will please to take off the manacles, good sir. I wish Martine to walk without losing her balance, and I am in a hurry."

The auctioneer hurried to comply. Martine was soon stepping down from the dais, rubbing her wrists. Tears slipped down her face. "I didn't know I was worth six hundred whole pounds," she said, sniffing.

"You are worth much more than that," Madame said, "but it's a good thing he agreed, as that's all I had with me! Now come, let us get out of the sun before my skin becomes as brown as yours!"

She twirled her parasol and led the way across the street to a coffeehouse frequented by ladies of the elite social set of New Orleans. Lyse, Daisy, and Martine followed like ducklings behind a particularly elegant hen. Inside the coffee shop, Madame furled her parasol and seated herself at a little round iron table with graceful wrought iron chairs. Lyse and Daisy joined her, while Martine stood awkwardly to the side.

"Now," Madame said, "please explain to me what is all the excitement about."

"Oh, Madame, thank you so much for interceding," Lyse said fervently. "I was so frightened! And I'm sorry you had to spend so much money. But I only wanted to know about Martine's son, Cain. He has been training my little brother, Luc-Antoine, who was indentured to Martine's owner, Madame Dussouy, to be a blacksmith."

Madame looked a bit confused. "Madame Dussouy is a blacksmith?"

Lyse laughed. "No, she is the harpy who owned Martine and

Cain, and also my cousin Scarlet. Cain is her blacksmith slave, who was Scarlet's . . . mate."

"Ah. Harpy I understand. Go on."

"Well, Madame Dussouy sold Scarlet, perhaps two years ago, and she ended first on a plantation in Natchez, then here at the market, where Rafa—I mean, Don Rafael bought her for you and then—but then, you know how all that happened. What I want to know is what Martine can tell me about my brother and Scarlet's Cain."

"Wait a minute, miss," Martine blurted. "Excuse me, but are you telling me Scarlet is here in New Orleans?"

"Yes! She has a baby—Cain's baby! His name is Nardo, after the governor—" Lyse smiled at Madame—"and he looks just like Cain. That's how I recognized you so easily, I think."

Martine stared for a moment. "Cain's baby?" The tears started falling again. "Oh, my. My grandbaby." After a moment, she pulled herself together. "Cain's alive. A troop of American militiamen raided the Dussouy plantation, and they brought several of us slaves here, but Cain managed to get away from them. I think your little Luc-Antoine must've followed and helped him. I don't know where they went, though."

Lyse pressed her knuckles to her mouth. Luc-Antoine and Cain were alive. They had gotten away. "W-What about Madame and Monsieur Dussouy?"

"They escaped to the fort, I guess." Martine shrugged.

"I don't guess you've heard anything about my grandfather, or my stepmother and the other children? Or—or my papa?"

"Your grandpapa and that bunch are fine, as far as I know. Not much there for the Americans to carry off. But your papa . . ." Martine flicked a glance at Daisy. "I heard terrible things happened after Miss Daisy ran off."

20

New Orleans, Gálvez mansion
Christmas Eve 1779

All the women were in the finest of their finery. Lyse no longer had anything fit to wear to such a grand occasion as a Christmas Eve ball at the Gálvez mansion. But she wasn't the only one with barely a change of clothes this year. The hurricane had wiped out many ladies' entire wardrobes, and there had been neither time nor extra funds to have more made. Material was always expensive, and in this time of war it was especially dear.

The Gálvezes owned one of the few residences that sustained only minimal damage to the ground floor; thus Madame looked as elegant as ever in a butter-colored sarcenet dress over a lace petticoat of the same color, her hair dressed high and fastened with topaz jewels. She stood greeting guests with her handsome father, the famous French planter and spy, Gilbert de St. Maxent, by her side in the absence of her husband.

Lyse greeted Madame after Daisy and Sofía, and was rewarded with a warm kiss on the cheek.

"You will be happy to know," Madame whispered in her ear, "your friend Martine is happy as a clam in my so-big kitchen, and she has created those spectacular cream puffs on the table over there. You must be sure to have one."

Lyse agreed that it was a requirement and moved on feeling happier about being here dressed in nothing more elegant than Scarlet's blue Sunday dress, which had been turned and retrimmed four times since rescued from a charity bin last summer. To give Scarlet credit, it was actually a lovely dress, albeit a little threadbare, if one didn't look at it too closely in the light.

Besides, since Rafa was not here to see it, a little of the shine had worn off the evening. She had looked for him, as she always did when she entered a room, but there were very few men here at all. All the soldiers had gone to the Mississippi with Don Bernardo, except for the few who worked night and day with Rafa and Simon, getting ready for the offensives against Mobile and Pensacola. There were a few civilian men still available to dance with one, but they were mostly elderly—all of fifty at least!—or infirm.

Sofía kept complaining that it was quite depressing, when one thought about it, and Daisy would nod absently. She watched the door when she thought nobody was looking, clearly hoping Simon would slip in unexpectedly.

Lyse kept her chin up, determined to enjoy herself, no matter whether Rafa stood up to Doña Evangelina or not. If he couldn't choose a bride without his maman's good opinion, Lyse didn't want him anyway. And he deserved to be beaten about the head daily, for good measure.

Smiling at the thought of tiny Doña Evangelina whacking her tall, muscular son with her beaded reticule, she turned to go for the cream puffs and smacked right into him, nose to chest.

Rafa caught her by the shoulders, held her away, and gave her a pirate grin. "What are you smiling about, *prima*? Oh, I see. It's the pastry. Are you going to chuck that at me too? Lots of little missiles this time, instead of one big one."

She scowled at him. "Let me go, or I'll find a Mardi Gras king cake somewhere. Then you'll be sorry."

"Sorry for what? I haven't done anything! However, if I'm going to be battered—haha, battered? Get it?—then I might as well have something to show for it." He swooped and planted his mouth on hers. Before she could protest, he lifted his head, winked, and disappeared.

She stood sputtering like a landed fish until Sofía walked by and said, "You'd better get out from under the mistletoe—you look like you're issuing invitations."

She looked up and, sure enough, clever Madame Gálvez had attached a nice little clump of the green parasite, woven into a ball, to the chandelier. "Oh, my goodness," she muttered, fanning her face.

But she moved.

Just before midnight, the grandest surprise of all came when Governor Gálvez walked in his own front door, went straight to his wife, and kissed her in front of the whole company. "My dear, I'm home," he said simply. "We accomplished what we set out to do—the Mississippi River is clear for Spanish and American transport. Mobile and Pensacola are our next objectives. What do you think of that?"

Madame clung to him. "I think I missed you."

Lyse wanted to melt into a puddle. Oh, to be loved that way, with a man staring at one as if he wanted to consume her like a grand feast.

"A woman like that could get anything she wanted from a man." Rafa's voice came from behind her shoulder.

"A man like that would deserve whatever she gave." Lyse plied her fan and watched the Gálvezes begin the minuet.

Rafa's hands cupped her shoulders. "Lyse, we leave for Mobile in two weeks time."

"But you will stay here again?"

"No. I'm going this time. Pollock will remain here, and Gálvez needs an ordnance officer."

She all but crushed the fragile sticks of the fan. "Then . . . I will go too."

He laughed. "This is not a joke. Look at me."

She whirled to face him. "I'm not joking. I know the bay of Mobile better than anybody in New Orleans, except maybe Simon. And I could be a nurse."

"Lyse, I'm not discussing this with you. I wanted to say goodbye, because Gálvez will have me very busy after tonight. Please don't make this any more difficult than it already is."

"It *is* difficult! I'm tired of saying goodbye." She swiped the back of her hand across her wet cheeks. "Being a woman, wearing skirts, getting left behind—I'm sorry, but I'm very angry right now."

His voice gentled. "But I'm very glad you're a woman. I can't say more, here in this crowd. And no, I'm not taking you outside to be alone, because I couldn't—don't look at me that way—" He swallowed hard and stepped back with a shaky laugh. "I'm trying very hard to be the man you deserve. So tell me you'll pray for me, and let me go. *Te amo, prima.*" He kissed his fingertips, laid them upon her mouth, and backed away into the crowd.

The fan snapped in half.

New Orleans, Fort San Juan
January 11, 1780

He was gone.

Lyse stood at the highest point of Fort San Juan, the bell tower of its little chapel, and watched the last sail fade into the sunset. She put her fingers over her lips, holding onto Rafa's last touch, and tried not to weep. He wanted to be the man she deserved?

Ah, Father in Heaven, how she loved him. He was courageous

and strong and faithful, and infinitely better than she had any right to expect in a lover. She wanted to be with him, to hold and serve him, and to laugh with him.

But it was time to think beyond herself and what she wanted. It was time to grow up a little more—a lot more—and become a woman who deserved a man like Rafael Gonzales. There were families without homes still, after the hurricane. There were children roaming the streets with no place to go, hunting for food in the garbage heaps. And there was Mr. Pollock, left to mind the warehouses and field messages for the governor. She knew every inch of the warehouses, as did Daisy and Scarlet—and surely he would need help.

She could accomplish those things, because every difficulty of her life had prepared her to do so. She smiled. Like Esther of the Bible, she was in New Orleans, now, for just such a time as this.

Dauphine Island
February 10, 1780

Rafa, making notes in a leather journal, followed Gálvez around as he inspected the wreck of the *Volante*, run aground on Dauphine Island, a spit of sandy ground that all but enclosed Mobile Bay.

On the twentieth of January, the Spanish fleet had been joined by the American ship *West Florida*, captained by William Pickles and holding a crew of fifty-eight men, just off the coast of Biloxi. The French had built their first fort there at the turn of the century, but the old wooden palisade had long since crumbled and washed out to sea. The British apparently cared nothing for defending the spot.

Rafa had to wonder if the British took defense of the Gulf Coast seriously at all. Perhaps the strategy of combined French, Spanish, and American commanders—that of stretching and spreading British forces thinly between the New England and southern coasts—had begun to take effect. In any case, there had been nary a shot fired as Gálvez led his armada east along the north boundary of the Gulf of Mexico.

But the forces of nature seemed determined not to make Gálvez's campaign easy. Three days ago, winds had begun to blow contrary, making progress difficult, and then the rain and lightning came. On the third day, visibility was zero, the twelve ships scattered in all directions of the compass. One of the brigantines went down, three others ran aground on sandbars, and Rafa, aboard the flagship *Volante*, had been cast overboard when it snagged on an underground shoal. Fortunately, he was a strong swimmer and had managed to hold on to a cask of wine washing to shore, narrowly avoiding the debris flung about by the wind.

Even now, he surreptitiously kissed the cross hanging about his neck in gratitude. Lyse and his mama must have been praying for him. Four hundred of the twelve hundred regulars and militia Gálvez had brought had died in the storm. One of those could easily have been him.

Gálvez paused beside a debris-covered dune, took the kerchief from about his neck, and wiped his sandy face. He sighed. "There's no repairing this one. We'll take it apart and carry as much of it as we can to make ladders and other structures as needed." He looked at Rafa. "Are you sure you're all right after that wild ride you took yesterday? I've never seen anything like it."

"You always told me I'd see adventure in your command, sir."

Gálvez smiled. "Indeed I did."

"Have you had any response from your request for reinforcements from Havana?"

The general's smile faded. "Not yet. It appears we're going to have to do this on our own. Well, let's get back to the *San Miguel*. We've a lot of work to do."

Many commanders would have given up and set sail for home. Not Gálvez.

Filled with admiration and renewed determination of his own, Rafa stuck his pencil behind his ear and followed.

~

Dog River, eight miles outside Mobile
February 28, 1780

The weather had continued to gnaw at them like a dog with a sore tail. Dawn came in a gray pall that barely lightened the eastern skyline. Rafa, like all the other men, was wet, chilled to the bone, and dressed like a ragpicker. His boots squished as he walked to the mess camp for a chunk of hardtack, and he'd given up on drying his socks.

For the last two weeks, sleeping had been a hellish business of rolling up in a tarp to keep the rain off, and fighting off the gnats that buzzed around one's face, twenty-four hours a day. At least as an officer Rafa was allowed to trade out stints in one of the longboats that had been dragged up the Dog River to their bivouac point. The infantry were required to find their rest wherever they could, in the mud.

By the twelfth of February, they had made it as far as Mobile Point, abutting Dauphine Island, where they set up the guns salvaged from the wreckage of the *Volante* to guard the entrance to the bay. Eight days later, just as they were ready to move on, the misery and frustration was mitigated by the arrival of reinforcements from Havana. Rafa had witnessed Gálvez's herculean effort not to rip into Generals Ezpleta and Míro—who commanded the four Spanish frigates containing over a thousand experienced infantrymen—for their lackadaisical response to his repeated requests for aid. After all, both men were technically his superiors, as they were of higher rank.

However, there was no question as to the real leader of the campaign. Gálvez was everywhere, encouraging, berating, and joking with everyone from cabin boys to General Girón. Rafa wondered if the man ever slept—then concluded that if he did, it was standing up, with his hat dripping rain, boots cracked and dull from the constant whirling of sand and salt.

Rafa's thoughts went often to Lyse. He hoped she was dry and safe, perhaps just waking up beside a banked fire in the little house the soldiers had built for their three beautiful young laundresses—the Sirens of San Juan, as he had called them in a song he wrote in their honor one late night before Christmas. His duties seemed lighter, knowing that Lyse waited for him at the end of the campaign.

At least, he hoped she waited for him. She was just as likely to hire a boat and row herself after him, if she felt he was taking too long to get back. Lyse wasn't one for doing what she was told in every situation.

Grinning to himself, he was about to round a stack of ladders he had helped build, when a familiar voice on the other side brought him to a dead halt. At first he thought it was Simon, which wouldn't be so surprising, of course. But then the voice rumbled again, this time more distinctly. He stepped around the ladders.

"Antoine?"

Antoine Lanier, sitting on an ale cask, chewing on a piece of sausage, looked up with an expression so like Lyse's it hurt. "Rippardá! I don't know whether to shake your hand or punch you in the gut."

"I prefer the former," Rafa said, extending his hand. "How are you, sir? And—how did you get here without getting shot?"

Lanier gripped Rafa's hand and stood up. "I'm much better, now that you Spanish boys have shared your provisions. We slipped in under cover of dark, through a little series of bayous I've been fishing since I was a boy. Simon could take you through that way."

Rafa looked at Simon, who sat on another keg close to the fire. Gálvez was nearby, engaged in conversation with a young Negro dressed in clothes every bit as ragged as Rafa's. In fact, they all looked as though they'd been dragged through briars backward.

Simon saw Rafa's curious glance at the black man. "That's Scarlet's man, Cain. He's the one got my father safely from the fort here. Well, him and Little Bit there."

For the first time, Rafa realized that a small lump under a tarp near the fire was a human being. A mop of curly hair was just visible at one end. "Is that Luc-Antoine?"

Antoine nodded, the firelight glinting across the pride in his face. "After the Americans raided the Dussouy plantation, Luc and Cain lived in the woods for a couple of weeks. Finally Luc started scouting around the fort to see if they could find a way to get to me. Eventually, an officer named Tully spotted them and convinced Luc to meet him near the edge of the Dussouy property. Tully has been kind to me, made sure I ate at least once a day and didn't drown when the water rose in the guardhouse. He said Lyse was always a favorite of his, and it was a shame the way the major had treated her and Daisy.

"Anyway, he told Luc that Redmond had more or less lost his mind since Daisy disappeared. He blamed her running away on us Laniers and had made up his mind to force my execution. Tully didn't hold with hanging civilians, and he wanted to help get me out of the fort. So he had Joony, one of Burelle's women, bring in an extra dress and cap with a load of clean uniforms, plus a tin of lamp black. I blacked my face, put on the dress and cap, and walked right out in broad daylight during a changing of the guard.

"'Course I was in pretty bad shape, after being locked up for such a long time, but at least I was stone-cold sober! My boy and Cain over there, they took care of me in a little shelter they built in the woods, fed me a little at a time until I got my strength back. Meanwhile, they watched and listened from the shadows and heard bits of news. In January, Redmond was recalled to

Pensacola, and they sent Colonel Durnford to replace him. If Durnford had been in charge a month earlier, I don't know that I'd have gotten away."

"That's—remarkable," was all Rafa could think of to say. Wait until Lyse heard what her little brother had been up to.

Antoine nodded. "And then rumors started to fly that you Spaniards had taken back the Mississippi River and were headed for Mobile next. We heard you'd landed at Mobile Point in spite of that nasty storm, and figured you'd camp here and prepare to attack." He lifted his shoulders. "So here we are. There's only a garrison of maybe three hundred men at Fort Charlotte, and they're running low on ammunition. I know Durnford has sent for reinforcements, but they will have been slowed by the same weather as you. We'll do whatever we can to help."

A smile took over Rafa's face. Gálvez would now have the advantage of an eyewitness who had observed daily preparations inside the fort, not to mention three individuals—four, counting Simon—who were familiar with every stone and hill and creek in the surrounding area.

Nothing was a foregone conclusion, but things were looking a shade brighter.

New Orleans, St. Louis Church
March 1, 1780

Lyse awoke with the splashing of gold, purple, and indigo light across her cheek and onto the marble floor of the St. Louis Church. She had come there late last night to pray, and had fallen asleep at the altar, crouched on all fours, her arms wrapped about her head.

Aching in every muscle and joint, she rolled to her back, spread-eagled like a living sacrifice, and stared up at the beautiful domed ceiling. One of the priests would be here to shoo her away, if she didn't move soon. But her thoughts continued to wheel like butterflies in the stained-glass dust motes.

Rafa was a hundred miles away, waking up, she hoped, to a rare day of sunshine. Perhaps he was putting on his boots, laughing at another man's joke, that roguish crease in his cheek, his hair coming loose from its queue.

Or maybe he had been wounded and lay in a muddy ditch, his precious lifeblood seeping into the ground.

She sat up, flattening her hands at her temples, as if to block out the sounds of his rasping breath. Oh, God! Why had she not told him how she loved him? Why had she been so insistent on a proper proposal of marriage? What did that matter, when he told her with every touch of his hand, the very timbre of his voice, that he wanted and loved her?

God, if you will bring him back to me, I will never again be so silly as to throw cake at him. Or refuse to kiss him. Or make saucy remarks.

Well . . . he actually seemed to enjoy the saucy remarks.

And one couldn't spend one's life kissing, though it might be fun to try.

At any rate, I most humbly ask you, Holy Father, to guard and protect him this day. Give him wisdom for whatever task he takes on. Oh, and give him dry socks.

Amen.

~

Fort Charlotte, Mobile
March 4, 1780

For the fourth day in a row, Rafa marched through the gate at Fort Charlotte under a flag of truce, bearing gifts from General Gálvez for Colonel Durnford. Rafa had been chosen for this important mission for several reasons. Because of his close connection with

Oliver Pollock, as well as his extensive travels through British territory, his English was the best of all Gálvez's officers. Also, Gálvez remembered Rafa's original report on his first stay in Mobile in the fall of 1776, which recounted the dinner with Redmond and, fortuitously, Durnford's family. Gálvez determined that Rafa's previous acquaintance with the British officer must shed a favorable light upon his intentions.

Gálvez hoped by this extended polite parlay to avoid a costly attack, encouraging instead a peaceful surrender of Fort Charlotte. Every day the negotiations continued, this hope became less and less a certainty.

Still, Rafa remained proud of his commander's gentlemanly conduct. When he arrived at Durnford's quarters, he saluted the adjutant, Tully, who had notified Rafa when Lyse's situation became desperate, and who had so humanely assisted Antoine Lanier. Tully returned the salute, but by no flicker of an eyebrow or twitch of mustache did the stodgy corporal betray any recognition; in fact, he might have been some inanimate block of stone as he held the door for Rafa's entrance into the commander's office.

Durnford, considerably grayer about the temples than the last time Rafa had seen him, rose upon Rafa's entrance and invited him to take a seat. Rafa did so with a smile, but first presented the handsome lined basket Gálvez had sent. In it were a freshly plucked chicken and a leg of mutton, two loaves of French bread, a dozen corn cakes, and a batch of tea biscuits—all purchased from the bountiful kitchen of Justine Lanier—and to top that bounty off, Gálvez had provided, from his personal store, bottles of Spanish and Bordeaux wine with a box full of premium Cuban cigars.

After poking eagerly through the basket's contents, Durnford set the basket aside and showed all his bad teeth in a gratified smile. "You must express to General Gálvez my deep appreciation for his generosity, Don Rafael. The chicken especially is a most appropriate manifestation of the don's character. My officers enjoyed the wines he sent yesterday, but I think I must keep this fresh batch of courtesy for myself."

Rafa pretended not to notice the buried insult. "I assure you, Colonel, that Don Bernardo is fully cognizant of the depths to which a British officer will go if there is a leg of lamb offered as reward. Perhaps that is how a certain prisoner managed to escape a few weeks ago."

Durnford's smile froze. "I do not know what you mean. It is true, however, that we were infested with cockroaches not too long ago—but we have rid ourselves of the pests finally."

"Oh—roaches. One never knows when they will attack." Rafa brushed at an invisible speck of lint on the knee of the pristine breeches he'd borrowed from the general for the occasion. "Speaking of inconveniences, my commander would like to remind you that our army is still camped quite uncomfortably near the gates of your little fort here. He hopes that you will be so kind as to vacate the premises so that we may have respite from your lovely little swamp. In fact, he is quite concerned that you do so before sundown today, lest his men become impatient and make their own doorway through the wall with a little cannon fire."

Durnford's blue eyes iced over. "Is he indeed? Then I'm sorry you have to be the bearer of bad tidings. You must return at your earliest convenience—let us say in the next ten minutes—and inform your master that his bone-bearing puppy has been whipped. He is advised to make himself comfortable in the swamp, because that is the only place I have available to offer as accommodations." He stood. "And if his men should try to create a doorway, my own men will respond with like enthusiasm. Do I make myself clear?"

Rafa rose as well, and nodded stiffly. "Abundantly, sir. And in that case, I give you good day. I will not disturb you again." Resisting the urge to poke his fingers into those chilly bug-eyes, he bowed and sauntered from the office. He saluted Tully, who looked away in obvious discomfort, then exited the building.

The gauntlet had been thrown. Gálvez would pick it up, and the battle would begin. And in the aftermath, the city of Mobile, Lyse's home, was going to fall.

21

New Orleans, the Cabildo
March 9, 1780

Lyse had been waiting in the anteroom of the Cabildo since noon, waiting for Oliver Pollock to have time to see her. He had sent a message to the fort this morning, requesting that she honor him with a visit at her earliest convenience, as he had some information that he thought might be of some interest to her.

Of course she had rushed right over, barely taking time to brush her hair into a neater braid. But here she had sat, in this chilly room, with its stone floors and cold stucco walls, and not a comfortable chair in sight. She rubbed her arms absently. She shouldn't complain. Rafa had been enduring untold miseries for nearly two months. Out of habit, on the thought, she whispered a prayer. Perhaps God kept her in discomfort to remind her to pray.

She thought of the night she'd brought Rafa's dinner to him here, when he'd said, *Don't be ridiculous—of course we're betrothed*. Why hadn't she believed him? She might have had four more months of kisses. They might even have been married by now.

Why did she always have to have everything exactly her way?

Suddenly the door of the governor's office opened, and Pollock's round, ruddy Irish face appeared. "Miss Lanier? I can see you now, if you'll come in."

She had come to know this kind, energetic man a deal better since the new year. She understood why Rafa liked and respected him so much. His passion for the new nation of the United States of America was infectious. Perhaps one day, when Rafa retired from service to His Spanish Majesty's army, they might emigrate, and establish a home somewhere in those free colonies. Surely someone as creative and determined as Rafa would be able to find a way to—

"Miss Lanier? If you please, I have much work to be done this afternoon after I see you."

"Oh! I beg your pardon!" Blushing, Lyse jumped to her feet and followed Pollock into the office.

"Please, sit there," he said, indicating the chair in front of the governor's desk, then seating himself behind it.

She stared at the desk, picturing Rafa's sleeping face. He had been so overworked and so tired that night. How could she have been so . . .

Oh, she was woolgathering again. She met Pollock's bland gaze and pressed her hands together. "What is it, Mr. Pollock? I know you're busy . . ."

"No, it is quite all right, my dear. Rafael's lady must always be a priority. In fact, my wife has reminded me repeatedly that we must have you over for supper one night. I shall make that happen. But first, this letter came for you, included in one addressed to me." He handed her a folded paper, sealed with red wax.

She took it and examined the seal. It looked like . . . It was! Rafa's signet!

She burst into tears.

Pollock stood, horrified. "My dear! What is wrong?"

"Nothing!" Desperately she hunted in her pocket for a handkerchief. "It is only that I have missed him so much, and I didn't think he would have time to think of me, but here is his signet, and I am so very happy!" She blew her nose.

"Oh, well, if that is all." Pollock sat down again, observing her dryly. "I am terrified of what will happen when you actually read it."

Lyse laughed, stuffed the handkerchief back in her pocket, and broke the seal.

Dear Lyse, she read.

I have only a moment to write this and send it with Gálvez's report to Pollock, but I want you to know how much I miss you, how I love you, and can't wait to return to you. We had a bit of a miserable time for the first couple of months—did you know it rains a lot in Mobile?

She laughed again, hiccupped, and kept reading.

Anyway, I must first tell you that we have your father, your little brother Luc-Antoine, and Scarlet's Cain safe with us. I'll tell you the story of their escape when I see you, but for now just know that I shall protect them with my own life. Simon is well, too, by the way, and insists I give his love to Daisy. The other news I must share is a little more difficult. Major Redmond has been recalled to Pensacola, to be replaced by Colonel Durnford. I know you remember him from that first dinner party where I fell in love with you. Actually, I think it was the cornbread, but I digress.

Durnford is an obstinate man, typical of the British race. He has determined that we Spaniards should in our victory—which I must say is certain—have no place to lay our heads. He has ordered the entire town of Mobile to be burnt to the ground. There is no explanation for this sort of insanity. So when you next come to the town of your birth, you will find nothing as when you left it. I dreaded to make you aware of this tragedy, and Durnford has much to answer for with regard to his cruelty and intransigence.

On a happier note, Luc-Antoine bids me tell you that he has learned to make horseshoes, and that he intends to become the most skilful blacksmith in New Orleans.

Now, mi corazón, the courier is giving me the famous New Orleans "evil eye," so I must close. The next time you hear from me, I will look in your eyes and pray there isn't a knife in your bodice or a cake in your hand!

With all my love,
Rafa

MOBILE
MARCH 12, 1780

For four days, Rafa and the other officers had supervised the Spanish forces as they dug trenches and built earthworks around Fort Charlotte, while the British emptied on them some rather paltry cannon fire, easily dodged for the most part. The Spanish surgeon had bandaged up a few gunshot wounds, amputated a leg caught in a misplaced bear trap, and generally eaten himself into a stupor.

Two days ago, a Spanish scout reported that British reinforcements, under General John Campbell, to whom Durnford had written several days earlier, were mired on the other side of a swamp somewhere between Pensacola and Mobile. There was little likelihood that they would arrive before Gálvez had completed the taking of Fort Charlotte.

Bolstered by this good news, the Spanish army had opened fire on March 10, bombarding the crumbling fort with eighteen- and twenty-four-pound cannons at a rate impossible for the undermanned and underprovisioned forces inside to withstand. As of yesterday, Fort Charlotte was out of ammunition.

Rafa stood atop a stack of cannonballs, watching for Gálvez's signals and keeping an eye on the fort itself. She had to surrender soon, for the air was thick with smoke from the cannon fire, the embrasures of the fort falling in in huge chunks, the sound of screaming artillery a hideous accompaniment to the boom of the cannon. Sweat poured down his face, his neck, and his arms, making puddles of mud and gunpowder which clogged his nose and stung his eyes. He reached for an already filthy rag in his coat pocket and wiped his eyes.

There. It wasn't a mistake, or a result of warped, faulty vision. The white flag had gone up the flagpole in the center of the fort. With a whoop, he raised his arm, whirling like a madman as he ran for Gálvez.

"Surrender! They just surrendered!"

The cry echoed, over and over, from soldier to soldier, across the battlefield, even as the cannon blasts continued until the officers should relay Gálvez's order to cease fire.

At last the order came.

Eerie silence settled with the smoke.

An enormous cheer went up from the Spanish army.

Victory!

Rafa bowed his head and wept for Lyse's home.

~

New Orleans
March 17, 1780

The bells of St. Louis began to ring as Lyse stepped onto the bank of the bayou with an armload of clean, wet shirts. Startled, she slipped and nearly splashed backward onto her seat, but managed to right herself at the last minute. Laughing, she dumped the shirts into her basket, then bent to lift it onto her head. Something wonderful must have happened for the padre to ring the bells on a Friday morning.

"Hey, miss, I'm looking for a place to sleep tonight. Can you help a soldier out?"

With a shriek, she did fall this time. The shirts went with her, back into the soapy, mud-roiled water of the bayou. She sat gasping, bottom aching, lye-tainted water stinging her eyes.

"Lyse! I'm sorry! I thought you saw me."

Fiercely she rubbed her eyes. Rafa's face hovered above hers. He was reaching for her.

She grabbed his hand and yanked. He tumbled in, headfirst, and came up sputtering beside her. Flouncing out of the water, she stood on the bank, sopping, dripping, arms akimbo, while he sat and blew water out of his nose like a dolphin.

"That'll teach you to sneak up on me!"

"Lyse! I didn't sneak! For the love of all that's holy, I had the padre ring the church bells!"

"Well. Well, I didn't know it was you. Could've been for anybody."

He propped his arms on raised knees and stared at her, one side of his mouth curling up. "Anybody?" He crooked a finger. "Come here."

"No."

"I am a conquering hero. You have to do what I say."

She thought about that. "Oh, well, in that case." Hands on hips, she sashayed into the water and stood over him. "Now what?"

His mouth was curling on both sides now. "Now you kiss me."

"You know the rules."

"Hang the rules. Your papa says I can have you. He's tired of worrying about you. Now kiss me."

"Oh, all right. You're such a bully." She splashed down beside him and puckered her mouth.

Very soon it went soft and warm. "Rafa," she said, when she could breathe again. "Your mama isn't going to like this. She will beat you about the head."

"I don't care what my mama says anymore. You are the one who will get to beat me from now on."

"Is that right?"

"Yes. I get my cake, and I get to eat it too."

Lyse laughed, perfectly happy.

A Word to the Reader

I always begin a book with questions that I must answer before my characters can come to life—questions about terminology, cultural and racial influences, literature and music, political power struggles, behind-the-scenes movers and shakers. But then a weird thing happens. As I immerse myself in the period and get comfortable with my imaginary people, I sort of forget how shocking some of those historically accurate words and ideas can seem to contemporary readers.

Which is where my editor comes in. It is one of her jobs to help identify places in the story where the reader may have difficulty swallowing some arcane or politically incorrect phrase, or where the context isn't quite obvious enough to explain it. Then it's a delicate dance, deciding how much is too much—which explanations can most effectively be woven into the story, which should be relegated to this type of afterword. After all, the goal of storytelling in a historical setting is to sweep the reader into an unfamiliar era, surround her with people of long-forgotten customs and language and dress, and make her forget for a time that life is zooming by at warp speed.

If you've hung with me this far, I assume you're the kind of reader who wants to know a little more. You wonder which characters are the "real" ones, and which are strictly from the author's imagination. You're curious about background forces that led people to think a certain way or make decisions that seem bizarre in twenty-first-century hindsight. Or maybe you want to know where I got my information so you can do some further reading. Just for you, I'm pulling back the curtain a bit!

First of all, I should note that, during the period of *The Creole Princess*, the American Gulf Coast—which, for my purposes, includes everything from present-day Florida to the eastern coast of Texas—developed under a confusing succession of European monarchies. Every American schoolchild knows that the thirteen British colonies along the Atlantic seaboard rebelled and formed the United States of America. But few are aware that two other British colonies remained loyal to the Crown—East Florida and West Florida (which came into England's possession in the 1763 Treaty of Paris at the end of the French and Indian War). Loyalist refugees from the rebelling colonies flocked to the largest settlements of the time, Pensacola and Mobile. Some also settled along the eastern shore of the Mississippi River, near Natchez, Mississippi, and Baton Rouge, Louisiana.

Meanwhile, Spain had taken control of the Louisiana colony lying west of the Mississippi River (along with Texas, Mexico, and most of Central and South America), with New Orleans as its seat of administration—and France had pretty much given up its stake in the American continent (for the time being, anyway).

Like players in a giant Monopoly game, the nations who held various pieces of American property rolled the metaphorical dice with regard to alliances, trades, and declarations of war, timing their moves for maximum economic advantage, and withholding and releasing information (both true and misleading) with an eye to manipulating friends and enemies alike. The history surrounding the American Revolution is complex, fascinating, and surprising—much too complicated to distill into a one-paragraph explanation. The best I can do is roughly set the geographical stage, as outlined above, and let the story speak for itself.

Regarding characters, there were a few fascinating heroes and villains of American Revolutionary history that I couldn't resist plugging into my story. Front and center looms Brigadier-General Don Bernardo de Gálvez, governor of the province of Louisiana and commander of Spanish forces out of New Orleans which captured the British forts at Natchez, Baton Rouge, Mobile, and Pensacola. Gálvez was an extraordinarily effective politician, military strategist, and administrator who was universally respected and admired by his own superiors in the Spanish chain of command, as well as those who reported to him, and who effectively negotiated the delicate relationship between the Spanish court at Madrid and the American Continental Congress. A short biography of Gálvez can be found on Wikipedia, but most of my information about his extraordinary life came from Thomas E. Chávez's excellent *Spain and the Independence of the United States* (University of New Mexico Press, 2002).

Gálvez's wife, María Feliciana de St. Maxent d'Estrehan, makes an appearance in my story, as does Oliver Pollock, the Irish-American merchant who served as liaison and supply agent between the Spanish government and Philadelphia. Pollock, whose significant personal fortune financed weapons, ammunition, and uniforms sent to the American militia, is a little-known hero of the Revolution. He eventually retired in poverty to his daughter's Mississippi plantation, after unsuccessfully applying to the Congress for redress of his debts. The two governors of New Orleans previous to Gálvez, O'Reilly and Unzaga, are mentioned in the story, as are Spanish minister of state Floridablanca (stationed in Madrid) and Captain-General Navarro, governor of Cuba.

On the British side, the real governor of West Florida, Peter

Chester, is mentioned in my story, and Lieutenant-Governor Colonel Elias Durnford plays an important role in the first and last few chapters during the siege of Fort Charlotte. Durnford was apparently a man of many talents—he was the civil engineer who redesigned the city of Pensacola after the Spanish decamped in 1763 (at the same time the French ceded Mobile)—and that he was given command of Fort Charlotte during the Spanish attack is a testament to his administrative and political skills (ignoring the fact that the fort turned out to be unprepared to sustain the determined onslaught of Gálvez's marines).

Beyond those few, all characters are strictly from my imagination.

One might well ask, Why have I never heard of these people? Early American history is full of the exploits of French allies like Rochambeau and Lafayette, but the contribution of Spain to the success of the American War of Independence is only recently coming to light—probably because it was of a necessarily clandestine nature. Spain's aid to the Patriot cause remained under wraps until late in the war, in order to give her time to outfit her navy with sufficient strength to engage and overcome the significantly stronger British fleet. But catalogs and records available in Spain and the National Archives in Washington (as well as other sources cited by Chávez) reveal that Spain's financial contribution to the American cause mounted into the thousands, probably millions, of *pesos fuertes* before her official declaration of war against Britain, and contributed significantly to the American victory at Saratoga. Perhaps most important, the fact that Spanish forces effectively split the British navy between two theaters of war became a deciding factor in the American success at Yorktown.

So much for the political and military aspects of the setting; the next most obvious questions surround the lumbering elephant in the room—slavery. It is probably true that the twenty-first-century American will have difficulty wrapping her brain around eighteenth-century attitudes (those of slaves, slaveholders, and free objectors to the practice) about this most deplorable of human interactions. It might be helpful to remember, however, that by the time of the American Revolution, slavery had been in practice since prehistoric times, not just in the American colonies but all over the world. Still, as I developed this book, I was highly conscious that modern readers have become justifiably sensitized and guilt-stricken that America, *the cradle of freedom*, somehow managed to deny that beautiful right to some of her own citizens—for nearly a century after the Declaration of Independence.

And then it occurred to me that the eventual abolition of slavery, and the convulsions of the Civil Rights Era, must have actually germinated right along with the struggle for freedom from British tyranny—that those two major revolutions developed, not *in spite of* Americans of European origin, but *because of* their passionate investment in man's God-given right to self-actualization. They were indeed a continuation of the Revolution, requiring a great deal more time to effect because those practices and attitudes had been entrenched for *thousands of years*. It is rather more miraculous than not that slavery in America was abolished as quickly as it was.

In any case, I chose to take my heroine, Lyse Lanier, straight through the middle of that quagmire of guilt, frustration, bitterness, and victory. I gave her a family tree rich with complex cultural roots and branches—French, Indian, African, aristocratic, slave, and free—much like many modern-day Gulf Coast natives. I matched her with a man of adventurous, generous, humorous spirit—and then let the story pieces fall where they would. I prefer not to prompt the reader to interpret the story in any particular way, but I hope you will find human truth in the characters. And while I tried not to go overboard in insensitivity, I hope some eighteenth-century terminology that may seem a bit politically incorrect to our modern ears can be accepted as historically accurate. Anyone interested in further study on the subject of slavery in the Deep South should check out a fascinating true story called *The Lost German Slave Girl* by John Bailey (Grove Press, 2005).

A more specific question I wanted to address here is in reference to the non-marriage between Lyse's cousin Scarlet and her "mate," Cain. In brief, it wouldn't even occur to Scarlet (let alone her owners) to want a marriage ceremony. Slaves were property and could not take part in any legal contract, even marriage ("jumping the broom," which one sometimes reads about as a substitute for formal marriage ceremonies, seems to have started in Scotland and Wales and became somewhat of a custom in the mid-nineteenth century). It appears that when the great noise of abolition controversy spread in the 1800s (several decades after my story), southern slave owners slyly began to encourage marriage between slaves, in order to counter the abolitionist argument that slavery was destroying human family units—which it was—and also to discourage slaves from running away and thus abandoning their families. It was despicable, of course, that human beings were treated so cavalierly, but it shouldn't be surprising for the time period.

Let me address one more item, and I'll wrap up this treatise. My leaping-off point for *The Creole Princess* was "How did a person become an American Patriot?" Or, as my editor asked it, "What *was* an American? Did they call themselves that at the time?" In a word, yes. The continents of North and South America had been called America since 1507, when the first world map that included the New World appeared in Europe. Thomas Paine's first collection of *Common Sense* essays, published in April 1776, is titled *Writings of Thomas Paine—Volume I (1774–1779): The American Crisis* (I highly recommend reading this collection—it's in public domain and thus free!).

And remember, the purpose of the Declaration of Independence was to establish the new republican government, *The United States of America*. So . . . an *American* colonist was a British citizen who lived in one of the fifteen British colonies in North America. Citizens of the thirteen rebellious colonies called themselves Americans or Patriots or Continentals, depending on context.

So, am I a complete and unashamed history nerd? You bet! And even more so after reading some of the writings that actually jump-started the Revolution. Before I go, I'll recommend one more excellent resource for my fellow nerds: *American Exceptionalism: An Experiment in History* by Charles Murray (AEI Press, 2013).

I certainly hope you have enjoyed *The Creole Princess*, and if you haven't read its prequel, *The Pelican Bride*, by all means do so! And look forward to more adventures of the Lanier family next year with the release of *The Duchess of Navy Cove*.

May you live long and prosper,

Beth White
Mobile, Alabama
August 2014

Acknowledgments

In one of those wonderful, unexpected acts of friendship and obedience to the Holy Spirit, a church friend approached me last spring to ask if I'd ever thought about recruiting a prayer team for my ministry and work as a writer and teacher. Being in the mood for gut-level honesty about my spectacular stupidity and lack of faith, I said no. Which was especially egregious, given that I was in the middle of one of the most difficult school years I've experienced in over thirty years of teaching, plus this book that would. Not. Get. Written.

Was I prideful, not wanting to admit aloud how desperately I needed support? Was I too busy to ask? I don't know, but you can be sure I rectified the situation immediately and went to the women closest to me spiritually, who had demonstrated interest in my adventures in public school and publishing, and asked them to join a little email loop. There I would post specific prayer requests, and report back with successes and further challenges.

I suppose it goes without saying that sharing those needs instantly lifted the weight and anxiety. The book got done, hallelujah, school broke for summer, and I had a lovely, long vacation, culminating in the birth of my first granddaughter, Rozalyn. So I would like to publicly thank my dear friend Elizabeth Grizzle for her sensitivity and gentle prodding. You'll never know how much that conversation changed the course of my life.

I would also like to thank my extraordinary extended family for your love and interest in my writing, and your patience for my crazy non-schedule as a writer. The quilting and the laughter and the gumbo and the music and stories keep me sane and give me things to write about. And calluses on my fingers.

Finally, thanks to the obvious three: Lonnie, my editor; Chip, my agent; and Scott, my love and my best friend (you are the only one who is, in Rafa's words, allowed to beat me about the head). I am blessed to have you all in my corner.

Don't Miss Book 3 in the

GULF COAST CHRONICLES

Coming Spring 2016

1

August 1814

She could set fire to the letter in her pocket and it would still be true.

Smearing away tears with the heel of her hand, Fiona slid down from her buckskin mare, Bonnie, and landed barefoot in the sand. She led the horse to the water's edge and splashed along beside her, knee-deep in waves chugging straight up from the Gulf of Mexico. At Navy Cove, on the other side of the isthmus, the beach was quieter and gentler, but here the wind tore at her hair and the salt mist stung her eyes. Perfect.

Her brother was on a British prison ship lurking off the coast of North Carolina.

The words from that terrible piece of paper floated like sunspots in front of her eyes. Her twin, the other half of herself, wasn't coming home this time. Sullivan had been at sea since he'd turned fourteen, and in six years had worked his way up to lieutenant in the new American maritime service. His letters had been full of adventure and optimism, and twice he'd managed a few weeks' leave between assignments.

But this . . . this was so final.

She of all people knew what the British did to prisoners of war.

Grandpére Antoine's stories of Revolutionary War days, when he'd been held in the guardhouse at Fort Charlotte, were burned in her brain. Short rations, rancid water, little sleep. Beatings.

She shuddered. Her older brother Léon said a prisoner exchange might be arranged. But who would do that for an insignificant young lieutenant from the backwaters of West Florida?

There had to be a way. Every day since Sullivan left home, she'd prayed for his safety, and God had protected him so far.

There *must* be a way.

She threw her arms around Bonnie's damp neck, pressed her face into the warm, quivering hide, and let the tears come. *Please, God, don't take my brother.*

Bonnie blew out a breath and nuzzled her shoulder, while the waves rolled in, rocking her, wetting her dress from the knees down. Eyes closed, she let her thoughts drift to long-gone, lazy summer days when she and Sullivan had wandered Navy Cove beach, crab buckets banging against their legs and never a care in the world. Then came the year she went to England with Aunt Lyse and Uncle Rafa, leaving Sullivan behind. By the time she returned, he'd become a sea-crazy young man, determined to travel the world on anybody's ship that would take him.

With a sigh, she looked up at the steely sky. What was done couldn't be undone, even by prayer.

The wind picked up, a gust that nearly knocked her off her feet, so she took up the reins once more. Grabbing Bonnie's mane, she hopped on, her sodden skirts slapping the horse's flanks. She'd lost track of time as usual, so probably she'd better head for home and get the men something to eat for supper. Yesterday's storm had put them behind at the shipyard. They'd be working until dark tonight and would come home hungry as bears.

She'd guided the horse a ways down the beach, lost in thought, when Bonnie suddenly shied and stopped. Absently Fiona kicked her in the ribs. Bonnie shook her head and refused to move.

"Bonnie, what's the matter?" Fiona leaned to the side.

Bonnie had almost stepped on a pile of black seaweed all but covered with wet sand.

Wait, not seaweed. Material. Clothing. A body. A roll of surf washed up, stirred the folds of cloth, but the body did not move. Dead?

Oh, dear Lord, please not dead.

She slid down, throwing the reins to keep Bonnie in check. The body was facedown and hatless. A young man, judging by the thick, wet blond hair, though his face was turned away. She knelt beside him, flipped him over just as another wave crashed in, sousing her thoroughly. Coughing, shivering, she struggled to her feet and grabbed the man's arms to drag him farther up onto the beach. He was tall and muscular, unbelievably heavy, inert as a sack of potatoes, and the tide was quickly rolling in, but she managed to get him out of the reach of the waves. Bonnie wandered after her, snuffling in irritation.

"I know," she panted. "This wasn't in my plan either." Léon was going to grumble about supper being late.

She let go of the young man's arms, stood up to ease the strain on her back, then dropped to her knees. She put her ear to the wet wool covering his chest, praying for a rise and fall of breath. Maybe . . . maybe there was a faint thud under her cheek.

Tugging and shoving, she got him turned over facedown again and pressed the heels of her hands against his back. Push, push, push, wait. He didn't move. She tried again.

He seemed to be dead.

She sat there with her hands flat against the broad back, praying for wisdom. What would her brothers have done? She'd heard them talk about breathing into the mouths of men pulled from the sea. Should she try that?

First she pushed against his back again. When he remained inert, she started crying. There was nobody to tell her what to do, so she hauled the poor dead man onto his back and knelt above him. All but blinded by tears, she pushed his hair back from his face to look at him.

She stifled a scream. "Charlie!" Grabbing his face in shaking hands, she tried to make sense of what made no sense. Charlie Kincaid would be across an ocean, in England, not washed up on a beach in West Florida. "Charlie, Charlie, don't be dead! Dear God, don't let him be dead!"

Because she didn't know what else to do, she put her mouth to his and breathed, willing him to come to life. Again she blew air into his lungs. She sat up panting, searching the familiar but man-grown face. The same, but not the same, as the boy she had known nine years ago. His face had lengthened, with slashing angles of brow, cheekbone, and jaw, and he'd grown into the commanding nose. But there were the same ridiculously long, dark eyelashes and a mouth made for smiling and teasing a bookish, horse-crazy little girl.

"Wake up, Charlie," she muttered, "or I'm going to tell your grandfather you're ditching your lessons again."

She bent to seal his lips with hers again, but his chest lurched under her hands. He gave a strangled cough, and water bubbled from his mouth. Relieved, terrified, Fiona scrambled to shove at Charlie's shoulder and back until she had him half turned. He continued to cough, weakly at first, then with agonized hoarse gasps. Fiona pounded his back with all her strength, helping him rid his lungs of the suffocating seawater.

"Don't die, don't die, don't die."

Finally she heard him whisper something, and she paused to bend close to his lips. "What?"

"Sto . . ." He wheezed.

"What?"

"I said st . . . stop hitting me," he choked out. "Headache."

Abruptly she straightened. "You're alive! Oh, thank God, you're alive!"

Charlie winced. "Yes, but would you mind lowering the volume?" He opened his eyes, those familiar, piercing cerulean eyes that she saw in her dreams.

Well, one was blue, and the other had that odd hazel-brown splotch. Perfect, Charlie was not. She sniffed back tears. "It's so good to see you."

"Er . . . you too." He coughed, then frowned as he stared at her. "You look an awful lot like someone I used to know."

"You don't remember me?"

The stare intensified. His face was sunburnt, sand-encrusted, and there was a large bloody gash over his left eyebrow. But of course he was Charlie. Nobody else had those oddly colored eyes. And likely she looked just as unrecognizable as he, for nine years had made a significant difference in her appearance.

As if following her thoughts, Charlie's gaze traveled downward from her face, and one eyebrow rose with that droll quirk she'd loved so much. "I think I'd remember you, if we'd met before."

Suddenly aware that she all but sat on him, Fiona jumped to her feet. "Oh, you! You haven't changed one bit—except it used to be Maddy you were drooling over."

"Maddy who? If there's another one as pretty as you, I've landed in heaven." He got an elbow underneath him and levered himself to a semi-sitting position. "What's your name?"

She stared at him in chagrin. "You really don't remember?"

"Right now I barely know my own name." He looked around irritably. "If I haven't broken down the pearly gates, where are we? Did I fall off my horse?"

Fiona looked around and found Bonnie ambling closer. Probably looking for food. "This is *my* horse, Bonnie. You seem to have washed in from the Gulf. There was a big storm last night." She paused. She'd heard of people losing their memory after a head wound. "You had to have been on a ship." But where was it? Frustrated, she scanned the empty horizon. There wasn't a hunk of wood or other detritus anywhere to indicate the type of vessel he'd arrived on. She shifted her gaze to the east, where an Indian trail ran toward Perdido Pass and on to Pensacola. Could he have come overland and then gotten injured and washed into the Gulf during the storm? It didn't seem likely.

Clearly no more enlightened than she, Charlie didn't bother to answer. Shutting his eyes, he simply lay back, as if too exhausted to even look at her any longer.

Now what was she going to do? She wasn't strong enough to lift him onto the horse, and she certainly couldn't drag him back to Navy Cove by herself.

"I should go get Léon," she said aloud.

"So there's a Maddy and a Léon, and a horse named Bonnie. I'll just call you Duchess."

She whirled to look at him, and found one eye open—the solid blue one—and his lips curled in a smile. "Then you *do* remember me!"

"No, I just—" The smile faded. "Your name isn't really Duchess, is it?"

"Of course not, but everyone—that is, my family—But I told you about it the night you—" Drowning in memory and anxiety and confusion, she dragged in a breath. "My name is Fiona Lanier. My cousin Maddy and my aunt and uncle all stayed at your grandfather's estate the summer I was eleven years old. It was a long time ago, but I would have thought . . ."

"If I hadn't gotten brained and nearly drowned, I'm sure I would remember you," Charlie said gently. "But do you think, Miss Fiona, we might find a way to get off the beach? Because, and I hate to mention it, I think the tide is going to carry us back out to sea before very long."

"Oh!" With a start Fiona realized he was right. The surf had crawled inland until the waves had almost reached Charlie's feet.

He was on his elbow again, clearly intending to stand up.

She shrieked. "No! You'll faint—or . . . or something!"

But he rolled to his knees. "I'll be fine," he managed, panting. "Do you have a saddle for that horse?"

"Of course I do, but it's at home. I just came out for a quick ride on the beach." Suddenly she remembered the letter. How could she have forgotten Sullivan? She wrung her hands. Now she had an injured British aristocrat to care for, and Léon was going to be apoplectic.

"All right, well, bareback it'll be then." Charlie was on his feet, swaying like a man coming off a five-day bender. He lurched at Bonnie, who quite understandably pranced away from him. Charlie landed on his rear and began to curse in Spanish. At least she thought it was Spanish.

Laughing in spite of their predicament, Fiona grabbed Bonnie's reins. "Shhh, it's okay, girl, he looks like a lunatic, but he can't hurt you."

Charlie snarled and began again in French.

She let him run down, then said, "I'm sorry she hurt your feelings, but she doesn't like to be mounted from the right." She reached down a hand. "If you can stand again, I'll give you a leg up."

"She didn't hurt my *feelings*, it's my *bum* that aches." But he laughed and grasped her wrist, coming to his feet with surprising agility for a man who had nearly succumbed to Triton's fury. She let him regain his balance with a hand on her shoulder. He was so tall that the top of her head barely reached his lips. She looked up at him, trying to find the boy she'd known in this mysterious stranger.

He stared back down at her, his expression just as muddled as she felt. "I *do* know you, somehow," he muttered. "I just can't remember . . . You said my name is Charlie, and that feels right. You mentioned my grandfather. Where is he? Did he bring me here?"

"No, he's—" Should she tell him he was English? Did he know

there was a war between their two countries? "I don't know how you got here." She shrugged. "This is Mobile Point, the isthmus that separates Mobile Bay from the Gulf of Mexico. I live about two miles across on the bay side, at Navy Cove."

Charlie squeezed her shoulder in friendly fashion. "All right, then, duchess of Navy Cove, if you'd be so kind as to cup your hands, I'll endeavor to boost myself onto your trusty steed. Then I'll swing you up, and we'll away." He grimaced. "We'd do it the other way 'round, except I fear I'm not exactly in fine fettle at the moment."

The deed was accomplished with more comedic effect than grace, but in a few moments Fiona grasped Charlie's extended hand and let him swing her behind him onto Bonnie's back. She put her arms around Charlie and took the reins, clicking her tongue to give Bonnie leave to walk.

She had ridden astride behind her brothers all her life, but this—clutching Charlie-the-stranger round the waist just to stay on—was another kettle of fish entirely. Not only was it awkward and uncomfortable, but she had enough sense to know that it was highly improper. Mama would not have approved. Maddy would definitely not approve. Léon would likely challenge Charlie to pistols at dawn.

None of them must ever know. She and Charlie would enter the barn from the back side, put the horse away, and hope nobody saw them. She could pretend Charlie had walked all the way from New Orleans. Or something.

There had to be some way to explain his presence, his injury, his obvious Englishness.

Oh, dear Lord, what was she going to do?

Beth White's day job is teaching music at an inner-city high school in historic Mobile, Alabama. A native Mississippian, she is a pastor's wife, mother of two, and grandmother of two—so far. Her hobbies include playing flute and pennywhistle and painting, but her real passion is writing historical romance with a Southern drawl. Her novels have won the American Christian Fiction Writers' Carol Award, the RT Book Club Reviewers Choice Award, and the Inspirational Reader's Choice Award. Visit www.bethwhite.net for more information.